First Edition
First Printing, 2014
ISBN 978-0-9909432-1-1

www.al-barrera.com

Darker Shadows Lie Below

The oldest and strongest emotion of mankind is fear, and the oldest and strongest kind of fear is fear of the unknown.

H.P. Lovecraft

Chapter 1

The last nine years of his life shrank in the rearview mirror. Michigan, medical school, and everything north of the Mason-Dixon Line would be past tense in less than a day. He looked over at Julia, and she smiled back. "Are you excited?"

She fidgeted with the radio. "You know, it's not too late to just dump all of this and go to New York instead." Cat Stevens blared from the speaker loud and proud as she leaned back in her seat.

"And let our baby grow up in educated luxury? I forbid it."

She shook her head and rubbed her belly. "I can't wait to see Little Ben."

Only a few weeks until they were parents. He couldn't believe it. For that matter, neither had Julia's parents. "Engaged was not married," or so they had informed the couple numerous times. Old-school Catholics had very specific ideas about *that* kind of thing.

Eddy, ever the consummate best friend, had asked if Ben was sure it was his kid. "She's just too good for you, brother."

1

Al Barrera

"You have the map, right?" Julia asked for the fifteenth time that morning.

"Yeah, it's right—" Ben reached to the center console of his new 1972 Sportwagon. A gift from Julia's father. Perfect for a new family. "I just had the darn thing."

"Are you serious?"

He smiled big and pulled it out from under the seat. "Kidding."

She slapped his shoulder.

"We aren't going to get lost. It's a straight shot down I-75 and then a turn onto I-24." The highway went all the way down to Florida. Eddy called it the run from the freezer to the grave.

"I worry, that's all. I've never done a cross-country move before."

"Worrying's my job, sweetheart. You're the brains of the operation."

The morning Ann Arbor traffic gave way to the bustle of the Interstate. Vacationers and students were off the road, and the September traffic turned light and then non-existent as they sped south toward their new home in Tennessee. The moving truck lagged behind, but that was to be expected. They'd arrive a few hours after and unload all of their things into the new apartment in Umber Gardens.

"Did you call … What was his name?"

"Dr. Howerton. And yes, I called the Home and let them know we were leaving Michigan."

"Are you nervous?"

He was, but she didn't need to know that. On the phone, Howerton hadn't sounded like the nicest guy, but new doctors were taught to expect a cool reception, especially psychiatrists. Knowing that hadn't helped Ben sleep over the past few weeks. "Of course not, darling. You know me. Nerves of steel." He waggled his eyebrows at her.

Michigan passed by quickly, and within two hours, they were back in Ben's home state of Ohio. The views didn't change much. Open fields, endless road, and blue skies forever. Cat Stevens gave way to Bob Dylan and the Beatles, the music lulling Ben into an almost hypnotic trance. He rubbed the sleep from his eyes and took a sip of the Tab they shared.

Halfway through Ohio, Julia poked him in the arm. "If you're tired, I can drive."

"You shouldn't even be in the car when you're this pregnant. You'll mess up the upholstery if you have that kid in here."

She laughed and rolled her eyes as the countryside moved by.

Morning turned to afternoon, and by evening, they were through Kentucky and into Tennessee. Knoxville rolled by out the windows. After that, it was all open road and trees as the highway climbed up into the mountains. By the time they reached I-24, the evening had given way to night.

Stars already shone overhead when they turned off the interstate and into Umber Gardens. The city appeared in the hills. Buildings twelve stories or more rose up from the forest like brightly lit giants.

The city's bustle noticeable, cars and headlights moving like ants in the distance, could be seen even from far away.

"That's gorgeous," Julia said. "Maybe it won't be as bumpkin as I thought."

Ben rubbed his eyes for the third time in twenty minutes. "Hey, little lady. I'm a bumpkin. You've got the son of a bumpkin kicking around in your belly." He arched an eyebrow at her in mock seriousness. "You better be careful with talk like that, city girl."

"Yeah, but you escaped the bumpkin life of a coal miner, and now you're going to be a world-famous doctor." She grabbed one of his hands and kissed it.

He smiled at her. That place, the Umber Gardens Home for the Mentally Unstable—the Home—paid new doctors what only surgeons made. Jean Piaget and Philip Zimbardo could keep their front-page pictures. Ben wasn't going to be poor anymore, and that was enough for him. Those thoughts danced through his head as they hunted downtown for their apartment.

Twelve stories tall and not more than a few years old, the building might have been out of place in another small Tennessee city. Not here though. Here it was just another up-and-coming project in an up-and-coming city. Fancy. New York fancy. Good enough for Julia, who was accustomed to the finer things in life. He parked the car and made his way around to the rear to grab the paperwork.

"Shall we, Miss Kent?" He offered her a hand as she stepped out of the car. She took it, and they walked through the double glass doors and into the lobby.

A security guard, old by even the most generous standards, sat behind a desk near the elevator, poring over a book.

"Hey, there." Ben walked up to the desk. "I'm Dr. Benjamin Kent." He savored the word. Doctor. A decade in the making. "We're supposed to be moving into four-a today."

The guard put the book down and smiled. "Well, welcome to Umber Gardens." He scratched at his chin and squinted as if he'd heard something funny. "You folks from up north?" His own accent dripped southern charm.

"As a matter of fact, yes." Ben set the paperwork on the desk. An agent for the rental company in town had already taken care of everything. A few weeks of playing mail tag and their new home was waiting for them when they showed up.

The guard took the packet and thumbed through it. "It's a nice little town we got here, and Tennessee is a helluva place." He opened a drawer and pulled out a pair of keys. "But y'all look beat, and it's late. Why don't I show you up?" The man started to stand, but Ben put up a hand.

"We can find it just fine. I appreciate it though." Ben looked over at Julia and smiled. "This is our first place together."

"Young love, huh? Y'all gonna need a hand moving your stuff?"

5

"I think we'll be fine. The movers should be here in an hour or two."

"When they get here, I'll send them up." The man stood up anyway and extended a hand to Ben. "My name's Harry."

Ben shook it. "This is my fiancée, Julia. You can just call me Ben."

"Well, Ben." He sat down. "If you two ever need anything, you let me know. Maintenance and everything else is handled right through this desk." Harry tapped on the wood.

"Thanks. We will." Julia and Ben walked to the elevator as Harry returned to his book. The door slid open, and they entered.

"Let me press it." Julia barely contained the laughter in her voice.

Ben stepped aside and gestured toward the panel with a wave. Julia ran her fingers down the buttons from twelve and stopped at four, pressing it. The doors closed, and the box took them up to their new life.

"Did that guard look like he was about to keel over?" Ben asked once the elevator started moving. She slapped his shoulder and laughed as it took them.

It opened onto a short pastel hallway with four apartments. The lights illuminated the golden signs etched with numbers upon the doors. They walked to four-a, and Ben pulled the keys out of his pocket. "You want to do this one too?"

She thought about it for a moment. "It's your turn."

He put the key into the lock, turning it. Before he could get his hand around the knob, she grabbed it and twisted it open.

"The lock was your turn," she said with a smile.

"Oh yeah?" He tried to grab her for a kiss, but she danced away and into the apartment, laughing. He followed her, wondering how she could still be that graceful nine months pregnant.

They took it all in as his shoes echoed across the hardwood floor.

"The living room is bigger than my dorm was." A living room with a breathtaking view of the mountains, an open dining room, and a cozy kitchen took up half the apartment. A short hallway led to a bathroom and two small bedrooms with a larger master bedroom and bathroom in the back. All of it painted in an awful green that had to go.

"This is amazing!" Julia said, running up and showering him in kisses.

He returned the last one and put his arms around her. "I think this place is going to be pretty great."

Ben spent the next half hour lugging stuff from the car to the apartment. The first thing he brought up was the folding chair he'd hidden away for Julia before they left. He set it in the living room. "I figured you might want to take a seat while we waited for the movers."

She shook her head, trying to keep her balance. "You just think of everything don't you, Dr. Kent?"

He couldn't afford to lose the rest of the stuff he pulled from the car, so he hadn't chanced putting it in the moving truck. His paperwork for the new job, family photos, and the antique lamp Julia's grandmother had given her for her birthday two years before. The little knickknacks, trivial until someone lost them.

In the back of the trunk, in a big black case, was the revolver that Julia's father had insisted they buy. Ben didn't want it. He'd grown up in the country, and was more than familiar with how they worked, but guns made him uncomfortable. He didn't like killing tools, especially now that he was a doctor. The idea of preparing to end a life while saving them every day struck him as more than a little hypocritical. Still, when daddy paid for everything, daddy got what he wanted, and so Ben had caved and bought the damn thing.

Julia and Ben spent the next hour looking around and planning while they waited for the movers. The couch would go there, the desk there. A new start in a new town, a new life in a new place. The movers knocked on the door shortly, and by eleven that night everything from Michigan was in the apartment. Ben thanked the movers, tipped them more than he probably should have, and closed the door.

He surveyed his new domain. "So what do you think?" He spread his arms out to indicate everything they'd accomplished.

She'd been messing around with dishes in the kitchen, despite insisting they not unpack until morning. She walked over to the couch and sat down slowly, letting out a sigh. "I think I'm beat."

He had to admit, he was too. "Well, what do you say we test out the shower and hit the hay?"

"That sounds like a great idea."

He helped her to her feet, and they went into the master bathroom. She took her clothes off and stepped into the tub, Ben just behind her. He loved showering with her. Not in a sexual way—although he liked that too—but because of the vulnerability. To stand naked in front of someone without fear of judgment touched something in him, something he hadn't known with anybody else.

"Little Ben just kicked," she said as the water splashed over them.

He put his hand on her belly, waiting to feel their son acknowledge that he too was a party to the moment. After a few seconds, he did. Ben leaned down as the water ran over his face and kissed the top of Julia's head. "I love you."

"I love you too." She put her arms around him and leaned her head against his chest.

Ben laid down to sleep that night as he had every other night over the last few weeks; full of trepidation. Julia turned the bedside light off and said goodnight.

Throughout the last month, something had changed. Sleep that once came easy now came slowly, if at all. He rolled over, trying to put it out of his mind.

If I keep turning sleep into a battle that needs to be won or lost, I'm never going to catch it.

He believed it. He knew it. It didn't help. Two hours after Julia began to snore, he still stared up at the ceiling, waiting for the night to carry him away. When it finally did, his dreams chased him down dark corridors. Fingers pressed against glass, and shadows shifted in the dreaming nowhere land. His dead mother whispered something to him, warning him. Afraid of whatever it was that no longer allowed him peaceful sleep, he ran. Unfamiliar voices screamed at him. Things reached out, trying to drag him down into the dark.

He found no rest.

They ate the last of their lunch from the day before for breakfast. When they'd finished, he moved furniture around while she unpacked boxes. "Grandma's lamp should go here, don't you think? The key holder needs to go by the door. Do you think we should put the baby in the closer room so we can hear him cry?" By the time afternoon rolled around, they'd done most of the unpacking.

"Do you want to go grab a bite to eat?" Ben asked as he surveyed their kingdom from the couch. A nice rug covered the floor, and a picture of him with Julia and her family hung on the opposite wall above the record player. Most of the furniture was a gift from Julia's father. Lord knew they had the money to spare.

"That sounds great," she said. "Why don't we go shopping?"

And they did. The daytime security guard, who looked about as ancient as Harry, informed them there was a Piggly Wiggly just up the block. They drove down the street and discovered that yes, Piggly Wiggly was in fact a real place. That gave both of them a good laugh. By the time they'd finished shopping, they had everything they needed to get through the first week in a new place.

"I guess all that's left now is to check out the town," Ben said as they got back into the car. He wanted to see it all, do it all. They had time, sure, but they'd watch it fly out the window once the baby came.

"Ugh! Not today. I can't handle anything that doesn't involve lazing." Julia leaned her head against the seat.

Ben acquiesced, and instead helped Julia cook an early dinner while Bessie Smith told them how hard it was to love someone who didn't love you back. Night cast itself over Umber Gardens. The long day of unpacking wound down into dinner on the couch.

"Looking forward to tomorrow?" Julia asked as the blues soothed away the day's troubles, few though they were.

"Yeah, of course." Not a lie per se, but not the truth. A new place, new friends, new co-workers.

He drifted away in thought as Julia looked over at him and smiled. "Good." She leaned against him.

He didn't want to be poor anymore. He didn't want to work to the bone so his family could eat dinner every night. *This is it. This is the good life now. I'm there.*

But he didn't feel there.

Chapter 2

He crawled out of bed when the alarm went off at seven. Another night, another nightmare. As Julia rolled over in her sleep, he walked into the bathroom and stared at himself in the mirror. *Just nerves. First day of the rest of your life jitters.* He let out a sigh and scratched his stubble. *Nobody walks into the hospital day one without thinking they're about to look like a jackass.* He slapped shaving cream onto his face, shaved, and proceeded through his morning rituals. Sit-ups and pushups until his muscles burned, buttered toast, and a shower to ease his mind. He wished he didn't look so tired.

By the time he stepped out, Julia was just waking up. "Good morning, Doctor," she said as she stretched in bed.

"Morning." He stepped into the closet to grab his suit. Had to look good on the first day. You never got a second chance to make a first impression. Or as his mother once said, *"You never get to screw it up twice."*

Julia picked up on his apprehension. "Shake off those first day blues, baby. You'll be fine." She scooted over to the side of the bed and stood slowly, her pregnant belly making it into a balancing act. "Why don't I make you breakfast?"

"Already ate."

She cocked her head and yawned. "Why don't I make me breakfast then?"

He didn't mean to be terse with her. Not only was she wonderful, but taking out his nervousness on someone else showed a stunning lack of character. He mentally chastised himself. "Coffee would be great though," he called as she left the room.

He finished dressing and checked himself out in the bathroom mirror. *Not bad.* He adjusted his tie and walked into the dining room, picking up his mug and taking a sip while she put some eggs into a pan. "Mmm. Good stuff. Just how I like my coffee and my ladies; hot 'n' sweet."

She brandished her spatula. "Dr. Kent, if you're going to be vulgar…"

He held his hands up in mock surrender. "Only the truth passes these lips."

"I'll feel a lot hotter when I don't look so round," she said, returning to her cooking.

He almost added, *"I like my women round too,"* but thought better of it. "I'm not sure what time I'll get home tonight. Might not want to wait up for dinner just in case." The clock in the kitchen told him it was almost eight ten. "I should go. This place is out a ways."

She set down her utensil. "You be safe today." She kissed him before re-adjusting his tie. "And try not to be nervous. You'll be fine."

He kissed her back. He'd be careful, but cool and confident wasn't going to happen. A little voice in the back of his mind reminded him that top of the class didn't mean he'd make a good doctor.

"I'll live, I'm sure." He grabbed his paperwork off the table. "See you tonight."

The downtown traffic wasn't as bad as he expected. His only other experience with a city had been Ann Arbor, and that place was gridlocked until ten. The heart of Umber Gardens didn't extend more than a dozen blocks in any direction. Past that were small suburbs and industrial complexes. He reached the city's eastern edge, where the lonely road that would take him to work stretched into the distance. Fields and pastures passed by as he did his best to keep his thoughts blank.

Yes, sir and no, sir. Keep up eye contact. Smile. Don't ask too many questions. Make sure they're the right ones. He mentally reviewed every technique he could think of for looking good on the first day. After a few minutes, he laughed. "And don't drill yourself like you have a stick up your ass," he said aloud.

The forest on his right loomed closer, the darkness of the woods absolute even in the sunlight. Old growth. The kind of forest that said it was there before you and would be after. He shuddered a little and shook it off.

The road climbed a gradual hill. At the top, the exit for the Home appeared on his right. A semi passed him going the opposite way as he turned, and the forest moved in to swallow him. The morning light vanished behind the trees. The effect, from the beautiful morning outside to a primordial overcast inside, stunned him. Perpetual dusk lived in these woods.

"Wow." He'd grown up in the hills and wilds of Ohio, but he'd never seen anything like this. *Eyes on the prize,* he reminded himself as the car sped along. *Plenty of time to stare slack-jawed at the flora later.*

Five minutes in, he thought he might have taken the wrong road. Halfway there he became certain. Just as he decided it would be best to turn around and call for directions, the road curved slightly. Past the curve, a large gate and a huge stone wall appeared out of the gloom.

Not a speck of rust marred the gate, but Spanish moss and cracks covered the stone wall like something out of a history book. The surrounding trees created an almost fairytale scene. Julia wasn't going to believe him when he told her about it.

Two men in white uniforms stepped out of the gatehouse. One looked to be in his mid-sixties; the other couldn't have been more than twenty. They blocked the road in front of the gate and waited for Ben to approach. Ten feet away, he opened his door to step out.

"Please stay in the vehicle, sir," the older guard said. His expression made it clear it wasn't a request.

Ben shut his door and rolled down his window. "Hey there," he said as the young man sauntered around to the driver's side. "My name is Dr. Benjamin Kent, and I'm supposed to start working here today."

The young man leaned against the car, placing his arm over the open window. Ben suppressed a wave of annoyance at the thought of someone putting fingerprints on his car, dirty from a cross-country drive or not.

"You got anything to prove it?"

Not a great first impression on your part either, Home. "Yeah, I've got all the paperwork right here." Ben handed the stack over to the kid. He walked back, and the pair conferred for a moment before the younger man unlocked the gate.

The older stepped up to the window. "Howdy, Doctor. Sorry about that, just a formality." He gave the paperwork back.

"No problem at all." *As long as you don't put your fingers on my paint too.*

He didn't. "Go ahead and pull through to the door. Someone will park your car for you."

The road continued for another fifty yards through the forest before veering to the right. The Home's grounds opened up before Ben. A stately, almost regal manor dominated the center of a huge clearing. The gardens and walking paths on the property stood empty, but Ben barely noticed. The manor itself drew his complete attention.

Châteauesque. The word came to mind from some long forgotten undergrad course. The three-winged building stood four stories tall. The road led up to a traffic circle with a porte-cochere on the far end and a huge fountain in the middle. The light gray stone and blue steeped roofs rose into points dotted with weathervanes and chimney stacks. The whole thing came right out of a Victorian romance paperback.

Or a horror novel. A chill ran up his spine. Daylight didn't touch the gardens. Clouds that he hadn't seen before blocked the sun. The red cobblestone road under his tires was conspicuously silent. The trees remained still, as if they weren't alive at all, just drawn onto the scenery. The lack of people made everything desolate. A motif of angels in heaven fleeing from a dragon below decorated the porte-cochere.

He put the thoughts out of his head as he approached. First day jitters, nerves and stress.

Two guards stood outside the doors. Ben pulled around the circle and stopped in front of them. He took a deep breath and let it out before grabbing his paperwork and exiting the car.

"Good morning, sir. Can we help you?" The guard on the left asked. He had about thirty years on the other one.

"I'm Dr. Kent. I'm supposed to start working here today." Ben stuck out his hand to shake with the guard when the paperwork slipped out from under his arm. The younger guard quickly stepped on the folder before anything had a chance to fly away.

"Hey, that was a close one." The guard bent to pick up the papers.

"Thanks." Ben dusted off the folder. *Auspicious start.*

"Dr. Howerton is expecting you," the older guard said. "If you head up to the desk, they'll take care of you." He moved aside and swung open the doors.

The reality of his situation settled over Ben. The rich marble floor, patterned in black and white, shone. Hallways spread out in every direction, both on the ground floor and the second story balcony. A massive white and gold chandelier hung from the engraved ceiling. It didn't just say wealthy, it said obscene. Decadent. This was kind of money Ben hadn't dared dream of in medical school.

A desk occupied the space between two sweeping staircases at the far end of the room. The middle-aged nurse sitting there said something to the orderly leaning against the counter. Judging by the look on her face, it wasn't very polite. They cut their conversation short as Ben entered the lobby and the doors shut behind him. His shoes made an outrageous amount of noise as he approached.

"Hello. I'm Dr. Kent." He flashed a smile and extended a hand to the nurse. "I'm supposed to be starting today."

She smiled back and shook it. "Welcome to the Home." Her New York accent could have come from one of Julia's sisters. "My name's Regina." She looked at the man nearby, and her smile faltered. "This is Scott, one of our orderlies."

Her smile could have melted butter. Nothing fake about that one, and Ben thought himself something of a pro on picking them out. The smile on Scott's face however, held no such warmth. "I can introduce myself just fine. Scott." He extended his hand, and Ben shook it.

"I was told to meet with Dr. Howerton. Is he available?"

"Yes, Doctor." Regina's practiced tone did nothing to mask her accent. "But first we need you to fill out some paperwork. You should have received a packet in the mail."

Ben placed the folder on the desk.

"Great." She opened a drawer, pulling out a separate stack of papers and placing them in front of her. "Dr. Howerton asked that you take care of all of this as soon as you came in. He's tied up in a meeting right now." She set a pen on top of mountain of loose leaf. "There's a waiting room just over there where you can have a seat and fill this out."

Being a doctor required endless paperwork; another thirty sheets wasn't going to dampen his spirits. "Thank you, Regina."

That smile flashed again. Scott said nothing. Instead, he did his best to look interested in something by the door.

Ben turned toward the waiting room she'd pointed out when Regina spoke up behind him. "Oh! I'll need your keys too."

"My keys?"

"Yes, Doctor. It's an access control precaution. One of the waivers you'll need to sign gives the staff permission to search you or your car when you leave."

Ben pulled them out of his pocket. Something about handing them over felt like giving up a lifeline; going past a point of no return. He set them on the desk without a word and turned back toward the waiting room.

As he walked away Scott mumbled something to Regina. "We'll talk about this later." Hospital drama. The more things changed, the more they stayed the same.

He crossed the lobby and pulled the door open. His apartment looked like a tree fort in comparison to the waiting room. A fireplace dominated the far end. Landscape paintings decorated the walls. Tasteful red couches and chairs lay near mahogany tables. Decadent wasn't even the right word. He knew the place catered to a rich clientele, but seeing was believing.

Until that letter had arrived in the mail three weeks before graduation, he didn't know places like this existed. They had asked for Ben through U of M. The letter said a lot about new blood and fresh ideas. The Home had to stay on top to continue catering to the high caliber of patients to which it was accustomed. He'd filled out the paperwork, certain they'd pick someone else. Nobody he spoke to had ever heard of the Home. Nobody paid the kind of money they talked about in the correspondence. But it carried on long past the point of joking. Letters of recommendation were written and signed, question after question was answered by mail, and finally, a phone interview by Dr. Howerton sealed the deal.

And now I'm here. He finished the paperwork in half an hour then walked back into the lobby. Regina still sat behind the desk, but now three older gentlemen chatted nearby. They all stopped to look at him.

Judging by the tallest man's hawk gaze, Ben guessed he was Dr. Howerton. The other two were equally old, but didn't possess his look of authority. "You must be Dr. Kent," the man said.

"I am." Ben approached the trio. "Are you Dr. Howerton?"

The man stuck out a hand. "Yes. Welcome to Umber Gardens." An iron grip. A no-bullshit kind of man. "This is the mayor of our little city, Tyler Carter." Howerton gestured at the shorter, slightly rounder man next to him.

Ben shook his hand too.

"And this is our local police chief, Richard Deetz."

Handshakes all around. The business way of sniffing a new dog's ass.

"We try to keep the local authorities apprised of our goings-on here."

"This place draws a lot of water in our town. We're glad to have it here." Mayor Carter winked at Dr. Howerton. "I trust you'll contribute to its sterling reputation?"

"Of course, sir." Ben faked a smile he didn't feel. Day one and the mayor stood before him. A sudden certainty that he'd gotten in over his head overcame him.

"They were just stepping out, and I hate to keep them."
Howerton turned to Regina. "Take Dr. Kent to my office." He turned
back to the mayor, shutting Ben out of the conversation. "The dinner
will be next Wednesday."

Ben took the cue and turned his attention to Regina.

"Follow me, Doctor."

Behind the sweeping staircase, a long hallway opened. Regina
navigated the hall, Ben in tow. As he walked off, the mayor spoke
behind him. "I'm very much looking forward to it."

The cavernous hallways leading away from the lobby gave way
to smaller ones. Huge wooden arches, lovingly detailed, hung
overhead. Posh sculptures and paintings of landscapes like those in
the waiting rooms lined the walls.

"This is quite the place," Ben said.

"It takes a little getting used to. It's pretty high-brow stuff."

"If I didn't know better, I wouldn't think this was a hospital."

She looked over her shoulder. "The west wing is where the
patients stay."

He hummed an acknowledgment and continued to eye the
scenery. The two-bedroom doublewide he'd grown up in would have
fit into one of the hallways.

Regina rounded a few more turns and stopped in front of a door
with a golden plate decorating the front, 'Dr. Richard Howerton'
written across it in bold print. She opened the door. "This is his
office. Do you need anything?"

"No, I think I'm fine."

She winked at him as she left. "Good luck."

Ben wasn't sure exactly what she meant by that, but it didn't sound promising. He couldn't help but think that the kind of guy with an office bigger than his living room probably didn't get there by being nice. He took a seat in one of the two high-backed chairs in front of the desk. The window behind it offered a view of a large floral garden and the mountains and forests beyond.

He didn't wait long. The door opened, and he stood as Dr. Howerton entered. He moved with authority. The kind of man who didn't ask for things, but demanded them. "My apologies for that, Dr. Kent. It's a very busy morning."

"Of course, sir. I understand."

Howerton stepped around to the other side of the desk. "Take a seat."

Ben did as instructed. "This is quite the place, sir."

Howerton crossed his legs and looked at Ben. Looked at him wasn't accurate, more like looked *through* him. That stare could peel paint. "It's the best in the world. Both for quality and care."

Ben smiled at that, but Howerton didn't smile back.

"Our fees to care for the loved ones of wealthy families are substantial. They expect the absolute best in all things. We are uniquely able to give them that because of our accommodations."

"I'm glad you've given me the opportunity to be a part of it, sir."

Howerton leaned back in his chair and appraised Ben. The silence stretched on for one minute, then two. Ben sat quietly, trying not to shift in his seat. Staring across the desk while his boss mentally picked him apart was the last thing he wanted on his first day. "What is it you're hoping to get from your time at the Home?"

He hadn't walked in expecting another interview. He reached for whatever answer came to mind first, unnerved somewhat by the long silence. "Experience, sir. I look forward to working with a staff that has years of knowledge." Trite, but he thought it would do.

Howerton waved that answer away and shook his head. "We brought a young doctor in for fresh ideas. Give me something more than that, Dr. Kent."

Ben didn't like being under the spotlight. Howerton would have fit right in with the medical boards that sat for psychiatrists certification. Those men had the same no bullshit expressions, and the same ability to ruin a career with a word.

"It's a good opportunity for me and my family, sir." Honesty might have been a bad choice, but it was already too late. "I didn't grow up wealthy. The Home will let me provide for them better than anywhere else out there. I intend to give back just as much."

Howerton raised his chin a bit and looked down his nose. The image of a hawk eyeing a rabbit couldn't have been more spot-on. "Tell me about your family."

They'd covered all of that in the phone interview, but if Howerton wanted to hear it again, Ben would give it to him. "I have a fiancée and a baby boy on the way. He should be coming any time now."

A small smile spread across his face. Not mirthful, but hard, like everything else about him. "I like people who have something to lose. People with something to lose work hard. They care about their jobs and the things that come with them." Howerton placed his arms on the desk. "Too many young medical students do it for recognition, or because it's what their family insisted on."

"You won't have that problem with me, sir."

Life growing up had been tough and poor, but back then he'd only had to deal with other poor folk. The mix of idealism and pie-in-the-sky American values at college had turned his stomach. It went beyond that though. His classmates honestly saw themselves as pioneers in a brave new world. Young men and women who would cure crazy one patient at a time. Give'em time and they might just fix death too. In medical school, entitlement went past the point of reason and straight to stupidity.

"That's good to hear. Very good, actually. Things are done a certain way here, and it's a way that works. If I can be frank, Dr. Kent, we aren't here to cure people."

Ben might not be looking to change the world, but being turned into a well-educated medication dispenser hadn't been in the cards either. Years of medical training amounting to nothing but a smile and a handshake while a nurse did all the work was the reason he hadn't gone the family medicine route. "Sir?"

"Our patients are all long-term. Schizophrenics, hyper-delusionals, the criminally insane— Wealthy families send us their dirty laundry so they don't have to deal with it. In turn, we provide a high standard of care so there isn't a burden on those families' conscience."

A lockup then, not a hospital. "What will my duties be, exactly, sir?"

"You will see patients, attempt therapeutic dialogue, and prescribe the necessary interventions. Standard fare for this sort of job. We have a small patient population, and it shouldn't be overly taxing." He leaned over the desk. "But you will treat the ladies and gentlemen here as ladies and gentlemen. We aren't some slipshod state hospital."

"I understand."

Howerton stood up. "Today I'd like to take you on a tour, get you familiar with the building."

"I have to admit, this place is fascinating. I've never seen anything like it."

Howerton left the office, Ben behind him. "There aren't other places like this. In the eighteen-hundreds when this place was built, it was one of the largest homes in the United States. It was donated to the state as a hospital building at the turn of last century." They passed a pair of nurses walking down the hall. Both smiled at Dr. Howerton, but didn't as much as look at Ben. "It was a general hospital until the early thirties, then it was unused until the mid-forties. I'm proud to say we've built quite a reputation around here."

They moved through the tangle of halls and back into the lobby. "We remodeled the east wing to be more like the original house. We use it for social functions, or guest space if a patient's visitors wish to stay the night. The west wing is the patient care wing. All of their rooms and facilities are there. The central building is used for staff and administration." They passed into the west hallway. Windows lined the wall on their right, offering a view of the front property. "There is a basement as well, but it's off limits to everyone but maintenance workers. Am I understood on that?"

"Yes, sir."

Howerton stopped and faced him square. "That isn't a rule to be taken lightly. The basement hasn't been renovated in years, and it could be dangerous down there."

Ben made eye contact this time. "I understand."

"Good."

They continued walking. Two massive doors dominated the far end of the hall, and a pair of orderlies opened them as they approached. "Security checkpoints are set up at the entrance to the west wing and at the landing on each floor. We take security very seriously here."

Ben heard him but didn't respond. The smaller lobby on the door's far side looked more impressive than the central section of the building. *This* was a home. Red carpet, red drapes, and the kind of furniture that cost more than his mother had made in a year.

"The third floor is residence for the mild patients, and the fourth is for the dangerous ones. This floor is administration."

A feeling of trepidation hung over the place. Ben chalked it up to first day anxieties, but he couldn't shake it. The shadows in the deep-set doorways were darker than they should have been.

27

Howerton showed him the kitchen and the dining room for the staff. The pharmacy came last. Ben couldn't relax, and his attention kept drifting. The phantom sensation of something watching him from those doorways wouldn't relent. He glanced behind him, expecting to see a staff member looking at him, but the hallway remained empty.

Nurses and orderlies passed by them occasionally, but the halls were largely unpopulated. "What's the staff size? I expected to see more people when I saw this place from the outside."

"Sixty people. You, myself, and Dr. Vitalie are the only doctors on staff. Dr. Bill Cray comes in to do the occasional checkup."

Fewer than Ben would have guessed. "How many patients?"

"Twenty-two." Howerton climbed the stairs to the second floor.

The amount they must have charged to keep a place like this open with only twenty-two patients made Ben's head spin, especially in light of what they were paying him. He'd found the goose, and all the patients were the golden eggs.

Howerton appeared to read his mind. "As I said, Dr. Kent, we sell peace of mind to wealthy families. Exclusivity is part and parcel of that."

Ben grunted an understanding. He stood on the other side of the looking glass, worlds away from the trailer park, in a place where people paid inordinate amounts of money for peace of mind. That kind of place didn't exist where he came from.

"The second floor is common rooms, libraries, and the space where Dr. Vitalie does the occasional group session. We have a small movie room set up for the patients as well. Violent patients aren't allowed on this floor at any time."

"How does supervision work?"

"Look around, Dr. Kent."

Orderlies sat at the end of each hallway that branched off of the main one. A nursing station was set up at the entrance to the stairs. *Eyes on everything around here.* "Will I receive privacy for my patient sessions?"

"Of course. Patient meetings are generally done on this floor. At least weekly, unless the patient requests a more intensive schedule." He looked back at Ben as he walked. "None of them ever do."

Howerton turned down a dark hallway with an elevator at the end. New, not some ratty old thing left over from the Stone Age. No windows let in light this far into the building, and the hallway's darkness unsettled Ben. "Are some of the bulbs out in here, sir?"

Howerton eyed the light fixtures and glanced back at Ben. "I think it's your imagination, Dr. Kent."

They continued down the hall. The hum of the elevator moving drew their attention. It set into place on the second floor, and the doors clicked open. The lights flickered overhead as the elevator revealed one small man inside, staring at the floor. He couldn't have been older than twenty-five. He wore a dark gray outfit that made it clear he was a patient. He had both of his hands behind his back, holding something.

"Robbie. Good to see you. How are you feeling today?"

Robbie didn't respond. He stepped off the elevator, and the doors slid closed behind him. The lights flickered again. Apparently, it wasn't Ben's imagination.

"Are you okay, Robbie?" Dr. Howerton asked. Robbie shuffled closer, but stayed out of reach.

Something wasn't right. Ben's head swam as the light bulbs continued to dim and brighten again. He rubbed his eyes. The first aching pain of a headache settled inside his skull.

"Robbie? What have you got?" A note of caution entered Howerton's voice.

"You aren't supposed to be here." Robbie peaked up at Ben as he spoke. His voice barely registered above a whisper. "You can't be here."

"This is Dr. Kent. He's a new doctor here." Howerton took a step toward Robbie, and Robbie stepped back in kind. "Are you feeling well today? Did you take your medicine?"

"They get you here."

The volume of his voice rose with each word.

"You can't be here. You have to go."

The words bounced off the walls around them.

"Bad place."

By the time he finished, he was yelling.

"Bad place!"

Ben had worked plenty of hospital rotations during his years at school. He'd seen unstable in all its forms, from delusions of grandeur to murderers sent by God. Nothing much got under his skin anymore.

"It's a pleasure to meet you, Robbie." Ben tried to ignore the buzzing that rose and fall with the flickering lights. He extended his hand for a shake. *Treat every patient like a person.*

"You can't be here!" Still yelling. "They'll get you here! They get you here every time!"

"That's enough, Robbie." Something subtle and threatening came across in Howerton's tone. "Maybe we should get an orderly to take you to your room."

For the first time, Robbie looked up. The unadulterated terror in his eyes startled Ben. He'd never seen anything like that. The eyes of a deer about to meet its maker on the front of a car. Ben stepped back.

"She won't let you have him!" Robbie screamed.

He lunged forward, the sharp handle of a broken broom suddenly in his hands, reaching for Howerton's chest.

Ben grabbed the middle of the stick, his own coordination and speed surprising him, as Howerton screamed for assistance.

Fear and determination stared out from Robbie's eyes. "You aren't supposed to be here!" He let go of the stick and jumped onto Ben. The sudden weight knocked Ben back before he fell to the floor, landing hard enough to force the wind from him. Howerton screamed something, but Ben didn't hear.

Robbie, still straddling Ben, bit down hard on the muscle between his shoulder and neck. Howerton hollered something again as Ben struggled to remove Robbie, grunting with panic. A patient had never attacked him before. Ben didn't want to hurt him, but his own animal instinct took over. His fingers found Robbie's face, and he sank his knuckles into the soft spot behind the ears, trying to do a jaw thrust to unlock the teeth from his neck.

Robbie howled in pain, letting go as two pairs of hands reached under his arms and pulled him off Ben.

The real world reasserted itself as the sudden altercation came to an end. Orderlies stood over Ben, Robbie struggling and screaming in their arms. *That was fast.* He chuckled at the absurdity of the thought as he sat up.

Dr. Howerton appeared above him and offered a hand. "Are you all right?"

Ben hardly heard him. A nearby nurse stared at his neck where Robbie had sunk his teeth in. Ben reached a shaking hand up and touched the spot. It came away bloody.

"Just hold pressure on it." Howerton put Ben's hand back over the wound and pressed it down. "We'll take care of that." He guided Ben by the shoulders down the hall, away from the elevator into which the orderlies were taking Robbie.

Ben looked behind him one more time before they rounded the corner. Robbie, Ben's blood covering his jaw, screamed down the hallway. "They get you! Shouldn't be here!" The sound followed Howerton and Ben down the corridor until the elevator doors closed.

Ben's heart beat hard in his chest as they walked toward the stairs.

"I've never seen Robbie violent," Howerton said. "He's been with us for years."

"It's fine." But it wasn't. The look in that man's eyes as he bit Ben wouldn't go away. Robbie hadn't just been agitated or scared. "He looked terrified."

"Well, Dr. Kent. That's sometimes one of the more unfortunate side effects of psychosis."

If Howerton cared that someone attacked Ben on his first day, it didn't show. They made their way down the stairs as blood seeped between Ben's fingers and onto his shirt. A medical office stood near the pharmacy. They walked in, Howerton ordering the nurse to retrieve sutures and a local anesthetic from the supply closet. Ben sat on the table.

"Move your hand." Howerton poked around, stretching the skin and examining the wound. "It doesn't look deep. I'm going to stitch it up." He turned his attention the nurse busy placing the supplies on a medical cart. "You can go."

Howerton opened the sutures and dug around in the drawers for what looked like a tiny pair of pliers. When he'd set up the needle holders, he retrieved the local anesthetic and injected it around the bite.

"What's that patient's diagnosis?" Ben asked.

"Extreme manic-depressive illness and paranoia."

"How long has he been here?"

"Five years." Howerton started stitching the wound before the anesthetic had fully set in.

Ben jumped as the needle pierced his skin. He did his best to suppress a wave of annoyance. He'd just been attacked, for fuck's sake. "Do people often get attacked on their first day?' Ben asked, his tone a little harder than it should have been.

"No." A note of irritation crept into Howerton's voice as well. "And you are expected to keep your composure even when such things happen." He pulled harder than he needed to on the suture, and Ben jumped again. "Am I clear?"

Ben wasn't sure how to respond, so he went with acknowledgment. "Yes, sir." He didn't think he'd lost his composure, but another tug on that suture and he might. "It won't happen again, sir." If that were any day but his first, Ben would've been tempted to tell the guy to fuck off. He kept that to himself.

"The staff here will look up to you as an example. Don't disappoint."

Howerton's hands were deft, and it didn't take long until the last stitch was in place and tied off. A knock came from the door as Howerton covered the site with a bandage. "Come in."

A short, portly man with a large mustache and combed-over hair stepped in. He looked about Howerton's age. "Hello, there," he said.

"Dr. Vitalie, this is our new doctor, Dr. Kent. Dr. Vitalie is the other staff psychiatrist."

"I'd shake your hand, but…" Ben held up his blood-covered appendage.

Vitalie laughed, but it never touched his eyes. "I see, I see. Who got you?" Ben didn't like that smile.

"Robbie," Howerton said. The way he said it implied it was expected.

Vitalie's mouth opened as if to reply. He glanced at Ben and then stared at Howerton. They held one another's gaze for a moment. "I see."

"Did you foresee problems with him?"

"I told you, Dr. Kent, he isn't violent."

Ben would have liked to point out that the man had lunged at Dr. Howerton with a sharp stick, but thought better of it. He washed his hands in the medical sink as Dr. Vitalie spoke. "We'll have to take care of that. Isolate him."

"Yes, we'll deal with Robbie," Howerton said. "But for now I think we should just deal with our new friend here. How're you feeling, Dr. Kent?"

Terrible and sleepless, but he wouldn't say that. "My legs are a bit rubbery, but I'm fine." Blood stained the front and side of his suit. He looked gruesome.

Howerton examined him up and down. "I think under the present circumstances, perhaps we should allow you the rest of the day to recover."

Ben didn't disagree. The three men walked out of the medical office. "We should have a nurse for you tomorrow," Vitalie said. "She'll have the files for the patients we assign you sent up to your office." He looked over at Ben's neck. "Unless something equally unfortunate happens, I don't see any reason why you couldn't meet your patients tomorrow."

"Do you know how many I'll be assigned?" The absurdity of asking so casual a question while covered in his own blood made his head spin. He didn't belong here, even the patients knew as much.

"Six. Just until you're more familiar with our family here." Vitalie laughed as if he'd told a joke, but again it didn't touch his eyes. "We have twenty-two, but seven are catatonic, or near so, so it's more like fifteen. Of those fifteen, six are held on the fourth floor permanently." He glanced over at Ben. "We've only given you one of those. The fourth floor can be a little… unsettling."

It couldn't be much more unsettling than being attacked. "I understand." They reached the lobby. "Are you sure you don't want me to stick around for the day, Dr. Howerton?"

Howerton looked him over again. "You look like a butcher. You'll have all the time in the world to get to know the place, Dr. Kent. It wouldn't be a terrible idea to keep a spare suit in your office."

That it might not be the last time a patient attacked him dampened Ben's mood further. Part of the job, maybe, but that didn't make the prospect any less frightening. Ben shook Howerton's hand, then Vitalie's. "I look forward to working with you both."

Howerton nodded and said nothing, and Dr. Vitalie laughed that humorless laugh again. "You'll never work at a place quite like this again, I promise you that."

Chapter 3

Ben watched the Home shrink in his rearview. Shrink might not have been the word he would use. Something that big didn't shrink, it just hid from view, crouching and waiting.

The men at the gate opened it for him and waved as he left. He returned a nod as best he could without hurting his neck. The bandage Howerton placed over the wound had already turned red.

"Damn." The first day couldn't have gone worse unless he'd blown up the building. He noticed a bit of blood on the side of his hand that he'd missed and wiped it on his pants. He'd held it together in front of his new colleagues—*bosses*—but now that he wasn't under scrutiny, the day collapsed in on him. Howerton thought him an immature young know-nothing, and Vitalie looked and acted like a caricature of Teddy Roosevelt.

That last part made Ben laugh, but the laughter only made him angrier. "Damn!" he yelled again, pounding a fist on the dash. He took a deep breath, trying to get a grip. Julia hadn't wanted to come here to begin with. "*Nineteen-seventy-two, and the south is still as racist as it was a hundred years ago,"* or so she'd said. The last thing she needed was him coming home covered in blood and stressing out. His lack of sleep already worried her enough.

Just cool off, Ben. Every week one day at a time; every day one breath at a time. His mother had told him that once.

When Ben walked into the lobby, Harry dropped his book onto the desk and stood up. "What happened to you?" Nothing fake about the concern in his voice.

"Just a little accident at work. Nothing a few aspirin and time won't fix."

Harry scratched his face as he sat back down. "Where are you workin' that what you got there's a little accident?"

Ben didn't feel much like talking after the day's events, but his mother would turn over in her grave if he disrespected a man three times his age. "The Home. You know it?"

"Yeah. I know it." Harry picked up his book and looked Ben over as if seeing him for the first time.

"I need to run upstairs and clean up. Sorry I can't stay to chat."

"You're all right, son. I expect I'll see you again." He smiled when he said it, but it showed too many teeth to be anything but a fake.

The elevator dropped him off in front of his apartment. He took one last deep breath and let himself in.

"Hello?" Julia said from the bedroom. She wouldn't be expecting him for hours.

"It's just me."

She turned the corner and stopped when she saw the blood. "Ben! What happened?" She walked over to him, quicker than a pregnant woman should, and put her hands on his arms.

"They said I wasn't right for the job."

She put her hand up to her mouth and drew in her breath.

He cracked a smile. "Joking."

"That's not funny." Her expression matched her words. She took a step back. "Tell me what happened."

He sat on the couch and told her about the attack, but avoided the rest of the oddness he'd encountered on his first day. He didn't want to upset her.

"I don't think Howerton likes me."

"Why?"

He shrugged. "Just a feeling I get." Ben stared off into space, trying to put his finger on it and failing. "Doesn't really matter."

He stripped off his bloody clothes and took a shower. The wound didn't look as bad as he thought it would. Howerton did a fine job of stitching, even if he did have a giant stick up his ass. Ben could deal with assholes though; he'd done it all the way through college. The poor kid from the trailer park on a full ride didn't make many friends in a wealthy school. His clothes were ratty, his accent was rough, and he didn't give a damn how much their parents made. He fixed the clothes and the accent, but not the rest.

Julia didn't care about any of that. She hadn't in their freshman biology class, and she certainly hadn't after her father demanded they get married.

"How're you feeling?" she asked as he picked out something less bloody from the closet.

"A little sore, but I'll be fine." He could deal with a lot of shit to make sure she didn't want for anything. "What do you say we have dinner early?"

They made dinner together and talked afterwards until the afternoon shadows stretched across the walls and the sun set behind the mountains. By the end of the night, things weren't as bad as when he'd left work.

Sleep came slowly. His mind moved between the waking world and the dreaming one. Visions of shadows on the wall became patients reaching out for him. He shook himself awake, and sighed in frustration. He needed sleep. The last few weeks had been brutal, and his first day on the job was worse. He rested his head again only to see the shadows slide down the wall and flood the floor around the mattress, leaving him and Julia adrift in a sea of black. Again, he shook himself awake. His mind was just trying to deal with the stress of a new career, moving, and a baby joining the family. Nothing to worry about. No reason to be scared.

Long after Julia started snoring, his waking mind finally gave up and swayed into dreams. He walked the empty the hallways of the Home searching for another person. Someone, anyone, to help him find the way out. His anxiety grew. If he didn't find a way out, he would spend an eternity wandering the halls of that place.

With that thought, a shadow shifted on the wall. Something sinister had lured him there, called him to work from home in the middle of the night. It chased him down endless corridors that reeked of age and neglect. He passed paintings of horrible men who'd done terrible things. The windows revealed a forest that stared right back at him.

He wanted to find a goddamn door, a way out, anything. Every turn brought him further into the building. The thing that chased him, a malignant presence that sucked all the hope from the world, filled the corridor. If it drew too close it would suffocate him with its pressure, push him against the walls until there was no air. Thinking about it sucked the breath from his lungs.

He had to get out. Another corner in his mad dash through the hallways brought him face to face with the basement door. There was supposed to be another way out of the hall, but this appeared to be the only way left to go. Trying to catch his breath, he turned to see how close the thing behind him was.

The jarring bell of his alarm pulled him from the dreaming world.

He groaned as he rolled over and hit the clock on the nightstand. The nightmares were getting worse, more specific. They homed in on him like a beast on the hunt. He shut the thought down quickly. A lack of sleep was bad enough; he didn't want to compound it with morbidity.

Julia moved, but didn't wake up. Probably for the best. Loving she might be, but not at seven in the morning. Ben performed the same routine he had every day for the last nine years. Workout, breakfast, shower, and dress. The wound on his neck didn't look terrible, but staring at it twisted his stomach into knots. Julia still snored by the time he'd finished. He packed up a few things for his new office and left.

Harry sat in the lobby as Ben walked out to the car. "Have a good one, Harry," Ben said as he walked by.

"You too. Have a better day at work, son."

"Thanks, I will." He meant it. At least he hoped he did.

At some point in the night rain had fallen, and a light mist covered the world. Once he passed into the forest at the edge of town, the mist thickened into fog. The deep shadows tucked away around the ground and the swirling wisps around the trees made the place into something primitive. The idea of getting stuck out in that primeval jungle made Ben uncomfortable.

Two orderlies opened the gate for him as he pulled out. No questions this time, just a friendly nod. The same malaise that coated the woods hung over the grounds. Stares from the windows followed him as he stepped out of the car and grabbed his things, but when he examined the windows, he saw nothing.

He walked into the lobby and up to the group standing around the desk. Howerton stared down a nurse who looked ready to flee as he finished whatever he'd been saying. "Ah, Dr. Kent. Good morning. How're you feeling today?"

Like I was bitten by a lunatic. Or like I haven't slept in a month. Dealer's choice. "Very well. A few aspirin and I was right as rain." Ben set his keys on the desk, and the nurse on duty took them. He wondered if he'd get used to that as she squirreled them away under the desk.

"Good, good. We'd hate to lose you on your first day to such an unfortunate incident." Howerton didn't show the slightest hint of humor when he spoke. "We have a nurse for you," Howerton continued. "You're familiar with Nurse Casey?" Howerton nodded at the woman Ben had met yesterday, Regina.

"We've met."

Regina smiled her winning smile at him.

"She's to show you up to your new office and help ease your transition into the Home." He looked at her. "You understand what's expected?"

"Yes, Doctor."

"I have a few things to attend to this morning. Administration in a place like this is never done." He nodded at Ben and left.

The rest of the nurses and orderlies around the desk scattered off to work.

Ben blew out a sigh as he watched Howerton walk away. "That guy's pretty intense, huh?"

Regina smiled at him, but only with her lips. Her eyes narrowed a little as if he'd said something particularly stupid. The older nurse behind the desk looked up and cocked an eyebrow at him. Apparently, he'd stuck his foot in his mouth. Rather than backpedal, he decided to retreat. "Care to show me to my office?"

"Of course."

They walked away, and the old nurse watched them go. Regina climbed the stairs to the second floor and went down a hallway on the east side with Ben behind. Not quite as lavish as the first floor, but the halls still had a touch of class Ben was fairly certain he'd never get used to. When he'd met Julia's parents on a spring break vacation in New York, she'd taken him on a whirlwind tour of the city's art and history museums. The Home felt like one of those with the lights off, even in the daytime.

"How does anyone ever find their way in this place?" Ben asked.

"I got lost all the time when I started here."

They made a few turns and ended up at another set of stairs. The third floor resembled the second, but without the people. After a few more turns, they arrived at the fourth-floor stairs. "All the way up?" Ben was in shape, but he didn't want to climb a hundred steps ten times a day.

She shrugged. "Dr. Howerton isn't the nicest guy with new people."

"Yeah, I'm getting that."

She glanced back at him, but her expression remained inscrutable. "You should keep things like that to yourself around here."

It didn't come off as anything but friendly advice, but it still struck a note of caution in him. "Yeah?"

"I don't care, but a lot of the people around here are a little more… conservative."

"How so?"

She shrugged as they walked down the fourth-floor hallway. "A lot of old timers work here. A lot of family, or friends of family. That kind of thing."

Ben understood. The same good ole' boys club that ruled the university campus.

They rounded another corner at the top of the stairs and came to a short hallway. One door read Janitorial across the plate, another Dr. Bill Cray. The last one brought a smile to Ben's face. Dr. Benjamin Kent.

Regina opened the door for him. The sense of class that pervaded the rest of the facility was lacking in the small office. Wallpaper, yellow with smoke and age, lined the walls. An old desk that had seen better days took up the back of the room. The only saving grace came from the window; a huge thing that looked down on an amazing view of the back of the property and the wilderness beyond.

Ben smiled as he took it in. It might lack charm in a building otherwise soaked in it, but it was his. His.

"Wow. Nice place," Regina said.

Ben laughed. "It'll do for now." He walked to the far side of the desk and sat in the chair. It squeaked dangerously as he put his weight into it. "I think I'll need a few more shelves in here."

"Dr. Howerton takes care of all that."

It didn't surprise Ben in the least that Howerton micromanaged everything. "I'll ask him about it. Would you mind bringing up my patient files before we get started today?"

"Sure thing. Do you need anything else?"

"I'm good, thanks."

He leaned back and surveyed his domain as the door closed behind her. There were a few hooks on the wall. He dug through the box he'd brought up from the car and hung his diploma on one.

He set a picture of his mother and the family dog next to one of Ben, Julia, and her grandmother on the Statue of Liberty. Her family had banished any concerns about being uptight when her grandmother hocked a loogie off the top of the statue and cackled like a mad woman.

Regina returned a few minutes later with a box full of manila files. "These are the treatment records for your seven patients." When she set the box down, the desk creaked almost as loudly as the chair. He really had pulled the short straw on offices.

"I thought I was only supposed to have six." Ben began digging through the box.

Regina shrugged. "Some of the people around here are about as organized as they are friendly."

"Yeah, I kind of picked up on the antisocial vibe. That nurse downstairs is a bitch, huh?" He froze for a second, unsure if he'd stuck his foot in it again.

Regina covered her mouth and laughed. "You're bad! But yeah, she's a real bitch. A lot of the staff's been around since the place opened. They treat the new people like dirt. I let it go. I didn't come here to make friends."

Ben kept digging around in the box. "Hazard of the profession I guess. Want to come back up at ten thirty? I'm going to need some time to look through these."

"Sure thing. I'll see you in a bit." She closed the door behind her.

He made three neat stacks of his patients. A few were catatonic and hadn't spoken in years. He pored over their medical paperwork and wondered if all the sedatives were to blame. He'd keep that opinion to himself until he got to know his patients. The one on the fourth floor had been diagnosed psychotic and had to be restrained in order to prevent him from hurting himself. Two were run-of-the-mill delusional.

The last one was the most interesting, and struck an odd note with Ben. She'd been at the Home for twenty-six years. She'd killed her family and spent nearly fifteen years in complete isolation before being allowed among other patients. Theresa Parker. She reminded Ben of his mother the minute he read her file, though he couldn't put his finger on why.

He decided to check on the three patients who would speak to him first, looking through his paperwork until Regina came back up just before ten thirty. She carried a clipboard with a stack of blank paper on it and set it down on the desk as she walked in. "Figured you might need one when you go see your patients."

"Thanks. Show me to my new patients? I'd like to start with Theresa Parker."

Regina led the way toward the western wing. "Theresa's yours, huh?"

"That she is. You've spent time with her?"

"All the nurses except for the doctors' private ones rotate around. I've spent time with everyone here. Most of them are too far gone to do much with. I just feed and clean them. Some of them are a little more… involved. You've got to be careful."

"Like Robbie?"

"You know, I can't believe he did that. Most of the time he's quiet."

"Really?" Ben couldn't imagine the screaming maniac that bit him sitting in a corner putting together a puzzle. "Could've fooled me."

"Yeah." The New York accent dripped off the word.

They walked in silence for a moment.

"So what about Miss Parker? How's she?"

"Just a little off. Smokes like a chimney, but never gives anyone any trouble." Regina brushed the hair from her face "I heard she killed someone when she first got here in the forties. Hard to believe, but I guess that's how she got locked up in the first place."

They moved across the lobby balcony and down the stairs, turning into the hallway that led to the west wing. "Anyone else I should watch out for while I'm here?" Ben asked once they were out of earshot of the desk.

She thought for a moment. "All the dangerous patients are kept isolated."

"And what about the staff?"

She smiled. "Anyone who's been here more than ten years is liable to make your life miserable."

They walked on in silence, passing by the security checkpoint and into the west wing. They made their way up the stairs and past the hallway where Robbie had attacked him. This time no mental patients waited in the shadows to strike. Ben wondered where Robbie was now.

They continued until they came to stairs leading to the third floor. *So many goddamn stairs in this place.* At least he'd stay in shape.

The third floor could have been a five star hotel. Tasteful decorations, fresh flowers in the vases, and a red and gold carpet pattern like something out of Buckingham Palace. Scattered orderlies kept an eye on the patient rooms. By and large though, the place was empty.

The west wing was still dimmer than the rest of the building, just like the day before. It wasn't a lack of light or windows. Every exterior wall let in sunlight. This was something different. Something Ben couldn't quite figure out. He blew it off. There was already enough on his plate for the day without adding vision troubles.

After a short walk, they arrived at a door with the name 'Theresa Parker' etched into a panel on the wall nearby.

"This is her room." Regina knocked. Ben nodded, but had serious doubts about finding it on his own.

"Come in."

Regina opened the door and stepped inside, Ben just behind. A large bed with a mahogany frame took up the far end of the room. Doors were set into the wall on either side. One opened into a bathroom as large as Ben's office. This wasn't a mental institution, it was the Viceroy Hotel. Just ring the bell and receive prompt service.

Theresa sat at a desk in the corner. Long gray hair cascaded down her back. She couldn't have been under sixty, but her presence commanded attention. She took a drag off her cigarette and eyed the pair as they walked in, the scent of cloves filling the air. That smell took Ben back to the trailer where his mother had smoked the same thing. She looked Ben up and down, but said nothing.

"Hello Miss Parker. My name is Benjamin Kent, and I'm a new psychiatrist here."

She stared at him a few seconds longer before speaking. "Did you go straight from kindergarten to medical school, Benjamin?" Her voice was so southern she would have made Scarlett O'Hara sound Californian.

"Ma'am?"

"You look about sixteen."

"I have all my adult teeth, if that helps."

Theresa smiled, but just a little. When she did, ten years dropped off her face. "Take a seat, Benjamin." She gestured to a chair near the door, and Ben took the invitation. "You can go," she said to Regina, fixing her with a frank stare.

Regina hesitated before Ben nodded at her. "I'll be just outside if you need me, Dr. Kent." She shut the door behind her.

"New Yorkers," Theresa said once the door closed. "Just as apt to rob you as look at you." She put out her spent clove on a nearby ashtray.

That stare of hers almost made Ben sit up straighter. Control was a tricky dance in the therapy game, and he resisted the urge. "I have to admit, Miss Parker, I'm not used to speaking with patients in their bedrooms."

"I've been here too long to give a damn." She took a pack of cigarettes off her desk and lit another one.

Trust took time. Ben knew that and respected it. Being too nosy, insensitive, or rushing a relationship was a good way to ensure one's patient never saw you as more than a talking head. He didn't want that. "Quite the accommodations they have around here."

Theresa continued to stare. She could give Howerton a run for his money. "It's amazing what endless money can buy, isn't it?"

"I didn't know places like this existed when I was in school."

She cleared her throat before finally looking away. "You'll have to forgive me, Benjamin. I'm just a little put off by your presence." She puffed on her clove. "I wasn't expecting a new doctor to come calling."

"They didn't tell you I was coming today?"

"They don't tell us much around here. I meant I wasn't expecting any doctor to come calling for me whatsoever. I've been here so long I'm almost part of the scenery."

Ben's puzzlement must have shown on his face.

"Don't be a dolt, boy. Patients are better unseen and unheard in a place like this."

"I don't understand."

"Obviously." She ashed her clove. "You're here to ask us how we're doing before they shut the door and collect the next check."

"I see. I won't be that kind of doctor, Miss Parker."

She turned to him and narrowed her eyes. "Be honest with me now, are you slow?"

"No." Ben tried not to smile. Quick wit and a tough exterior; Julia wasn't much different. "Miss Parker, I don't know how things are with Dr. Vitalie, but if you need me, I'm here."

"Call me Theresa, please."

He stood and walked over to her, extending his hand. She shook it lightly, like a lady. "I've got other patients to introduce myself to today. Do you want to set up appointments to see me?"

She thought for a moment, taking another long drag off her clove. "I will admit some company would be nice. There isn't much intellectual stimulation around here." She stared off into space for a moment. "Can you come by tomorrow?"

"I can do that." Ben wrote it down on his pad. "Anything in particular you want to discuss?"

"I'm sure I'll think of something. If you'll excuse me now, I have to finish my letters."

"It was nice meeting you, Theresa."

"Likewise, Benjamin," she drawled as she turned back to her desk.

Ben let himself out. Regina stood in the hall at a respectful distance. Once the door shut and they'd walked a little ways toward the stairs, he spoke up. "She doesn't strike me as the typical patient."

"I told you, she's different."

Different. Not the word he'd have used, but that summed it up.

The next patient, Mike Long, made Theresa appear downright normal. He clicked through an old box radio's channels in a second-floor room. "They send the messages this way," he informed Ben. "Fuckin' commies get their signals straight past the national defenses."

"Do you know where you are, Mr. Long?"

Mike opened his mouth to speak, but something caught his attention. He cocked his head to the side, listening to something that wasn't there. Ben pressed him further, but got nothing else. He left to see his next patient.

Miranda Kelly informed him that he needed to visit more often. "Daddy, I get so bored sitting around the house all day." She had twenty years on Ben.

"I'm not your father, Miss Kelly. My name is Dr. Kent. You're at a mental institution."

She twirled her hair in her hands and ignored him. Twenty minutes of that and Ben gave up for the day.

Two of his semi-catatonic patients listened to the sounds that weren't there, much like Mike Long. Their heads swayed in exactly the same way despite being in different rooms. Watching them loll back and forth, a faint smile on their lips, sent a chill down his spine.

"Does that happen a lot around here?" Ben asked after they walked out of the last room where soundless music played.

"Yeah. Dr. Vitalie told me it's called shared psychosis."

He'd heard the term before, but he wasn't sure it applied there. "I'll have to ask him about that when I get the chance."

They left the third floor and went up to the fourth. As they crested the stairs, a wave of dizziness overcame him. He grabbed the railing to steady himself.

"Are you okay?" Regina asked.

"I'm fine." The spell passed as suddenly as it came on.

The nurse at the desk station atop the stairs glanced over her newspaper at the spectacle.

"Just a little light headed, don't worry."

They walked past her, exchanging pleasantries. Up here the temperature dropped a few degrees, and goose pimples puckered up on his arms. "Cold up here, isn't it?"

"Yeah. It always is."

They moved down the fourth-floor hallways. All the windows were barred, and the decorations that adorned the halls below were nowhere to be seen. All business when it came to the crazy folk. Most of the rooms they passed sat empty, and orderlies were posted outside all the occupied ones. They stopped in front of Chris Clann's room.

The orderly stood up as they approached. He eyed them nervously and licked his lips. He couldn't have been over twenty. "He's agitated today, sir."

Ben looked at Regina then back at the orderly. "What do you mean, 'he's agitated'?"

The young man shifted on his feet. "He's been screaming all morning. One of the nurses finally had to sedate him."

Leaving a patient alone in a room by himself all day troubled Ben, though it was fairly common practice. "So you just stand out here all day and listen to it?" Annoyance crept into his voice.

"We sit in the room with them sometimes,, and the nurses go in to visit. But when he gets like this, having someone in the room only makes it worse."

The patient files made it clear that Chris Clann was a very dangerous man. Still, leaving him unattended all day was inhumane. "Keep me posted. I want to know if he gets worse."

"I will, sir."

If he found his patients were being left alone on a regular basis, he'd have something to say. But Ben already had a lot on his plate, and he didn't want to deal with that today. Besides, nobody liked a doctor that started making demands on day two.

They returned to his office. "Thanks for your help today," he said. He sat behind his desk and set his notepad down.

"No problem. Is there anything else you need?"

"I'm good. I just need to set my schedule."

"All right. When you're finished, drop it on the desk. We need to add it to the master list."

"Thanks." He sighed. Looking past her into the middle distance. "I'm not sure what I can do for most of these people." It came out like a guilty admission.

"I thought it was weird they brought on another doctor. Most of the people here aren't gonna get better." Howerton's words mirrored almost exactly.

Ben put his elbows up on the desk and rubbed the stubble on his face. "Yeah. Not what I expected for a first job." He picked up his pencil and tapped it on the notepad. "I'll have this on the desk tonight. Thanks again, Regina."

"No problem. I'd rather be a personal nurse any day." She smiled and waved as she walked out the door.

Ben set to work transcribing all his notes for each patient and inserting them into the appropriate folders. He spent the next few hours arranging his files and more carefully going over each. Eventually, his attention started to wane.

The small room with his name so proudly displayed outside the door was cramped now that he had to spend time in it. The yellowed, smoked-out wallpaper stopped looking like wallpaper when he stared at it for too long, instead taking on the hue of old flesh. Old like a patient that had spent too long on the fourth floor without sunlight or human contact. The morose thought chilled him. Shadows that stretched across his desk grew longer, reaching black fingers toward him.

At that thought, three hard knocks sounded on the door.

"Come in," Ben called, shaking the sleep away. He hadn't realized he was starting to doze off.

The door opened, and Howerton strolled in with Vitalie just behind him.

"Good afternoon, gentlemen."

"Dr. Kent. I hope your second day is going better than your first." Once again, not a hint of humor played across Howerton's face.

"It's been much better." Any day one didn't get attacked was apparently a good day. "Please, take a seat."

They did as he bade. "So, what do you think of our little facility so far?" Vitalie asked.

"I'm not sure I'd call it little."

Vitalie laughed, but it still didn't touch his eyes.

"It's quite the place though. How's Robbie?"

A shadow crossed Howerton's face. "He's been particularly agitated since the incident. We had to accommodate him on the fourth floor until he calms. It wouldn't do to have him get everyone riled up."

"You'll get no argument from me, sir."

"You have your schedule written out already?" Howerton asked.

"I'm just writing it down now. I was reviewing my patient's files in light of putting a face to them. Most don't seem like they'll benefit from a psychiatrist."

Howerton didn't react, but Vitalie laughed a robust, belly-shaking laugh. "You aren't wrong there. Most of these people aren't here to get better. They're here so their families don't have to look at them."

His sentiments mirrored Howerton's perfectly. This field wasn't one of instant gratification, but the prospect of helping nobody settled on his heart painfully. He tried not to let it show on his face.

"As I said yesterday, Dr. Kent, this isn't a place for idealism. If you can make these people more comfortable, you've done your duty."

They made small talk for a while. Vitalie and Ben did most of the talking, Howerton occasionally interjecting. "Where did you go to school? Who taught you? Oh, I've read his work, very sharp mind." With the spirit of etiquette properly sated, Howerton and Vitalie stood up. Both made apologies about busy schedules.

"By and large the plan is for the two of us to work independently," Dr. Vitalie said as he opened the door, "but if you have any questions about your patients, my office is on the first floor."

"Speaking of offices, is this my permanent spot?"

"It's what we have available for now, Dr. Kent. We'll look into getting you something downstairs when we have space."

Ben took Howerton's tone as final. He doubted the only space available in that giant building was a broom closet on the fourth floor, but he wasn't going to argue with his new boss. "I appreciate it. Thank you."

"When you're finished with your work, feel free to go home."

Both men left the office, closing the door behind them. Ben sat back down and penned out a schedule for the next month. It looked woefully inadequate. He decided it didn't matter and gathered up his things. The day was coming to a close, and while it had been interesting, he was ready to go home. He made his way down the honeycomb of hallways toward the front desk. Regina was nowhere to be found, but the older nurse from earlier chatted with two orderlies. He handed her his schedule.

She called over a security guard, wearing the outfit that made them all look like milkmen. When the man pulled his car around, Ben got in and left.

The building watched him go. *"I never said you could leave,"* it seemed to say. *"You can never leave."*

He shuddered at the thought. Nothing awful had happened, but he couldn't shake the feeling that it hadn't been a good day.

Chapter 4

He walked into his apartment half an hour later, arms loaded with the box full of patient files. The smell of chicken and broccoli greeted him. The living room had been rearranged in his absence.

"Sweetheart, I'm home," Ben called out as he shut the door.

"I'm in the kitchen."

He looked around at Julia's handiwork as he walked over. "Did you unpack all of that by yourself?" He set his things down on the kitchen table.

"Of course." She licked something off one of her fingers. He leveled a mock disapproving stare at her as she gave him a quick kiss.

"Julia, you're pregnant and ready to pop. You can't push furniture around here like a trucker."

She rolled her eyes and went back to cooking. "I wasn't moving furniture. I just unpacked a few boxes."

"All right, but if you end up giving birth on our new floors, you've got nobody to blame but yourself." He took his jacket off and draped it on a chair.

"Har, har, har, Steve Martin. Set the table." She stirred the boiling pot.

He grinned at her and did as she asked.

"I wasn't expecting you for a little bit yet. I wanted to surprise you with dinner on the table." She studied him up and down for a moment. "It doesn't look like anyone tried to eat you today."

"Thank god for that." He sat at the table and let out a weary sigh. "Not much to do around there when patients aren't out for blood."

She gave him a quizzical look.

"Most of my patients are not the sort to benefit from therapeutic dialogue. Totally disconnected from reality."

"But you have a few you can talk with, right?"

"One seems to be pretty lucid. A handful of others speak."

She shrugged. "So you won't be busy. There are greater tragedies, darling."

"One of them… I don't know. She reminds me of Mom."

Julia waited to see if Ben would say anything else before she asked, "How so?"

Ben sighed. "She killed her husband and infant son in the forties because there were monsters in them. She smokes cloves." He rubbed his face. "She doesn't look like Mom or anything, but that history kinda hit home, you know?"

Ben's mother had killed herself in his senior year of undergrad after a total psychotic break. He should have seen the signs. He should have known something wasn't right. He hadn't, and she died because of it. She cut her wrists in the bathtub to get the monsters out. The suicide note had said it all.

"Have you asked to have her switched to another doctor?" Julia asked.

Ben laughed. It reminded him of Vitalie's; mirthless. "Are you kidding? I've been there two days. It's not really the right time to unload the family laundry."

She kept silent, stirring the pot and not looking up. He didn't expect her to say anything. There was nothing to say. The only rough time in their relationship had been in the months following his mother's death, and neither of them were eager to drag up those memories.

"I'm going to go take a shower."

Julia nodded and kept cooking. By the time Ben showered and changed into something more comfortable, Julia had laid out dinner on the table. Broccoli, chicken, and biscuits from a can— Julia might not have been a culinary genius, but Ben was grateful all the same.

They made small talk and ate. "Did you get an office yet? That wallpaper sounds gross. Yeah, at least it has a view. Oh, you made a friend? That's good."

After dinner, Ben kissed the top of her head and cleared the table. They spent the rest of the afternoon, joking, teasing, and unpacking the last of the boxes while putting the apartment together.

Hours passed, and the workday tension slowly eased away. By the time the sun set, Ben had forgotten all about Theresa. They sat down and listened to old jazz records, appreciating the unpacked living room and making plans for their future.

They lay in bed that night and talked about the new city. She'd grown up in New York, and they'd both gone to college in Ann Arbor. Small town life was going to take some getting used to, at least for her.

"Are we going to have to start talking in southern accents?" she asked as they lay looking at each other, lights off, covers up.

"Better than that god-awful one your grandmother has."

She laughed aloud and slapped his shoulder.

He wrinkled his face. "Jes'! Do not hit meh! Da' hurts meh!"

She hit him again and snorted with laughter.

He smiled back. "I think we'll get by just fine without them. Wouldn't do for the doctor to blend with the yokels."

"Wouldn't do for someone to mistake you for a miner?"

He laughed. "Why do you think I left Ohio?"

She shook her head. "You're ridiculous, Dr. Kent."

"I'm ridiculous? You're having my baby."

"Oh... This is yours?"

He rolled over and showered her with kisses. She squealed in mock protest, giving up after a moment and kissing him back.

"Go to sleep. You have to be up in the morning," she said when the giggling had died down.

"All right, sweetheart." He looked into her eyes and leaned over to kiss her one more time. "I love you."

"I love you too."

He tried to sleep after that, but his mind raced from thought to thought. New jobs and new opportunities. Thoughts of taking care of a baby, and thoughts of his mother. It kept him up long past the point where Julia had fallen asleep. The clock read ten, then eleven, and still he couldn't get there. By midnight, his mood had turned sour. This couldn't go on much longer. He didn't have time for it with the new job and a baby on the way. Something though, unease in the back of his mind, wouldn't abate.

As he lay in that place halfway between sleep and wakefulness, his thoughts slowly came apart and gave away to dreams. Something wasn't right. Shadows wormed on the walls. The flesh on the back of his neck went ice cold as something leaned over the bed behind him.

"They don't want to sleep anymore," a voice whispered in his ear. A rasping whisper, dark and scratching, like a dying man's breath.

Ben opened his eyes and lifted his head. He sat up in his office chair, looking around, trying to get his bearings. A dull orange light bathed the room, but as the sun shifted behind him, it took on the color of rust, or blood, and set faster than it should have. The shadow across his desk became a hand reaching for the door. It stretched out and touched the sickly yellow wallpaper, creeping up it until the dark of full night washed everything in a sea of shadow and black.

Boom, boom, boom. Something slammed three times on his door. His mind screamed at him, warned him against opening the thing between him and nightmares. He couldn't help it. He walked around the desk, his heart racing and his legs moving of their own accord. He couldn't understand how he'd gotten to his office.

He glanced behind and saw his bedroom through the window, floating in the air four stories above the ground. The sheets of his bed were ruffled. Julia was nowhere to be seen. Something dangerous had come for them. It chased them out. Julia was nearby, he could feel it. She touched the edges of his mind.

"She's in danger." The voice came from everywhere and nowhere. *"Help her or they'll wake up."*

"Who's there?"

No answer. He had to go. He had to find her. He reached for the doorknob, but before he could touch it, the entire door vanished, leaving only a hole leading to a world of darkness. The gloom reached in and consumed him. He flailed in the black like a drowning man. All around him pieces of the Home and his apartment flew through the void.

"Have to get out of here. Not safe here." The same voice from before, further away now, drifting from nowhere.

The shadows diminished, receding no different than the tide. When they'd cleared completely, he stood in the lobby of the Home. His mind moved slowly. Julia, he'd been looking for Julia. She was in danger, and he needed to find her.

The dull light of a full moon illuminated the room, though he couldn't see the source. It cast an blue glow on everything. The black parts of the floor turned into gaping holes through the world, and shade shrouded the upper balcony. The windows in the room revealed nothing outside but a world made of fog. The smell of old dirt wafted up from the floors. A sense of dread grew in his gut. Julia was here somewhere, she had to be.

"I told you they'd get you." Robbie, hunched and pathetic, stood in the darkness of the hall behind the desk. The balcony's shadows obscured his face, but Ben could still see the blood on his shirt. "They get inside you so they can stop sleeping."

"Robbie? It's okay, Robbie. Come out here. We need to go." Ben didn't know why that last part was true, but he did. He reached out, hoping Robbie would come to him so they could find Julia together and escape.

"Too late. Too late." Robbie backed away and vanished into hall. Ben chased after him, running to catch up. A slow-motion echo followed his every step.

The unseen edges of the corridor closed in around him. Hidden things stared from the corners. Something moved on the wall, and shapes crept in the peripheral of his vision even in the constant, dim light. The paintings he'd admired earlier now watched him as he ran. He couldn't think straight. He'd been warned. Someone had tried to tell him.

Robbie fled around a corner, and Ben followed. He reached the next hallway as Robbie ran toward the back of the building. Another sound joined his echoing footsteps, something close behind, a sound like the slap of wet feet on tile. The air went cold. His breath hung heavy in the air.

He ran as fast as he could, the sound of his footsteps no longer fading, just building and building as he ran, the wet slaps always a little louder. He turned the corner, sweat and fear pouring off him. At the end of the next hallway, the basement door opened, and fog rolled out as thick as clouds. Standing there, smoking a cigarette, stood Theresa. All the sound stopped as Ben froze in place.

"It's hungry, Benjamin," Theresa said in her long drawl.

Terror seized his mind as the darkness closed in and swallowed him.

He woke up thrashing in his sweat-soaked sheets, his heart racing. His body knew it was awake now, but his mind hadn't quite caught up. An echo, just the barest nod on the edge of his consciousness, spoke. *"It's hungry, Benjamin."*

He put his face into his hands as the waking world asserted itself.

Julia turned over. "What's wrong?"

He sat in silence for a moment as he found his bearings. He looked at the clock on the nightstand. Six twenty-five in the morning. Another goddamn night with no real sleep. "Bad dream. Go back to sleep." He got up from the bed and left the room.

He didn't want to think about it. Couldn't think about it. Another day without sleep would be hard enough without torturing himself over nightmares.

After his mother died, they'd been just as bad. Dreams of her alone in the tub cutting her wrists. Dreams of cockroach swarms devouring her body before he could find it. Dreams of her coming back and telling him it wasn't his fault for leaving her alone. Time had healed those, and time would heal these.

When he'd finished showering, the dream was already a distant thought in the back of his mind. He made his breakfast and sat at the table, paging through his patients' files. He'd decided to skip exercise. His heart had gotten enough of a workout already. He needed something to focus his attention on, and sit-ups wouldn't do it.

He thumbed through the files, trying to get a feel for the new people in his life. His patients had been at the Home for more than a decade without visitors. More in some cases. Ben couldn't help but think about what a horrible life that must be. Confined to one room, never knowing the touch or love of anyone besides those paid to watch you like a dog in a kennel. That was no way to live. He set those thoughts aside and focused on treatment. *They aren't paying me to editorialize on their lives.* Solutions served better than statements.

Before long, he had to get ready for work. He went into their room to change, and when he'd finished he walked over to Julia and kissed her on the head. She mumbled something that may have been a question, but he didn't want to wake her. By eight twenty, he was on his way to work.

The forest on the road to work glided by. He needed to take Julia out to see the city, but he'd skip the woods. They loomed over the car like disapproving guardians. As he drew closer to the Home, what little beauty existed in the forest slowly drained away. Maybe it was lingering fear from the night before, or maybe the way the light caught the gate as he pulled up, but something about the place wasn't right. It was as if the wilderness, the whole world, ended at that gate, and some other place began.

Ben chalked it up to nerves from his bad dream as he waved at the security guard, who gestured for him to roll down his window. Three people were out there that morning, all dressed in the milkmen whites. Orderlies or guards, Ben doubted there was a difference.

He turned the crank, and the window slid down. "Good morning."

"Good morning, sir," the man said in a business tone. "We have an issue. A patient got out of his room on the fourth floor. Dr. Howerton is directing the search from the lobby. Once you're in today, you're in until Dr. Howerton says you can go."

"Alright. I understand."

"Thank you, sir." One of the other guards opened the gate and shut it behind Ben. It slammed, the echo of its finality following him up the path.

For the first time in his three days at the Home, he actually saw people out on the property. Looking for the patient, he supposed. Not that there were many places to hide on the big, open grounds. *How could anyone have gotten out of the building?* All the windows were barred, and the doors were guarded. Ben wasn't overly familiar with the Home yet, but he assumed it wasn't a cakewalk to escape.

He pulled up to the doors and grabbed his box of files off the passenger seat and thanked the man who took his keys. He walked into the lobby—no nightmare moonscape, just the lobby—and went to the desk where Howerton and Vitalie spoke to the older nurse from yesterday. Howerton held a radio that crackled and spoke up occasionally.

He looked up from his conversation as Ben walked in. "Robbie has gotten out of his room."

In spite of himself, a little jump of adrenaline coursed through Ben. The bite on his neck had turned into an ugly bruise with bloody teeth marks. He'd covered it up again to avoid agitating any patients who might see it. Ben had never been afraid of anyone, but he'd hoped it would be a while before he saw Robbie again. "I'm not familiar with the protocol here, sir. How can I help?"

Howerton reached behind the desk and grabbed another radio from an unseen nook. "Take this and drop your things off up in your office. We're doing a floor-by-floor search from top to bottom. I'll have an orderly meet you in your office, and you can come down together to help."

"Of course, sir." Ben set the radio in his box before heading to the stairs.

"Stay on channel two, Dr. Kent, and stick close to the orderly. The last thing I need is to have someone else get lost here today."

That guy really loads on the charm. Ben walked up the stairs, very aware of how easy it was to be alone in the giant building. The silence swirled around him, turning everything sinister. He couldn't hold Robbie accountable for the unfortunate incident on Monday. He suffered from mental illness. That didn't mean Ben was eager to run into him again.

He reached the fourth floor without incident. Scott, the orderly Ben met on the first day, stood outside his office.

"You know a shortcut I don't?" Ben asked, puffing a bit from the stairs.

"I took the elevator."

Ben stopped in his tracks. After a moment Scott laughed.

"I'm just kidding, man. No elevator on this side of the crazy line."

Ben forced a smile. Scott leaned against the doorway with his arms crossed as Ben set his things on the desk. The hungry look in his eyes reminded Ben of drunk frat boys with something to prove. Scott knocked on the doorframe three times—*boom, boom, boom.* The sound brought Ben back to last night.

"You okay, Doc?"

"Yeah, yeah I'm fine. Just a little chill is all." September in Tennessee was anything but chilly.

They made their way back downstairs, chatting as they went.

"How're you liking it around here?"

71

"It's great, man, starting to feel like home already," Ben lied.

"Good to hear! We're a big family here. We look after our own. Heard you were from a small town yourself."

It wasn't really a question, but Ben answered anyway. "A lot smaller than this, but yes."

"You know what it's like then. Gotta look out for each other. That's what this place is all about."

He would have thought a hospital was all about taking care of patients, but kept the idea to himself. They walked in silence before Ben spoke up, not out of real curiosity, but because the silence made him uncomfortable. "How long have you been here?"

Scott looked up and to the left for a second as if doing some particularly hard math. "I guess about twelve years now. My old man was a maintenance guy, got me the job before he died a few years ago."

"I hear a lot of the staff has been around a long time."

"Sure have. Some have been around since the place opened in the fifties. A few of the old timers back then were here when the place was a hospital. Lot of new blood running around since then, but most of them are relatives, or friends of people who worked here a while."

"Keeping that good pay in the family, huh?"

"Something like that," Scott said with a smile and a sidelong glance. That hungry look intimidated Ben.

Howerton explained the situation when they reached the lobby.

"Check the back areas and work your way forward. I want the two of you to stick to the hallways. We have teams of people checking each room. If Robbie is hiding somewhere, I don't want him to sneak behind a group into a room we've already searched."

It was going to be a long and monotonous day just walking around the halls with an orderly. *Is this why I spent nine years in school?*

They searched for some time, but soon they were walking the halls and talking. The doors had been guarded all night, and all the windows were barred. No way had Robbie gotten out, but gone he was. Harry Houdini couldn't have done it better.

Scott told Ben about growing up in Umber Gardens as they paced the halls. The bars to visit, the places where the single ladies liked to go, and the spots the big city hustlers threw their money around. "Those fuckin' people. I can't stand those people." He shook his head. "Snobs come down from Nashville and look at us locals like we're a bunch of inbred nothings. Makes me goddamn crazy." He looked over at Ben. "You know what I mean, right? You look like the kind of guy who'd go out for a beer."

The venom in his voice set Ben back a step, but he tried to cover it up. "I'd love to, but I can't anytime soon. I'm getting married. Got a baby boy on the way."

"Married, huh? She from Ohio too?"

"She sure is." The words New York would probably give this guy an aneurism.

Scott did most of the talking, and within an hour Ben was certain he knew the guy's entire history. By the end of the second hour, he wanted to scream. He needed to change the subject before he lost his mind. "I haven't seen any of the nurses around," he said, thinking of Regina. All the people they'd passed had been orderlies.

"When we got into lockdown, the nurses stay with the patients. They'll rotate by the front desk throughout the day, but the orderlies do the searches. Speaking of nurses, that one you're with—" He cut off as they walked into the back hallway. The two orderlies that had been on the back door the dozen times they'd passed were nowhere to be seen. The door outside stood wide open.

"Oh, what the hell?" Scott moaned. He stuck his head out and looked around. Ben peeked through one of the nearby windows but didn't see anyone outside.

"Fuck, man," Scott said. "What the hell were those guys thinking?" He stepped outside and looked further while Ben stood in the doorway. The guy was high-strung enough without something like this happening. Ben imagined Howerton wasn't the forgiving type. As a newly minted member of the upper staff, Ben wasn't thrilled either. Robbie could end up anywhere if he got out of the building. *If he isn't already. Why the hell am I doing this? I'm a doctor.*

"Where did those guys go?" Scott looked around. He blew out his breath in an angry huff. "Lock this door up behind me."

"I don't have keys yet."

Scott thought for a moment. "It'll be fine. Just wait in this hall in case one went to piss and needed the other to hold it."

"Alright. Whatever you think is best." He might get a lecture from Howerton about taking responsibility as a doctor, but he could deal with that. As long as it got him away from Scott and his inane stories for a little while, Ben didn't much care.

"I'll be quick about this." Scott went outside and pulled out his keys. "Dr. H. is gonna lose his shit if he hears about this." He shut the door behind him. The lock clicked, and Ben was alone again.

Finally, a moment of peace and quiet. If Robbie were on the first floor, someone would have seen him by now. Howerton coordinated two first-to-fourth-floor sweeps and was currently looking through the east wing. The occasional radio chatter confirmed Robbie wasn't in the west wing either. If he was still in the building, which was less and less likely every hour, he'd hidden well enough that they weren't going to find him. Everyone acted casual about the whole thing. The hospitals Ben had attended during residency would have been in an uproar.

The minutes stretched on while Scott searched for the other two orderlies. Ben looked around the hallway, appreciating the landscapes and portraits that decorated the walls. His gaze fell on the basement door a little ways down the hall. Large red letters had been painted on the door: *KEEP OUT*.

They'd been down that hall a dozen times since Ben's arrival, but this time the space between the door and the wall looked wider, as if someone had left it open. Ben walked over to check it. It had to be a figment of his imagination. No way they'd been so inept that they hadn't noticed the basement door was unlocked.

But it was.

"Fuck," Ben said quietly. He unclipped the radio from his belt and keyed it. "Dr. Howerton, this is Dr. Kent." He listened for a moment. No response. "Scott, this is Dr. Kent." Again, no response. "Can anyone hear me?"

Scott had done all of the talking on the radio. Just as well, since Ben's was apparently broken.

He had to admit, he was curious about whatever might be in the basement. As a boy, he and Eddy had once gotten lost in an abandoned coalmine for a weekend. Always going where he wasn't supposed to be. He wasn't a kid anymore, but he did have a responsibility to the patients. Robbie might have gotten lost down there.

He looked over his shoulder at the back door. *I'll leave this door open. Scott will see I went down there when he gets back.* He propped the door open with a nearby table and stepped inside.

The hallway on the other side didn't have the wide-open feeling of the rest of the building, just a narrow path leading to another door. He walked toward it quickly, not wanting to be gone longer than he had to. Three flashlights hung from a hook on the wall.

Better safe than sorry. He grabbed one. The nearby door had seen better days. It swung away with a foreboding creak as he twisted the handle, and a chasm of darkness yawned before him. Old stone stairs descended into perfect darkness. He clicked his flashlight on and made his way through the door.

The steps angled downward sharply, and the air grew chill as he went lower. At the bottom stood another door, more decrepit than the one at the top. He twisted the handle, but the door didn't budge. Slightly dismayed, he shoved on it and nearly tumbled through when it gave suddenly. He caught himself just in time to avoid spilling onto the floor.

While not as tall as the lobby, the room was easily as long. The beam from his flashlight didn't reach the distant walls. He tried to picture the building in his mind to figure out what would be above him, but gave up. He'd only been at the Home for a few days, and the layout remained a mystery.

The stone floor had been tiled at one point, but most of that was gone. The cracked and broken pieces reminded him of an old factory he'd explored near his home in Ohio. That place would rather have been left alone too. The ceiling towered eight feet above. Pipes and bundles of wiring passed in and out over him, but they looked as if no one had serviced them in years. He shined the light along the walls, trying to find a switch. Five feet away an old-fashioned turn knob jutted out. He walked over and twisted it. Dim light filled the room—not much, but enough to see by.

Despite the overhead lights, pockets of darkness remained. The eerie effect illuminated the piles of old equipment and debris like a spotlight. Hallways led off in several directions.

Dread stabbed his heart. The entire place stood empty and cold as a tomb, a testament to the past better left undisturbed. His head swam. The hum of old wiring keened above him. *I should go back now. This is stupid. I could get fired for this.* But he didn't. He wasn't wrong. Robbie could be down there. Someone needed to find him.

The scent of old dirt rose from the floor as he walked toward the passage at the far end of the room. Not the natural fragrance of a garden or grass, but the smell of an old grave. His footsteps echoed, but the sound didn't travel.

He passed under the arch, and the ceiling lowered considerably, now only a few feet above his head, pressing down on him. The walls of the hallway had been more than just stone once. Only in a few places did supports and rotted wood still cling. Everything else had been laid bare by time, revealing the old, colorless bricks underneath. He walked on, the overhead lights providing little illumination. A few doors opened into unused rooms. Most of them contained dilapidated hospital equipment.

Was this an old ward for the hospital? He swept his flashlight beam over the ancient junk. *What a terrible place to spend your last days.* The morbid brought to mind his mother's funeral. The black dress. The pale skin. The cuts peeking out from under her sleeves. He walked on, going slow and eyeing everything.

More than once, he turned around, expecting something behind him. It wasn't anything he heard or saw, just a sense that he wasn't alone. That feeling of being watched from across a room only to

78

look up and find a stranger staring. Down here, there were no strangers, and he tried to chalk the sensation of company up to paranoia. A missing patient, a new place, and a basement fit for the Addams Family. He shook it off with a shudder.

The hallway went on longer than he'd expected. He'd just decided to turn around when it poured into another cavernous room. He again scanned the walls for a switch, but didn't see one. His dread grew as he stepped into the blackness with nothing but his flashlight and what little illumination from the hallway leaked in. *Just a basement. Nothing new here. Relax.* He'd grown up exploring dark places much deeper under the earth, but something about this place screamed confinement, as if the walls themselves didn't want him poking around. He tried not to let the feeling bother him. Stubborn pride or foolish fear he wasn't sure, but he'd be damned if a spooky basement would chase him away.

He stopped in the middle of the room as his unease grew. While he peered into the blackness, a darker shadow moved off to his right. He jumped, and quickly flashed his light in that direction. The cone illuminated nothing but a brick wall with an old door set in it. He took a deep breath and blew it out slowly. *Get a grip, Ben.*

He pondered looking inside the room when his radio crackled to life. He let out an audible gasp and nearly dropped his flashlight. His heart hammered as if it wanted to escape his chest. Whatever was said on the radio came through only as static.

Anxiety washed over him, and ugly thoughts followed. Robbie could be watching him from the shadows. The idea was silly, not that it mattered. Robbie hadn't walked down there and wandered around in the dark all morning, not with all the shit lying around. He'd break his neck in ten minutes. Still, as soon as the thought entered Ben's head, the phantom sensation of eyes watching him from the unseen corners crawled over his body. The swimming sensation in his head hadn't abated since he walked down the stairs, and it was giving him a headache.

But he wouldn't turn back now. He couldn't look himself in a mirror when got home if he let a basement scare him. If he couldn't search the whole place on his own, he'd go back and get Scott.

He almost called out Robbie's name, but thought better of it. Yelling down here would be like yelling in a graveyard. Instead, he walked forward and opened the door in front of him. The old iron hinges creaked slowly as it swung toward him. *Of course, it would.*

File cabinets stood along the walls, and boxes of papers were spread across the floor. A records room.

He walked in and flashed his light around. It wasn't particularly large, and it reeked of mold and old parchment. He stepped over a pile of boxes filled with loose papers in the middle of the floor and up to the old filing cabinets, some of them made of wood. He opened the top drawer of the nearest one.

Old files, yellow and brittle with age, filled the cabinet. He thumbed through them, looking for anything that caught his eye. He picked out one file in particular and set it on top of the cabinet. 'Mary J. Hemsworth 1911' was written across the front in flowing script. He opened the file, careful so it didn't tear or crumble apart.

Mary's family had sent her to the hospital amid a wave of tuberculosis patients that year. She died within two months of admission. She spent her last days in the basement with the other tuberculosis patients in an attempt to stop the spread of the disease.

"Aha," he muttered softly. *So that was what they used the basement for.*

He closed the file and placed it back in the same spot. It was silly of course. Nobody had been down there in decades by the look of it, and odds were good nobody would ever look through these files again. Years from now, they'd be thrown out as trash and the people in them forgotten. Still, it felt like some small respect to the people whose names were written out in that flowing handwriting. He closed the drawer before walking around the edge of the room, examining each cabinet. He stopped in front of another promising wooden cabinet reading '1930' across the front.

As he reached for the handle, something moved outside.

The sound drifted faintly into the room— a shoe sliding against stone. Ben shined his light out the door. The flashlight swept as far as it could across the dark room outside. It wasn't far enough, and he could see nothing in the basement's black. All thoughts of old patients and hospital history fled from his mind. The quiet set his nerves on edge. He hadn't imagined that. Something was down here.

"Robbie?" Ben called into the silence. "Robbie, are you down here?"

He listened, hoping to hear something. After a few seconds of eerie silence, his radio crackled to life, the static drowning out anything he might have heard. The swimming in his head burst into a headache. He'd been expecting the radio to key up again, so he didn't jump, but what he heard made him stiffen and his eyes widen.

A quiet voice whispered through the static of the radio. "I told you they'd get you."

His fingers and toes went cold. *Did I just hear that? I couldn't have, right?*

Panic rose inside him. Visions of his dream from the night before came to his mind unbidden, and suddenly, he was back in the nightmare lobby. Every nerve in his body blared the message *'Get out!'* full blast.

He didn't second-guess himself this time. He ran from the room toward the dim illumination of the hallway that would lead him back to the stairs. Another door creaked open somewhere in the larger room, and the sound of feet scraping against stone hissed. Not the slow shuffle of someone walking, but the fast *skt skt skt* of running.

He sprinted into the hallway as a thousand horrible images flew through his head. Robbie behind him. The thing from his dreams. Something terrible that would drag him into the lightless depths forever. Any rational sense melted, replaced by fear. He looked back over his shoulder, expecting to see Robbie or some other horror hot on his heels, but he saw only darkness.

Something struck him at waist level. He tumbled over, his flashlight flying from his hand. Both Ben and the old gurney he'd run into crashed to the floor. He tried to get his hands up in time but failed. *That wasn't there before,* was the only thought he managed before landing hard on his chest and chin, knocking the breath from his lungs.

All sound stopped. He stared at the floor in a daze. He rolled over onto his back and took a few deep breaths, gulping in air. He lifted his head to look back the way he'd come and saw something moving in the shadows; a shape that filled the passage behind.

That was all it took to find his second wind. He jumped up, flashlight forgotten, and ran hard toward the stairs. Something heavy—the boom of thunder on a starless night—gave chase behind him.

He made it through the hallway and into the room, crossing it in seconds. The booms drew closer. He sensed a hand reaching for him, some impossibly long appendage that would drag him away forever.

The door upstairs stood open. He bolted through and up the staircase, taking the stairs two at a time. He sprinted past the door at the top of the stairs, slamming it shut behind him without looking.

The feeling of pursuit ended at the basement, but he ran on, needing the light of the sun and to escape whatever was downstairs. He charged across the length of the narrow hallway. As he reached for the handle of the door that would lead him back to the first floor proper, it swung open.

There stood Scott, smiling. It faded the second they locked eyes. "What happened to—"

Ben flew past him and shut the door to the hallway, stopping only once it was sealed. He gasped for air in the light from the rear windows. "Something down there," he panted as he leaned against the wall.

Scott glanced between Ben and the door. "What happened to your face, man?"

Ben touched his chin, and his hand came away bloody. "Did you hear what I just said? There's something down there!"

"Just hold on, man." Scott grabbed his radio. "Dr. Howerton, I think Dr. Kent just found Robbie in the basement."

"No. That wasn't Robbie." Ben was lightheaded from fear, but Scott wasn't listening. "Something chased me."

"What was Dr. Kent doing in the basement?" Howerton's voice held the deceptive calm of a tornado before touchdown.

"What are you saying? An animal?" Scott arched an eyebrow.

"I don't know. But there's something down there." Ben became very conscious of having his back against the wall next to the basement hallway and moved.

"Just slow down—" Scott started.

"I want some answers," Howerton said over the radio.

Ben grabbed for his own radio on his belt, only to find it wasn't there. He grabbed Scott's radio from his hand as Scott looked at him with a slack jawed expression somewhere between shock and stupidity.

"I was looking for the missing patient." Ben's temper flared as fear and adrenaline coursed through him. "Something attacked me down there. There's your answers."

Scott's mouth dropped open as if he'd been slapped, but he quickly recovered and snatched the radio back. "Hey, man! You look spooked, but you say shit like that on the radio and they'll lock you up in a place like this." He made a show of taking a deep breath in and letting it out. "Relax, and tell me what happened."

By that time, the two orderlies who had been guarding the exit—or who were supposed to have been guarding the exit—had walked inside and approached the pair. Ben walked to the back door, needing the fresh air, as he told the group what happened. He felt better with the wind and sunshine on his face. The property might be gloomy, but nothing was as gloomy as that basement. When he finished, the other three men looked at each other.

"It was probably just Robbie giving you a scare," Scott said with his hand on Ben's shoulder.

Ben shook his head, making the headache worse. One of the other orderlies had produced a handkerchief for Ben to wipe his chin. "I'm telling you, I heard a voice on the radio and a door open in pitch black. You think he can see in the dark?"

"I don't know, but look sharp." Scott nodded toward the hall. Ben stepped back inside to see Dr. Howerton striding toward them, a small group of orderlies and nurses in tow.

He walked up to the four men standing at the door. "Scott, you and Mr. Handley help the group going to check the basement. "You"—Howerton looked at the remaining orderly—"take Dr. Kent to my office and then come back here." He turned to walk off.

"Dr. Howerton, I—"

Howerton, his face a storm of anger, spun around quicker than Ben would have guessed he could. "Not a word from you."

Ben had taken about as much as he could, but he bit his tongue. Adrenaline-induced boldness would be a bad reason for being fired. He took a deep breath, trying to force himself to calm as Howerton strode toward the basement hallway.

The remaining orderly gave Ben that 'you're fucked' look troublemakers and wage workers knew so well. Ben's displeasure at the sudden turn of events must have been clear. The orderly quickly put on a stoic mask and led the way toward Howerton's office. He opened the door for Ben, who walked in and took a seat, then left him alone with his thoughts.

He fumed over his boss yelling at him in front of the staff. He wanted to give Howerton a piece of his mind. The audacity of the man, being that rude after his big speech the first day on setting an example.

The minutes dragged on, and the headache he'd acquired in the basement pounded at his temples. His anger turned to doubt as the minutes ticked by, and then to concern. He'd been told not to go in the basement. *The basement filled with shadows and monsters.* He scoffed at the thought, but became keenly aware of how alone he was. Uncomfortable with the building's silence, he fidgeted in his seat. After twenty minutes he stood and started pacing. The day had been mostly sunny, but the shadow of clouds passed over. The whole property turned silent and solemn despite the warm weather.

There wasn't anything down there.

The irrational part of his mind answered back. *You know that's not true. There was something.*

He shook his head. *That's idiotic. The building is creepy, but it isn't…*

He couldn't bring himself to think the word haunted. Instead, he rubbed his forehead. *You haven't slept well in weeks. It was just a lack of sleep. You need to get some real rest before you lose your mind.* He regretted that thought immediately. It hit too close to the mark.

Howerton interrupted as a light drizzle fell outside. "Sit down, Dr. Kent." Howerton walked past and sat behind his desk. His earlier rage was absent from his voice, but his eyes remained hard.

Ben sat down without a word, his hands on his lap. Howerton stared at him for a long moment. "Members of the staff are combing over the basement now, but it appears there is no sign of the patient down there."

Ben waited to be asked anything before he spoke up. He didn't know what to say anyway. *Sorry, Dr. Howerton. I heard a voice out of my dreams on the radio and got spooked.* Even now, as he sat there looking at Howerton, he became less and less sure of what had happened.

"Why were you down there?" There was no right answer. The tone of Howerton's voice said as much.

Ben answered anyway. "I found the door open and wanted to see if the patient was down there."

"And it didn't occur to you to radio that in or ask Scott to accompany you?" Howerton's voice grew louder as he spoke.

"My radio was broken. I just meant to poke my head in." Ben searched for the right words. "I got spooked. I wasn't alone down there, and I don't think it was Robbie."

Howerton leaned back in his chair and smiled. It was possibly the most condescending smile Ben had ever seen. "Are you saying you think another patient escaped, Dr. Kent?"

"I'm saying I don't know what happened. There was a voice over the radio that I couldn't identify, at the same time I heard someone walking around outside the room. When I… When I ran out, I heard a door opening behind me and thought I was being chased."

"You let a voice on a *radio* scare you?" Howerton shook his head, his smile fading. "You are a medical professional now, Dr. Kent, and you have authority over a staff full of people with more experience and wisdom than yourself." He rose from his chair. "You could have been hurt down there. More importantly, you've shown yourself to be insubordinate after only three days." He planted his hands on his desk, his face full of disdain "Don't ever, *ever*, disobey me again!"

Ben's blood boiled, and he stood up. "I get attacked in this place twice in three days, and that's how you speak to me? Is that the kind of operation this is?" He was ready to walk out on that job right now. He could find another one easy enough. The pay wouldn't be as good, but maybe it wouldn't be as miserable.

They looked at each other for a long moment before Howerton sat down and rubbed his eyes under his glasses. When the minute stretched on and Howerton continued to say nothing, Ben sat back as well. His heart beat out an angry march in his veins, but he kept silent.

New employees were a dime a dozen, and a hospital found few things as obnoxious as a new doctor who knew everything, or one disobeyed his more experienced co-workers. He'd heard it a million times in medical school. As the silence stretched on, his anger turned to embarrassment. It had been a day for sticking his foot in his mouth.

"It's been a trying day, Dr. Kent," The anger has vanished.

Ben didn't trust himself to speak. 'Cram it up your ass' was the only thing that came to mind, and that was a poor choice.

"Why don't you take the rest of the day off? You look terrible."

Ben seldom found himself at a loss for words, but he was then. He'd been certain Howerton was going fire him over the day's events. He was proud of his accomplishments, but sometimes one had to bite the bullet and admit that a job wasn't a good fit.

"I'm quite serious. It's been a long day for everyone, and I've taken it out on you."

"I understand, sir." Ben didn't know how to react to Howerton's shift in tone.

"I'm getting ready to call this search off and inform the local authorities if Robbie isn't in the basement. I'm going to have to call his family and tell them of this turn of events, and I'm certain they won't be pleased. Your… outburst on the radio was unexpected, and the basement is dangerous. There are pieces of old equipment and gas lines down there. I don't want the rest of the staff in a tizzy over this. They look up to the doctors as an example here. Next time you have an experience like that, come tell me in person. Don't announce it."

He'd let himself get scared in the dark while breaking the rules. Howerton had every right to be mad at him. He was being incredibly childish. His cheeks began to burn under Howerton's scrutiny. "I'm sorry, Dr. Howerton, I don't know what came over me—"

Howerton held up a hand. "It's fine, Dr. Kent. You are adjusting to many new situations here. Just don't let it happen again."

"I'll use more discretion in the future."

Howerton nodded and waved for Ben to leave. He did as he was told, but as the door closed, Howerton's words stuck in his head. *Next time you have an experience like that.*

He walked out to the lobby. Regina and a few other nurses and orderlies sat at the desk. They stopped talking as he walked up. They must have been discussing his episode.

"I'm leaving for the day."

One of the orderlies opened a cupboard hidden behind the desk, and the jingle of keys followed. He moved to the exit, not wanting to answer questions if any staff worked up the nerve to ask them. Regina approached him a moment later.

"I heard you had a scare downstairs."

He brushed aside his annoyance, not wanting to be rude to the only member of the staff that treated him with respect. "Yeah. I thought… I don't know. I thought I heard something down there with me." He spoke quietly so his voice wouldn't carry. "It was stupid."

She was silent for a moment before dropping her voice to a conspirator's whisper. "A lot of people see weird stuff around here. Don't sweat it."

"Do those people usually yell about it over the radio?"

She laughed, and looked guilty for it. "No, but relax." She put her hand on his arm. "It's going to be fine. Everyone expects a new doctor to act like a jackass."

He arched an eyebrow, trying to look serious, but blushed despite that. She laughed again. "Weird things happens here. You get used to it." She smiled her beautiful smile. "You'll be fine."

The orderly came back in. "Car's ready, sir."

"It's fine, Dr. Kent, really," Regina said. "Don't let this place get to you. You haven't been here nearly long enough."

Chapter 5

Ben tried not to think too much on the drive home. There was nothing particularly good to think about, and dwelling on the bad wasn't going to fix anything. He switched the radio to a random station and lost himself in the witless banter of lunchtime talk radio. He didn't want to revisit his discussion with Howerton, or think about the maybe-not-a-thing in the basement. Rain began to fall, indifferent to his dilemma.

Halfway through the drive, he gave up trying to ignore his nagging thoughts. Julia was right. They should have gone to New York. Any new job was hard, and a new job as a doctor was harder than most. He'd prepared for that during school, had it drilled into his head repeatedly. That didn't make it any easier to eat shit from his new boss. He tried to imagine what his mother would say to him in that situation.

"Life can be hard sometimes, Benji. You just have to keep trying."

She must have said it to him a thousand times when he was a kid. She'd come home from working late at one of her jobs and peak into Ben's room after he'd put himself to bed. On one occasion, he'd woken up while she stood there looking at him from the hallway.

"Why does it have to be like this, Momma?"

"Because life's hard."

Truer words were never spoken. He sighed as he stared at the road. He'd keep working at the Home because, as hard as it might be for now, it would get better, and it would let him provide for his family in a way he'd never dreamed about when his mother snuck into his room at night.

The light traffic on the way home did little to occupy his mind. His anger at Howerton gave way to confusion about what he'd seen in the basement. *It was Robbie. It couldn't have been anything else.* He tapped his finger on the steering wheel. *Could it?*

The implication was too huge to grasp. The feeling of being watched, the way the property felt like it belonged to some other world. Now monsters—*things,* he corrected himself— things in the basement.

He couldn't imagine what he'd tell Julia if she asked. She was stuck in an apartment all day, a thousand miles from all her friends and family. The last thing she needed was her future husband coming home every day and complaining about his job. The job he'd insisted on taking.

He pulled into their parking lot and walked up the stairs, needing the extra time to compose himself. The drive home had dulled his headache into a minor twinge in the back of his head. He fumbled the keys, dropping them to the ground.

"Just a second," came Julia's muffled voice from inside. A moment later, she opened the door, looking as beautiful as ever. When she saw him covered in dirt, she stared for a few seconds. "Jesus, Ben. Again?"

He walked inside and gave her a kiss.

"If you keep inciting rage in patients, you might need to find another line of work, Dr. Kent."

"It wasn't a patient." He sat down on the couch and rubbed his eyes.

She walked into the kitchen and started rummaging through the fridge. "What happened?"

Before he knew what he was doing, he lied to her. He'd been searching around in the basement by himself and got spooked. Something loud on the floor above scared him and he fell running out. Howerton had told him not to go down there and had yelled at him afterwards.

"Ben…" Her tone implied she pitied his situation or his intelligence. She hugged him, resting her head on his chest.

"I know." He hugged her back. "But I don't think he's mad at me." *Why lie?*

She slapped his chest playfully. "I don't mean that. He sounds like a jerk. He could drown in his bathtub for all I care."

He laughed. "You're a mean woman when you're pregnant."

"Shut up." But she laughed too.

He went to change, and when he returned she'd toasted a bagel for each of them, hers holding a conspicuously larger amount of cream cheese. They sat on the couch in the living room while they ate.

"So what was down there?"

"Nothing, really. Just an old storage area. It's huge though. It was a quarantine ward. Creepy too. I think a lot of people died down there."

"Ugh. I wouldn't be able to work there."

He raised an eyebrow. "Well, you might not be aware of this, Miss Falargio, but I'm the manliest man you know." He took another bite of his bagel as she rolled her eyes. "I'm more worried about Howerton anyway. I don't think he likes me."

"Well, don't think about it too much. If this place turns out to be awful, we can always leave after you collect your first few months' pay. It'll be more than enough to start up anywhere we want." She took another bite. "And we can always ask Daddy for help if we need it."

He let out a sigh. They'd had that conversation a lot since he graduated. "I'm not asking your dad for any more help. The last thing I want is him thinking I can't provide for my family." Her parents had done enough for him already. If they hadn't helped, he would have never made it through medical school. Ben hadn't gotten much from his family. They didn't have much to give. Pride, however, ran strong in the Kent line.

"Don't be so touchy." She gave him a stern look.

"Sorry." He turned away. He always did that when he was about to be stubborn. "We won't need his help though. I'm going to be making enough. More than enough. Soon."

She smiled. "I've got you." She snuggled up against him. "That's enough for me."

He didn't respond. Julia was sweet, but she hadn't grown up watching her parents work themselves into mania and an early grave. Thinking love would be enough to solve their problems was idiotic. Money mattered, and he was going to make sure his family never had to worry about it.

They finished their bagels, and Ben took the plates into the kitchen. "You know, I was thinking we could take a look around town this weekend. Maybe do a little walking at some of the local parks, if you feel up to it."

"That sounds fun. I was actually thinking the same thing."

Ben returned to the living room and sat down, landing hard and letting out a weary sigh.

"So what are you going to do the rest of the day?" Julia snuggled against him again.

"Read. Read and relax, I think." He put his arm around her.

Ben didn't get as much reading done as he would have liked. He spent the afternoon finishing the last of the unpacking and putting things together, most of it in the baby's room. Julia watched and chatted about nothing in particular. She held one hand on her pregnant belly, waiting to feel their son kick.

Ben helped Julia make dinner that night. After they ate and he cleaned up, they went on a drive around the city. They watched as the sun set over the mountains, and the firmament turned to starry black. By the time they returned, most of his thoughts of the Home were only minor points of stress in an otherwise fine evening.

When he went to bed that night though, the memories surrounded him, preventing him from sleeping. Things in the dark stomping just behind him. A phantom hand reaching out to take him away. He tossed and turned for hours, trying to put it out of mind. The only thing he could do was jump back on the horse tomorrow and hope nothing like that happened again—whatever had happened.

The lie he told Julia bothered him between bouts of waking and sleep. He couldn't remember ever having lied to her before. *Why now?*

As he lay in darkness, his mind turned away from the day's unpleasantness to his nightmare from the night before. He counted his breaths until the clock told him it was one in the morning. He finally fell asleep after losing count and starting over for the fifth time.

Only half-remembered impressions of dreams came to him when he woke early the next morning. The door to the basement. Robbie crying. Theresa smoking a clove in the darkness.

He climbed out of bed, angry and annoyed at another night with little sleep. Looking down at Julia, he found himself envious of her ability to let it all go.

Morning routine gave him small solace—exercise, breakfast, and a shower—and he was off to work by eight thirty. By the time he pulled in, the impressions of the previous night's dreams had faded into nothing.

He walked in, handed off his keys, and found Regina and an older nurse he didn't know sitting at the desk.

"Good morning, Regina."

"Good morning. How was your night?"

That question reminded him of something Eddy once said; *The world would be a bitch of a place if everyone always told the truth.* "Great." He noticed his lack of sleep in the mirror every morning. It amazed him nobody else did.

They do. They just don't say anything.

She came around the desk, handing him a clipboard with a few sheets of paper on it. He thumbed through it. Just standard forms for patient evaluations, typed up with his patient's names and information on them.

"You're amazing."

The old nurse at the desk wore a sour look, but Ben pretended not to notice. He supposed everyone there over age forty had a stick up their asses.

"Come up to my office around nine thirty, and we can get started."

"Yes, Doctor."

Ben walked up to the fourth floor alone. It astounded him that the Home could buzz with so much activity with a patient missing but be so barren otherwise. It felt solitary. Isolated. The half-remembered sensation of a hand reaching out behind him came to mind. From the top of the stairs leading to the third floor, he looked over his shoulder.

Of course, nothing was there. *Stupid.* He practically stomped up the stairs. *It's the middle of the day. Get a grip.* He didn't consider himself paranoid, but the last few days hadn't been his best. He touched the bandage over the bite on his neck, wondering if Robbie was still in the building somewhere, hidden away.

Or maybe he's dead. The thought came from nowhere, and it chilled him. It wasn't as if Tennessee's woods were inhospitable. Hikers and locals were out all the time. If Robbie had gotten out, he would turn up eventually.

He reached his lonely office with those thoughts on his mind. He turned the corner to the short hallway to find his door standing ajar. He tried to remember if he'd left it open, but couldn't.

Icy paranoia raised goose flesh across his body. He walked the rest of the distance, trying to be stealthy and failing miserably in his loafers. He reached for the handle, silently swearing to himself that if he was attacked again he was going to quit. He pushed it open quickly, ready to fight if he had to, but the room sat empty. Just his desk and the sickly wallpaper to witness his idiocy.

He shook his head and rubbed his eyes. "Stupid."

He shut the door and sat behind his desk. *The cleaning staff left it open. There's nothing to get anxious about.* He paged through his patients files. He'd be visiting all of them today, Theresa at the top on the list. He familiarized himself with each patient's peculiarities, trying to put the quirks of his new job out of mind.

Just before nine thirty, a knock sounded on the door. "Come in."

Regina poked her head in. "Are you ready, Doctor?"

"Yes." He hadn't been able to get the open door off his mind. "Do you know if anyone comes in these offices up here? Maybe a cleaning crew?"

"The maintenance guys and some of the orderlies do the cleaning around here, but I doubt they'd clean your office. They barely clean the places they're supposed to. Why?"

Ben gathered the few things he'd need. "My door was open."

She shrugged. "I wouldn't sweat it. Weird stuff happens here."

Simple as that. *Weird stuff happens here.* The basement hadn't just been weird; it had terrified him. And the dreams he'd been having since he started working weren't helping either. He rubbed his eyes and tried not to think about it. He had other things to attend to.

He made sure to shut the door behind him this time as he mentally reviewed his last meeting with Theresa. It had been brief, but telling. She wanted to control. In his experience, that was true of most wealthy people. She hadn't shown any signs of paranoia or delusions like her chart said, but complex delusions were usually harder to root out. *"The best lies are the ones you believe."* He recalled his mother saying that when he was little, followed shortly by, *"If lying to yourself was a paying job, we'd all be millionaires."*

They made their way down the floors, passing a few nurses and orderlies as they went. "Is this place empty, or is it my imagination?" Ben asked.

"Yeah. It's a big place, and there aren't a whole lot of people around."

"That's somewhat surprising too."

"I think the people that own this place prefer to keep things personal. You know, the fewer people, the easier it is to care for them."

"Awfully altruistic." Ben grinned.

"Nothing altruistic about what they charge here." They walked on in silence for a moment before she spoke again. "One of the other nurses told me this place was opened so that the guy who owned it had somewhere to put his crazy family."

Ben laughed. Hospital rumors were apparently the same everywhere. "I guess if you're going to be locked up, this is the place to be."

They crossed into the west wing and headed up to the second floor to meet Theresa. One of the orderlies guided them to where she waited in a small room facing the back of the property.

"I'll wait outside, Doctor." Regina took a seat in a nearby chair. "Just let me know if you need anything."

A small table and three chairs stood in the center of the room, and bookcases that reached up to the ceiling dominating all the walls. Hundreds, if not thousands, of books filled the room. Theresa looked out the window, her hands clasped behind her back. An ancient keeper of knowledge. A librarian at Alexandria before it burned.

"Good morning, Miss Parker." Ben set his things on the table then pulled out a chair. If he wanted her to relax around him, he needed to relax as well.

"I told you, Benjamin, call me Theresa," she said in her southern drawl. "As long as you don't call me Saint Theresa. The nurses call me that from time to time." The morning light framed her, making a halo above her head. She had been gorgeous once.

"I wouldn't dream of it. And I can promise you no nurses will call you anything but Miss Parker when I'm around."

She walked over to the table. "I'm too old to care, Ben. Don't trouble yourself." She pulled out a chair and sat down, taking a pack of cloves and a book of matches out of a pocket. She lit one, and the smell of spices filled the room. "Most of the patients can't carry matches." She wiggled her fingers in the air. "Fire hazard."

Ben smiled. "I can imagine it is."

"I've been here too long, Benjamin. If they're letting me carry matches around, it's been far too long."

"How are you feeling this morning?"

Eyeing Ben, she took a slow drag off her cigarette. "I'm fine. I sleep soundly most nights. The walls are soundproof here. A blessing, as you might imagine."

"None of the other patients bother you?"

"No. This place is a resort for the rich and crazy. The staff sees to our needs like a waiter on a cruise ship." There was something in her voice that Ben couldn't place. She was being sarcastic or bitter, maybe both. He could understand either way. "I've never been on one myself, of course, although I have sailed. My parents took my sister and I out often as girls."

Ben put his pencil to paper to take a note, but she interrupted. "Benjamin, if you must take notes, please do so after you leave. I don't get to converse with the sane very often anymore, and your scribbling is liable to make it impersonal."

"It helps me keep track of what we've spoken about." He was also likely to get details wrong if he didn't write them down.

"Your brain can do that for you just fine without a pencil. Come now, indulge an old woman." She raised her chin but kept looking at him. It was a demand, not a request.

He set his pencil down and pushed his notepad to the middle of the table.

"Thank you."

He leaned back in his chair. She did like to be in control. "Is there anything in particular you'd like to talk about today?"

Something about her stare unnerved him. Her steely gaze made his skin itch. "What's the world like outside nowadays?" she asked.

He thought about it for a moment. "The United States just got its first chess champion."

She rolled her eyes. "Chess, Benjamin? Come now."

He thought a little longer. "There was a meteor shower during the day last month, made quite the show. I missed it, unfortunately."

"Interesting," she mused. "The world does have its ways of making us feel small, doesn't it?"

"It does."

They were playing a game of chess too, though she apparently didn't care for the game. He guessed it was his move. "I was hoping to talk a little about you and why you're here today."

"Because I killed my family. I would have thought they'd mentioned that in a note somewhere." Neither her tone nor her posture changed when she spoke.

"Can you tell me what happened? I'd like to hear everything in your words."

She tapped the table with her fingers, lost in thought as she stared behind him. At length, she spoke. "Do you believe in monsters?"

"I believe sometimes people do bad things, but I don't think people are monsters."

"No. No, not people. I mean *monsters*." She said the word deliberately, like a mother explaining something to a child. "Things other than humans, with intelligence and cruel intentions."

"No. I think people are the only ones who can make decisions they might regret."

"What about things that don't regret?"

He kept his voice level. "No, Theresa, I'm afraid I don't believe in monsters."

She ashed her cigarette. "Have you spent any time here at night? Seen anything strange?"

The question caught him off guard. His mind traveled back to the basement, to the voice on the radio and the sounds in the dark. He put it aside quickly, but it must have shown on his face.

"So you have?" She gave him one of those steel-eyed looks again, as if she could see all the way through him. He'd had similar experiences in clinicals. Very intelligent patients could be charismatic in the extreme. It was easy to get lost in the stories that people wove when they believed them whole-heartedly.

Ben often wondered what that meant for his own sanity. "No. I only started working here Monday."

"You're lying." Her tone made it clear she didn't appreciate it.

"I was attacked by a patient on my first day. He appears to have since gone missing." He gestured at the bandage on his neck. "That sort of thing isn't unexpected in this field."

"Good Lord. Robbie did that to you?" A touch of honest concern entered her voice.

"Yes. He was having a bad day. How did you know it was Robbie?"

"Word travels fast around here." She took another drag. "I heard Mr. Ford had gone missing."

Ben might need to have a talk with Howerton about staff discussing things like that with his patients. "I'm sure he'll turn up soon enough."

"He's dead, Benjamin." She said it softly, as if the admission would hurt him.

He shifted in his seat. Maybe he'd been wrong about her not showing signs of delusion. "How do you know that?"

"Most people wouldn't notice one more ghost in a place like this, but I do. Robbie saw them too."

"Do you see a lot of ghosts in the Home?"

She stared at him for a full minute, weighing him. The silence went on uncomfortably long. If she thought he was patronizing her, she'd never trust him.

"Are you related to someone who works here?"

The quick subject change caught him off guard. "No."

"Why did they hire you?"

"I graduated highest in my class."

She put out her clove, leaning in as she did so. "Are you familiar with the history of this town, Benjamin?"

"Just what's in the tourist brochure. But I was hoping to talk more about you today, Theresa. I want to get to know—"

"Look into it."

He took the bait. "What do you expect me to find?"

"Monsters. What else?" Her drawl chilled him.

"Do you think the monsters killed Robbie?"

The perfect image of chess player weighing her options. "Maybe."

Ben tried to push the conversation for a few minutes after that, but she artfully dodged the questions. "Do you see these monsters? No, Benjamin. Do they talk to you? No, Benjamin. Are they here right now? Don't be an ass, Benjamin." Though he found her sudden shift suspicious, he wasn't going to push her in their first session.

"I'm tired. Forgive me if I ramble. Do you mind if we continue this tomorrow?"

"I'd like to go on. I can't help you if you don't let me get to know you."

She sighed. "It's fine. You'll find there's a lot of time available here. I just need to lie down for a bit."

Ben considered his schedule. He did indeed have plenty of time to visit her whenever she wanted. He didn't expect his other patients were going to be as conversational as she was anyway. "What time would you like to meet tomorrow?"

"Same time. In here, please."

Ben picked up the few things he'd come in with and stood up.

"Thank you for indulging an old woman. It's nice to have someone to talk."

"I'm here to help. I want you to get better." He walked to the door and left. She watched him go, weighing him, looking through him.

Regina stood as he left. "How did it go?"

"She was feeling tired." He walked to the stairs, Regina in tow. "She also wouldn't let me take notes. I need to go back to my office to write a few things down."

"She's a strange one, but not half as strange as most of the people in this place."

"She asked me if I'd seen anything unusual here. You said something about that yesterday."

They passed a pair of orderlies as they descended.

"Dr. Howerton doesn't like people talking about any of the weird stuff here," Regina said once they were past. "There was a nurse here when I started who told everyone she saw a shadow following her on the fourth floor. She got fired the next week. Never heard why, but I don't think it was a coincidence."

"Please tell me you're not spooked by shadows, Regina."

"Tough talk from the guy who got scared by a radio."

Ben's cheeks heated up, and he cleared his throat.

She smiled. "It's more than that. Things aren't where you leave them. Whispers at night when you're sure you're alone. It's creepy here sometimes. You get used to it."

Ben opened his mouth to tell her about the bad dreams, but shut it before he could. He'd been there less than a week. She might be sweet, but if he told her this place was giving him nightmares, she'd think he was nuts. If a nurse could be fired just for telling people about shadows on the wall, Howerton would almost certainly can him for that; especially after recent incidents.

Ben hadn't spent a lot of time thinking about ghosts before. Whether they were real or not, it didn't change life much either way. Still, if his boss would fire him over it, then it certainly wasn't worth bringing up. Better to keep those cards close to the chest. "This place does give me the heebie-jeebies," he said instead.

They passed through the security checkpoint and toward Ben's office. "What time would you like to see your next patient?"

"Ten thirty." He started up the stairs.

Regina nodded and turned to walk away.

"Regina," he said. "Do me a favor and find any other files you can on Theresa, would you?"

"Like what?"

"I don't know. Anything you can find outside of her treatment file."

"Yes, Doctor."

"Bring me Robbie's file too."

As he walked alone through the second-floor halls, he thought about whispers and shadows. A woman like Theresa, who had delusions about monsters, would certainly not be helped in a place as dark and overbearing as the Home. A place where the administration was more concerned with keeping its mouth shut than with the health of its patients.

His mother had been a Baptist and raised him the same way. She'd believed in evil and the devil as real things to be recognized and avoided. She might have looked the same as Theresa in a place like this. Worse. Sitting alone in a room, screaming prayers at monsters as they closed in around her. Chanting scripture at the whispers that spoke to her in the night. The image gave him chills, and set off a pang of guilt in his chest.

He couldn't judge the place too harshly. After all, he was there for a paycheck just like everyone else. He had no plans for changing the way this or any other place was run. He thought about all of that while the notes he wanted to write on Theresa were stuck in his head. Delusions. Not dangerous ones, but delusions.

They're never dangerous until someone acts on them.

He puffed his way up the stairs. He had work to do. He could lament his poor character later. Still, it was hard not to feel the gloomy building bearing down on him as he made his way through the empty fourth floor.

He rounded the corner and stopped dead in his tracks. His door was cracked open again. He knew he'd shut it this time. He recalled doing it very deliberately.

"Hello?" he called out, his voice small. He walked to the door and pushed it open.

Nothing. An empty room. Just yellow wallpaper and an old desk.

Regina came back up at ten thirty to walk with Ben to his next appointment. He'd written down all of his notes on Theresa. She did indeed suffer from delusions and control issues, but he felt she'd opened up to him. Given time, he was confident he could win her trust.

They left his office and walked back to the west wing. Ben didn't tell her about the door.

Miranda Kelly smiled when Ben walked in. The session didn't go much better than the last.

"I'm not your father, Miranda. My name is Dr. Kent, and you're in a mental institution."

"Dad, you know I hate it when you talk down to me." An old woman who thought she was a teenager, she brushed her hair in a mirror.

"Do you know what year it is, Miranda?"

She smiled dreamily and kept brushing. "I think Zachery is going to take me out on Saturday. I know you don't like him, but he's a good man." She stopped and listened to something that wasn't there, the brush forgotten. It lasted only a moment before she continued and started to hum.

Ben wrote it all down in his notebook. By the time he left half an hour later, he hadn't made any progress. Vitalie had tried several medications in her treatment. Their effects ran the gamut of results from anxiety to near suicidal depression. Nothing snapped her out of her delusions. She refused to acknowledge anything but her fantasies.

Mike Long was next on his list. He sat in the same room he'd been in on Tuesday, listening to the radio and waiting for the communist spies to make their presence known. Ben sat in a rocking chair. Mike, not saying a word, stared at him with open spite in his eyes.

"Do you remember me from Tuesday, Mr. Long? My name is Dr. Kent."

"Yeah, I bet it is." Mike leaned back in his seat and looked Ben up and down. "Pinko."

"Do you remember me?"

"Yeah, I remember you, and I got your number too. I got a line to McCarthy's office." Mike smiled, the smug expression sliding across his face. "My family funded him. I know a commie when I see one."

"Senator McCarthy passed away in nineteen-fifty-seven. Do you know what year it is, Mr. Long?"

"Yeah, it's nineteen seventy-fuck yourself, comrade."

That meeting only lasted twenty minutes, until Mike became agitated. He jumped from his chair and stomped around the room, raving about politics. Regina poked her head in to make sure everything was okay. Mike's record said he had a history of violent behavior, and Ben didn't want to trigger an episode. He informed the orderly sitting outside the room with Regina that he might have trouble later.

The visits with his catatonic patients were brief, just checking in on people who needed constant care. He expected no results from those visits, and his expectations weren't exceeded. By the time he'd finished, he was frustrated. Howerton had given him patients he could do nothing for. Granted, he was new, but he wasn't incapable. In college, he didn't think that was what the real world would be like. Visiting vegetables to while away the morning. He felt stupid for being so glum about a job he'd just started, but it had been a glum few days. The lack of sleep wasn't helping.

When he'd finished with his catatonic patients, he and Regina walked downstairs for lunch. A turkey sandwich, a salad, fruit, and pudding. The patients ate well, and so did the staff. They sat in a large, brightly lit break room near the kitchen. Three orderlies and a nurse sat at a table on the far side of the room talking quietly when Ben and Regina walked in. They chose at a table near the door, Ben not particularly up to meeting new people.

Regina didn't share his sour mood. "So what do you think so far? Is it everything you dreamed of?"

Ben found her phrasing amusing, given the unpleasant nature of his dreams. He took a bite out of his sandwich. "It's going to take some getting used to."

"I get that. I wanted to quit when I started here. I was right out of nursing school. Between the staff and the patients, I was fed up by the end of my first month."

"What kept you around?"

"Are you kidding? I can work on some floor in a hospital and struggle to get by, or work here and make three times as much. Not a hard choice." She took a bite from her apple. "Besides, I like some of the patients here. The place has a quiet that I'm used to." After a few minutes of silent eating, she took a sip of water and asked, "You got any family here?"

"My fiancée. She's from New York."

Her eyes brightened. "Me too!"

No kidding. She couldn't hide that accent if she tried. "I'll have to introduce you two." He remembered what he'd said to Julia about going out that weekend. "We're going to explore a bit on Sunday. You want to come with? Maybe show us around?" It would be a good chance to help Julia meet someone around town too. Ben was good company, but one friend in a city wouldn't do.

"That sounds great, I'd love to. It's been forever since I've seen another New Yorker. I visit my parents sometimes, but it's a long trip, and I don't like to fly."

"Well, now's your chance." Ben smiled. "She's pregnant, so we can't do anything too strenuous."

"How far along is she?"

"Eight-and-a-half months. She's due in a few weeks. I didn't want her to travel in her condition, but I didn't have much choice."

"You got an OB yet?"

"Yeah, Dr. Essex. She's going to meet him Monday to go over the birth plan." He chewed on a bit of salad. "What about you? Married?" Ben asked as he polished off the last of his salad.

She held up her hand. No ring. "I'm not really the marriage type. This is Tennessee. A woman in her thirties without a husband is an old maid." A look of annoyance flashed across her. "Suits me just fine."

They finished lunch while chatting about Julia's pregnancy. Regina wanted to know everything. "What's his name? Got a room? Private schools or public?" Two months ago talking about his new baby would have sent him into a panic. He could barely take care of himself most of the time, let alone a little person. The sheer terror of it had come and gone though, replaced with excitement. Excitement mixed with anxiety, true, but still excitement.

They dropped their trays off in the kitchen. Ben had only his high-risk patient left to visit. As they walked up the stairs, the fourth floor's oppressive malaise struck him again, like going under cold water. He looked over at Regina, but if she noticed it, she showed no sign. He would keep that to himself then. He needed to shake the somber feelings if he was going to last here.

They walked along the too-dim hallways to his patient's room. He saw more staff up here than anywhere else in the building, but that made a sort of sense. All of his patients had been in the Home long enough that a good reading of their symptoms and peculiarities would've been made long ago. If someone needed to be locked away in the attic, they were almost certainly put there for their own good.

The same nervous young man sat outside Clann's door. He informed Ben that the patient was lucid. "I'm supposed to sit in there with him sometimes, but… he makes me awfully uncomfortable." He looked nervously back and forth between Regina and Ben. "He got locked up for killing some kids, you know."

Christopher Clann had been incarcerated for murdering two little girls several years earlier. His admission to the Home had created a scandal in the national papers. *Rich white man kills two black girls and gets vacation in prestigious facility instead of death penalty.* In truth, the man had been disturbed long before the murders. The patient's file stated it all clearly. Ben gave the orderly a disapproving look regardless.

"We talked about this last time."

"I know, sir." He looked like he wanted to say more but held it back. Ben shook his head and stepped inside.

"Hello, Mr. Clann, my name is Dr. Kent." The door closed behind him. "I'm your new doctor."

Christopher Clann smiled at him, showing too many teeth. He sat upright in his bed as if he'd been waiting for a visitor. Aside from a bed against the far wall and a chair by the door, the room was bare.

"Hello, Doctor." His eyes, searchlights in his face, locked onto Ben.

"I'm glad to finally get a chance to speak with you. How're you feeling today?" Ben sat down in the chair near the door. Leather straps connected to Christopher's ankles and wrists bound him to the bed. He had enough room to move around, but he wouldn't be going anywhere. Those were there for his protection, but Ben had learned early on in his career that restrained didn't always mean secure. A similarly restrained man had stabbed one of Ben's classmates with a pen during his first year of medical school. He'd keep a safe distance.

"I'm feeling good, Doctor. Very good." Christopher's huge smile put Ben off. The way he sat in the bed didn't look human.

He looks like a doll. Ben tried to ignore the thought. He wasn't there to pass judgments on his patients. "Are you treated well here, Christopher?"

Christopher licked his lips. "Oh, yeah. You know it, Doctor." He blinked slowly.

Ben looked through his notes to check what medication Christopher was taking.

"What about you, Doctor? Seen anything interesting? Had many good dreams?"

Ben jumped in his seat at the uncomfortable impression of Christopher looming over him. He looked up quickly, but Christopher sat in the same spot. A human doll on the bed, set there by some unfathomable giant.

Ben took a few seconds to compose himself. "I'd rather talk about you."

Christopher threw his head back violently and laughed.

"Christopher, would you like to talk to me?"

He laughed on, ignoring Ben's question.

The dull ache in the back of Ben's skull that had been threatening all day finally blossomed into a headache. "I'm here to help you." Ben rubbed his eyes but dropped his hand when the sensation of someone standing over him started again.

Christopher laughed harder.

A buzzing filled the room. Ben looked around for the source but couldn't find it.

Christopher's laugh made the headache worse. *He knows about the dreams and the basement.* Ben became very aware of how uncomfortably small the room was, and he didn't care to be alone with Chris anymore. "I'll set another appointment for Monday. If you need me for anything or just want to talk, please ask for me."

Christopher's laughter hit a peak. Ben didn't know how he could breathe, cackling like that. He stood up and knocked twice on the door. It swung open, and the monotone noise followed him into the hallway. The orderly closed the door, and the sound abruptly cut off. This place really was soundproof. For some reason, that didn't comfort him.

The orderly wouldn't make eye contact with Ben. "Told you."

Regina and Ben walked across the fourth floor and down the stairs, heading back toward Ben's office.

"That man is unsettling," Ben said.

"Yeah. Whenever a nurse has to give him meds or clean him, orderlies have to be in the room. And the way he looks at you…" She hunched her shoulders in a small shudder.

"Well, that should cover everything I need for today. I'm heading back to my office to jot down some notes."

"I have to fill out some paperwork in the main nursing station. I'll have those files for you tomorrow."

Ben had almost forgotten about that after seeing Christopher. "Before I forget, can you get me the entire medical history of these patients too?" Ben handed over a sheet of paper with some of his patient's names on it. "I won't need them until tomorrow."

"Yes, Doctor. I'll leave them at the desk. You can pick them up in the morning."

They parted ways in the lobby. As Ben was about to climb the stairs to his office, Howerton came out of a hallway on the first floor.

"I'm glad I caught you, Dr. Kent. How has your day been?"

The day had dragged on forever, and Ben had slept like shit. "Good. Very good. I met with all of my patients today."

"Excellent. Is there anything you need?"

"A bookshelf and a filing cabinet in my office would be nice. I'm still keeping all my patients' files in a box on the floor."

"I'll see to it. While I've got you, we've planned a small get together to celebrate your addition to the staff. Will Wednesday of next week work for you?" It sounded like an offer, but something in Howerton's tone suggested it wasn't.

"Of course, sir. We'll be looking forward to it." Ben looked forward to dinner with Howerton as much as he looked forward to a dentist appointment.

A smile crept across Howerton's face; a slow, crawling expression that wasn't friendly in the least. "Good, Good. I have work to attend to, Dr. Kent. Have a nice evening, and tell the missus I said hello."

Ben climbed to his office to drop his notes in his patients' files. The door was closed this time, but he still felt like something might be lurking up there, waiting for him. The same uncomfortable impression he'd had in the basement plagued him; that someone watched him from across a crowded room.

His initial feeling about the building had been one of trepidation, and his experiences so far that week hadn't proved him wrong. He only had to get through one more day. A relaxing weekend at home would do him good. He hadn't had a chance to unwind in weeks, and it was certainly catching up with him.

He left his office and closed the door. As he was about to walk down the hallway that led downstairs, a thump came from the closet marked Janitorial.

He stopped dead and looked at the door, listening for it. Nothing moved. He steeled his nerves and reached for the door handle. He wasn't a child, and monsters in closets wouldn't scare him. Enough was enough.

The cold knob triggered a memory he couldn't quite recall. It spun freely and squealed loudly. A click followed, but when he pulled the door, it wouldn't open. Dead bolted, and of course he didn't have the key.

The invisible eyes of his unseen stalker bored a hole into the his back. The hairs on his neck rose up. He couldn't help but wonder; if something happened to him up there, would anybody hear him yell? *Soundproof walls, remember?*

That thought brought him back to the basement and the shadow that moved in the darkness. After sleeping on it, he thought he might have imagined it, but as he stood before that door, he wasn't so sure. He let go of the handle. *Mice.* An old building as big as the Home almost certainly had them. He left the hallway and made his way toward the stairs.

Maybe it was Robbie.

Theresa's words returned to his mind from nowhere. *He's dead, Benjamin.*

Before his foot touched the first step, a loud squeal and a click emanated from the hallway behind him. His skin danced under his clothes, and his eyes watered. He kept walking, determined to ignore it. He'd cleared the fourth floor when the sound of a door opening echoed in the hallway above.

He didn't feel safe until he was back in the lobby among the handful of nurses and orderlies. He requested his car be brought around. An orderly hopped to and walked out the door with his keys.

A black-haired nurse in her forties sat behind the desk. "Are you okay? You look like you just saw a ghost." She smiled at him.

He didn't return it.

Chapter 6

As Ben drove home, he tried not to think about it all. If he worried too much, he'd end up telling Julia, and as much as he needed to share his thoughts with someone, he didn't want to worry her. It'd been a long few weeks.

Current science drew a strong link between genetics and psychological disorders. Julia would think he was cracking under the pressure, and nothing scared him as much as madness. Losing all sense of self. Losing awareness as a thinking creature. Never really knowing if you're truly mad. Ironic when he thought about it, given his career choice.

Worrying about something he couldn't control wasn't doing him any favors. He turned on the radio and listened to a local newscaster talk about tomorrow's all-day rain.

He walked into his apartment half an hour later.

"Hi, sweetheart," Julia said. She gave him a long kiss. "The phone was installed today. Number's on the fridge."

Julia wasn't a big fan of phones. She thought nothing was so urgent that she had to be reached at a moment's notice. Ben insisted he needed one because of work. One of the downsides of being a doctor.

"Great. I had a patient mention the history of the town today, and it got me thinking it might be worth a look. Could you grab my address book?"

"Taking tourist advice from mental patients?" Julia walked back into the hallway and toward their room.

"Har, har. Howerton invited us to a swanky dinner next Wednesday. Does that work for you?"

"Fine by me," she said from the bedroom. She came back a moment later with a tattered leather bound book. Eddy had been there when Ben's mother gave him the book the day before he left for college. His number and address were on the first page, albeit crossed out and updated several times. Eddy had studied history at the University of Chicago. After he graduated with his bachelors, he enrolled in the U.S. history doctoral program. He had received his doctorate the year before and was teaching at a small college out in California. If anyone would be able to tell Ben about Umber Gardens, it was Eddy.

Eddy's house phone rang. Of course, there was no answer. Eddy was a busy man now. Ben smiled, trying to imagine Eddy teaching a room full of people only a few years younger than him. Eddy, who had once hit another student with a chair in their high school English class. Eddy, who had mooned the audience during their school production of *Alice in Wonderland* in which he played the Mad "Mooning" Hatter.

After another moment he gave up and called Eddy's work number. The phone rang twice before a young woman answered. "History department," she said in cheerless tone.

"Hello, I'm trying to reach Professor Webber."

"Professor Webber is in class the rest of the day. Can I take a message?"

"Yes, tell him Dr. Kent called. I want to ask him about the history of Umber Gardens in Tennessee."

"Okay, I'll make sure he gets it. Thank you." She hung up.

Ben hung up as well. He shouldn't buy into Theresa's delusions. He loved history, but he hadn't given Umber Gardens a second thought until she said something. He couldn't tell her he'd taken her up on looking into Umber Gardens. It would only make her think she might be onto something.

But I'm sitting here looking it up. He rubbed his eyes. The last few days were getting to him. The move, the lack of sleep, the new job, and the odd experiences were certainly taking their toll. He needed to relax, just one more day, and he could—

"Are you okay?"

Ben jumped. He hadn't heard Julia walk into the room. "Yeah, I'm fine. Just thinking."

She looked at him for a moment. He could never get a lie past her, but she let it slide.

"You know, why don't we go out tonight? You must be going crazy cooped up in here for the last four days."

She mulled it over. "That sounds wonderful."

Ben waggled his eyebrows at her. "No secrets from me, sweetheart. I have a doctorate in mind reading." He pulled an imaginary cloak across his body.

She smiled tolerantly and walked back toward the bedroom. "I'm going to change into something nice."

"Good idea. I was thinking we could try a barbeque place I've driven by a few times. The smell is driving me wild." He stretched as he stood. "Maybe we could catch a movie if you're feeling up to it. There's a theatre in town."

He let her think it over while he took a shower and changed into something casual. Julia wore a maternity dress that wasn't flattering. Ben told her she was beautiful regardless, and he meant it. Even with everything that had happened in the new city, when he was with her, he thought everything might just be all right.

Julia eyed the fifteen-foot-tall pig on the roof, complete with a sign on his apron that promised the best barbeque in Tennessee. "Porksters?" she asked with doubt in her voice.

Ben smiled. "I do declare, the best barbeque in Tenn-o-see!"

She laughed and looked away, embarrassed enough for both of them as he found a parking spot.

Inside wasn't much better, but the smell was divine. They followed a waitress to a booth, layers of peanut shells cracking under their feet. Ben immediately grabbed a peanut from the small bucket on the table and shelled it, smiling at Julia as he threw it to the floor.

She reached across the table and grabbed his hand. "So how was work?"

"I asked my nurse Regina to join us on Sunday," he said, trying not to think about the squealing door on the fourth-floor, or the echo of it opening in an empty hall.

Julia cocked an eyebrow. "Oh, really? Is she prettier than me?"

"Not by a long shot." He popped the shelled nut into his mouth. "I wanted to introduce you to her though. Do you mind?"

"No, of course not." She reached across the table and grabbed his hand. "Now why don't you tell me what's bothering you."

She knew. Of course she knew. He might have the doctorate, but Julia was smarter than he was. He debated if he should share everything with her. They were getting married, but a part of him would always wonder if she would stick around no matter what. Nobody wanted to be with a guy who couldn't relax. Nobody liked to be around someone who heard phantom noises when they were alone. He was being ridiculous, but he was tired, and the week was weighing down on him. As far as excuses went, they weren't bad.

And just like that, he told her everything. The odd feeling he'd gotten from the building since the first day, the thing in the basement, and the lie he'd told. He told her about Theresa, and how he couldn't help but entertain her delusions in light of what he'd experienced so far. He hadn't realized that last part was true until he said it aloud. He finished by telling her about Clann and the noise from the closet.

She looked at him for a long moment. "Sweetie, it's fine. You're stressed out, is all. We're on our own for the first time, and you have a baby on the way."

"We," he corrected. But she was right. Maybe having a baby bothered him more than he thought. Some psychiatrist he was.

"*We* have a baby on the way." She squeezed his hand.

"I've just never felt like this before. Ever since Mom died, I've just been terrified that the same thing's going to happen to me. I feel like I haven't slept in weeks. I shouldn't feel like work is beating me down this much already. I just started there."

Julia didn't say anything; she didn't need to. Nothing was going to make him feel better but time. He wasn't losing his mind. There had been a few odd coincidences, sure, but he wasn't crazy. Mice in closets and panic attacks in basements could play all sorts of tricks on the mind. Julia squeezed his hand again, and he squeezed back.

Ben wanted to see the newest Burt Reynolds movie, but Julia was tired. They drove around instead, enjoying the calm quiet of a late September night in Tennessee and each other's company. Sometimes the simple things were better.

Ben looked at his watch as they walked into their apartment. They'd killed most of the evening. He set out everything he'd need for work tomorrow and lay down in bed, Julia joining him after taking a shower. She wore nothing but a towel on her head. Her body looked wonderful, even nine months pregnant.

He rolled over to go to sleep as Julia climbed in bed. She kissed him on the cheek. "I love you," she said.

"I love you too."

She was out within minutes, but he just stared at the wall. The same old song and dance. The anxieties of the week stampeding through his mind. The endless self-criticism. Worst of all was the fear. A nameless thing that crept into his mind every time his eyes closed, no matter how sleepy he was.

I'm never going to get to sleep. But for the first time in a month, not twenty minutes after Julia fell asleep, Ben did as well.

He sat in the living room of the ten-year-old trailer he and his mother shared. She leaned over a stack of paperwork at the kitchen table, tapping a pencil on the vinyl as she concentrated on her homework from the supermarket manager. His mother had been a whiz with numbers, and she earned extra income by helping the him keep the paperwork in line. A woman who ran the kind of numbers his mother had should have made twice the money, but a trailer park mom with bill collectors harassing her all the time could hardly afford to barter.

Those had been happier times, and in Ben's dreaming mind, they still were. Days spent playing with Eddy, who lived across the road. The days before he knew about things like poverty and guilt, before he understood how lonely his mother had been while he was growing up, and well before he realized he didn't want to be anything like her. He loved her with all of his heart, but the toll that hard living took on her was obvious even to a child. It became more obvious when he found her corpse.

His mother, still young and pretty, but with the hard lines of a hard life already showing on her face, stood up from the table. "Do you want to go on a walk, Benji?"

He nodded, and like that they were walking down the country road he'd used every day to get to the bus stop. That road had been the main vein through the town, the artery on which all the money to and from Rapid Hills travelled. The road stretched on for miles, empty. They walked for hours, hand in hand, happy. They strode on long past the point the road should have ended, into an ancient oak forest not part of the place he'd grown up.

A shadow of dread covered Ben's heart when he realized where they were going. A buzz in the air turned to music, soft and sad, as they walked on. A siren song. Something to lure people to crash upon the rocks in a dark sea.

They rounded a bend in the road, and there stood the Home. Ben tried to tug away from his mother. She looked down at him. "It's okay, Ben, trust me."

And he did.

They passed through the gate and down the drive toward the building. The sun shone overhead, but night shrouded the building itself. A Francisco Goya painting, all shadows and soft edges. It didn't belong there, even in the dream world. Looking at it was like looking at the mirage of a shadow on the highway. The presence of the place touched him with a wave of cold. They walked hand-in-hand across the property to the door, her warmth giving him strength.

Robbie stood outside the door, but not the Robbie who'd attacked Ben. This Robbie was clean cut in jeans and a white T-shirt. His eyes shone with intelligence, and his skin glowed like that of a young man who spent all his time in the sun.

"It's okay, Ben, it's sleeping," Robbie said, his voice authoritative. Ben knew he was dead. Dead like his mother. He looked up at her, expecting to see a corpse. Only his mother, younger and healthier than he remembered her ever being, stood before him.

"We have to show you something," she said. "We have to show you, and you have to remember."

Robbie opened the door and stepped inside. The music became hard and ugly. Ben and his mother followed Robbie across the threshold, and night overtook them. A different dream lived inside the Home. A nightmare.

The world drifted away into fog as the doors slammed behind him. Shadows of people wandered by. Some moaned in pain. Some screamed in terror. The sound threatened to block out everything else. Ben could only move forward by holding onto his mother's warmth and watching Robbie, whole and alive, as they walked through the specters and into the hall behind the desk.

The dead pressed in, but Ben glided through them as they made their way toward the back of the building. They followed the hallways deeper. Before long, the door to the basement loomed before them, a mouth that descended into madness. Ben tried to tell his mother and Robbie that they couldn't go down there, but the words wouldn't come out.

Robbie took Ben's other hand. "It's okay. Just this once, it's okay."

They walked side by side, though the hallway should have been too small for it, and descended into the basement together. Darkness cloaked the barely visible walls down here. The oppression of the nightmare world suffocated him, trying to get close, feeling its way toward them in the black. He glanced up at his mother and Robbie, both of them older now, unhealthy, closer to how he remembered them.

"Momma?" Ben said, his voice just above a whisper. The music grew louder, drowning out his words.

"It's okay, Benji, just a little more."

They walked on as something circled them outside the edge of vision. It grew closer. They walked deeper, deeper than Ben had when he was alone. Here the walls bled shadows made of wet tar. Puddles of blackness on the floor dripped upward, forming pools of midnight on the ceiling. The warmth of his mother's hand began to fade. He was losing her all over again.

"Momma," he said in his child's voice. His throat caught. She was going to leave him again.

"Shh, baby, it's going to be okay."

An opening appeared on one of the walls. Piles of broken brick and stone littered the ground around it. At one point, it had been covered, but any protection that offered the world outside was gone. Beyond the doorway, a stone slope descended. The walls moved like a creature taking breath. The music rose to a fever pitch, a discordant piano slamming out the ugly song of something ancient.

"It's down there, Ben," Robbie said. "That's where it sleeps."

"Momma," Ben whimpered.

"It's okay." Her hand went cold. He couldn't bear to look at either of them. Somehow, he knew what he would see. They would be dead things they were, not the living beings they had been.

They walked back the way they'd come, taking another turn instead of heading toward the stairs. They entered a room filled with rusty pipes, and the door slowly shut behind him. Whatever slept in that hole was awake now, and it could see him.

Both Robbie and his mother let go of his hands. "Burn it down, Ben," Robbie said. "Burn it all down before it's too late."

Shadows flowed down the wall like waterfalls. Ben could discern only his mother and Robbie through the blackness. The music stopped as something massive screamed below them, a bass note that shook the world.

They stood behind Ben, both looking like he had last seen them. Robbie, hunched down and staring at Ben with crazed eyes. A man who remembered what he had in another life, blood pouring from a wound on his neck and staining the front of his hospital gown. Ben's mother wore her black funeral dress, her face painted into a death mask. The cuts on her arms, nearly white without blood, stood out against the fabric.

But it was his mother. He could sense it even through the nameless nightmare that flooded the world around them. "Please, Momma. Please don't leave me again." Tears filled his eyes.

She smiled a sad smile. "It's going to be okay. It's going to be all right."

"Don't leave me here alone, Momma." Hot tears streamed down his face.

Shadows saturated the world. Robbie was gone, another soul lost in the twilight place. His mother stood alone in the darkness.

"I miss you, Momma! I love you!" Ben screamed as she faded from sight.

Ben woke as tears streamed down his face, but his mind caught one last echo. "I miss you too, baby. Don't forget."

His head pounded to the beat of a hammer, but nothing hurt as much as the hole the nightmare had punched through his heart. He hadn't dreamed about his mother since she died, not once. He missed her so much. He hadn't realized just how much in a long time.

He turned over and sobbed silently into his pillow.

He looked over at his clock. It was only four thirty in the morning. Julia breathed the deep rhythmic breath of the unconscious, and he didn't want to wake her.

At least one of us is getting some sleep. Wiping his runny nose on his arm, he got out of bed. He left the room as quietly as he could and sat on the couch, staring at the opposite wall for a long time, his thoughts too raw to examine clearly.

He and his mother had been very close. He'd always felt childish about it, but he'd called her Momma long past the time when most young men switched to mom or mother. It had been one of his embarrassing secrets growing up. Coal towns tended to be places filled with hard people. Ben had been in more than his fair share of fights as a kid, and if the other kids had known that, he'd have been in more.

But his mother was all he had growing up, and the same was true for her. No gentlemen came calling for the trailer park woman with a child, certainly not for women with very Christian ideas about sex before marriage. He wondered what she would say about his baby.

But she wouldn't say anything. She was gone. She'd died scared to death. A wild animal caught in a trap. Just as frightened as all those people locked up in the Home.

Maybe someone just like Mom is up on the fourth floor now. The thought almost brought fresh tears.

The nightmare had been ugly, but he'd gotten to see his mother again as he remembered her; happy and strong. He'd really felt as though she was there holding his hand. The rest of it was fading fast, but the beginning, him happy and at home, remained clear.

Ever since her death, he couldn't remember those good times. He only remembered the feeling on the phone when he dialed nine-one-one, knowing it was too late. That sinking in his heart. That sudden wave of guilt. When he pictured her, he thought about the corpse at the funeral, not the woman with whom he'd grown up. It wasn't healthy, but he couldn't help it. The guilt weighed him down. He'd left her alone and run off the first chance he got. He wasn't there when she needed him the most.

He'd never shared those thoughts with Julia, but he suspected she knew. She never brought up his mother. He hadn't brought it up either. Five years and he hadn't spoken about her once.

That bothered him. He retrieved a photo album from the hallway closet. As he cracked it open, the smell of age wafted out. Inside were pictures from his youth. Him and his parents playing on the playground when he was just a toddler. Him on his first day of middle school, his mother standing next to him. His favorite one was of him graduating high school. Her covering her mouth and laughing as him and Eddy tossed their caps into the air.

He ran his hand across the pages as he turned them, savoring the memories, trying to feel them as much as he could through a photograph. By the time he'd finished looking, his heart was heavy, but a good heavy. He hadn't revisited those memories in a long time.

Julia was still fast asleep. He changed into running clothes and left the apartment, hiding the key under the doormat. Running drained him physically, but it always cleared his head, and he desperately needed some of that. He passed the sleeping night security guard on his way out the door.

He sucked in a deep breath of the early morning air, taking off at a good pace and checking out mentally as the city passed by. The streets were vacant. Ben had grown up in an empty town, but Ann Arbor had been bustling, even early in the day. He ran under the streetlights, imagining himself the last man on Earth. He wondered if Dr. Neville had gone running on the empty streets of Los Angeles. The Omega Man out for a jog, all alone.

His thoughts became pleasantly dull. He wasn't thinking about his dream or anything else. Nothing but one foot in front of the other and the pavement to keep him company.

Chapter 7

By the time he returned to his apartment, it was closing in on seven. The city had slowly blossomed into life around him. Cars appeared, lights in stores turned on, and the first trickle of foot traffic bled onto the street. It had been a long run, and his body screamed in protest. He took a slow walk around the building to cool down then went back inside.

Harry had replaced the napping security guard at the door. He gave Ben a cheerless, "Good morning." All Ben could muster in return was a wave. He took the elevator up to his floor and walked into the apartment to the smell of breakfast.

"Good morning," Julia called from the kitchen.

Ben grunted his greeting and sat on the floor to stretch. "Couldn't sleep?" he asked.

"No. I woke up right after you left."

Ben growled out an affirmation and continued reaching for his toes. A few minutes later he took a lukewarm shower and changed into his robe. He walked to the dining room table and sat down. "That smells great."

She set a bowl of corned beef hash and a plate of toast in front of him then walked back to the kitchen, taking a pan full of eggs off the stove. "All for you."

"Not hungry? You shouldn't have morning sickness this late in your pregnancy."

"I'm not. I just don't feel like eating." She sat down and placed the eggs on the plate next to his toast.

"Don't have that baby yet. We haven't met the doctor," Ben said around a mouthful of toast.

"Your concern is touching."

"I'm just worried about the floors."

Apparently, she didn't think he was funny this morning. "Well if you're that concerned about our apartment's hygiene, you can clean the dishes." She got up from the table. "I'm taking a shower."

Ben finished his breakfast and did the dishes as Julia asked. He went into the bedroom afterward. His bed looked damn good. His run had only tired him out more, but he'd needed to clear his head. It was going to be a long day. He changed for work, wishing it were Saturday and not Friday. It couldn't be a good sign if he wanted his workweek to end after just four days.

Julia sat at the vanity, brushing her hair. "What got you up so early?"

"Just couldn't sleep." Another lie. Just piling them on.

She gave him a look halfway between concern and pity. "I'm sorry."

"Not your fault." He screwed with his tie. His mind slow, his hands clumsy. Julia stood and adjusted it for him.

"I think I'm going to head to work early. There are some records I wanted to look at." Ben faked a smile for her and leaned in for a kiss. She kissed him back and finished fixing his tie.

"One more day and we can lounge away the weekend." She patted the knot as she finished dressing him.

"I'll see you later."

"Have fun at work."

He closed the door and walked to the elevator. He doubted the word 'fun' had ever been used to describe anything at the Home.

Ben got into his car, but he didn't go to work early. He didn't want to be in the Home any longer than necessary. Instead, he drove around the city, trying to clear his head. He mentally chastised himself for lying to Julia again as he pulled up to a red light. They'd been together more than half a decade, and he'd never lied to her. Now he'd done it three times in as many days. *Something's wrong with me.*

Lack of sleep dulled his thoughts. He rubbed his eyes, trying to chase away the sleepiness. Whatever his problem was, he needed to get over it. The stress wasn't going to go away once there was a baby in the house. At least then he'd have a good excuse to be up all night.

Someone laid on a car horn behind him, and Ben jumped in his seat. The light had turned green, and his mood was quickly turning black. It would be a very long day.

Storm clouds drifted in overhead as Ben drove around town. The wall of angry clouds that filled the sky was shocking in its swiftness. He'd been told that could happen in the mountains. Valleys hid clouds until they were right on top of you. Umber Gardens Valley was no exception. Ben turned on the radio. Within minutes, what might have been a beautiful morning turned drab. It didn't help his mood.

"All day rain, folks. If you don't have to go out, don't do it. Low visibility expected."

Great. He pulled a U-turn toward the direction of work. Rain or no, Howerton would have a few choice words if he were late. He didn't want a lecture today.

The sky turned sinister, and the first distant peal of thunder boomed overhead. He switched his headlights on. He left the city heading south toward work when the first drops of rain fell. Half a second later, a roar of thunder shook his car. Within moments, he turned on his wipers.

The road to the Home stretched on as empty as ever. He realized with a sense of déjà-vu that he'd never seen another car going either way on lonesome path. His skin crawled. Rain poured harder as he passed beneath the canopy of trees that marked the end of the civilization. It was another world. The sky overheard wasn't visible, but rain fell regardless. A primordial jungle hidden away in a quiet corner of Tennessee. A place where old and ugly things slithered through the cracks in places man hadn't ever set foot. His head swam with the unreality of it all. Thunder rumbled and crashed above him as he journeyed south.

He walked into the lobby half an hour later and dropped his keys off at the desk. By that time, rain cascaded from the sky in thick sheets. The building's quiet struck an odd juxtaposition with the world outside.

"Do you have anything for me from Regina?" he asked the older nurse sitting behind the desk.

"Just a moment, Doctor." She continued to look at the newspaper in front of her.

That was the last straw. The staff hadn't been overly polite to him since the first day, and he'd be damned if he was going to eat shit from them today. "No, you'll check now."

The nurse gave him a foul look that said, "*I've worked here twenty years,*" clear as day.

"Did I stutter?" he yelled over the desk as thunder grumbled outside. The nurse jumped in her seat, and several people walking by turned to see what the shouting was about. Lack of sleep and the sinking suspicion that he was seeing things at work had worn his patience thin. He hadn't gone to medical school so that some spoiled nurse at a rich hospital could throw attitude at him first thing in the morning.

The nurse put down her paper immediately and looked under the desk. She pulled out a large box full of files from one of the hidden cubbies and set it on the counter with a *thud*. She covered her dirty look with a condescending smile. Without a word, he grabbed the box and walked up the stairs.

The rain darkened the world, and without the light from the windows, the grim second floor cast deep shadows in the doorways, like portals to the night. His mind otherwise occupied, he barely noticed. *These people aren't ever going to like me. I'm not part of their little club.* He shook his head.

In part, the sleeplessness made him think that way. He'd read the studies. Sleeplessness caused a myriad of mental and physical health problems. Stress factored into sleeping habits, and he had stress in spades. He swore to himself that if it kept up for another week, he'd see a doctor about it. *Oh? Having trouble sleeping? Don't have a family history of mental illness, do you? Oh, really? Better quit that job, son. Maybe something in manual labor?* He squashed the thought, but it didn't make him feel better.

He climbed up to the third floor, huffing as he lugged the box with him. The second floor was sparsely populated, but the third was barren. He didn't want to be alone up there. The same sort of childish fear that plagued kids when they were alone in the dark closed in on him as the rain pounded its angry cadence on the roof. Knowing something was childish didn't stop it from worming under his skin, or making him check behind to ensure he wasn't being followed. He thought about the odd noise from the closet the day before, the click and squeal as the door drifted open on its own.

He'd just walk by and do his best not to think about it. He'd have one of the orderlies take a look for rats later.

Or it could be Robbie.

He dismissed the absurd thought immediately as he climbed to the fourth floor. Robbie hadn't hunkered down in a locked closet for three days.

The water on the roof roared above, and adrenaline panged in his chest as he turned the corner. Part of him had expected to see his office door sitting open. It wasn't, and Ben stepped inside. The world outside the window looked as if God had ordained another flood to wipe out Tennessee.

At some point during the night, Howerton, true to his word, had two shelves brought up for the office. They stood on either side of Ben's desk, cramping the small office further. Ben shut the door and sat down, pulling out his patient files and putting them in stacks. Underneath everything else sat another folder with 'Theresa Parker' written across the front.

He opened it and paged through the contents. Newspaper articles, witness statements, and affidavits from workers at the Home. She really had killed her husband and infant son. She stabbed Eric Parker to death with a knife after he came home from a meeting at one of his local business interests: The Home. She had drowned her infant son in the kitchen sink. She confessed to both crimes, claiming her husband had put a monster inside of her.

That old woman did this? It happened nearly thirty years ago, but it was still hard to imagine. He set it aside. He'd focus more on that when he didn't have a pile of work in front of him.

The rest of the folders were medical records for his patients, and Ben was looking at a few days' worth of going through them to get everything he needed. The thought made him sleepier. He sighed as he considered all the work he had to do.

It's not going to get done if I just sit here thinking about it. He dug in and started taking notes, kicking himself within minutes for not bringing his reference material. He read about the inane details of every patient, from his catatonics to Christopher Clann. The files had every scratch they'd acquired, both before and during their stay at the home, chronicled in great detail. All of his patients had been there for years. As he paged through the file after, he wondered if anyone ever left this place.

Someone walked down the short hallway to his office and knocked on the door.

"Come in," he called.

Regina entered. Ben checked his watch. Past ten, he'd lost track of time.

"Good morning, Doctor. You got the files?" She was giving him a look, which he picked up on immediately. The old woman downstairs must have said something.

"That nurse at the desk is a bitch." He returned to the papers spread across his desk.

"You aren't wrong. Theresa wanted to meet with you this morning, remember?"

Ben had completely forgotten about that. He set his pen down and rubbed his eyes. "You remind me when I'm a half hour late?" He stood up from his desk and gathered his things.

She didn't miss a beat. "I'm sorry, Doctor, I thought you had a watch."

Ben looked up, his jaw clenched. His attitude didn't impress her, and it passed quickly. He scratched absently at his forehead. He shouldn't be taking this out on her. "I'm sorry, Regina, I didn't sleep well last night."

"You look like you haven't slept in a month."

Longer, but he wouldn't tell her that. "Let's head down there." He shut the office door behind him. "Did you forget about Robbie's file?"

"No. It wasn't there."

"It's just gone?"

"Yeah."

"How the hell does a hospital lose a missing patient's file?"

She shrugged. "No idea. That's the third patient to go missing since I started working here."

His foul mood wasn't exactly subtle, and the walk to the west wing passed silently. The old nurse at the desk glanced up briefly from her paper and put her head right back down when Ben walked by. She wore the same expression she had earlier. *She'll get over it. Or not. Who cares?*

The normal oppression that hung over the west wing only worsened in the rain. The first signs of a headache wormed behind Ben's eye. He took a deep breath and tried to clear his head. Theresa had done nothing wrong, and he wanted to be professional to her.

They walked to the room they had used the day before, and Ben knocked on the door.

"Come in," came the long drawl from inside.

Ben entered. Unsurprisingly, Theresa stood smoking by the window. The room smelled of clove, which brought Ben back to the dream of his mother the night before. He put it out of his mind as he sat at the table.

"Good morning, Theresa."

"Hello, Benjamin," she said without turning around. "How are you feeling this morning?"

"I'm well."

"I was wondering if you were going to show up for our appointment." She took another drag and blew it onto the glass in front of her. The torrent of rain continued.

"I apologize. I was going over some paperwork and lost track of time." He shifted in his seat.

"Don't fidget, Benjamin. Just don't be late again."

His mother had always said that to him as well. *"Don't fidget unless you have ants in your pants."* He smiled as Theresa said it, and he thought he saw her smile in the glass' reflection.

For a long moment, she did nothing but stare outside, giving the impression she was lost in thought. He didn't interrupt. People always felt the need to fill in the quiet, but Ben found silence very therapeutic. The truth usually hid in the places between words.

"I keep expecting the lightning, but it never comes," Theresa said after a while.

It hadn't occurred to Ben that there was no lightning. He tried to recall if he'd seen any on the drive in, but couldn't. "I don't think I've ever seen a storm this bad that doesn't have lightning."

"You get used to it here. There isn't a lot that brightens this place up." A roll of thunder roared its agreement. She turned around and sat across from him. "Why should I trust you?"

"I don't see any reason why you wouldn't, but at the end of the day it's your decision, not mine."

She locked eyes with him and continued smoking. She was unusual alright. She showed clear signs of delusions and paranoia, but none of the more severe symptoms that indicated a tendency toward murder. Her presentation didn't match that of a deranged killer. She looked to be a normal old woman on the outside, but Ben suspected there was something hard under the surface.

She leaned back. "What do you want to talk about, then?" Her grip on the cigarette loosened, and the lines on her forehead eased up. The consummate chess master. Unfazed. Waiting.

"I want to hear why you're being kept here, in your own words."

"I was sent here because I killed my son and my husband."

147

He'd expected that. Heaven forbid anyone in the building answered a question directly. "Can you elaborate further for me?"

Blowing the smoke toward the light, she put her free hand to her temple, and her gaze drifted up to the ceiling. Pondering. She stayed that way for a moment before she looked back at Ben and put her clove out in the ashtray. "You have to understand a few things before I can get into that. There are things in this world, dark things. Older than people. Things that might be older than the world. Those things live, in a way, but they aren't alive like you and me."

He hadn't expected *that*.

"They're all different, but they all have some things in common. They are creatures of the night, and their being is not compatible with a world where the sun shines."

Ben nodded and kept any sign of judgment from his face. "What does this have to do with why you're here?"

She took another clove from a box in her coat and lit it. Her hand shook as she placed the matchbook down. A peal of thunder sounded in the distance. "Bear with me."

He wouldn't push the point. She needed to trust him, and if listening to her delusions would gain her trust, he would.

"They don't sleep, but sleeping is the best way I can think to describe them. They live all around us. When you get cold sweats at night for no reason, or when you hear a noise and your hair stands up, that's one of them passing close to you. Some are small things, like an ant or a rabbit, and they don't do much harm."

148

She looked up at the ceiling again. "Some of them are big." She fixed her gaze back on Ben. "And they're hungry, Benjamin." A roar of thunder rocked the building as she spoke, and he shuddered despite himself. If she noticed, she didn't comment.

Her words tickled something on the edge of his memory, but he couldn't reach it. "And how does this affect you, Theresa?"

"It didn't before I met my husband. As I said, those things are asleep. When we dream we might see them, or we might be closer to wherever it is they stay, but in the light of day they can't touch you, and they can't hurt you." She inhaled a puff and blew it out slowly, calm as a cat. "Sometimes they get close enough to do harm. I don't know if they're all evil, or if they just don't have the sense of right and wrong like we do. They aren't nice, and even being near one is unpleasant. Are you familiar with the concept of possession?"

"I'm familiar with the term, yes." Religious babble at its finest.

"I think most all of that is nonsense, but sometimes I think it's one of those dark things that get inside someone and turn them into a puppet, pulling strings and making them do things they wouldn't otherwise want or be able to."

She was quiet for a full minute before Ben finally asked, "Do you think you or your family were possessed?"

She sighed. "I think that some people hear those things and are drawn to them."

"If these things are as unpleasant as you say, why would anyone want to be close to them?"

She shook her head. "I don't know. Why do people do any of the things they do? People have vile streaks in them, and sometimes those streaks come out in terrible ways." She took another drag from her clove. "I also think there is a perverse sense of power there. I think people see the ways those things affect the world around them and want to use it, want to be a part of it."

"What does all of this have to do with why you're here?"

"My husband was a man that wanted to be close to the dark things. I suspected after I became pregnant that Eric was not the man he wanted me to think he was. I started to feel strange. Near the end of my pregnancy, I started to see things. Something wasn't right. Eric became cold. I hired a man to follow him. The detective was killed in a car accident." Theresa took a deep breath and let it out slowly. "I learned enough though. I learned what Eric and his friends did, right here," she tapped the table, "In this place. They put something inside of me. Changed my baby."

Her file had included notes from the trial that put Theresa into the Home. There was no mention of a detective.

"By the time I found out, it was too late. It was inside of me already, and it got into my baby. I knew it wasn't my son when I looked into its eyes." She squinted at the wall behind Ben. "I killed it. I drowned it in the sink so it wouldn't get out. So that it couldn't pretend to be my little boy anymore. And when Eric came home, I killed him for using me and taking my baby away from me." She put out her clove.

He didn't know what to say to all of that. Complex delusions took a lot of time to work through. If he tried to break them down on their third meeting, he would lose her trust forever, and then he would never be able to help her.

Theresa walked back to the window to watch the world drown for a few moments. "You need to get out of this place, Benjamin."

"May I ask why?"

"You're in danger. I've seen you in my dreams. They want something from you."

She dreamed it? His thoughts raced back to his nightmares over the last few weeks. Danger. Something chasing him. The headache behind his eye exploded into stars of pain. He rubbed it as a hum filled the room. "Who is 'they?'" He tried to keep his composure. A coincidence. Many people had bad dreams, especially mental patients.

She sighed, and for a moment, she looked every bit her age. "The staff are as much members of that… that… whatever you would call it, as my husband was. Some of them anyway. Richard Howerton and Larry Vitalie for certain. They were friends with my husband."

And there was the paranoia. "So you believe members of the staff here are part of a cult?"

"Some, yes."

"Do you think I'm a member of this cult?" The pain behind his eye throbbed.

She faced him. The way the window silhouetted her—wings of dark clouds and rain spread out on either side— made it look like the world was ending. Thunder grumbled in the distance as if to enhance the effect. "No. If I thought you were, I wouldn't be speaking to you." She pulled out another clove and lit it.

"Do you think if there was some kind of a cult here, they would let me speak to you?"

"I don't know everything, but I know you are in terrible danger in this place."

He leaned forward, trying to ignore the pain in his head and the buzzing in the air. It had to be the wiring in the room. "I want to help you get better."

"Get better, Benjamin?" Her voice grew stern. "Get better? Do you think there's a 'get better' for a woman who killed her son? Do you think that story can have a happy ending?" She shook her head. "Let me help you. Look around this place. "

"Yes, Theresa. I do. I think that if you can accept what happened, you can move past it."

"I accepted what happened years ago. You will too, eventually." She pursed her lips, clearly ill pleased by his response. "Those dark things are here. They are in this building, and they want out. As long as you're here, you're in danger. Don't trust anyone. Get as far away from this place as you can." She turned back toward the glass.

"Is that why you asked me about monsters yesterday? You think that they live in this building?"

"I think you know it's true."

Ben had seen many strange things since he came to the Home. The deeper-than-they-should-be shadows, the noises in the basement, the closet upstairs; it was a strange place. But it had been a long few days and longer nights. Only his sleeplessness saw any sense in her words.

"No, I don't. I think you did some things a long time ago that you regret, and I think that if you can see that, you have a real shot at recovery."

She shook her head. "I think we're done for the day."

"I'd like to continue talking to you."

"No. I've said enough, and you aren't listening." She crossed her arms over her chest and leveled a gaze at him that said she had spoken the final word on the matter.

Ben considered pushing the point, but decided against it. He wouldn't do any good if he made her angrier. He could already see his denial of her story upset her. She needed time to think. A weekend between them would do some good, and he could revisit the issue next week.

"Alright, I understand. Would you be willing to meet with me again on Monday?"

She took a drag from her cigarette and blew it out against the glass. "That'll be fine."

He gathered his things and left. Regina sat in a chair outside reading a magazine as he walked out.

"Lunch?" he asked as shut the door behind him.

They ate in silence as Ben wrote down the notes from his meeting with Theresa. It had been interesting, to say the least. He was now certain of her delusions and her paranoia. She bought into them too, not attempting to cover up her crime. She created an entire fictional world in her mind, one populated by monsters and madmen. Modern medicine dictated that she be put on antipsychotics, but Ben wasn't a fan of that approach. Evidence was building that therapy was the key to recovery for most non-psychoses psychological problems. Theresa spoke clearly, she was aware of her surroundings, and all her fantasies were at least somewhat grounded in the real world. He was confident that he could reach her, given time.

He finished his notes and mulled over them while he ate. Grouper and rice. The entire facility's decadence struck Ben once again. Even on a rainy and miserable day like today, the building exuded a touch of class that made him feel out of place. He wondered if that wasn't where some of his discomfort came from. "I don't think I'm going to see my other patients today. None of them are expecting me, and I need to catch up on those medical files."

"Whatever you think is best, Doctor."

He could tell she was picking up on his mood. Being a good nurse meant reading a person's vibes. Sometimes that involved being engaged and friendly, and other times being quiet.

"If you want to just pop in and check on them, that should be fine. I'll do full rounds on Monday. You can go home afterward, unless there's a problem."

"Sounds good to me. Did you still want to meet up on Sunday? I'm looking forward to meeting your fiancée."

"Yeah, definitely." Ben tore off the bottom of a blank sheet of paper and wrote down his phone number. "Just give us a call Sunday morning. We'll figure something out."

Regina smiled. "Good. There are some great views we can drive to. I think you'll like it."

"I'm sure I will." Ben stood up from the table. "I'm going to head up to my office and keep doing my homework."

Rain continued to fall outside. Nature liked to put everything in perspective, and his problems always felt smaller during storms. The older nurse still sat behind the desk as Ben walked through the lobby and up the stairs. She gave him another sour look and kept reading.

The roar of thunder and the pounding rain normally soothed him, but today the sound only reminded him of his isolation on the fourth floor. He wanted to get his work done soon so he could go home and try to get some sleep. If he had to, he would ask one of the other doctors to prescribe him something on Monday.

He walked into his office and looked over the papers spread across his desk. Records of medical history, surgeries, medications, and reactions for all his patients. He picked up Theresa's files and started reading. No medications of any kind were ever used on her. Every other patient file he browsed showed a long list of anti-psychotic, anti-anxiety, and anti-depressant medications.

That struck Ben as odd, and he pulled out her treatment file to compare the two. She had received almost no treatment except therapy since her trial. *She said nobody came up to see her anymore.* According to her records, she was seeing Dr. Vitalie every week. It didn't line up.

She hadn't received any other psychological treatment, but that wasn't surprising. The Home didn't utilize the more aggressive therapies like electric shock. Only the most humane intervention techniques could be administered. A part of the peace of mind for the wealthy families who sent their undesirables to be locked away.

Ben tilted his head back and closed his eyes, reclining in his chair as best he could. Regina said Theresa had killed a nurse at the Home. After their meeting, he could believe it. She didn't just *think* monsters roamed the Home; she was convinced. He waved it away with a shake of his head. *That's how you get locked up in a place like this. Ghosts and rumors become hallucinations and voices.*

Get a grip. Focus on your work.

Sleep would help. Some fringe psychiatrists thought a large portion of mental diseases might root from a lack of regular sleep patterns. Ben had read their studies in school and found the evidence compelling, though the rest of the mental health community had largely panned it.

His eyes grew heavy. He thought about Theresa locked up on the fourth floor for killing a nurse. Christopher Clann laughed in the corner as Ben drifted to sleep.

He sat at his desk as a long line of patients came to see him. It ran out the door, down all the stairs, and straight to the basement where it stretched on for miles. An endless line of dead that wanted out; out of the Home, out of the world.

"When can I go home, Doctor?" the woman at the front of the line asked. The others directly behind peered around her, trying to hear his answer. The Hemsworth woman he'd read about in the basement stood before him, a corpse asking questions.

"I just want to see my husband again." She spoke with no lips. Old and rotten, her eyes had long since decayed, and her flesh sagged from the bone. A few strands of hair that time hadn't yet destroyed remained on her skull.

He tried to explain he couldn't send her home, but when he opened his mouth, the wrong words came out. "You can't go home. You're dead, Mary, and you'll be here forever."

She stared at him without eyes for a moment that stretched on into hours. Disdain and hate radiated from her. He became hot.

She opened her mouth, and a noise like wind in a canyon poured out. A piercing shriek rising impossibly loud. A denial from somewhere deep inside the dark heart of things. The others in line echoed the scream, first the ones behind her, then farther back. The voices of hundreds, maybe thousands of dead, leveled their damnation at him.

Ben tried to cover his ears, but couldn't. His hands wouldn't move. He screamed words that weren't his back at them. "You're dead! You're all dead!"

They howled in return, not needing to take a breath.

"All of you, dead!"

A cacophony of voices damning their fate, they paid him no mind.

"Leave me alone!"

Thunder shook his office, and he was alone. He jumped in his chair at the sudden solitude. He'd yelled and they'd left. The lights in the office were dark. *Did they turn them off? They were on just a second ago, weren't they?*

The world outside was darker than it should be. Not full night yet, but close. He looked down at his watch, but it was stuck at exactly three p.m.

He couldn't think straight, and his head pounded. A ghostly howl of wind buffeted the windows. He stood, the chair falling and his heart in his throat.

I'm dreaming still. I just need to wake up. He touched the edges of his desk. They felt real enough. Another crack of thunder shook the building. Rain pounded the roof just above him.

He couldn't tell if he was awake or asleep. It scared him somewhere deep inside; a primal fear. He set his chair upright and walked around the desk to turn the light back on. It was well past time to get the hell out.

Something moved with a loud squeal and a click in the hallway. Thunder rocked the building, drowning out everything. The sound of a door opening outside followed.

Everything went quiet except for the rain. Something hit the floor outside his office loud enough to rattle the door. Cold sweat broke out all over his body.

"Who's there?"

The creaks of old wood emanated from the hallway. Quiet at first, the noise a foot made when touching a squeaky floorboard, but the sound grew louder. So loud, so quickly, that Ben thought the floor might be breaking apart. Similar creaks joined the noise, some from the ceiling outside the door, some from the walls. The impression it gave, of something growing too big for the hall, maddened him.

Ben held his breath, and his eyes widened. Waves of nausea coursed through his body. The pounding in his head spun the room.

The door expanded inward, joining the chorus. The smell of moldy paper, of a basement filled with rotten files, seeped through the cracks. Moans of the dead from his dream called out to him, the sound of a thousand voices in the wood crying for relief that would never come.

The chorus of screams drowned out the thunder and wind. *I've died. I've died and now I'm in Hell.* Ben backed up until he hit his desk. The door kept caving inward. Soon it would fall, and nothing would stand between him and the thing outside.

Time lost all meaning. It might have been hours or minutes. The thing moved. The creaking faded and stopped as the screams and moaning voices receded into the distance, drifting down the hallway.

The door returned to its normal dimensions as if nothing had happened.

He let out his breath and drew another deep one, dizzy from holding it for so long. Thunder again rattled his windows. His mind kept working on some animal instinct. *I can run. I can run by and get out of here.* If he could make it down the hallway, he could get to the stairs and escape. If it returned, he would die or go mad. He wasn't dreaming, but he pinched himself to be safe. It hurt.

He crept toward the door, listening for something, anything, outside. He couldn't hear it anymore. Ben ripped the door open, expecting the endless dead to be waiting for him.

The door to the janitor's closet sat closed, the hallway empty. Nothing to suggest any sort of disturbance. He ran down the hall, staring straight ahead. If there was anything to see, he didn't want to know.

He sprinted to the stairs and down to the third floor with nothing chasing him except a feeling of impending doom. The whole building closed in, as if he were in the belly of some unfathomable, angry monster. It felt alive. Electric. It wanted him to stay.

He looked behind him as he reached the second floor stairs, and returned his gaze to the front just in time to avoid running into Scott.

"Woo, Doc, where's the fire?"

Ben nearly fell to stop from colliding with him.

"Holy shit, man, are you okay?"

"I don't… I don't know." Ben's hands shook. He thought he might puke.

"Jesus, Mary, and Joseph, take a seat." Scott put his hands on Ben's shoulders, trying to sit him down on the stairs.

"No. No!" Ben pulled away from him. He couldn't stop there, not now. They had to get away. They had to flee from the monstrous building and its ghastly inhabitants. In a distant place, his mind was telling him he was in shock. He had all the classic signs of having the mother of all panic attacks.

"All right, Doc, all right. Come downstairs with me, okay?"

Ben didn't resist further when Scott put a hand around his shoulder and guided him down the stairs. The building was hot. Too damned hot. His mind wasn't working quite right. He had just seen a ghost upstairs.

It was a ghost, right?

He wasn't sure. He couldn't think. His head hurt too much. His temples pulsed with every move. If he could look in a mirror, he was certain he'd see his veins popping out with every beat of his heart.

"I need to go home."

Most of the staff had gone for the day, but two nurses sat at the desk. Ben had never seen either of them before. Scott sat Ben behind the desk next to one of them. Both stopped speaking and stared at him.

"Is he okay?"

"I'm not sure. This is Dr. Kent. He almost ran into me coming down the stairs. I'm going to go get him some water."

The nurses looked at each other. One knelt down next to Ben. "Dr. Kent, my name is Veronica. You look very ill. Are you feeling all right?"

Ben just shook his head. The urge to flee the building came over him, and he shifted uncomfortably in his seat, looking away from her. She grabbed his hand.

"You're burning up. Nikki, go get me a thermometer."

The other nurse vanished down one of the hallways.

"How long have you been feeling like this?" She took his pulse.

"I don't know. I fell asleep in my office and…" He couldn't tell her. She'd think he'd lost his mind. They locked people up in places like this if they saw ghosts and heard noises.

"And what?"

"And I don't know. I woke up confused." Just confused, he had to be. It couldn't be real.

Scott returned to the lobby alongside Nikki. He set a glass of water and two aspirin on the table next to Ben. Veronica took the thermometer that Nikki held and put it into Ben's mouth.

"One hundred five degrees. You're burning up." She grabbed the aspirin and water and held them out to Ben. He took them without thinking and swallowed both, chasing it down with two mouthfuls of water. "You need to get home. Can you call someone?"

"No. My fiancée doesn't have a car." He put his face in his hands, trying to sort out his thoughts. "I need to go home."

Veronica looked at Nikki. Ben was out of it, but he still caught the look. "He can't drive like this. Doctor, that fever is dangerously high. Maybe you should go to the hospital."

Why is she talking about hospitals when there are monsters in the building? Monsters. "I'll be okay. Just let the aspirin do its thing."

"Are you sure? I can drive you," Scott said.

"No, I just need to go home." He wanted desperately to get out of the building. *Why am I still here?* A wave of panic rocked him. *Whatever was upstairs is still around.* Everything had become unreal. His senses were working properly, but what they were telling his brain couldn't be anything other than fiction. He was sleeping. He'd wake up and everything would be okay. He needed to get as far away from this place as he could and never look back before that happened.

Veronica must have noticed the panic in his eyes. "It's fine. You're just running a nasty fever. If the aspirin doesn't knock it down, one of us will drive you to the hospital."

Ben nodded. *Was it just a fever dream?* Everything hurt. *Did I imagine it?*

"I've got work to do. You ladies call me if you need anything."

Ben had the insane urge to warn Scott, to tell him something was lurking on the fourth floor. "Be careful."

Scott gave him a strange look, the kind one might give a mental patient, before continuing up the stairs.

Fifteen minutes passed as Ben sat at the desk, listening to the two nurses chat quietly. They tried to act casual, but it sounded as if they were shy about talking in front of him. Hushed voices. No eye contact. The kind of nursing that happened around the soon to be dead or clinically insane. He didn't care. Monsters roamed the halls of this hospital. Or he thought they were, which amounted to the same thing.

"Your color is looking a little better. Let me take your temperature." Veronica popped the thermometer into his mouth then looked down at it when she pulled it out a moment later. "One hundred and one. It's still high, but it's breaking. Do you feel well enough to drive?"

"Yeah, I should be all right. I just need to get out of here."

Both nurses glanced at one another. Once again, the urge to tell them everything nearly overcame him. *But what then? What do I expect to get out of that? Validation?*

Veronica called over an orderly who'd been standing by the door. The orderly took Ben's keys from her and came back a few moments later drenched from the rain.

"It's a little better out now, but I'd still be careful on your ride home."

Ben nodded as he rose from the desk. He didn't say a word as he walked out the door, but he could feel their stares on him. He felt the stares of others too, thousands of others watching him as he left the Home. He didn't look back as he drove down the long driveway to the gate.

He was too afraid of what he might see.

The rain had reduced to a reasonable drizzle. Still, Ben was scared of getting stuck out there in the woods if a tree had fallen across the road. He assumed he would have heard about it at the desk, but he wasn't sure of much right then.

Is this what happened to Mom? The empty road held no answers for him, and he didn't really want them. He could have snapped. A fever, the lack of sleep, the crazy stories Theresa told him. Maybe it was all just too much for him and he'd had a minor breakdown. The thought turned his stomach. He was going to be sick.

He pulled over onto the shoulder and got out of his car. He walked around to the passenger side and hunched down, hands on his knees. Being stuck on the side of the road in those surreal woods at night did little to help his panic and nausea, and soon he was heaving up what little was left in his stomach from lunch. He waited a few moments and puked again.

He got back in his car, wiping the vomit from his lips with the sleeve of his suit jacket. *What am I going to say to Julia? I can't tell her I've seen monsters. Can I?*

He drove to his apartment complex, pulling in as the clock turned to seven thirty. By the time he got there, the rain had almost stopped. He walked into his building feeling like a wreck. The not-Harry ancient security guard gave him an appraising look as he walked by. Ben didn't as much as nod at him.

He tried to compose himself before Julia saw him. He fixed his tie, which had become lopsided at some point. He adjusted his jacket so it sat right, and tried to wipe some of the puke off his sleeve. All he did was spread it around. The effort nearly brought him to tears. *What the hell am I doing?* He was losing his mind. Or he'd seen ghosts. Maybe both. He took a few steadying breaths as he stepped off the elevator. He didn't want Julia to see him like this. He didn't want her to feel the awful fear rising inside him.

He stepped off the elevator and put his key in the lock, but the door flew open before he could turn it. Julia stood in front of him. Her hair stuck out as if she'd been running her hand through it all night. Her eyes were puffy. She'd been crying. Her expression didn't soften when she saw him wet, pale, and with puke on his clothes.

"Oh my god, I was so worried something horrible had happened to you. That storm was so bad."

Ben walked past her to the couch, put his head in his hands, and began to sob.

Chapter 8

"What happened?" She sat next to him and grabbed both of his hands. She was warm, but he was warmer. "You're burning up."

"I'm all right." He wiped the tears from his eyes and calmed his breathing.

"Get to bed, Ben, right now."

Maybe it was the delirium talking, but the words poured out regardless. "No. I can't." She didn't understand, and he didn't know how to explain it to her. There were things out there, things that watched him while he slept. He'd finally seen them, and now he understood. *I can't sleep anymore.*

He knew the thought was crazy as soon as it crossed his mind. He moaned his displeasure.

"You're sick. Get up, and I'll help you take your clothes off and get you in the shower." She knelt down and took his shoes off while he stared into the middle distance, his thoughts raw and ugly. Madness and monsters danced through his mind, leaving terror in their wake. She grabbed his hands again and gently pulled him to his feet.

Sick. I'm sick… Did I imagine everything? Everything in his mind came through in a fog. He couldn't believe he'd driven home like that. He could've killed himself. He would have left Julia all alone with a new baby.

"I'm sorry," he said as he got to his feet.

"It's okay. Let's just get you in the shower." She helped him take off his tie and jacket. His white button-down shirt, soaked with sweat, smelled terrible. She sucked her breath between her teeth. "You might be dehydrated too." She walked him to the bathroom and ran a hot shower, helping him step out of his pants as she did. She placed him under the water and took her clothes off to join him, washing his body and trying to soothe him.

For the first time since he walked in the door, he really looked at her. She might be putting up a brave front, but he could see fear in her eyes. She held herself so rigid she might break if he didn't do something. He wrapped his arms around her, and she laid her head against his chest. "It's okay. I'm just sick." He couldn't tell her what had happened. He wasn't sure himself.

She said nothing.

"I was fine and then I… I fell asleep at my desk. When I woke up, I had a fever."

"Okay." She kissed his chest. "I want you to get in bed. I'll get you some water to sip."

Ben got out of the shower and dried off, walking naked to the bedroom and crawling under the covers. The thought of going to sleep made him want to run away screaming. He couldn't take another one of those dreams.

He pushed it back down. He wouldn't let Julia worry about it anymore. She walked back into the bedroom with a big glass of water and another aspirin. Ben swallowed the aspirin and sipped the water as she climbed into bed with him.

"I'm all right," he said after a moment.

"I know." She stroked his cheek, rubbing the stubble. "Get some sleep. If you aren't feeling better in the morning, we'll go to the doctor."

Part of him knew what he would see when he closed his eyes. Darkness and shadow, creaking wood and screaming voices. He couldn't handle it. He felt fragile. A strong wind would blow him away.

He pulled in a deep breath, willing himself to be calm, telling his heart to beat slower and let him sleep. Eventually, his body obeyed.

He slept in fits. Asleep for an hour, awake for ten minutes. His mind drifted in and out of dreams half-recalled. Dark rooms and dead people, old hospitals and mental patients. Every time he woke up in fear, he'd feel Julia resting against him and force himself back to sleep. He didn't want to worry her anymore. He'd done that enough.

His mind stopped separating fiction from reality as his fever dreams carried him through the night.

"You killed me, Ben," Regina said. Her body laid on the lobby floor, but her mouth moved as if she was alive. "You killed me."

Julia leaned on the desk only a few feet away, her robes covered in blood from an unseen wound. Howerton's body sat propped in a chair behind the desk. The charred remains of dozens of people littered the floor.

One of them, Scott, stood. "You killed all of us, Ben." The bodies crawled on burnt and bloody hands toward him. Howerton's eyes opened, black as midnight.

Ben woke in sweat soaked sheets. The dream faded as soon as he spied the light from the bedroom window, but the image of Howerton's black eyes stuck with him as he stared at the ceiling.

Julia woke half an hour later. "How're you feeling?"

"Alright, I guess." And it was true, at least a little. He wasn't as delirious as he'd been the night before. The way Regina had stared through him in the dream. The smells of the charred remains. He wished it scared him as much as it should, but after the previous night, it didn't.

"Do you think you could eat?"

"Yeah."

She kissed him before getting out of bed. He stayed there for a while still, trying to sort out his thoughts. The night before was a fevered mess, dimly recalled. The office, the lobby, the drive home, and the shower with Julia all blended in a sweat-drenched catastrophe. The episode in his office had the same fever hue as his dreams. Though it still made his heart beat faster, he was certain he'd hallucinated it.

That didn't make it any better. Real or imagined, it still said something alarming about what was going on in his head. Hallucinations were often the tipping point for full-blown psychosis. Still, other than being warm and mentally sluggish, he didn't feel crazy, and doubting his sanity marked a sure sign that he still had it.

He got out of bed and joined Julia in the kitchen. He kissed her cheek before he reached into the cabinet to grab the aspirin. An ounce of prevention, a pound of cure.

"You look better today."

"I feel better." He sat down at the table. Everything about last night was less alarming with the sun out.

"I want to take you to the doctor anyway, just to be safe."

The lack of sleep was killing him. If he could get something prescribed, that would go a long way toward making him feel better.

Julia went through the motions, but there was a terseness to her actions. She wasn't happy, and he could blame no one but himself. Coming home last night as he had must have really scared her.

When they finished breakfast, they went downstairs to the car. Julia suggested they call around local offices, but Ben pointed out they didn't have a Yellow Pages yet.

"Driving it is then," she said. "But I'm doing it in case you pass out on me."

The sun shone down on the city. People walked the sidewalk, and birds sang in the sky. Warm weather had settled over the land, a product of the previous days rain. By midafternoon it would be hot. A perfect day for driving around with the AC on if you weren't sick and tired.

Neither of them spoke much, but Ben held her free hand as they cruised around the city. They spotted a doctor's office on the outskirts of town and pulled into the parking lot.

Ben read the sign as they walked up to the building. "Dr. Cray," he said under his breath.

"Hmm?"

"Dr. Cray does exams for the Home."

"Do you want to go somewhere else?"

Ben considered it. He hadn't had the chance to meet Dr. Cray yet. *Will he turn out to be another Howerton?* "No, it's fine. I've got to meet him sooner or later, might as well be at my worst."

Julia smiled and slapped his arm.

The same sort of non-descript art and furniture as every office Ben had ever been in decorated the small lobby. A receptionist sat behind the desk, doing her best not to look bored. Other than her, the room was barren. When Ben and Julia walked in, the receptionist put her magazine away and smiled. A decent fake.

"Welcome to Dr. Cray's office. How can I help you?"

"I need to see the doctor."

She looked him over. He wanted to tell her it was none of her damned business why, but he held back. It wasn't her fault he felt like shit. The question didn't come. "Of course, sir, I just need you to fill out a few things. He'll be able to see you right away when you're finished."

Ben sat with Julia on a small sofa and filled out the paperwork. He didn't have an insurance card yet, but if he had to pay out of pocket, he could afford it. Julia's father had insisted they couldn't move to a new place without a few months of money in case something happened.

He took his completed paperwork up to the desk as another woman came out of the back. He handed it to the receptionist, who checked it over. "This looks good, Dr. Kent. If you would just follow Miss Jenny back, she'll get you all set up to see the doctor."

"Thanks." He turned around and forced a smile at Julia.

"Right this way, Dr. Kent." The door opened into a hallway, and the nurse took Ben to the first door on the right, setting the paperwork in a basket outside.

"Just sit on the table for me. I'm going to get your vitals and ask you a few questions."

Ben did as he was told, and the nurse asked him questions. Had he ever had a serious illness, had his family, was he allergic to anything... the list went on. When she finished, she took his temperature.

"That's not good. One hundred." She washed the thermometer and placed it back in its case. "How long has it been like that?"

"Since last night. It's why I'm here."

"Have you had any other symptoms?"

"I…" Ben almost told her everything, but he couldn't imagine how that would look to his new colleague. He didn't want Dr. Cray to think he was crazy, and more importantly, he didn't want word getting around his new job. "I've been a bit delirious. In and out of it since yesterday."

She nodded and took his pulse. "Everything else seems normal. I'll let the doctor know you're ready."

Ben composed himself as best he could. He couldn't do much to hide a month without sleep. Still, he wanted to make a good first impression.

A few minutes later, someone knocked on the door and an elderly voiced called, "Dr. Kent, are you ready?"

"Yes. Please, come in."

The door opened, and a very old man walked in. His skin had the same texture as a prune, and his hair had thinned almost to non-existence, but intelligence shone in his eyes. He extended his hand.

"Nice to meet you, Dr. Kent. I'm Dr. Cray. Just call me Bill."

"Ben. Nice to meet you, Bill."

Bill sat in a chair near the bed. "I hadn't heard there was a new doctor moving into town. I hope you aren't here to take my business." He smiled.

"No, not at all. I'm a psychiatrist. I just started working at the Home."

Ben caught the slightest falter in Bill's smile, but it disappeared as fast as it had arrived. "Not a terrible place for your first job.

Watch out for Dr. Howerton though. Guy's got a stick in him a mile long."

Ben smiled a genuine smile, and when he did, Bill laughed. His laugh was infectious, and Ben laughed too. He couldn't believe it; laughing after last night.

"I see you know what I'm talking about."

"He's a little rough around the edges."

Bill patted his knee. "Good on you, son. Keep up that diplomatic front and you'll go far around here. It's all a good old boys club these days."

"I was told you do some work down at the Home."

Bill scratched his face and squinted a bit, as if thinking took great effort. "Yes. I just do checkups on patients and refer them to other facilities if I can. Howerton fights me tooth and nail on it, but I was practicing medicine before that man knew what his pecker was for."

Ben laughed. "Why refer them?"

"Nobody gets better at that place, son. You'll see that soon enough."

That hit a little too close to home. After being there for a week, Ben could understand. Christ, that place drove the sane to the edge. He couldn't imagine what it must be like for the sick. Instead of trying, he changed the subject. "How long have you been practicing?"

"I worked with Theodore Howerton—that's Stephen's father—and Dr. Ross when that place was still just a hospital. Guess it's been about fifty years now."

The idea that this man had seen so much of the Home's history took Ben aback. Thoughts of the basement ward and the thousands of patients who'd passed through the Home burned in Ben's mind. A million questions must have stamped themselves onto his face, because Bill laughed again.

"Slow down. How about we see what's wrong with you, and then we chit-chat about what it was like to walk with the dinosaurs."

Ben went over the same things he had with the nurse, and Bill did all the same tests. He took some gear out of a drawer and drew some of Ben's blood. "I'll have a few tests run to see if you've got any serious bugs, but my bet is you just caught the business end of a nasty cold."

Ben saw no reason to disagree. He only came to the doctor to soothe Julia's fears ."That reminds me, I haven't been able to sleep well for months."

"That would weaken your immune system." Bill looked through the chart. "What about this delirium you mentioned?"

Bill reminded Ben of the grandparents he'd never gotten to meet. Still, he didn't know if it was wise to lay all his troubles on one of his colleagues. "I was in my office last night, and I had a few auditory hallucinations. My fever was one hundred five."

"What was the nature of those hallucinations?"

Once again, Ben was at a loss for words. *Why is that important?* "I thought I heard some noises outside my office."

Bill squinted again as if he was trying hard to think. "Where's your office?"

"Right next to yours on the fourth floor."

Bill laughed, easing the tension. "That's half the reason I don't spend more time at that place. My knees just about fall apart when I have to walk up those stairs. Any particular reason for the bad sleep?"

Lying to your doctor didn't advance your treatment very far. Still, Ben feared the question that always came up when assessing a patient's mental state. *Do you have a family history of mental illness?* And that would be it. The new job would vanish, and he would be back to begging money from Julia's parents to make ends meet. No self-respecting hospital would hire a mentally ill psychiatrist. Hard to treat the crazies when you have a nasty case of it yourself. "Stress. New job, new place, new baby on the way. I was hoping to get something to help me sleep."

Bill shook his head. "I don't prescribe sleeping medication. The body wants natural sleep, not pills."

The answer hit Ben like a punch in the gut. Natural or not, he needed some goddamn sleep. "I understand."

Bill patted Ben's knee again. "You're sick, you're stressed, and your new boss is a horse's ass. When things settle down, you'll be fine." Bill reached into a nearby drawer and pulled out a prescription pad. "I'm going to give you some antibiotics just in case it's a bacterial infection." He scribbled a prescription and tore it off, handing it to Ben.

"I appreciate it."

"You're too young to be so stressed out. Are you working this weekend?"

"No."

"Good. I want you to go home and rest. Drink plenty of fluids. If your fever spikes again, call me. I've written my home and office number on the back."

Ben found that oddly touching. He looked down at the numbers on the back. "Thanks, Bill." He felt silly for letting a simple gesture touch him, but it did.

"Rather than keep you here all day while you're sick, why don't you and I have dinner next week? We can talk all about the Home then."

Ben folded the number and put it into his pocket. "I'd like that."

"My receptionist mentioned you didn't have an insurance card yet. Don't worry about this visit. Consider it a welcoming gift."

Too often, old doctors treated new doctors like pests to be brushed aside. It felt nice on the rare occasion that Ben found one who treated him like a colleague instead of a child. "Thanks. I appreciate it." Ben shook his hand. They walked out to the lobby, and Julia stood up as they entered.

"And who is this lovely young lady?" Bill asked.

"Dr. Cray, this is my fiancée, Julia. Julia, Dr. Cray."

Bill shook her hand. "Bill, please. I feel ten years older every time someone calls me Doctor these days. I want you to make sure Ben here gets plenty of rest and fluids. He should be fine."

"I will."

Bill said his goodbyes as Ben and Julia left the building. They stopped at a corner pharmacy to fill Ben's prescription. He didn't have much hope for feeling better, but it would be a cold day in hell before he ignored medical advice from someone fifty years his senior in the field.

Once they had his antibiotics, they returned to the apartment and spent the rest of the day following Bill's advice. They sat on the couch, catching up on their reading. Neither had ever owned a television, and neither wanted one. Ben's mother once told him that when you had something tailor-made for distractions, you never got any work done.

Julia made him lunch and later that night ordered pizza for dinner. By eight, they were both in bed. Ben didn't sleep for a long time, and when he did, it was restless.

Ben awoke at six in the morning, but lay quietly in bed until Julia got up at eight. He'd had bad dreams, but he couldn't remember them. He woke up with his pulse racing, thinking he was on the fourth floor of the Home. That place had certainly put its hooks into him.

His fever broke completely at some point in the night. He felt world's better, but still wanted more sleep. It wouldn't come, and he didn't bother trying. Bill wanted him to get natural sleep, but the way things were going, he wasn't sure he'd ever get it again.

When Julia sat up, he did the same. "Good morning," he said.

"Good morning." She kissed him then placed a hand on his forehead. "You feel better this morning."

"I do," he agreed.

She looked at him for a long moment. "It doesn't look like you slept at all."

"I'm not sure I did."

She hobbled out of bed and fished around in the closet for something to wear. Open concern was becoming a regular look for her. "Think breakfast will make you feel better?"

"Maybe."

She left the room, and Ben found himself alone with his thoughts. *What if this is the rest of my life?* Everyone had that thought at some point in their twenties. Going out into the world and cutting loose from any anchor you've ever known would scare anyone. How a person dealt with that fear defined who they would become.

He put clothes on, wanting to chat with Julia and distance his mind from his anxieties. As he left the room, the phone rang.

"Can you get that, Ben?" Julia called from the kitchen.

He walked into the dining area and picked up the receiver on the wall. "Hello, Kent residence."

"Dr. Kent? This is Regina."

Ben had completely forgotten about going out with Regina today. "Hey, Regina, how are you?"

"I'm good. Still feeling up to exploring the city?"

She couldn't have known about Friday's events. "Just a second." He put the phone down to his chest and covered it. "Do you want to go out with Regina and see some sights today?"

Julia poured the pancake mix into the pan. "I'd love to if you feel up to it. Ask her if she wants to come over for breakfast."

Ben put the phone back up to his ear. "Sounds like a plan, Regina. Get here soon and there's breakfast in the deal."

She asked his address and said goodbye. Ben excused himself to take a quick shower. By the time he finished, breakfast was nearly done. He took over for Julia so she could shower and change. As she stepped out of the bedroom, a knock sounded on door. Julia answered it.

"Hi. You must be Regina."

"Julia, right?"

"Sure am. Please, come in. Breakfast is just about ready."

"It smells amazing."

"That's because I cooked it," Ben said from the kitchen.

Julia rolled her eyes. "He did no such thing. Please, sit down, Regina. Do you want coffee or orange juice?"

"Orange juice sounds great."

Within a few minutes, everyone had dug in. "How long have you been a nurse, Regina?" Julia asked.

"Ten years. I started at the Home right out of school. Dr. Kent—
"

"Ben," he said around a mouth full of bacon.

"Ben told me you're from New York." That New York accent really came through. It happened much more whenever two or more of them got together. Julia's family sounded like caricatures of New Yorkers when they ate at the dinner table. Except her grandmother anyway. That woman refused to give up the Old World.

"Brooklyn. You?"

"Yeah, me too."

Julia and Regina traded stories about New York and the places they'd been. It turned out that they'd run in a lot of the same circles growing up, but they'd never met. In a big city like New York, that wasn't surprising.

He found himself shut out of the conversation. Occasionally one of them would ask him a question, and he'd give a quiet reply. He didn't mind. Julia needed a friend in this town, and Ben was glad he could help her with that. Besides, he didn't feel much like chatting. He hadn't lied to Julia, he did feel better, but he didn't feel great. His temperature had leveled out, but the lack of sleep weighed heavily on him.

Half an hour later Ben was cleaning the dishes while Julia and Regina continued to chat.

"So what do you want to see today?" Regina asked.

"I don't know. What's the most Tennessee place in town?"

"Porksters," Regina said without missing a beat.

Regina and Julia both laughed, Julia until she snorted. Ben couldn't help but crack a smile as he scrubbed the grease from the frying pan.

"Okay, okay," Julia said when the laughing had died down. "Besides that, where are the must-go places in Umber Gardens?"

Regina leaned back in her chair. Ben was thrilled at how quickly Regina had clicked with him and Julia. Making friends was a process, but laughing over breakfast was a sure sign you were on the right track.

"Most of the good hiking trails wouldn't be great for a pregnant woman. You could do worse than a doctor and a nurse delivering your baby in the woods, but I'd rather not."

Julia smiled again. "At least the little guy would have a great story to tell. Still, I agree. What else?"

"Well. It's not exactly local, but Fall Creek Falls is a state park about an hour away. Minimum walking for maximum viewing pleasure."

"What do you think, Ben?" Julia turned to look at him.

"I think"—he toweled off the last of the dishes—"that sound like a great idea."

Julia made sandwiches so they'd have something to eat. Thirty minutes later, everyone piled into the Sportwagon. Ben drove so the women could chat. They were really hitting it off, though their backgrounds couldn't be more different. Julia, a rich girl from an immigrant family. Regina, the rebellious daughter of a World War

183

Two NCO. Ben wondered if back in New York they would have been friends. Anything familiar looked like a lighthouse when you were far from home.

"What about you, Ben? How did you grow up?" Regina had just told several stories about growing up in a Marine Corps sergeant's house. She didn't have many kind words to say about it.

"I was raised by my mom in a town a lot like Umber Gardens."

"Did moving here feel like coming home?"

Ben chuckled. "Hardly. The town I grew up in had about five hundred people."

A quiet settled onto the car for a few minutes as they drove along. Regina spoke up as the silence stretched on. "So how did you two meet?"

Ben looked at Julia in the passenger seat. "In college. When we met she thought I was the biggest asshole in the world."

Julia smiled and stared out her window. "That's because you said I looked like an ethnic Barbara Eden."

Regina laughed.

"Well, to be fair, you told me I was so skinny I could be a Third-World refugee."

Regina laughed harder. "Oh my god! How did you two end up together?"

Ben glanced at Julia, but she spoke up. "He can be a charmer when he wants to." She squeezed Ben's hand.

The Tennessee landscape flew by. All the car's windows were down so they could enjoy the weather. It was easy to forget your troubles looking at the wilderness out there. The mountains closed in around them, and steep hills opened up onto breathtaking views of valleys from on high. The clouds stretched on forever, and the forests below ruled the world. The leaves hadn't started to change color yet. They wouldn't for a while in Tennessee.

Regina pointed out the exit they needed to take, and Ben pulled off. The highway's Sunday bustle slowly gave way to the towering trees and streams of Fall Creek Falls. "Take a left up here. I'll show you what this place is named for first."

Ben did as Regina said and moved through turns and loops as they passed deeper into the park. Within ten minutes Ben became hopelessly lost, but Regina knew exactly where she was going.

"Been here a lot?" Julia asked.

"I come up here all the time. I grew up in the city. I didn't realize how closed-in my world was until I left."

"I miss it," Julia said. "I liked the rush and the noise. Not being able to go out at three in the morning and get a pizza is going to take some getting used to."

Ben laughed. "You went out for pizza at three in the morning?"

She smiled. "No, but I could."

That started a conversation about which New York pizza place was the best. It lasted until they pulled into a parking lot surrounded on all sides by trees.

Ben had never been to a state park before. A dozen other cars sat in the parking lot, and in the distance, he could hear a waterfall. A family ate their lunch on a nearby picnic bench, and the smell of nature hung heavy in the air. It looked exactly like Ben had always imagined a state park would.

Julia stretched as she struggled out of the car. *She has good balance for a woman that's nine months pregnant.* Ben always expected her to fall over looking like she did.

"Are you ready?" Regina asked. "This way."

Countless feet had worn a trail into the grass just outside the parking lot. It led down a hill littered with trees, past signs and posters encouraging visitors to respect the park. As the path steepened, the trail gave way to steps carved into stone. Ben and Julia walked hand-in-hand, as much out of love as to make sure she didn't fall. The sound of the waterfall grew louder. The picturesque park had a tranquility Ben missed. It was almost enough to make him forget how tired he was.

Almost.

The trees opened up, and they approached a cliff that crested a breathtaking view of the Smoky Mountains. Regina led them up an outcropping of rocks with a wooden fence around it. As they approached, they could see the waterfall below dropping from a cliff and into the river.

Julia gasped when she saw it. A fine mist settled over the bottom of the cliffs, making rainbows that were present year round. Unlike the woods around the Home, this place was pristine. Nature untouched by man or any other contaminating hand. Ben couldn't remember seeing anything so pure.

They were silent for a long time before Regina finally spoke up. "So what do you think?"

"I don't think I could have asked for a better nurse," Ben said.

"I think that I feel better about not being in New York," Julia said.

"Yeah, all it needs is an all-night pizza joint at the top, and you'd be in heaven." She slapped his shoulder.

"If you follow this trail, you can get to the river." Regina pointed at a path that ran alongside the edge cliff before it veered off and disappeared into the woods.

"Do you want to go check it out?" Ben asked Julia.

She looked at the path. It descended steeply, and, judging from the expression on her face, she wasn't keen on the idea of walking down that far in her condition. "Why don't you two go take a look? You can bring me back a river rock or something."

"I don't want to leave you up here alone." He pulled her hand to his mouth and gave it a kiss.

"There's a family having a picnic within shouting distance. I think I'll be okay."

"Might be a family of bears between them and you, darling."

Julia rolled her eyes. "Regina, will you take my overly protective fiancé down the path before I show him the short route over the cliff?"

Regina laughed and grabbed Ben's free hand. "Come on, hero, we'll get her a souvenir at the bottom."

Ben followed. He couldn't remember the last time he'd smiled this much. "Mind the bears, sweetheart!" he called over his shoulder as he and Regina started down the path.

Shafts of sunlight fell on them as they walked. The steps were dirt and stone, with the cliff and the river on their right and the woods on their left. The waterfall turned into a distant roar. The climb steepened, and the path grew more rugged. The cliff side became unnavigable; a sudden drop gave way to the river forty feet below as the path turned left and continued down.

"I wish I could live down here," Regina said as they veered off into the woods.

Ben hummed in agreement. The trees towered above them, and Ben experienced the same feeling of being in an alien world as he had Friday morning on his way to work. Here though, that world didn't press in. No hostile malice radiated from the ground under his feet. Just light in the air, and the relaxing sounds of nature.

"I've explored all the parks around here. This state has everything you could want if you like the outdoors." Regina ducked under a low branch, and Ben did the same. "Or if history is your thing. There are a million Civil War monuments in southern Tennessee."

"Yeah, Howerton mentioned this area had some history."

"Umber Gardens is old, but that's all I know."

Ben couldn't understand how history didn't fascinate people. The lives of countless men and women who came before, all their love and hate, hope and tragedy, all that humanity had deemed fit to remember was encapsulated in the history books. Not looking at where you came from, not caring about the stories of people who'd come before, was like letting them die twice.

They continued in comfortable silence, and the path looped back around toward the river, moving steadily downward. Ten minutes later the trees parted, and the river opened before them, stretching to the opposite shore where only trees lived. The forest went on around them for miles. The roar of the waterfall grumbled in the distance. There was no way to reach it from the shore. The cliffs made an impassible barrier. Ben looked up behind them to try to see Julia, but it was impossible from the side of the river. For the moment, he and Regina were the only two people in the world.

Ben sat in the dirt and took it all in as Regina walked to the bank where moss and grass hung down to touch the water. It must have been at least seven feet deep. Wading in would be stupid, but its enchantment called to Ben. The sun shining off the surface mesmerized him. He lost all track of time.

The world didn't look ugly from here. He forgot his fears of insanity and dark things somewhere else. Somewhere that didn't matter. He wished Julia could see it, but he wouldn't bother to explain it to her. Sometimes words just weren't enough. You couldn't explain to someone what it was like to see the first people leave Earth and go into space. You couldn't explain to someone what it had been like to be in the trenches in World War One. Places like that riverside on that day couldn't be explained either. It soaked into him, and he let it.

"Are you okay?" Regina asked.

Ben hadn't realized she was staring at him. "I'm fine." The spell of the place broke apart, and the inexplicable moment passed.

She sat down next to him, gazing off into the world the same as him. "Is it new job jitters or something else?"

He liked Regina, but he wasn't sure he wanted to share his fears with her. "I don't know." The silence stretched on as birds flew overhead and the occasional cloud blocked the sun.

"You know, most people think they're the wind. But really, we're all just clouds. We don't really have any control over where we are or where we're going."

Ben laughed. He couldn't help himself. "What does that mean?"

"It means life is better when we just go with the flow."

That was the worst kind of sentimentality, but he knew she was trying to make him feel better. "The best part about being a cloud is getting to piss all over the nurses when you have a bad day."

She laughed so hard that she snorted, and soon they were both laughing. "I'm serious though, Ben. I've seen people come and go from the Home because they let the place get them down. You've got to let it roll off you if you want to stay."

He wasn't sure he wanted to stay at all. "You mentioned you'd seen creepy stuff around the Home. I saw Bill Cray yesterday and he said it too. What have you seen there?"

"Well." She got up and offered a hand to Ben, who took it and stood as well. "It's not just about what I've seen. It's more about how it feels." They walked back toward the trail, away from the river and its enchantment. "Whispers when I'm alone, and patients who've told me that we aren't by ourselves in a room when I had just had the same feeling. And it feels so dark there."

He couldn't have said it better.

"Some of the other staff is weird too. It's like their whole lives revolve around that place. They talk about it like it's a church. To be honest, it creeps the hell out of me." She looked over at him. "But I wouldn't turn down the money for anything."

Ben could appreciate that. Times had changed a lot over the last fifty years, but it was still a lot harder for a single woman to make it than for a man.

"Obviously I don't want any of that repeated around work," she said.

"So you trust me with all of your secrets?"

"Some of them. You seem all right." She smiled. "And Julia seems like she's on the up and up. I doubt she'd be marrying you if you were an asshole."

"New Yorkers stick together, huh?"

"Every time."

Silence filled the space as they walked, until Regina spoke up. "So what did you see?"

Ben almost missed a step.

"I'm not going to say anything," she added.

He let it all out before he could stop himself. "I had a fever Friday night and thought I heard voices outside my office. Earlier last week, when I was in the basement, I thought something was down there with me." His cheeks grew hot as soon as he told her. "Just weird stuff like that."

"I…" She stopped herself and stared into the middle distance where there was nothing to see. "I saw a ghost in one of the third floor bathroom mirrors my first week." She waited for Ben to say something. When he didn't she continued, "An old woman behind me when I looked up. She was trying to say something and crying, and when I screamed, she vanished."

"Jesus. Really?"

"Yeah. I think a lot of the staff see and hear things but don't mention it. Howerton doesn't want to hear about it."

"Why?"

"I don't know. They're a weird bunch. Most of the staff is 'senior' staff, and they don't associate with newer staff at all. There's an in crowd and an out crowd, and unless you've been around here for a few generations, you are always going to be in the out crowd."

"What about Dr. Cray?"

"He's all right. I get the impression the other doctors don't like him much."

In a few moments, they were back at the top of the trail with Julia, stood at the cliff looking down at the waterfall. "Where's my river rock?"

"Whoops," Ben said.

They spent the rest of the day driving around the park, seeing sights and buying souvenirs from a small shop along the road. They ate their lunch on a bench outside. As they left the park that night, the sun was setting, bathing the world in crimson and gold. When they arrived home, Regina said goodbye and gave Julia a big hug.

"She seems like such a sweetheart," Julia said as they rode the elevator up to their apartment.

"She is. I'm glad they paired me up with her."

Julia hugged him, leaning her head on his chest as the elevator rode up. "Do you feel better?"

Physically, he felt fine except for being tired, but he didn't want to sleep. Anxiety wormed its way through his guts at the thought of putting his head on the pillow. He wasn't going to burden Julia with that. The day had been too good. "I'm fine. I feel great." He kissed the top of her head.

Sleep avoidance behavior was the clinical term for it. The irrational fear of sleep. Usually a sign of post-traumatic stress disorder or similar form of anxiety. Therapy and drugs were the preferred interventions. Drugs were a bust for him, and he wouldn't go to therapy in a town where he worked. He wasn't going to risk word getting around that he couldn't hack it. Too many people in the Home already looked down their noses at him.

They ate a small dinner before taking showers. Ben sat in the bedroom, getting ready to lie down, when he heard Julia scream from the bathroom. His heart skipped a beat, and he ran to her. "Julia! What's wrong?"

"What the hell is that?" She pointed at a tick on her leg as she threw the curtain open.

Ben didn't mean to laugh at her, but he couldn't help it.

"What the hell is it, Ben?"

"It's a bug." He got one of her sewing pins and a lighter from the living room. As he walked back to the bathroom, a chill ran down his spine and he stopped in his tracks.

The air grew heavy, and the certainty that something was watching him from the corners overwhelmed him. The impression that something *other* had walked in the door and made itself at home tickled his mind. He wasn't alone.

He looked around the living room. Nothing out of the ordinary presented itself. He went into the kitchen and turned on the light but found nothing unusual there either. *Just anxiety. Everything's fine.* The first twinges of an ugly headache caressed the inside of his head. He went into the bathroom. "All right, let me see your leg."

Julia grabbed onto the towel rack and stuck her leg out of the shower. "Is this going to hurt?"

"No." He heated the tip of the needle and poked the tick. It moved on her leg, leaving a little blood behind. He grabbed it between his fingers and squished it.

"See, all bett—"

A creature loomed out of the shadows of the hall in the mirror. The skin of its face hung black and rotten as if falling off, its one visible eye milky and bloodshot. It wore a half smile, the other half-hidden by the doorframe. The visible teeth ended in sharp points.

Ben yelled and tried to face the door, expecting the thing to come into the bathroom for him and Julia. He lost his footing on the wet floor as he spun, falling and hitting his head on the edge of the tub. His vision blurred.

"*Ben,*" said a voice in his head. "*All mine.*"

He tried to yell, to warn Julia, but only a groan came out.

"*All mine, Ben. Ben. Ben!*" It was shaking him now. Screaming his name.

"Ben!"

Julia stood over him, tears in her eyes.

"Ben!"

The world snapped back into focus. He grabbed her arm and used the edge of the tub to jump up, ready to face whatever was in the bathroom with them. There was nothing.

It's here for my fiancée and me. Ben knew it, but he wasn't going to let it get Julia. Survival overcame fear. "Stay here." He strode past her and shut the door.

"What's going on?" Julia yelled through the door, her voice trembling.

His head pounded, and something hot ran down the side of his face. He went to the bedroom and pulled the handgun out from the bedside dresser before searching the apartment for the intruder. A moment later Julia emerged from the bathroom, a towel wrapped around her, to find him reaching under the bed, looking for a thing that wasn't there.

"Ben!" She was crying now. Ben couldn't remember ever seeing her cry before. "Ben, you're scaring me."

"I told you to stay in the bathroom," he said, harsher than he meant to.

"What's wrong?"

He looked up at her. Tears filled her eyes and her lower lip quivered. He must have seemed crazy to her with blood running down his face as he checked under a bed for an intruder, gun in hand.

"I'm sorry." He sat against the bed and touched his head. His fingers came away red.

"What's wrong? What happened?" She sat in front of him, grabbing his wet towel out of the hamper next to the bed and dabbing it against his head.

"I thought I saw someone behind me in the doorway."

She sniffed back tears. "I was looking in the doorway the whole time. Nobody was there."

Fear washed over him. *Did I imagine it? Am I seeing things at home now?*

She finally lost her composure. "Tell me what's happening with you!" Tears streamed down her face.

Of course his mental state would be getting to her. The last week he'd been on edge, and the last two days he'd been a crazy wreck. He couldn't imagine how it must all look to her. Alone in a new place, the father of her unborn child coming unhinged before her very eyes.

She thinks I'm going to crack like Mom did. The thought made his heart ache. He pulled her in close to him as she sobbed, trying to comfort her, whispering platitudes in her ear. "I'm okay. I'm okay. I'm just a little stressed is all. I promise it's going to be fine."

She cried for an hour, finally falling asleep after countless reassurances. It was a long time before sleep found Ben.

Chapter 9

Ben woke up the next morning from another half-recalled dream. Endless hallways and locked doors, something wicked chasing him as he sought an escape. He rubbed his eyes and looked at the clock. Five thirty in the morning. He lay back down and stared at the ceiling until seven, when the sun started to invade the room. He thought no good thoughts, and felt no good feelings.

At one point last night Julia had accused him of shutting her out, keeping his problems locked inside where they would fester and rot. Stress, he'd said, it's all just stress. Lying in his bed that morning, Ben couldn't help but wonder how true that was.

Is it just stress? Am I going crazy like Mom did? Is this job too much for me?

Once again, he thought about the alternative. Living in New York and finding a job there that didn't involve mental health. A doctor working construction, or helping Julia's family run the business. He pictured the look of shame he'd wear when he saw her father, who would know Ben couldn't live up to the expectations put on a man caring for a family.

It killed him. He didn't want to be a failure. He didn't want Julia or their son to know the strain he'd experienced growing up. Julia's family had enough money to support them both, and they thought of him as a son. But he was better than that. He knew it, and he'd make sure everyone else did as well.

He left the bed and dressed. He barely recognized himself in the mirror anymore. The bags under his eyes were heavy, his color off, and his eyes bloodshot.

He skipped breakfast, his appetite gone with the problems of the last few days. He snatched the book on the coffee table, hoping to lose himself in a story for a little while before he woke Julia. She was going to drive him to work so she could use the car to get to her obstetrics appointment.

The book failed to grab him. The only thing that could occupy his attention was his dread of going back to the Home. He knew that place was responsible for at least some of his sudden problems, even if he didn't know why.

He thought back to what Theresa told him about monsters living there. It drew out the image of the creature from the night before, standing in the hallway, looking at him and Julia. *What if she's right?* He'd have a lot of questions for her today.

Another thought followed closely after. *What does it mean if you're going to crazy people for answers?*

It meant you were crazy.

He woke Julia at a quarter to eight. She dressed quickly but said little. He didn't think she was mad, but she was certainly upset. The short drive to the Home was longer in silence. When they passed out of the city and into the forest around the Home, she finally spoke up. "This is creepy."

"Just wait until you see the building."

A few minutes later they waved at the security guard and pulled into the gates. The Home presented itself in all its unsettling glory. The odd carving on the porte-cochere, the heavy atmosphere of the property within the walls, and the forest crowding in around the place, pressing in on all sides as if trying to hide it from the world— Julia saw it all.

"Why would anyone want to be here?"

"Exclusivity. It's the same reason people buy thousand-dollar pens." They drove around to the entrance. Ben gave her a kiss before getting out of the car. "Have fun today, sweetheart."

The front doors opened. "So, this is the future Mrs. Dr. Kent?" Howerton asked as he stepped out of the building.

Ben wondered how this guy always managed to pop out of nowhere. "Dr. Howerton, good morning."

Julia stepped out of the car as Howerton came around and extended a hand. "Nice to meet you, Dr. Howerton."

"That's quite the grip you have, young lady. Please call me Stephen."

"Stephen."

"I understand you have a little bun in the oven. May I?" Howerton gestured at her belly.

Julia looked nonplussed but nodded. She hated people thinking it was okay to touch her just because she was round as a beach ball. The smirk on Howerton's face turned into a smile as he placed his hand on her pregnant belly. Once again, Ben found himself not liking that smile.

"I hope the little guy kicks." Howerton leaned in close.

Julia gave Ben a, "What the hell is he doing?" look over Howerton's head. Ben just shrugged.

"Oh, yes. He is going to be a strong one. Do you have an OB yet?"

"Yes, I'm going to see him this morning, actually."

"Good, good." Howerton took his hands off Julia and gave Ben the creepiest smile he'd ever seen. "Yes, I think he's going to be very strong. I understand you'll be joining us for dinner the day after tomorrow?"

"I wouldn't miss it." Julia smiled.

Ben had known her a long time, and if that smile was real, he was Benny Hill. The strain of the last few days must have gotten under her skin. *And why wouldn't it?* He'd come home from work half-crazed and searched their apartment for invisible monsters. She was nine months pregnant with his child. It was a wonder she'd tolerated the last week as well as she had. He silently swore to himself that he would make it up to her somehow.

"Good. It's a very special dinner, just for the two of you. We want to give a warm welcome to the newest members of our family."

"We appreciate it. It's hard being in a new place," Julia said.

"I know, dear, I know. But if you need anything, anything at all, please call me." Howerton pulled out a small notepad and pen from his jacket and wrote down his information, tearing it off and handing it to Julia. Ben didn't know how to feel about that, but Julia's smile looked genuine this time.

She can't seriously be taken in by this nice guy act. But apparently, she was.

"Thank you, Stephen."

"Of course, my dear. We're all family here."

Julia shook his hand again and got into the car, saying her goodbyes to both of them. She pulled away in the Sportwagon, and they watched her go.

"Quite the little family you have there. I very much look forward to chatting with her over dinner." Howerton walked toward the door and gestured Ben to follow. "I understand you were ill on Friday. Is everything all right now?"

"I'm fine, sir. Just a nasty fever."

Two orderlies opened the doors for them, giving a courteous nod to Howerton but not to Ben. The same old nurse from last Friday morning sat behind the desk. Otherwise, the lobby stood empty, as brooding and uncomfortable as ever. A headache started the moment he walked through the doors.

"I hope so, Dr. Kent. We don't want any of the patients getting sick."

"I wouldn't dream of it, sir. Dr. Cray prescribed me antibiotics on Saturday."

Howerton gave Ben a distasteful look. Apparently, whatever dislike Bill had for Howerton was mutual. "I need to get back to work, Dr. Kent, but if I could give you a piece of advice?"

"Of course, sir."

"Don't associate with the wrong people around here. It isn't good for your career."

The almost threatening statement struck Ben silent as Howerton walked away. *He really does have a stick up his ass.*

Odd that Howerton could be so sickly sweet to his fiancée and treat him like he was beneath consideration. Ben had more pressing concerns. He dropped his keys at the desk and walked up the stairs to his office, thinking of the thing he heard in the hallway Friday night.

Maybe I'll just grab my things and use one of the break rooms downstairs for the day. Halfway up the stairs to the third floor he decided that was idiotic. He was a medical professional and soon-to-be father. He wouldn't let noises and silly fantasies scare him. *So you won't believe there are monsters in the building, but you'll ask your patients about them?*

"Crazy."

Ben stopped in his tracks at the top of the third floor stairs. The word had come from in front of him. Just the barest caress of an unseen voice.

"Hello?"

No reply except the occasional creak and the wind outside. The pressure in the hallway changed. Charged, as if a lightning bolt would strike. He'd heard it. It hadn't been in his head, he was sure of that.

"If someone's here, speak up."

No response. He started walking toward the fourth floor stairs again. The unseen gaze weighed on him from shadowed doorways and corners despite the daylight spilling in from the windows. Goose bumps pimpled his arms. The headache began to pound.

Thinking of what Regina told him the night before, and determined not to let it bother him, he continued to his office. *I'll just grab my things and go back downstairs. There's a lounge just outside of the lobby I can use for a few days. I'll tell everyone I'm not feeling well and didn't want to walk up the stairs.*

As far as excuses went, it wasn't bad. He'd been sick Friday. People would believe him. It didn't matter that he was rationalizing his behavior. Either his mind was slipping or something very dark roamed the halls of the Home. Either way, he didn't know how to deal with it.

He climbed the stairs to the fourth floor and walked down the short hallway to his office. A strange smell hung in the air. It reeked of old dirt, like a basement with an earthen floor that hadn't seen the light of day in years. The invisible audience cut closer, leaning forward in their seats to make certain they didn't miss anything.

He stopped when he saw both the office door and the door to the janitor's closet cracked open. The smell was coming from one of them. If he hadn't needed to get the notes and paperwork from his office he would have run down the stairs. He found the thought attractive anyway. Not for the first time since he'd started at the Home, he considered walking away. Go downstairs, call a cab, grab Julia, and just get the hell out.

He took a deep breath and walked on, keeping his gaze directly ahead. As he passed the closet, he grabbed the handle and gently closed the door. He pushed the door to his office all the way open. The paperwork sat on his desk, exactly where he'd left it.

Sunlight caught the window and illuminated the glass. Handprints, what looked like thousands of them, littered the window on both sides. They hadn't been there before.

He pretended not to let it register. He couldn't.

I can't believe I ever looked at this room and thought anything good about it. The color of had the same hue as diseased flesh, and the smell made him sick. Glad he hadn't eaten breakfast, he quickly gathered everything from his desk and placed it in the box. He tried to keep some semblance of order, but ended up mixing patient files. He could fix it downstairs.

As he picked it up and turned back toward the door, cold overtook him. He ignored it and didn't bother to close the door behind him. *It'll just be open if I ever come back up here.*

If. The thought rang in his head as he walked down the hallway. *If I come back up.* When he reached the end, the smell, like rotten eggs rolled in dogshit, gaged him. The headache grew behind his right eye, more painful by the second. The slow squeal and click of the closet door shattered the silence behind him.

The urge to turn around and look overcame him, but he didn't want to. Something had been growing in his mind, a malignant presence that had shadowed him since his first day here. If he saw it now, he didn't know if he'd be able to stop himself from running out the door screaming.

He gave in.

Peeking through the small crack in the door stood the same figure he'd seen the night before in his apartment. Eyes bloodshot, sharp yellow teeth set in a piranha grin.

Ben, his eyes wide, bolted. He expected to hear the door opening further, but it didn't. As he ran down the stairs, another whisper followed him.

"All mine."

He ran through the third floor, puffing as he held the box. *All in my head. I'm still just a little sick. Everything's fine. There's nothing there.*

He reached the second floor and managed to compose himself slightly before he walked into the upper part of the lobby. He wasn't sure why it mattered, but he didn't want people to see him running through the hallways like a crazy man. *They'll lock you up in a place like this.*

The nurse behind the desk stared at him. He realized he wore a huge grin on his face and quickly fixed it.

Grinning like that. Coming down the stairs sweaty after walking up them ten minutes before. They'll lock you up in a place like this.

"Is everything okay, Dr. Kent?" the nurse asked. An orderly standing next to the desk nodded at him. Both looked condescending.

"Everything's fine. I just don't want to walk up the stairs all day. I've been sick."

"Of course, Doctor."

"I'll be in this lounge if anyone needs me."

"Yes, Doctor."

Ben walked into the lounge. Nobody there. Good. He wasn't sure he could handle a face-to-face conversation right now. He shut the door behind him and put the box down. His hands shook, and sweat beaded on his head.

Am I having a heart attack?

Just panic. He knew the signs. He closed his eyes and took a few deep breaths. His mind wasn't coping with what just happened. This wasn't something seen in a mirror, or a fever dream. The creature in the closet had been real, and it had been only a few feet from him.

Not real. No way. It couldn't be.

But his senses disagreed.

I need to get out of here. He stood up to leave. He would grab his keys and flee, get away from the Home. His hand rested on the knob of the door when he remembered his car wasn't there.

Just a panic attack. Stress. It's not real.

He chanted it under his breath, "It's not real. It's not real."

He sat on the couch and tried to clear his mind. Deep breath in, slow exhale out. One at a time until his heart rate resembled something close to normal. He needed something to distract his mind. He took patient files out of the box and laid them out on the table, organizing them, putting the proper papers back in the proper folders. That would occupy him for a little while. He'd never go back up to that office, and if he saw something else in his apartment, they'd move. He wasn't going to lose his mind and everything he'd worked so hard for.

A knock came from the door. "Come in."

Howerton walked into the room with Regina close behind. Ben thought he must have looked half a mess, because the scowl on Howerton's face became sterner than usual. Regina was a little more composed, but she wore her concern openly. She gave him the same expression you might give a new friend you just found out was nuts.

They'll lock you up in a place like this.

"What the hell is this, Dr. Kent?" Howerton gestured at the room. When Ben didn't say anything, Howerton continued, "One of my nurses just came to get me saying that you look like a half-mad patient."

Gee, sorry, Doc, I just saw a monster in my office. It was at my house last night too. "I'm sorry, sir. I got up to my office and felt dizzy. Given how sick I was all weekend, I wasn't feeling up to walking up the stairs all day. I thought this would be fine, since you told me we don't get many visitors."

The shake in his voice was obvious to his own ears, but Howerton bought it. "If you aren't feeling well, you should leave, Dr. Kent."

"I'm fine. Just a little woozy is all." His heart rate jumped as he spoke. He should be running away, not trying to stay. "If it would be more convenient, I could move elsewhere."

"We provide you with an office so that you don't leave your messes all over our hospital like an over-privileged child."

He wanted to tell Howerton he could take this job and cram it up his ass. He didn't need this shithouse. He'd go to a real hospital, one that actually helped people.

Howerton let out a loud sigh. "This is a onetime occurrence, Dr. Kent. Clean this up." He walked out of the room, nearly shoulder-checking Regina, who stood right behind him. She shut the door.

"My god, Ben. You look like terrible."

He didn't want anyone, certainly not the only friend he'd made in town, to see him like this. His knee started jerking again, and he rubbed his eyes. She sat next to him, placing her hand on his leg.

"Jesus, you're shaking. What happened?"

They'll lock you up in a place like this.

"I don't know." He finally turned to her, having avoided eye contact as long as he could. She stared at him as Julia had the night before. It said everything he needed to know. He looked like a madman. He tore his gaze away again, trying to control his erratic behavior.

"What happened?"

Unable to stop himself, he let it all out. "Last night I thought I saw something in our apartment after we got home. I went upstairs, and I saw it in the closet outside my office. I heard voices."

She put her hand on his forehead, leaving it there for a moment. "You don't feel feverish."

Her touch eased some of the tension from him. Human contact could go a long way to heal a wound, any kind of wound. His heart slowed down. He felt like himself again, at least for a moment. "I don't know what's happening to me. I feel like I'm cracking up."

He didn't know what to call her expression; disbelieving, perhaps. He waited for her to tell him that he'd lost his mind. *This place was too much for you. Maybe working construction in New York would be a better choice.* But it never came. The silence stretched on into minutes, and he put his head in his hands, unable to bear that look any longer. He wanted to tell her he wasn't crazy. He wasn't like his mom.

"Just… try and keep it together until you get your work done and go home."

Matter of fact, the way Ben imagined every nurse from New York would be. The idea of trying to get any work done felt ludicrous, but he did as she said. He'd been in the middle of checking medical charts for his patients Friday night. He started doing so again.

What am I doing here anyway? The whole place struck him as insane, even for a mental asylum. Patients that never recovered, hostile staff, and things roaming the halls. He idly flipped through a few of the pages in Christopher Clann's file, but nothing registered. Regina noticed.

"Ben, let's just go for a long walk and see one of the patients." She didn't know how to help him. Years spent working with craziness didn't prepare you to deal with crazy co-workers.

"Yeah, I think that's a good idea." He cleared the papers off the desk and into the box, careful to keep them in order this time. When he'd finished, he placed the box on the side of the couch, but thought better of it. The last thing he needed was Howerton finding patient files left unattended in a public area. Based on that morning's interactions, Ben assumed he was only a mouse fart from being fired.

Maybe that wouldn't be so bad.

Ben and Regina walked to the desk in the lobby. "I need you to hold onto these for me while I go attend to my patients." Ben sat the box on top of the counter, pulling his clipboard out. The nurse gave him a look that said she would rather be doing something else, but Ben wasn't going to rise to the bait. He didn't need another blowup today. Without saying anything else, he turned and walked with Regina toward the west wing.

He wanted to go for a long walk on the grounds. Some fresh air would do him good. There wasn't a doubt in his mind that the second he walked out the front door someone would run off and tell Dr. Howerton. "Regina, are patients allowed to walk on the grounds?"

"Yes, as long as they're accompanied by staff."

Good. He'd ask Theresa to join him outside. Having Regina with him helped soothe his panicked mind. He wanted to distance his thoughts from whatever was going on, but one conclusion was clear: he didn't need the job that badly. Whatever he'd seen, real or not, this was clearly too much for him. He would sit down with Julia and seriously discuss leaving at home that night. He didn't let the thought go any further than that. He couldn't. But begging her parents for money was a better alternative than being locked up in a looney bin.

That thought steadied him. With a plan, he could make it through the day without cracking up in front of the staff.

"I want to see Theresa first," Ben said once they were past the security checkpoint. "Alone."

"Yes, Doctor." Her demeanor said nothing was wrong.

They walked up the stairs and down the hall where Robbie attacked him only a week ago, then took the stairs to the third floor.

"Where is Miss Parker?" Ben asked an orderly on the landing. His hands were full of trays, but he stopped to answer. The orderly couldn't have been older than twenty, and Ben didn't doubt that was the only reason he hadn't received a snide comment.

"She's in her room, sir. I just saw her."

Without acknowledging the man, Ben walked on. Three days ago, that would have been unthinkably rude, but Ben's only concern presently was getting Theresa and getting out of the building, if only for an hour. He walked down the hallway, ignoring the stares of the nurses and orderlies. He couldn't blame them. He looked like hammered shit.

He knocked three times on Theresa's door.

"Come in," she called. Theresa sat in her chair before the vanity, penning a letter much as she had been the first time Ben met her. She turned to look at him. "Jesus, Benjamin. You look terrible."

Ben ignored the comment. "Would you care to go for a walk on the grounds with me?"

She searched his face for a moment before nodding.

Twenty minutes later, Ben and Theresa strolled the paths between the main gate and the building. Regina waited in the lobby at Ben's insistence, but she wasn't very happy about it.

"I'm not sure that's a good idea, Ben."

"It's my call." He'd looked her dead in the eyes when he said it. "Howerton won't fire you for something I do."

She didn't look so certain. He didn't know if that was out of personal concern for him or their shared professional life. As he walked out the door, it occurred to him how crazy all of this was. He was honestly taking a patient for a walk so that he could question her about the things he'd been experiencing.

Outside, neither spoke more than a dozen words. He couldn't shake the feeling that she knew what was coming.

"I have a few questions for you."

"Feel free to ask." She pulled out a clove and lit it. Ben wondered how a woman as old as her who smoked as much as she did could still get around so well.

"How are you feeling?"

"Well enough. When you're my age, not everything works like it did thirty years ago."

They walked quietly for a little while, Ben pretending to enjoy the gardens, Theresa keeping her gaze ahead, staring at nothing.

"What is it? You're acting like a child about to wet his pants."

He took a deep breath before plunging in. "You mentioned things that live in the Home last Friday. Can you tell me more about them?"

She took a long drag from her clove and sat on nearby bench. She stared at him with that appraising eye, a chess player planning her next move. That expression made Ben feel even more ridiculous about the whole thing.

"Sit with me." She patted the bench, and he sat next to her. The old and the young, equally insane, relaxing side by side. "I thought you didn't believe me."

"I don't know what to believe anymore." Ben rubbed his eyes. "I haven't slept in weeks. I keep seeing things."

They'll lock you up in a place like this.

He didn't know what he expected from her. An old woman who'd killed her family wasn't going to provide him with answers. He needed to get out. He needed something, anything, that could make him feel like he wasn't cracking up. Everything hit a little too close to home here. *I should have listened to her.*

"What sort of things?"

"I don't know." He'd lose his job. He didn't know this woman. She might run back in the building and tell every nurse she saw that one of the doctors had cracked up on the lawn. He looked over at her. Her face didn't hold a hint of malice, but that did little to comfort him. "Things in the closets here. Bad dreams. Voices."

"I told you before, you should leave. Pack up your car and get out of this town."

"Why did you tell me there are monsters here, Theresa?"

"Because there are. Something lives in that building." Theresa gestured at the Home. The building loomed in the distance, darker than it should be on such a sunny day. A gargoyle standing guard over the forests of Tennessee. "And it's not your friend. What did you see?"

Any sense of professionalism was gone, but there hadn't been much to start with. From day one, this hadn't felt like a job. Dr. Cray's words rang in his mind: *"Nobody gets better at that place."*

He told her everything. The dreams, the basement, the thing outside his office, the fingerprints on the glass, and the creature in his apartment. By the time he'd finished, she stared at him, her clove forgotten in her hand. Ben sat silently, looking down at his feet, ashamed but not knowing why.

"What did it say to you?" she asked.

"What?"

"You said it spoke to you in your home and upstairs. What did it say?"

He looked her in the eye. "It said, 'All mine.'"

She threw her clove down on the stone and crushed it under her slipper. "You need to leave here. Leave here and don't ever come back."

"What is it?"

"It doesn't matter. Get away from this place and pretend you never heard of it."

He wondered if his mother had seen the same sort of monsters before her descent into madness. He could picture her alone in the trailer where he'd grown up, cowering in fear from monsters in the closet and fingerprints on the glass. His mother going in her room with a fresh load of laundry and seeing a sinister face peer at her from the closet. Whispers in the dark, things outside the bathroom edging her toward suicide until she finally slit her wrists.

"I feel like I'm cracking up."

"You look it too." She produced another clove from her pocket and lit it, taking a drag before she continued. "You aren't beholden to this place or anyone in it." She offered him a clove from her pack. He'd never smoked in his life. His mother told him time and again growing up that those things were bad for you, despite her two-pack-a-week habit.

He accepted, and she lit it for him. It tasted awful, but he imagined it helped calm his nerves.

"I know," he said. "I think I've already made up my mind. But what about the patients? And the staff? Why aren't they all…" He groped for the word. "Experiencing things like this."

"You don't think a house full of crazies sees things in the closets? And as for the staff? I think a lot of people here know more than they let on."

"So you know all their secrets, and they just let you speak to every new Joe that walks through the door? Only the two of us notice it for some unexplained reason."

"If you're going to be snappy, don't come asking for me, young man. I'm trying to help you."

"I'm sorry, Theresa." He tried to look appropriately bashful. "This is all just a bit hard to swallow, even with some of the things I've seen. I'm your doctor. I could lose my license for having this conversation."

She stared at the building. "Your sanity and your soul are more important than your money."

It amazed him how much her words echoed his earlier thoughts. Ben clasped his hands between his knees as if it was time for prayer, the clove sticking out of his fingers. He doubted any prayers were answered in that place. Even sitting out in the sun, it felt wrong there.

The real world took one step to the left, leaving Ben and Theresa sitting in its shadow. The sun smiled like it always did, but its warmth didn't penetrate the Home. The building leered down at him. The porte-cochere became a snarling mouth, and the windows held countless specters trying to hear what they said. The image flashed through his mind in an instant, but chilled him even in the heat.

Theresa spoke after a moment. "Some people are more sensitive to these things. I think it gets inside you." She looked up at the sky. "I remember when I was pregnant, near the end, feeling that way. It was like living in a dream."

"How can you tell?" Ben had only taken a few drags off his cigarette. He followed her example and crushed it under his heel.

"It's in the eyes. Sometimes you can see it. Black spots. I like to think it's where the soul used to be."

Ben looked away. That was crazy talk, not medical work. Theresa apparently sensed his doubt.

"What do you think is going on here? Do you think they just hired a preschooler because you look so handsome in your photos? Do you think you're imagining things? Monsters in the closets? Ghosts in your room?"

Ben understood what she was getting at despite her haughty tone.

"I don't know why you're here, but if I were you, I'd get out." She stood up. "If whatever is here is paying you any attention, you're in more danger than you know." She started walking toward the building.

"What about you? Why does it leave you alone?"

She turned and stared at him. The light in her eyes had died, leaving only two pools of indifference. "I'm its mother."

The panic that had nearly driven him out of the building had subsided, but talking about ghosts and monsters with one of his patients like that was unprofessional by any stretch. It only made him more conscious of how screwed up his life was becoming. He couldn't argue with her though. A place like this should have had a list ten miles long of doctors beating down their door to get a position. Howerton mentioned bringing in fresh blood, but he'd also been very clear that Ben was better seen than heard.

The first dark tendrils of paranoia wrapped themselves around Ben's mind. *What if she's right? Is it possible they brought me here for something?* The implications made him dizzy. Not because he thought Theresa might be right, but because it was all too much. He was seriously entertaining the idea of some sort of conspiracy at his new hospital to… *To what? To get me to join their cult? To scare me until I snap?* It didn't make any sense.

Regina stood by the desk, talking with the nurse. Ben wondered if she was talking about him. He gestured for her to join them as they walked back to the west wing. Regina said a few last words and walked after Ben and Theresa. "How was your session?" she asked as she caught up.

"None of your business, darling," Theresa said without looking at her.

If the comment bothered Regina, she didn't show it. If one thing could be said about people who grew up in the city, they had thick skin. Still, Ben couldn't help but note Theresa's hostility. Yet another sign of her deteriorated mental state. *This is the woman I confide in about my mental breakdown?*

They walked through the west wing and up the stairs. The buzzing and the headaches began almost immediately. If he saw something in the company of other people, he assumed it would bring him a sense of comfort. If Regina and Theresa didn't see anything when he did, then he would know beyond any doubt that he'd lost his mind. At least then he wouldn't have to wonder anymore.

They took Theresa to her room. "Do you mind waiting down the hall?" Theresa said to Regina.

Regina looked at Ben, who nodded. Without a word, she walked to the end of the corridor and smiled at the orderly standing there. Theresa and Ben watched her go, and when she was out of earshot, they faced one another.

"Consider what I said," she said in a hushed voice. "Don't get stuck in this place. The staff isn't much better than the patients."

Ben snuck a glance at Regina. "Not everyone here seems that bad."

"That woman is thick. Some people don't see things that are right in front of their noses. You're sensitive to it, and if you don't get away from this place, it'll suck you in."

Ben understood what she meant. The Home was a lake at midnight, and he was drowning. "I'll come see you again before I leave." As soon as the words were out of his mouth, he realized what he'd said. The decision was made.

"I'm a crazy old woman, remember? Don't concern yourself with me or anyone else here. It's too late. Just listen to what I told you." She walked into her room, shutting the door behind her.

Yes, she showed clear signs of paranoia and delusions, but then, so did he. The very fact that he entertained her ideas meant that she was either very charismatic or he was easily taken in.

Or she's right.

Ben walked down the hall and joined Regina. She spoke once they were out of the orderly's earshot. "That was all very cloak and dagger."

"She's a very personal woman."

Regina didn't respond. Ben got the impression she wasn't referring to Theresa. "You have a scheduled appointment with Chris Clann today. Do you want to do that next?"

Ben felt a little better than he had downstairs in the waiting room, but the idea of talking to Chris was daunting. That guy gave Ben the creeps. Still, he was one of Ben's patients, and even if he was going to quit the place, he needed to do his job while he was here. He needed to keep his bridges unburned.

If he starts laughing again, I'm leaving. "Let's go see him."

They walked up to the fourth floor. The phantom watchers, those unseen eyes gazing at him from nowhere, had faded after Theresa disappeared into her room, but on the fourth floor, they returned in full force. The sudden plunging in his gut was like missing a step and finding only open air, or going into a haunted house. In those places, a rubber ghost could pop out and say, 'Boo,' at any moment. In the Home, the ghosts weren't plastic.

The same orderly from Friday stood guard outside the room. "How is he today?" Ben asked.

"He's really quiet. He actually asked for you an hour ago."

Ben looked down at his watch. It was approaching ten. He'd spent more time with Theresa than he'd meant to. "I thought I asked you last week not to leave him alone all day."

The orderly shifted on his feet. "I just stepped out actually, sir. I've been sitting with him most of the morning." He absently scratched his chest. "He's, uh, just been staring at me. I tried talking to him, but the only thing he said after breakfast is he wanted to see you."

Ben nodded and walked past the orderly, opening the door and stepping into Christopher's room. The temperature dropped five degrees. He closed the door as the smell of old earth wafted past his nose. His mind reeled. It was the same smell from his office earlier and the basement last week. The urge to flee came over him. He forced his frayed nerves to stand down. All he had to do was make it through one or two more days, the rest of the week tops. He took a seat by the door.

Ben looked across the room at Christopher, who stared right back. His eyes reminded Ben of a snake's. "How are you today, Christopher?"

"Oh, I'm good. Real good." He stretched a little, pulling his restraints taut as he did. Ben absently wondered if Christopher was restrained year round. He made a point to check the file for that, his training kicking in despite his decision to leave the Home.

"Would you like to talk for a bit?"

"That's why I called you up here, Doc. I want to talk." He licked his lips, his gaze never leaving Ben.

"What do you want to talk about?" The headache that had been growing all day wouldn't relent. His temples were about to explode.

"You, of course," Chris said with a smile.

Ben shifted in his seat, his head like a jar of pennies. "Don't you think our time would be better spent talking about you?"

"Stop fidgeting, *Benji*."

Ben jumped in his seat. Chris sounded just like Ben's mother. The hair on Ben's arms stood up, but he tried not to let it show. It was just his imagination. Chris squirmed in his bed, moving his hips in an almost sexual way.

"I'm not as interesting as you are, *Benji*."

"I don't think that's true. I think you just need someone to listen to you." Ben kept his voice level, but the pressure in the room steadily increased. It felt too small again, just like the Friday before. Theresa's voice played in his mind. "*Your soul and your sanity are more important than your money.*"

"Is that why you're here, *Benji*? Talk to everyone until they're all better?"

"It's more complicated than that, but yes, I want you to get better."

"You couldn't even help your mommy."

The words struck him like a bolt of lightning. He rose from his chair, his clipboard dropping to the floor. "What did you say?"

"Mommy all alone, bleeding to death in the bathtub—"

"What?" It was the only word that Ben could find.

"—cut herself to get it out. Bleed out all the bad feelings—"

Ben strode over to the door and pulled on it. He didn't need this. He would walk out of this building and not look back. The door didn't budge. His head would split open from the pressure. A buzzing noise filled the air.

"—get all the monsters out of her. Make that dirty bitch clean again, *Benji*."

The way Chris kept saying his name, the nickname his mother had used… He'd never told Chris his first name. He began to shake, his fear overcoming any sense of propriety left as the walls closed in. He knew. He knew everything.

"You know she fucked the manager at the store, right?"

"Open the door!" Ben yelled as he pounded on it. His heart leapt in his chest, and his fingers and toes went cold. He was trapped. Isolated. The whole world empty except for him and Chris.

"Of course you knew. Sucked his fat cock to keep food on the table." Chris made a slurping sound.

"Open the goddamn door!" He pounded the door so hard his hand hurt, then he tugged on the handle.

"She liked it, you know. Every time."

"Shut the fuck up!" Ben screamed as he pulled desperately on the door.

"And you ran off and left Mommy all alone. Small wonder she killed herself with an ungrateful, selfish kid like *you*." Chris laughed.

"Open the fucking door!"

"Careful, *Benji.* They'll lock you up in a place like this." The words were in Ben's ear, the hot stink of Christopher's breath on his cheek

Ben spun around, putting his back to the door, expecting Christopher to have broken out of his restraints. Instead, the creature from his closet sat in the bed, staring at him with dead eyes, its legs crossed Indian-style. His body went cold. It drew its lips into a tight, ugly smile when his eyes widened.

Ben opened his mouth to scream, but the door opened behind him, spilling him into the hallway. He backed away from the room, kicking his feet, his guts tightening in terror. He looked back in the room to see Christopher sitting on his bed, smiling.

"Close the door," Ben said as evenly as he could.

"Are you—" Regina began.

"Close the goddamn door!"

The orderly quickly shut the door and locked it. Ben sat up, shaking all over, his mind reeling in panic.

"Are you all right? We heard you scream, but the door was stuck. Didn't you hear us?" Regina offered her hand. Ben ignored it and stood on his own.

"You all right, Doc?" the young orderly asked.

Ben barely registered what they were saying. Every nerve in his body screamed at him to leave, and this time he was going to obey.

"I've got to go," he said in a shaking voice. The walls closed in around him. He put a hand out to steady himself. He felt colder than he could ever remember being.

A nurse sat in a chair near the stairs. "Are you okay?"

He didn't respond, just passed her and ran down the stairs. If he'd eaten earlier, he would have thrown up. He might do it anyway. He made it to the bottom floor, distantly aware of Regina saying something behind him. He ignored her and power walked past the orderly at the checkpoint. He burst into the lobby, making for the front door, then remembering he didn't have his keys.

"I need my car," he said to the old nurse behind the desk. Scott sat nearby in a chair, talking to Dr. Vitalie.

Vitalie looked up from his quiet conversation. "What's the trouble, Dr. Kent?"

He didn't want to explain. He couldn't. If he tried, he'd crack up. "I need to go home."

"Are you all right?"

All eyes were on him now. No, he wasn't all right. Nothing was all right. "I don't feel well." His voice shook as he spoke. "I have to go."

"Your car isn't here, Doctor," the nurse said.

"Fuck." The word slipped out before Ben could stop himself. If it offended anyone, they didn't show it.

"Scott, why don't you take our friend here home?" Vitalie said. "Dr. Howerton mentioned he was feeling ill."

Feeling ill. That place felt ill. The nurse rummaged for keys and pulled out a pair, handing them off to Scott. "Don't worry, Doc," Scott said. "We'll take care of you."

Vitalie kept talking as Scott walked off, but Ben didn't hear anything, couldn't look at him. "I have to go."

"Get better," Vitalie said in a jolly voice.

Regina caught him by the door. "Jesus, Ben," she said quietly. "What's wrong with you?"

They'll lock you up in a place like this. The voice in his head sounded like Chris Clann. "I have to go. I can't be here anymore."

Regina looked over her shoulder at the old nurse and Vitalie behind the desk, both of them watching intently. "You're just gonna leave like this? In the middle of the day?

Ben shook his head. "Let them fire me, I don't care. I'm not coming back here."

"Ben." She lowered her voice even further. "Is there anything I can do for you?"

She thought he'd lost his marbles. Maybe he had. "I just need to get out of here," he said as Scott walked back into the building.

"I'll call you tonight."

"I'd get out of here if I were you, Regina." He did his best to keep his composure as he left the Home and walked into the sunlight.

Chapter 10

Every bump in the road aggravated the raging headache.

After it became clear that Ben wouldn't be answering any questions, they drove in uncomfortable silence. Ben didn't need to talk, he needed to think. Needed to make a plan.

But you've made a plan already. He had. He would leave. He'd pack up everything and get out of this crazy town with Julia.

Once he reached that conclusion, his calm surprised him. He didn't know if what he'd seen in the Home was his sanity finally leaving him or something darker. He couldn't get his mind around it. Everything was like a dream. He reminded himself that he was real, that all of this was really happening, as Scott made another pass at conversation.

"What spooked you, Doc?"

Ben continued to look out the window. "I don't want to talk about it."

Scott shrugged. "I like you, Ben. You're one of us. Some people been here a long time, and they can't say the same." He glanced over. "Just something to think about."

Theresa had warned him. Dark things lived under Umber Gardens. The implications made him lightheaded. Possibly hundreds, even thousands, of mental patients and religious nuts were right. They weren't crazy, they could just see things other people couldn't; get closer to whatever place those shadows lived in.

He was losing his grip on reality. He kept checking the car's side mirror, convinced he would see Chris, or the monster-that-wasn't-Chris, sitting on the side of the road.

Only a few blocks from the apartment, doubt crept into his plans. Rational people didn't do this kind of thing. *What's Julia going to say when she comes home and I'm sitting on the couch?* He didn't want to think about it. He couldn't deal with it.

They pulled into the parking lot. "Don't forget what I said, Doc," Scott said. "You're one of us now. We take care of our own."

Ben didn't like the look in Scott's eyes. He got out without saying goodbye. He made his way through the lobby, ignoring Harry's half-hearted wave, and took the stairs. He wanted the extra time to think. He hoped Julia was still at her appointment with the new doctor.

Halfway up the stairs, the lights flickered. The blinking momentarily blinded him, and shadows played across his vision. He ran the rest of the way up the stairwell, gripping the railing for dear life. The bottom door opened as he made it to his floor and grabbed the door handle. It stuck for half a second, and Ben imagined the thing from the Home crawling up the stairs. One rotten hand in front of the other, its stink wafting up to him. Suffocating him. Killing him. He pulled harder, sweat forming on his head. The door gave with a soft whoosh, and Ben was through it in a flash.

Stomps ascended the stairs from inside. Ben ran to his door, fumbling his keys and dropping them. He reached down, sure that something horrible would burst through the door behind him and drag him into the dark stairwell. The keys shook in his hand as he picked the correct one and thrust it into the deadbolt.

As soon as he unlocked it and opened the door, he rushed through, closing it behind him and slamming the deadbolt into place. He put his eye to the peephole and watched the hallway. Nothing happened.

He ran into the bedroom, grabbing the gun from the dresser. He didn't know if it would help against the things he'd seen, but he wanted the comfort of its weight in his hand. The killing tool he hadn't wanted. He slumped onto the floor, putting his head into his free hand and rubbing his eyes. Nothing followed him. No noises came from outside.

His job would almost certainly fire him after that outburst, and his fiancée would think he was losing his mind. He wasn't sure he disagreed with her. He wanted to blame that place, but if it ran in his family, it was only a matter of time before it affected him.

He needed to do something, keep himself busy somehow. They hadn't thrown out the boxes they'd used to move. He started putting them back together, finding a small amount of comfort in the repetition. They were getting out. He would make Julia understand when she returned home. She loved him, she knew him, and she would see that he needed to escape before he lost his mind. As he worked, he thought about what he'd say to her.

His lack of sleep and food, combined with an abundance of fear, made him clumsy. It took him thirty minutes to put them all together. When he finished, he considered grabbing something to eat, but his stomach might rebel at another scare. Just thinking about what'd he seen on the fourth floor of the Home made it difficult not to be sick. He opted instead to start taking down all the things they'd unpacked.

He packed up the living room, putting everything away except Grandma's old lamp. Julia had commented on how depressing it was that they could fit all of their belongings into half a dozen boxes when they left Michigan. Now Ben was grateful for it. He did his best to keep his mind carefully blank as he worked, but as he moved into the kitchen to pack up all their kitchenware, the absurdity of what he was doing overcame him. He sat on the floor next to the box and took a few deep breaths. He heard the key in the front door as he kicked the box across the kitchen and into the living room.

"Ben?" Julia called out hesitantly.

"I'm in here."

She shut the door and walked into the kitchen, confusion crossing her face. "What? What's going on here? How did you get home?"

He put his head back down, not able to take the look she was giving him.

"Ben, what the hell is going on?" She set her things down on the kitchen table but didn't come any closer to him. Her eyes fell to the gun on the counter nearby.

Is she afraid of me? Given how he felt, he could almost understand. His eyes were heavy and sore, his lips chapped. A vein on his neck throbbed with each pulse of his heart. His clothes were rumpled, and although he'd left the apartment that way earlier, it only accentuated his feeling of disconnection. He felt like he'd just escaped from the Home, not come back from work.

"Ben!"

"A co-worker dropped me off. We need to get out of this place." He wanted to make a more eloquent argument, but any carefully planned speech was gone the moment he saw her. The lack of sleep made him sluggish and stupid.

"What?"

"I can't stay here anymore. If I do, I'm scared I'll lose my mind."

"What are you saying? Listen to yourself!"

He slammed his fist onto the floor so hard it hurt. "I can't stay here, Julia. I'm seeing things, and hearing things. Today at work…"

"What happened, Ben?" She wrapped her arms around herself. "You're scaring me."

She'd never said that before. It broke through the fear and made him really look at her. He could see it in her eyes. She meant it.

He stood up. "I'm sorry, Julia. I've… I feel like I'm cracking up. I'm having a hard time telling what's in my imagination and what's real. I need to get out of here. I think this place is driving me insane."

She walked over to him, her brow furrowed, her jaw set, and put her arms around him. "Just tell me what happened." Emotion strained her voice.

"I can't. I don't want to, not right now." He looked around at the apartment. Boxes packed in the living room, cabinets in the kitchen ready to be unloaded. What he was doing struck him as the actions of a madman.

"Can we go for a little bit?"

She leaned away from him, her eyes wet and confused. "Ben, sweetie, slow down."

"I'm sorry. I just need to get out of here." Fatalistic thoughts ran through his mind. *You're crazy. She'll leave you. They'll lock you up. You're dying. It's all real. They're coming to get you.*

"Talk to me."

"I will." He gently pushed her to arm's length and grabbed the keys from the kitchen table. "As soon as we get out of the house."

She nodded, consenting without a word. They walked out, and he locked the door. The ride down the elevator was oppressive. He wanted to explain himself. He wanted her to see that he wasn't doing this on a whim. If he could get out of the apartment, get some fresh air, he could make her understand.

Julia looked out her window, arms over her chest. He didn't know how to read her. Two weeks ago, he could have told her exactly what she was thinking. He grabbed her hand, but she didn't hold his back, just left it loose in his grip. They drove like that for twenty minutes before she finally spoke.

"Now we're out of the apartment. Will you tell me what happened?"

He took a deep breath, careful to keep his eyes on the road. "I saw some things today at work. Things that I don't think were really there. Things that couldn't be. I heard voices when nobody else was around. I don't know what's going on, but I'm done. I need to get away from this place. If we have to ask your Dad for money, we'll do it. I don't care anymore." The words were out before he'd really thought them through, and he was surprised to find he meant it. If keeping both his family and his sanity meant swallowing his pride, he'd do it.

"What did you see?"

"The same thing I saw at the apartment last night. And a patient..." She'd think he'd lost it. "A patient talked to me about Mom. Said some things he—"

"About your mom? What?"

"Yes."

"Did you tell anyone there about her?"

"Are you kidding me? Why would I?"

Silence settled over them for a moment. "And now you want to leave?"

234

"Yes."

"You think it's this town?" It came off like an accusation.

He brushed it aside, but it hurt. He tried to remind himself that she was scared too. "I think it's the Home. Either that or I'm losing my mind like Mom did. I don't want to be here anymore." When she didn't respond, he continued, "One of my patients told me there were things in that place, things that sounded a lot like what I'm seeing."

"Jesus, Ben. You're listening to mental patients?"

"Yes. That's my job, in case you've forgotten." He let go of her hand as his temper flared. "What the hell am I supposed to do, Julia? You want me to go back there?" He didn't bother to tell her it was probably past that point now.

"No, I don't. Not if it's doing this to you." She looked out the window again. "I just don't like to hear you talk like this."

"I don't either. That's why I want to get out of here."

She knew he didn't want to take her father's money. She must have known how hard it was for him to admit defeat and walk away. "Are you really just going to leave the job like this?"

He rubbed his eyes. "Whatever I saw today was real, or at least real to me. I'm never going back to that place." He glanced at her. "Not ever."

She grabbed his hand again, squeezing it, doing her best to put on a brave smile. "Okay. I'll call Daddy tonight and tell him we're coming."

Ben didn't want to make the twelve-hour drive as pregnant as Julia was, but they couldn't help it. It would take a few days to coordinate everything, but worst-case scenario, they could be out of town by Friday. Ben would call Howerton in the morning and tell him the plan. If he didn't like it, he could go to hell. He didn't give a damn if he ever worked again if it meant holding onto his sanity and his family.

He didn't know what was going to happen next, doubly true with all the terrible things he'd experienced that week, but as long as Julia was on his side, he might be okay. They drove around for a long time, talking—haltingly at first, and then a little more comfortably once a plan began to form—about what they would do when they got to New York.

"Do you think your dad would mind if I worked for him for a little while?" Ben wasn't comfortable with being idle. If something was actually wrong with him, then he'd have to re-think the plan. He was working under the assumption that getting away from Umber Gardens would solve his problems.

"I'm sure he wouldn't. But you know he's going to ask why we changed our mind."

Her father had insisted they get a job in New York. Ben had been adamant about taking the job at the Home when they'd contacted him. He wished he'd listened. "We'll just tell him it didn't work out."

Several hours passed before Ben calmed enough to head back to the apartment. The phone started ringing as soon as they walked in, and Julia moved to answer it.

"Don't. If it's work, I'm not ready to talk to them yet."

The phone stopped ringing a moment later. Julia went to the kitchen and made sandwiches, taking the time to put the gun back in the bedroom without a word. Ben felt better after he ate, and once an hour had passed, he'd successfully put his problems out of his mind as they worked on packing.

"You chose a great time to have a nervous breakdown. Couldn't do it a week ago when the boxes were packed?" She sat on a chair in the kitchen, carefully wrapping each piece of glass in newspaper they thankfully hadn't thrown out yet. Ben didn't have the patience for that sort of work, so he divided their clothes into two separate boxes.

The phone rang again.

"I've got it," Ben called from the bedroom. He'd have to deal with it sooner or later. He walked into the kitchen and picked up the phone, expecting to hear Howerton berating him for a laundry list of offenses. "Hello?"

"What's new, Big Ben?"

Ben hadn't expected that. "Eddy? Well how about that."

"Yeah, sorry it took so long to get back to you. I've been swamped at school. This professor thing is for the birds. How's Julia?"

"She's fine." Ben pulled up a chair.

237

"Are you all right, man? You sound weird."

"Yes, I'm fine. I've just been having a long week." Ben rubbed his eyes with his free hand.

"Tell me about it. My secretary told me you asked about Umber Gardens. Isn't that the town you moved to?"

"Yes."

"Brother, let me tell you. You sure know how to pick 'em." Eddy laughed, but Ben didn't. "That place is a mess."

"What do you mean?"

"Jesus, man, where to begin—" Someone started talking in the background. "I'm on the phone, Mr. Lewis. You can wait outside the office just like everyone else. Close the door behind you... These rich kids, let me tell you. This brat's dad runs the—"

Ben's patience was thin enough already. "What were you saying about the town?"

"In a rush, are we?"

"Sorry, it's been a long day."

"Lot of that going around, brother. I can't talk long anyway."

"All right then, let's hear it."

"Well, that town has one hell of a past. It was founded by some religious nut job family before the Revolutionary War, when they were kicked out of Boston."

"The city kicked them out?"

Julia looked at Ben, but he just shook his head. She went back to packing the kitchen.

"Yeah, man. Apparently, they wanted to hang the patriarch, Jedidiah Black, but he and his church skipped town. Supposedly, the city denies that they lived there."

"What?" Ben wouldn't put it past Eddy to make something like that up.

"Sinister, I know. It gets better. This Jedidiah guy was supposed to be some mystic who could lead the chosen people to God. He claimed they had to go west to find him. So they headed out over the mountains."

"Are you pulling my leg, Eddy?" Ben shifted in his seat, finding the whole story very uncomfortable. "This isn't really a great time for that."

"No way. You can't make this crap up." Ben heard the strike of a match followed by Eddy taking a puff off a cigarette. "So in the mid-eighteen-hundreds there was this huge craze for mystics and—"

"Mystics?"

"Yeah. Tarot card readers, spirit mediums, shit like that. The Umber Gardens community was huge on that. Umber Gardens became the mecca for spiritual freak shows, including a mining magnate named Carl Saggers. He finds it choked full of valuable metals and brings in his business, turns that place into a city almost overnight." Eddy took a drag from his cigarette and blew into the receiver. Ben could almost smell it. "The guy was a Class A weirdo. Said he'd only bring in his business if the town agreed to never build another church."

"I call bullshit. There are churches all over the place here. And how do you know all this anyway?"

Julia again gave Ben another odd look.

"Firstly, the agreement was repealed at the turn of the century. Turns out you can't ban churches in the United States no matter how much money you have. Secondly, I know all this because this is hands-down the coolest thing I've read about. Saggers' wife wrote two books before she died. I could send you my notes if you want."

"No. I don't think so." Still, a morbid sense of curiosity drove him to ask, "Does it mention anything about hospitals?"

"Yeah, actually it does. How'd you know?"

"Lucky guess. What does it say?"

"When the last member of the Black family died, they left the Black Mansion which, I shit you not, was called *Macula Umber,* to Saggers and his wife. They converted it into the first hospital in town."

Ben had taken four years of Latin. *Macula Umber*. Black stain. The Black Mansion couldn't be anything but the Home. "Was the community down with all that voodoo?"

"Spiritualism—different thing—and the book I read doesn't say. I would guess so, judging by how quickly they all adapted to the new lifestyle." Eddy took another drag. "I did a quick search of it in more modern books. The 'official' history is very, very different from the one in the Saggers books, which I was lucky to find. The head of my department had a copy in the historical fiction section of our collection. I'm thinking of doing a study on it if I can find the other book."

"What? Really?"

"Yeah, man! Readers eat that kind of stuff up. That hospital, is it still around?"

Ben sighed. "Yes. I work there." *Worked.*

"No kidding? Wow. Is it as creepy as it sounds?"

Another knock on Eddy's office door spared Ben from answering that question.

"Hey man, I've got to take care of a ton of stuff here. I got excited and wanted to tell you about it though. Can I call you tomorrow?"

"Sure, Little Eddy, you can call anytime."

Eddy laughed, and the sound made Ben smile. "Look, Doc, you're never too big or important for me to slap. I'll call you tomorrow." Eddy hung up.

Julia couldn't contain her curiosity anymore. "What was that all about?"

"Nothing. I just wanted to ask Eddy a few questions about this area."

"Sounds weird."

She wasn't wrong. Magic and a crazy cult. All the things Theresa had mentioned. Maybe he wasn't crazy at all. Maybe it was real.

He wasn't sticking around to find out.

Julia called her father and arranged everything. He was glad to have them back, according to her. They should have never gone to Tennessee. People weren't right down there. His daughter coming home with his new grandbaby was the best news he'd heard all day. Ben wished he felt the same.

They finished packing the apartment as the sun set. Ben kept expecting Julia to come to her senses, to tell him how crazy all of this was, but she never did. They packed the baby's room last, and that was the hardest.

Julia sat in a chair, sipping iced tea, while Ben dismantled the crib and stacked it in the corner. It felt like giving up. All his dreams for raising a family and being a man, all the desires to provide for them in a way his parents couldn't; all gone. Julia, showing no hint of strain, smiled when he looked up at her. Ben felt it though. He felt it keenly. His new life, putting the morbid past behind him, and overcoming the problems he'd always known, all washed away in less than two weeks.

"Julia, I'm sorry—" His voice caught as he spoke. "I'm sorry about all of this."

She got up, balancing herself with the chair back so she wouldn't fall. "Don't be sorry. It's going to be okay." She hugged him.

The phone rang.

"I've got it." Ben walked out into the kitchen and picked up the phone. He needed to get out of there anyway. He didn't want Julia to see the tears in his eyes.

"Hello?"

"Hi."

"Hi, Regina." Ben glanced down at his feet, bashful after his earlier breakdown. He'd been raised with in a house where the golden rule had been, '*Keep your dirty laundry off the lawn.*' He'd aired all his dirty laundry in the lobby, in front of his only friend in town and a handful of co-workers. Regardless, he was glad she cared enough to call.

"How're you feeling?"

"A little better. I'm sorry about my outburst earlier. I…" He wanted to tell her what he'd seen, but she wouldn't believe him. He looked out the living room window at the darkness over the city. Superstitious or no, he didn't want to talk about it at night either. "I just needed to get away. I hope you didn't get into any trouble."

"No, not really. Vitalie told Howerton right after you left. He seemed pissed at first, but when I explained what happened, he calmed down. He wanted me to talk to you and let you know you aren't in trouble."

Ben arched an eyebrow. "He said that? You're kidding, right?"

"No, I'm serious. I thought for sure he was gonna say you're fired and couldn't come back. He told me to call you and tell you to take a few days off."

Ben couldn't believe what he was hearing. Howerton had been nothing but a hard ass the entire week he'd known him, and now he was breaking out a compassionate side. "It doesn't matter anyway. I'm quitting."

Silence filled the line between them. "Are you sure?"

"Yes. They can keep the money. That place has gotten under my skin, and I just want out."

"Have you told Howerton already?"

Ben shifted on his feet. "No. I'll call him tomorrow and let him know."

"That's a shame, Ben. I liked having someone around who doesn't seem like a total bummer." She clicked her tongue. "What did Julia say?"

"She's concerned about it—we both are—but she's on board. We're going to go back to New York and staying with her family."

"When are you guys leaving?"

"We want to be out of here before the end of the week."

"Jeez, that's quick."

The silence grew awkward. He barely knew this woman. He couldn't blame her for thinking he was odd. "Alright. If you need anything, just call me."

"I will. Thanks, Regina."

"I'm serious. Anything at all."

Ben smiled. "Alright."

"Bye." She hung up, and he did the same.

She'd tried. She'd really tried to reach out to him, and he'd done nothing but show her his crazy side. He stared at the phone for a long moment after he hung up, wondering what she must think of him.

The day had dragged on long enough. Ben took a shower and lay down in bed, Julia joining him a little later. They chatted for a while, until she drifted off to sleep. The clock told him it was after nine, but fear kept him from sleeping.

As soon as you close your eyes, it'll be there. The thought continually raced through his head. He didn't want to sleep. He wanted it to be Friday, so that he and Julia could be safely on the road, away from Umber Gardens and its dark past.

Everything Eddy had told him played again in his mind. Theresa's warnings called out in his ears. *Get out of here, Benjamin.*

He couldn't help but think about what she'd done to her family. *If she told the courtroom the truth, that monsters were inside them, did that justify what she'd done?* Just thinking about it made him uncomfortable.

Sleep finally caught him while he pondered the question. His rest passed dreamlessly, until Julia's shifting woke him at midnight.

She pulled the covers over, leaving him exposed. He tried to pull them back and failed, losing more in the process. The cold night air stung his bare skin. It was as if she was doing it on purpose. He rolled over to face her, not in the mood for games.

She slept soundly as the thing from the hospital, naked and feral, perched on her like a cat. It grinned down at him with its sharp teeth, leering with its milky eyes. He opened his mouth to scream, but he couldn't make a sound.

It crawled off Julia and into the space between them. The smell of rotten eggs filled his nose. He could see inside the thing's mouth and down the endless blackness in there.

"You're all mine, Ben."

Its voice was cold and ugly. Inhuman. It pulled away a piece of dried, leathery flesh from its face. Ben struggled to escape, but a pure, unadulterated fear he hadn't known since childhood paralyzed him. It reached toward his mouth, trying to put its flesh inside him.

"This is the flesh of my body, and the blood of my blood. For my flesh is real food and my blood is real drink. Eat of me. Take me in you. Be me."

It touched his lip, and his body went cold. He put everything he had into one last surge of resistance, desperately trying to move.

He woke, sitting straight up in the bed, spitting and trying to get the taste from his mouth. The thing's putrid smell lingered in his nose for a moment, and then it was gone.

Just a dream. Just a dream.

Julia didn't move. He looked over at her, expecting to see it sitting between them. Nothing. His whole body shook. He glanced at the clock on the nightstand. It was after three in the morning.

He let out a shaky sigh, trying to convince himself it was just a dream. *What the fuck is wrong with me? What's wrong with this place?* A dull ache between his ears beat in time with his heart.

The phone let out a single ring, its echo filling the apartment.

He needed to be somewhere with a light. The moonlight from the window cast the room in a glow that hid monsters in the corner. He threw off the covers and made his way toward the kitchen.

He felt his way through the dark hallway. His foot hit something in the dark, and a rush of adrenaline nearly made him yell aloud.

Just a box. We left the damn things everywhere.

He chastised himself for letting a dream make him so nervous. They were leaving soon. He didn't need to worry about it. Once the city was behind him, everything would be better. Crazy or no, it would all be over soon. It had to be true. He needed it to be.

He wanted to believe it, but it didn't stop the sensation of something watching him in the dark. He flipped on the living room lights, taking in his life all packed away and ready to go.

The phone rang again. This time it didn't stop.

He froze where he stood. Something nagged at him. A dream half-remembered. A feeling as if he'd done this before. The humidity had jumped tenfold in the short walk from the bedroom to the dining room. Sweat poured off him.

It would wake Julia if he didn't get it. He walked to the dining room and flicked the light switch. Nothing happened. The phone rang twice more as he toggled the switch. Up, down, up, down. Nothing.

His sweat turned cold. *This is how it starts.*

The phone continued to ring. He had the sudden terrible feeling something was stalking him. Some unimaginable *other*, watching him from the darkness, imposed itself on his imagination. He strode into the kitchen cast in shadows from the living room light. He picked up the phone and put it to his ear, the cold plastic chilling him further.

"Hello?"

A woman accompanied by a violin and a piano sang in the distance, but otherwise nothing answered.

"Hello?" he said again, more forcefully.

A door opened in the hallway. He hung up, expecting to see Julia wondering why he was up at that ungodly hour. His head throbbed with every breath. Julia didn't emerge.

"Julia?"

No response. He crept toward the hallway despite himself.

There was nothing in the hallway, but the door to the baby's room stood wide open. Some small voice of reason, lost in the madness of the last week, told him to get out. Wake Julia, grab the keys, and just drive away. Get the hell away from Tennessee before things worsened.

He'd made enough concessions in the last twenty-four hours. He wouldn't be a victim in his own home. He crept toward the door, afraid to break the silence. The floorboards creaked under his weight. Whatever phantoms watched him from the shadows felt closer there, as if they would reach out any moment and drag him back to wherever they came from.

He tried to turn on the hallway lights, but again, nothing happened. It wasn't a coincidence. Heedless, he continued until he stood in the doorway. It took a moment for his eyes to adjust.

In the center of the room, the crib that he'd taken apart just a few hours ago sat fully assembled. He backed out, his mind reeling like it had in Chris's room the day before.

This isn't real. I'm still dreaming.

But he wasn't. The cold wall against his back told him he was wide awake. Out of the corner of his eye he caught movement. Something further back in the hallway, toward the third bedroom. A shadow of deeper darkness in the black.

This isn't real. I'm not seeing this. This isn't real.

The phone began to ring again. He tore his gaze from the shadow in the bedroom as his headache hit a crescendo. He strode into the kitchen, trying to calm his fragile mind. He picked up the phone before it rang three times. "Who the fuck is this?"

Laughter, the cruel giggling of a child, answered. The woman's voice still sang in the background, but the violin was gone. A piano hammered out a discordant tune.

"Is this a prank? You think this shit is funny?" His voice rose as he spoke.

"All mine, Ben."

The creature from his dream. He dropped the phone, letting it hit the wall. The receiver knocked once against the wall, then swung silently back and forth.

"Jesus, Ben."

He jumped and yelled as Julia walked into the kitchen, pulling her robe around her.

"What the hell are you doing?" she asked, her voice heavy with sleep.

"The phone…" He didn't trust his voice not to waver. He picked up the receiver and placed it back in the cradle. "The phone rang."

"What the hell? What about that?" She pointed at the cupboards behind him. He turned to see all the cabinets and the fridge wide open, all the dishes Julia had packed away neatly stacked on the counter.

"I didn't do that! It wasn't like that two minutes ago!" He put his hands up to his head. His headache drilled into his brain. "What the fuck is going on?" His heart raced as he leaned against the wall, staring open-mouthed at the kitchen.

Julia pulled her robe tighter around her. "What are you talking about?"

He shook his head. "I didn't do this, Julia, I swear!"

The phone started ringing again as he stared at the dishes. He grabbed the cradle and ripped it off, slamming it down on the ground where it gave one final, ugly ring as it bounced. The silence that followed was deafening.

Julia stepped away from him. "What the hell is going on?"

"We need to go. We can stay at a motel or something. I'll pack bags." He went into the bedroom and pulled out a suitcase from the closet. He started throwing shirts and pants into it. "We can tell the movers where to get our stuff when they show up."

Julia walked into the bedroom and stared at him. "I'm not going anywhere. It's three in the morning!"

"We aren't staying in this place. Something's here with us."

She stomped her foot, shaking the floor. "Goddammit, Ben, listen to yourself!"

He stopped and looked at her, panic twisting his insides until he thought he might be sick.

"There's nothing here." She stormed out of the room, turning on all the lights, even the ones that hadn't worked for him. "Nothing." She switched on the bathroom light. "Nothing." She turned on the light in the baby's room. "Nothing!"

"Okay then, what's this?" He walked toward the baby's room.

"What's what?"

"The crib is…" His words died in his mouth. The crib sat dismantled in the corner, exactly where he'd left it earlier. "It was… It."

"You had a bad dream," she said after a moment, anger still coloring her voice. "We're leaving in a few days. Packing everything up and moving across the country. Again." She pulled the chair from the wall and sat down, staring at him. "I can't handle all of this right now. I need you to hold it together until we get to New York."

"I'm telling you—"

"Hold. It. Together."

He didn't know what to say. She'd never spoken to him like that before. The crib standing in the middle of the room hadn't been a hallucination, and he certainly hadn't stacked the dishes up on the counter. *I'd remember doing that.*

Or at least he hoped he would. He paced around the room, frantically searching his mind for an explanation. The only one that came to mind was the craziest. Theresa was right. He stopped pacing and closed his eyes, bearing down and trying not to let it overwhelm him.

Julia watched him, a mask of stony discontent covering her features. Whatever was going on, she was right. He needed to hold it together.

"Okay. We'll—" He remembered he'd ripped the phone from the wall. "We'll use the phone at the desk downstairs and call the movers tomorrow. And… I don't know." He rubbed his eyes. He didn't want to be there anymore, he didn't want any of it.

He knelt at her feet and grabbed her hands. Once again, he'd managed to terrify his very pregnant fiancée. The panic hadn't died down, but he couldn't stand the look she gave him. With time, maybe he could make her understand he wasn't crazy. He would hold it together for her. Just a few more days and he could put it all behind him.

He pushed down the fear. "I'm sorry." He kissed her hand. "I don't know what's going on. I didn't mean to scare you."

"Let's just go to bed. We can deal with this in the morning." She got up, brushing his hands aside, and walked to the bedroom without saying another word. The only thing that scared him more than whatever was happening was losing Julia. The way she'd said that... *We can deal with this in the morning.*

She fell asleep with the bedside lamp on. Ben didn't fall asleep until the sun came up, fearing what might happen once he closed his eyes. He managed to get only two hours before Julia began to stir.

Chapter 11

Ben rose from bed, groggy and unhappy, to repack the dishes. He didn't want to touch them. They were unclean after the previous night. But Julia was rapidly approaching the end of her rope, and he wanted to do everything he could before it ran out. Looking back on the last few days, he was amazed at how well she was holding up. Another incident like last night would put both of them over the edge.

She won't have to worry about leaving me if they lock me up in the Home.

No, not the Home. Anywhere but there.

By the time she got out of bed, he'd packed everything and cleaned up the mess he'd made in the kitchen the night before. He expected the phone to ring as he dumped it into the trash.

When Julia walked out of the bedroom, she wore a serious expression. "Ben," she said as she sat at the table. "We need to talk about last night."

"I'm sorry. I didn't mean to—"

"It's fine. I know… I know something's wrong. I want you to promise me that when we get to New York, you'll get checked out."

He blinked at her, taken aback by the suggestion.

"I'm serious, Ben. I'm scared. I'm scared something is happening to you."

He closed the last box he'd finished packing. "I don't think I'm crazy."

"Good. But that doesn't mean something isn't wrong. Please, promise me."

Ben stood at the counter, not saying a word. His thoughts were unpleasant. Fear and paranoia had been struggling for control all morning, now she was dropping this on him.

"I don't want our baby to grow up without a dad."

That hit close to home. "You think I'm going to kill myself? Like Mom did?"

"I don't know. I don't know what's going to happen. You tell me monsters are after you, you insist we leave town, you wake up in the middle of the night screaming about getting out of the house. What would you do if you were me?"

He hung his head. A long time passed before he spoke. "Do you want to leave me?"

She raised her eyebrows and opened her mouth as if she'd tasted something foul. "No. No, I don't. That's why I need you to promise me you'll get help."

He didn't know what to say. The thought of Julia leaving him twisted his stomach in knots. He'd do anything to make sure that didn't happen. She was all he had left. "Okay. I promise," he said quietly.

"Alright." She took a deep breath and let it out. "Whatever's going on, we'll get through it."

He hoped she was right. He'd always considered himself a strong man. His father had died violently and young, he'd grown up poor, his mother had killed herself—He'd been through more by twenty-nine than most people had by fifty. And still, this.

"I'm going to call the moving company. Where did you leave the number?"

"It's on the notepad by the phone." She corrected herself. "By where the phone *was*."

"I should call Dr. Howerton too. Let him know what the plan is."

He walked to the kitchen and flipped through the notepad. He found the page with the movers' number and jotted it down, doing the same with the number for the Home. As he turned the pages, the piece of paper with Dr. Cray's number fell out, fluttering to the floor.

Ben picked it up. He'd only met Dr. Cray once, but he liked him. He decided to call and say goodbye before he left. It might be odd, but everything about his failed first foray into the medical field had been. He slipped the paper into his pocket. "I'm going downstairs to use the phone. I'll be back in a bit."

Julia didn't say anything. *Why would she?* She'd gotten little sleep, and she was nine months pregnant. *Not to mention her fiancés' losing his mind.*

Ben closed the door and walked across the hallway to the stairs. As he closed his hand around the handle, he recalled the lights blinking in the stairwell the day before. *Nope.* Instead, he took the elevator. It opened into the brightly lit lobby.

"Hey there," Ben said to Harry behind the desk.

"Hello, sir. How're you today?" That friendly southern charm was gone, replaced by cool, unflinching politeness. Harry clearly didn't think much of his new tenants.

"Fine, fine." Ben scratched the five o'clock shadow on his face. "Our phone keeps cutting out on us, and I have to make a few calls. Would you mind letting me use the one down here?" The lie was better than the truth.

"Of course, sir." Harry reached under his desk and pulled out a phone, setting it on the desk.

"Thanks."

Ben called the moving company first. They would charge extra for a rush job. He didn't care. Money had very quickly gone from being one of his primary concerns to the last thing he gave a damn about. He arranged for the movers to take their things on Friday. The side of Ben that grew up poor cringed at the estimated cost.

He considered calling Howerton afterwards, but decided against it. The full weight of a month without sleep crushed him, and he didn't have the mental energy to deal with that. He called Dr. Cray's office instead.

The phone rang twice before the receptionist picked up. "Hello, Dr. Cray's office."

"Hi, this is Dr. Kent. I was there on Saturday. I need to speak to Dr. Cray."

"Just one moment."

Ben heard the phone being put down. A moment later, Dr. Cray picked up the receiver. "This is Dr. Cray."

"Hello, Bill."

"Well hello there, Ben. How're you feeling?"

Ben suddenly felt silly for calling. The old man might be nice, but he didn't know Ben from Adam, and he wouldn't care they were leaving. "I'm good. Whatever that bug was, your antibiotics knocked it right out."

"That's good to hear. Make sure you take them all."

"I will."

Silence clouded the space between them for a moment. Ben didn't know what to say.

"I get the impression this isn't a medical call," Bill said.

"No. Julia and I have decided that this job isn't for us."

"Oh?"

"Yeah. We're leaving town at the end of the week, and I thought I'd call to say goodbye."

"I'm sorry to hear that, son. Do you mind if I ask why?"

Ben ran his hand through his hair. "Have you got an hour?"

Bill laughed, an old man's laugh, time-tested and used often. "Actually, I do. Want to meet me at the office for lunch?"

"Sure." He cringed after he spoke. The last thing he needed was face time with a stranger.

"Good, good. I'll see you around noon?"

"Alright, I'll see you then."

They said their goodbyes and hung up. Too late for regrets, Ben handed the phone back to the Harry.

"Thanks."

When he returned to the apartment, Julia sat on the couch, reading a book. "Everything all set up?" she asked.

"Yeah. I called Dr. Cray. I'm having lunch with him today."

"Do you want me to come with you?"

"No, no. I think it's just going to be a handshake and a goodbye."

She shrugged, eyed him a moment longer, and went back to her book. Her expression said he was a ticking time bomb, set to go off before the disposal unit could arrive. He rubbed his eyes, trying to get the feeling of sleeplessness to leave him alone, if only for a moment.

He busied himself as best he could the rest of the morning. He stacked boxes, put things in the living room, and cleaned. He needed to be doing something. His anxious pacing was certainly getting on Julia's nerves, but she kept silent about it. He'd never felt like that with her before. Things had always been easy between them. Even during the rough patch in college, neither of them had been angry per se, just distant.

"I think I'm going to go for a drive," Ben said.

"Alright." She didn't look up from her book.

"Want anything while I'm out?"

"I'm fine."

She's fine? Nothing here's fine.

Ben drove around the city, losing himself in the side streets and back ways. He loved the scenery, and Tennessee's mountains felt like coming home. He wanted to go hiking in them, to see all the things had Regina told them about on their Sunday drive. That wouldn't happen now. Nothing he'd planned for this place or his family was going to happen as he'd wanted.

Lost in thought, it took him a moment to realize he was driving toward the Home. He shook his head, trying to rid his mind of the nagging drowsiness that had become mental background noise. He didn't want to go anywhere near that place. Something there had worn his mind down to a nub over a single week. He wouldn't piss on that place if it was on fire, and he certainly wasn't going back.

When he reached the turn that would take him into the woods he flipped a U-turn. A horn blared at him from nowhere.

He didn't see the semi until he was close enough to meet the driver's eyes. He looked as scared as Ben, who screamed and overcorrected, pulling to the right and narrowly missing the truck that would have killed him. He cursed as his heart skipped a beat and his car went off the road, coming to rest at the bottom of the hill.

He sat there gripping the wheel. *I almost died. Jesus Christ, I almost died.*

He got out of the car and took a deep breath, shaking as he leaned against his door. He could hear Julia telling their boy how his father was in a better place after being smashed by a truck on the way to work. Too poetic. Too similar to what happened to his father.

Ben laughed at how stupid all of this was. The new job, the new place, all the shit going wrong. He laughed until tears formed in his eyes and his stomach hurt.

"I've got to get the fuck out of here," he said aloud once the laughter tapered off, telling his story to the mountains. "I'm losing my fucking mind." If the mountains cared, they showed no sign.

A car drove by, and the driver looked down at Ben as if he'd gone nuts. Maybe he had.

He pulled into Dr. Cray's parking lot and walked inside. The same receptionist from Saturday sat behind the desk.

"Hello, Dr. Kent," she said with the same fake smile she'd worn then.

Ben nodded. "Is Dr. Cray around?"

"Yes, sir. He—"

Bill walked out of the door behind her, smiling. "Well hello there, Ben." He eyed Ben up and down. The look on his face plainly said, "You look like shit."

"Ready for lunch?" Ben forced a weak smile.

"You bet." Bill gave instructions to his receptionist. When the door closed behind them and they were safely alone, Bill examined him again. His gaze lingered on the bags under Ben's eyes. "Still not sleeping?"

"No." Ben rubbed his face.

"I'm sorry to hear that."

Ben chuckled a little as they entered Bill's car. "I'm sorry to say it."

"How's Julia?"

Ben saw no reason to be anything but honest. "She's a little pissed. I've been… I've been having a bad week."

"I guess that means it was your decision to leave."

"Yeah, I suppose that's right." He always thought of himself and Julia as a team when decisions had to be made, but she hadn't really been a part of this one. Ben didn't know if he would have stayed even if Julia had insisted. He tried to imagine himself walking out on Julia, nine months pregnant or not. It was easier for him to imagine flying.

Bill directed them to a small diner nearby. "So do you have a plan already?"

"We're going to stay with her family for a bit in New York."

"Do you have a job lined up?"

"Not yet, but I'll find something."

Bill scratched his chin. "I wish I could help with that, but anyone I've known in the industry is dead or retired by now."

"I appreciate it. I might work for Julia's father for a while. He owns a construction company."

"A doctor building houses, huh? Can't say I've seen that before." He was quiet for a moment. "Is it the job, son?"

Ben blew out his breath and avoided looking at him. "Honestly? I don't know. This all stacked up a lot faster than I thought it would."

Bill nodded, and they drove in silence for a few minutes. Ben couldn't blame him if Bill thought he was crazy. They'd only met three days before, and Ben was laying all of his problems on the guy.

"You'll be fine. It's a tough business, and that place you've been working makes it tougher than most."

"What do you mean?" They pulled into the diner's parking lot and walked toward the restaurant.

"I mean you wouldn't be the first medical worker to up and quit that place. It's happened a dozen times since the Home opened."

That piqued Ben's curiosity. "Did you know any of the other people who quit?"

"I met a few of 'em. Couple nurses, one doctor in your position. Like I said before, nobody gets better there. I think that has a lot to do with it. And that place... there's something not quite right about it. Do you know what I mean?"

Ben knew exactly what he meant. "Yes, I've gotten that feeling as well."

The restaurant had a certain rustic charm to it. A pie rack sat on the corner of the counter, and the kitchen looked to be one cockroach away from winning a place in a record book somewhere. Ben and Bill had the corner all to themselves. The waitress took their orders for coffee and left them alone with the menus.

"I'll be honest with you. I've never liked that place. I think it's good that you're getting out of there. Once it gets its hooks in you, it's only a matter of time before you end up like Stephen."

Ben summed up everything he knew about Howerton as best he could. "An asshole?"

Bill laughed his well-worn laugh. "Bitter. More concerned with numbers than patients. That said, he's been like that as long as I've known him. What did he say when you told him you quit?"

"Well…" Ben suddenly felt very stupid for not calling Howerton. "I haven't actually told him yet. To be honest, I had a bad day yesterday and walked out."

The waitress, whose expression made it clear she'd rather be somewhere else, brought their coffee and left.

"I'd be careful about that." Bill put cream and sugar into his mug. "The medical field is smaller than you might think. I know you're not keen on working in it right now, but sooner or later you might be. Don't burn any bridges."

Ben took his coffee straight. "I don't know. This has been hard on me, a lot harder than I expected. I'm not sure if I'll do this when I get to New York." He couldn't imagine how this nice old doctor might react if Ben told him he'd been seeing things. The questions would come next. *Do you have a history of mental illness? Does your family? That doesn't sound good, son. You'd better get checked out.* It'd be too much.

"Well," Bill said. "You're young. Things change. My advice is to get the hell away from the Home. Take a long break and then try your luck again somewhere that isn't filled with ghosts."

Ben stopped, his coffee mug halfway to his face. "Ghosts?" He must have misheard. It couldn't be that this guy had seen anything like what Ben had. Regina, Eddy's story, and now Bill. Coincidence was one thing, but this…

"I'm a good Christian man. I've gone to church every Sunday my entire life. I believe in God, the Devil, and everything in between. Thousands of people died in that place. There's more than one wayward soul there."

Suddenly, it wasn't silly to ask. "Have you ever seen anything odd?"

Bill leaned back in his seat. "Lots. I've spent twice as long as you've been alive the Home. Right after I started there a flu epidemic killed five hundred people in town. It was one of the worst outbreaks in the state. We used the basement as a quarantine ward." He stared into his coffee as he spoke. "I wouldn't go down there for all the money in the world."

He looked up at Ben. "Don't let that place sour you on your job. Do things the right way. Make sure you leave on the best note you can."

They ate their lunch and chatted about the town and its history, but Ben found it hard to focus. Ghosts. Bill had said there were ghosts in the Home. He hadn't put it as Theresa had, no mention of monsters or cults, but something was wrong there. Ben might not get another chance to question him about it.

"So why is everyone at the Home either older or related to someone who worked there?" The question had been rattling around in Ben's mind since day one. Theresa mentioning a conspiracy certainly hadn't helped.

"Tennessee and nepotism go together like ham and cheese." Ben laughed.

"It's just how things are run around here. Stephen's father was the same way. That family's been around these parts since before the Civil War."

They finished their lunch. Bill paid for everything. "Call it a good luck in New York gift. I've heard it gets rough up there."

They drove back to his office, and Ben stepped out of the car to shake Bill's hand. "Well, short as it was, it was good knowing you, Bill."

"Same to you, Ben. I hope you land on your feet. Try not to let this get to you. If it's the worst thing that happens in your medical career, you're doing pretty well."

He wanted to believe that was true.

"And don't forget what I said. Don't burn your bridges."

"I understand."

If he'd stuck around, they might have been friends. Between Bill and Regina, Tennessee wasn't such a bad place. *Doesn't matter now.* Ben returned to his car and watched Dr. Cray head back into his practice, wondering if they'd ever meet again.

When Ben returned to the apartment, he laid on the couch, hoping to sleep during the day since he was incapable of doing it at night. Julia said little to him, but he could do nothing about that. The wheels were in motion. They would to New York no matter what.

Part of him wanted to be upset with her as he tried to fall asleep, a towel from the kitchen over his face to block the light. She'd tried to convince him New York was the right decision after he graduated. Moving because you wanted to and moving because your fiancé was cracking under pressure were very different, he knew that. Still, he needed her right now. He told himself the shock of the whole thing had upset her. It was understandable. He fell asleep with those thoughts in his head, and he dreamed of Julia staying in Tennessee while he went on to New York.

His two hours of sleep were more restful than any he'd gotten since coming to Tennessee. When he woke, Julia was in the bedroom with the door closed. He stared up at the ceiling, trying not to think of anything and failing miserably. Bill's words rang in his ears. *"Don't burn your bridges."*

Ben grabbed the notepad with the Home's number on it. He took the elevator down to the lobby. "Mind if I use that phone again?" he asked Harry.

He looked at Ben over his book with an expression bordering on rude, but he didn't say no. "Sure thing, sir." He placed the phone on the desk.

Ben dialed the Home's number and listened to the ring. He didn't know why Harry had soured on him, and he didn't care. Just one more reason to leave this place. A woman picked up. "Umber Gardens Home, this is Nancy, how can I help you?"

"I need to speak with Stephen Howerton."

"Just a moment." The line switched over, and the phone rang again.

"Dr. Howerton."

"Dr. Howerton, it's Dr. Kent."

Silence halted the conversation for longer than was strictly polite. "Dr. Kent. We missed you this morning. Is everything alright?"

The genuine concern in Howerton's voice threw Ben off. He wanted to choose his words carefully, but they poured out. "No, Dr. Howerton. A few unexpected things have come up. Julia and I have decided that we can't stay here."

"You're quitting?"

"I'm afraid so. I'm really sorry about the short notice, but with Julia as pregnant as she is, we needed to make the decision before the baby is born." *Nice. Use your fiancée and unborn son as an excuse.*

"Is there anything we can do to change your mind?"

Ben hadn't expected compassion from the man who'd been nothing but rude, sometimes downright hostile, since Ben set foot in town.

Dr. Howerton continued, "I know things have been rough here for you. Dr. Vitalie and I were just talking about that this morning. You could take a week off to adjust, come back to work fresh when you feel ready."

He was bargaining. "No, I don't think so, sir. We've already made plans, and Julia's quite insistent." He cringed after saying the words. It was wrong to use Julia like that. He hoped she never found out.

"If the pay is an issue, we can always talk about raising your salary."

He had to be kidding. His salary was already twice what he'd get anywhere else. The thought of that much money would have boggled his mind any other time, but memories of ringing phones and ugly monsters were more powerful. "We can't stay, sir. Once again, I am very sorry about the short notice."

Ben could almost hear Howerton thinking. "I'm sorry to hear this, Dr. Kent. I really am."

Bill's words played themselves again in his head. *Don't burn your bridges.* Ben scratched his stubble. "Everything's been great there. The staff is fantastic, and the facility is outstanding. I'm really sorry to do this, I would have loved to stay." The lies tasted sour, but Bill was right. Better to lie now than be a jobless doctor later.

"I understand. Things happen. It really is unfortunate." He paused for a moment. "Do one thing for me, Dr. Kent."

"Yes, sir—if I can."

"Come to dinner at the Home tomorrow. We've prepared very expensive plans, and I'd hate to have to cancel it all now."

His pulse quickened at the very idea of going back to the Home. In his mind he saw Chris Clann sitting on the bed, telling him about the cock his mother sucked. Things in the empty basement moving around. Ghostly handprints on the glass and monsters in the closet.

"Hello?" Howerton said when the quiet went on too long.

Don't burn your bridges. "Yes. We'll join you for dinner tomorrow. It'll be a good chance to say my goodbyes and pick up my things."

"Excellent!" Howerton's enthusiasm took Ben aback. "We'll see you around seven. Formal attire."

"Will do. We'll be looking forward to it."

Ben felt as if he'd just signed a deal with the devil. When he entered the apartment, he told Julia about his call with Howerton.

"I thought you'd never go back there."

"I need to. I can't risk pissing off a place like that six months into my career."

She took in a deep breath and let it out slowly. "I'm glad. I think it'll be a good thing to get some closure and put it behind you."

"You sound like you're married to a psychiatrist," Ben said with a strained smile.

She didn't smile back. "I'm serious."

He put his arms around her. "I know you are. And I swear I'm going to make sure everything is okay one way or another. I promised, remember?" He held her out at arm's length and smiled for her again. This time she returned it, just a little.

Since the dishes were packed, Julia didn't make dinner that night. Instead, Ben took her to the diner he'd been to earlier with Bill. The same waitress was still there, and Ben wondered if she wasn't a permanent part of the scenery.

The sun set on Tennessee, casting the world in an orange and red glow. He looked across the table at Julia bathed in the amber light. If they could just make it through the next few days, if they could just get to New York, everything would be fine. He wouldn't go crazy like his mother. He wouldn't end up in a place like the Home. He reached across the table and grabbed Julia's hand. She stared into his eyes, searching for something.

"It's going to get better," he said. "I promise."

She squeezed his hand and forced a smile. It was fake, but only a little.

Chapter 12

Ben dreamed of dark depths in the Earth below the Home, and things in the fathomless black that had never seen the light of day, things never before seen by men.

He floated on, going ever deeper, until he was at the heart of the world. Giant serpents with the heads of humans wormed their way through eternal twilight. White-skinned and white-eyed, they tasted the air around them with their tongues. They were as ignorant of world above as Ben was to their realm below. Dark masters whipped their backs as they slaved away to further the machinations of some unfathomable will.

Even those beasts feared the dark things. Twisting masses of horror without form that had lived in the void before God created the firmament. The dark things knew about the lands above. They hated it and loved it. They wanted to be in it, and they wanted to destroy it. Ben saw it all, and his sleeping mind knew what he was seeing wasn't for the land of the wakeful and the living. By the time he woke, he remembered none of it.

Things weren't as gloomy Wednesday morning. Julia hummed as she brushed her hair after her shower, a sure sign she was in a better mood. No nightmares meant Ben slept better than he had in a month. The bags under his eyes still drooped alarmingly—it would take more than a good night's sleep to fix that—but he felt worlds better. Getting a little rest gave him some hope that things might be getting better.

The sun shone outside, and as soon as Ben said goodbye to the Home that night and got his things, he'd never have to set foot there again. Everything might actually be okay.

They spent most of the day around the house. At noon, they went out for lunch at a small Italian place near their apartment. They wandered a nearby park afterwards. Ben couldn't help but appreciate what a great place it would have been to play with his son.

Julia held Ben's hand as they walked. They sat down on a bench and watched cars go by. Words would come later, when they were far from Umber Gardens.

Julia finally spoke up. "When we get to New York, I'm going out at least every other day."

Ben gave her a sideways glance. "Oh yeah? Going to be a socialite mother?"

"I'll have you know, Benjamin Kent, I was quite the social butterfly growing up."

"Think a lot of your friends will still be there?"

"It's the city. Nobody leaves, and if they do, they come back."

"Think they'll like me?" He meant it as a joke, but it came out desperate.

She smiled. "Of course not, sweetheart, you're a country bumpkin."

His mouthed dropped open in momentary surprise before he scrunched his face into that of a wrinkly old immigrant woman. "Do nut make fun uf meh!"

They both laughed for a long time, first aloud and then quietly. The afternoon sun watched their tender moment, looking down without judgment as it always had.

Ben dressed in the only tux he owned. He might be overdoing it, but better safe than sorry. This would be the last time any of these people saw him, and he wanted to leave a good impression, if such a thing was possible.

As he combed his hair, he had a dreadful premonition of something happening during dinner. He would see Chris Clann in a mirror, or a rotting creature in a closet. He'd scream and run out of the building, and everyone would know he'd lost his mind. Nobody would hire him, and Julia would leave him for someone who wasn't a total nutcase.

She put her hand on his shoulder, snapping him from his fatalistic fantasy. She looked good—great even—despite the fact that her dress was slightly less formal. She couldn't fit into her nicest clothes at all anymore. They had to buy her something when they were out for lunch.

"Are you almost ready?" she asked.

"Yeah, just finishing up." He set the comb down and turned to kiss her. "You know we could blow this off and just leave for New York tonight. Leave the key at the desk and let the movers pick everything up themselves." He was only half-joking.

"Let's just get it over with. We'll be out of here in two days, and everything'll be fine."

Twenty minutes later, they were on their way to the Home. A light rain started to fall, and the sun set rapidly. Julia flipped on the radio and adjusted the knob until she found a local weather station. Rain all week.

"Sounds like a great time to make a cross-country trip."

Ben watched the road. Tennessee's forests loomed large, devouring the path like a great green monster. He tapped the steering wheel nervously as they made the final turn that would take them to the Home, just past where the semi-truck had almost killed him the day before. He couldn't agree with Julia more. It was the perfect time to get the hell out of this state. He hoped those last two days would go by quickly.

The forest swallowed them. No sky showed overhead, and the trees wept rainwater as the Sportwagon sped along the lonely path. The only visible lights in the world were the headlights, giving the eerie impression they'd entered a land without stars.

"It's so gloomy here," Julia said.

"You aren't kidding." He stared at the road, imagining the Home ahead of them, seeing the things he'd seen there in his mind's eye. "I'm not going to miss it."

They approached the gate. A single guard stood outside, waving and opening it as Ben passed. The sun had set behind the mountains, and the cloud cover obscured whatever light the moon might have offered. The only visible illumination after the guardhouse came from the Home itself.

"Why would anyone build something this far out in the middle of nothing?" Julia looked over at Ben. He gripped the steering wheel tight, his jaw set. "I'm sorry." She put hand on his knee. "We don't have to stay long."

The closer they drew, the less he wanted to be there. They drove around to the doors. Scott, dressed to impress in a nicer suit then Ben imagined an orderly could afford, manned the doors.

"Hey, Doc, glad you could make it." Scott flashed a smile at Ben, who returned it with a polite nod.

They entered the lobby, taking a moment to adjust to the difference in light. A small crowd stood around chatting. Most of them were Howerton's age or more. Their finery said money, and they all glanced at Ben and Julia as if they were the newest exhibit at the zoo.

Howerton strode out of the east wing passage as Ben and Julia walked in. "I'm so glad you two could make it. I wish it was a welcome to the family party, but a nice to know you party will work just as well." He took one of Julia's hands in both of his and beamed a smile. "How is your baby?"

Ben hadn't asked her how her OB appointment had gone. He kicked himself mentally. *Is that why she's been frigid?*

No, it's because I've been acting like a crazy fuck.

"The baby is very good. He should be coming anytime now," she said.

"I know it's not my place, but are you sure you want to travel in that condition? We'd be more than happy to keep Ben on salary until you two are comfortable moving." The sickly sweet honey of Howerton's words crawled under Ben's skin.

Julia glanced at Ben and smiled. "The plans are already made. We'll be fine."

Howerton turned his attention to Ben. "Good to see you, Dr. Kent." He extended a hand, which Ben shook.

"Please, just call me Ben."

Howerton smiled. Ben caught the fake right away. *Guess he wants to keep it formal.*

"You'll be missed around here. We've quite enjoyed having you."

For Julia's sake, Ben resisted the urge to roll his eyes. "I'm sorry to go, I really am. I felt like I was really making a connection with some of my patients." Ben saw Chris Clann in his mind, sitting on his bed, his smile unnaturally large. He pushed it aside as his stomach turned. "Theresa Parker especially."

Howerton's smile faded. "Theresa Parker? I didn't realize she'd been assigned as one of your patients."

"Yes, I've seen her almost every day since I arrived here. She's a very unique woman."

"There must have been some mistake," Howerton muttered. Ben didn't see why it mattered now.

Howerton introduced them to everyone. A few Ben already knew: nurses from around the hospital, Dr. Vitalie, and a couple of the orderlies. The mayor beamed at him when they shook hands before apologizing profusely for Ben not staying.

Most of the faces were new though, and Ben wouldn't remember any of their names in ten minutes. Julia found her stride while mingling. She was back in her own world. A rich businessman's daughter socializing with the upper crust. Ben watched her as much as he watched them, appreciating the grace she displayed in the social dance. He'd never seen her in that kind of element before. He wondered if living with her family in New York would be like that. He hoped not. It wasn't his kind of scene.

The partygoers asked many questions and made many comments. "I've heard you're leaving, whatever for? What part of New York? My father lived there! Heard the market's flooded with doctors there. You should stay." Ben only half-listened. He couldn't relax in the Home. He felt like all eyes were on him and Julia, and he wasn't wrong. All the fossils who'd come to rub elbows with each other weren't the ones who concerned him though. He didn't want to spend any more time here than he had to. Fortunately, he was spared thinking about it too much when Howerton spoke up.

"Dinner is ready. Would everyone like to join me in the eastern dining hall?"

The small crowd made its way toward the eastern hallway. Howerton explained the history of the building to Julia as they shuffled toward the dining room. Ben didn't pay attention. He couldn't shake the idea that the whole dinner felt like a wake. *The funeral procession will now make its way toward the eastern hall.* All these old men and women dressed in black tuxes, old dresses, and jewelry made Ben feel like he'd stepped into someone else's world.

In a few minutes they arrived at an enormous room that reminded Ben of something from a movie. It looked like a converted ballroom. A high ceiling, two stories tall, peaked in intricate woodwork and chandeliers. Huge windows at the eastern end illuminated a rainy garden outside. Solemn paintings of old men dressed in black were spaced around the room—Black family heirs, Ben guessed. Two huge tables had been set out in the nicest silver Ben had ever seen, and one smaller table was closer to the window. A headpiece to the affair. A place of honor for the guests.

"Stephen," Julia said. "This is gorgeous."

"Thank you. My great-grandfather was actually a cousin to the Black family. I've always enjoyed the portraits." He looked out at the crowd, the whole group moving through familiar motions. "I hope you don't mind joining us at the head table. It's reserved for the senior staff and esteemed guests."

"Of course not," Julia said for both of them. Ben just smiled and nodded.

Howerton led the way to the table where Dr. Vitalie and his wife were already seated.

"Is Dr. Cray joining us?" Ben asked.

"No. He's made it clear in the past that he isn't keen on these sorts of get-togethers."

"Is there a Mrs. Howerton?" Julia asked as Ben pulled out a chair for her. He took the seat next to her.

"I'm afraid she passed away giving birth to my daughter."

"Oh. I'm sorry."

"Don't be." Howerton sat beside Julia. "It was a long time ago."

Howerton entertained Julia as Ben took a closer look at the room around him. He tried to imagine what the place must have looked like with hundreds of people gathering for a ball. Instead, he saw what it was when epidemics hit the city. Cots lining the walls, people suffering and dying all around that room. Buckets of vomit and the stink of bedpans overwhelming the senses.

He turned his attention to the guests, and his unease grew. Theresa told him that the people of the Home wanted to be close to the dark things. His paranoia wouldn't ease up. He saw these people, all this old money, dressed up in black robes and chanting out of a book. Painting profane symbols in the blood of animals. He shook the image away. It was ludicrous. Stupid. Even knowing that, he couldn't help but wonder if Theresa was right. He wasn't supposed to have met her after all.

Wasn't I the one that asked her why they would let me meet her if she knew all their secrets? We could be surrounded by monsters right now.

He shifted in his seat. He hadn't wanted to come, and the more time he spent, the less he wanted to stick around.

Julia laughed at a joke Howerton told her. She glanced over at Ben. She must have seen the discomfort in his eyes. She held his gaze a moment longer than normal and grabbed his hand. It didn't help. Paranoia burrowed into his mind, and he suddenly felt stupid for coming back. He'd already gotten away scot-free, and yet here he stood, back where he started. *For a goddamn reputation I don't care about.* He took a deep breath and let it out slowly. Not for a reputation, for Julia. So she would be able to look him in the eye without seeing something crazy there.

"Are you all right, Ben?" Howerton asked.

"I'm fine. Just not feeling too well."

Howerton looked down his nose in his hawkish manner, a bird of prey eyeing a rabbit. "Still feeling that bug you had over the weekend?"

"I'm not sure."

"Maybe something to eat will help."

"They get inside you so they can stop sleeping."

The thought came from nowhere, almost a whisper in Ben's ear. Robbie's voice. Ben shifted in his seat and peeked behind him, expecting to see Robbie standing outside in the rain. The garden sat empty.

The first touch of a headache settled in the back of his skull. Cold sweat broke out across his body. The din of the dining room quieted too much, as if nobody wanted to be overheard. Julia and Howerton's conversation was the loudest thing in the room. Vitalie and his wife weren't saying a word.

His discussion with Theresa came to mind. *I think a lot of people here know more than they let on.* He swallowed hard. *I think it gets inside you, I think it makes you want the same things it wants.* He didn't want to be here anymore. This wasn't a dinner celebration, it was a painting of a Sunday funeral—somber and officious, Death hanging over everything.

Howerton tapped a spoon against his champagne flute. "Can I have everyone's attention?" The statement was pointless; everyone stared at Ben and Julia already. "Despite the fact that our newest friend and co-worker won't be remaining with us, we wanted to express how grateful we are for the time we had together." He raised the glass. "A toast."

Ben picked up his glass, going through the motions, following the same song and dance as everyone else. He couldn't have wanted anything less.

Howerton continued, "To new family, unfortunate circumstances, and new life." He winked and smiled at Julia.

Everyone else in the hall drank, including Julia. Ben didn't. Something wasn't right. *They get inside you so they can stop sleeping.*

What if they get inside through the food? What if they poison you? What if they're trying to poison us right now?

Ben put his flute to his lips and took a discreet sniff. He caught only the bubbly sweet smell of champagne. Julia sipped daintily from her glass. He wanted to tell her not to. He wanted to slap the glass out of her hand, grab her, and get the hell out.

The pattern revealed itself to him for the first time in a sudden moment of clarity. The headaches. The feeling of something looking at him from the shadows. The hum in the air. It all started right before whatever was in this place revealed itself. Theresa had been right all along. Something dark roamed the halls.

He didn't leave though. Julia already thought he'd lost it. Screaming about poison in the punch might finally chase her away. He mimed drinking and put the glass back down. Maybe there was more to it than nerves, but he wouldn't make a scene. He'd cornered himself in the cage like an idiot, and now he'd just have to deal for another hour.

"We're ready for the first course," Howerton said.

A short line of people Ben recognized from around the Home emerged from a back door carrying pots and ladles. They started at the front table where Ben and Julia sat, pouring helpings of what looked like delicate pea soup with chunks of rare, dark beef into the bowls. Ben stared into his soup as the orderlies continued along the rest of the tables.

"This looks great. What is it?" Julia asked Howerton.

"It's a local favorite. Pea soup with venison."

A warning alarm went off in his brain. Again, the feeling of eyes on his back bore into him. Julia saw him turn around and look out the window. She cocked her head and raised one eyebrow as if to ask, *'What is it?'* He shook his head and looked back down at his bowl.

What if it's Robbie?

The morbid thought flashed through Ben's mind quickly, and was gone. That was stupid, his paranoia was getting the best of him. *It's just soup,* he reminded himself over and over as the guests placed napkins on their lap. Once the last person was served, the rest of the gathering started to eat.

"I'm famished. This looks divine." Julia picked up her soupspoon and dipped it into her bowl as Howerton took the first bite of his own. Ben stared at the dish before him. The smell was intoxicating, but he wouldn't touch it. If it was poison, they weren't going to get him. He could just grab Julia and get the hell out of there. Julia raised her spoon to her mouth and blew.

If it's poison, it'll kill her. Kill the baby.

Julia stopped with her utensil partway to her lips when she saw Ben hadn't touched his. "Are you okay?" she asked quietly.

Howerton overheard her and looked over. "Is something the matter, Ben?" He put more emphasis on Ben's name than was strictly polite.

"No." Ben had the spotlight on him. "I'm just not feeling well is all."

"You should eat. It may help you feel better. This dinner was prepared just for the two of you." Howerton gave him a hard look.

The first waves of anger rose in his chest. He might eat shit from this guy if he was going to work there, but he certainly wasn't going to do it if he was quitting. Howerton had a stick up his ass, and if he talked to Ben like that one more time in front of his fiancée, he would have a boot up there too.

"I said I'm not feeling well," Ben said with steel in his voice. Vitalie stopped eating and looked over. Mrs. Vitalie stared ahead as if no one had said anything. Julia's eyes grew wide. She stuck her spoon into her mouth, as if to buy time for a response. A jolt of fear and adrenaline ran through him as she did.

My God. What if they just poisoned my fiancée?

"I'm sorry to hear that, Ben." Again the emphasis on his name. "Maybe you'll be feeling better when the main course arrives." Howerton went back to eating his soup. Julia looked at him out of the corner of her eye.

He wanted to go. He wanted to get the hell away. He leaned in close to her and whispered, "We need to leave."

She put her spoon down. "Let's just finish dinner, and we can go."

"I don't think we should. I think we need to get out of here."

"Sweetheart, we aren't getting up and walking out in the middle of a banquet for you."

"Don't you think this is weird? Something's wrong here." His voice rose as he spoke. If Howerton noticed, he pretended not to.

"Hold it together, Ben," she whispered before returning to her soup.

He sat in silence, looking around, doing anything but making eye contact with the other guests. *It was a mistake to come back here. I should have just dragged Julia to the car and left last week. Something bad is going to happen.*

But it didn't happen while they ate their soup. Howerton made small talk with Julia, mostly questions about the baby. Ben wasn't comfortable with it, or with anything else for that matter. A few minutes later, the main course, what looked like roast beef and carrots, rolled out of the kitchen on carts. When the orderlies pushed it past, Ben caught the strange smell—a sickly sweet odor that reminded him more of blood than meat.

"What is that?" he asked.

"Another local favorite," Howerton said.

The staff cut off slices and placed it on everyone's plates. Ben hadn't seen roast beef like that before. The smell turned his stomach.

"This looks delicious." Julia cut a small piece off one corner.

Everything spiraled into slow motion. Julia raised the fork to her mouth. A feeling of impending doom washed over Ben. "Don't eat that," he said aloud.

"Ben, don't be impolite," Julia said. She forced a smile. All eyes were on them.

"I'm serious, Julia. Don't."

"Ben." Her no-bullshit voice. "Stop."

Her tone cut through his paranoia, but did little to ease his nerves. He shouldn't have come back. He should have listened to Julia and never come to Tennessee in the first place. He focused on his plate, watching the juices ooze off the meat and puddle beneath it. Howerton said nothing. He stared straight ahead as he cut the meat and forked it into his mouth. The only sound in the room came from knives and forks on porcelain. The *scrape, scrape, scrape* of animal flesh being cut apart.

Julia took the small piece she'd cut off and chewed it slowly. "That's a very interesting flavor."

Howerton smiled from ear to ear. "I'm glad you like it. We made it special for you… both of you. Please, eat it, Ben."

Julia glared at him with everything she might have said. She'd had enough for the day. She might not want to leave him during his nervous breakdown, but she was quickly reaching the boundary of what she could stomach. If she could smile and nod through the embarrassing dinner, so could he.

He looked down at the meat again. The blood mixed with the water on the plate and turned everything pink. The outside edges were black and burnt, and that smell—dear lord, that smell! How any of them could eat it when it stank like road kill was beyond him. Julia could be a sweetheart, but even she had her limits.

Maybe it's in my head. Ben cut off a strip of meat from the side. He skewered it with his fork and stared at it.

If they could just get through dinner, they would be fine. He'd get help, find out what the problem was. Within a few months, they'd be happy again. They'd have a new baby boy to love. He raised the fork to his mouth.

"Don't eat it!"

Ben spun around, dropping the fork. Robbie stood outside the window, a gnarled claw from some unseen monster covering his mouth. He'd transgressed, and he would pay. The image almost immediately faded to a dark outline, then vanished.

Ben's vision tunneled to where Robbie had just been. The blood covering his shirt, wet from the rain. The fear in his eyes that now mirrored Ben's own. The room shrunk in on him as he jumped from the table, spilling his chair. They should never have come here, and now it might be too late to get out.

"We're leaving." Ben grabbed Julia's arm and dragged her to her feet, knocking her chair over too.

"Ben! What are you doing?"

Everyone in the room stared. Howerton smiled. "Is there a problem, Ben?" Again the emphasis on his name.

Ben dragged Julia toward the exit, ignoring him. They had to escape now. Whatever body that claw belonged to lurked nearby. It was the same impossibly long appendage from the basement, and it would take them away if they didn't flee, away to some nightmare world.

"Ben. Ben! What are you doing?" Julia said, trying to whisper. She didn't understand, and it didn't matter. They had to go. "Ben!" She yelled this time, putting her feet down and resisting. Nobody in the hall moved. If they tried to block the exits he wouldn't be able to get past them all.

Ben faced her, fully aware of all the stares. "Do you trust me?"

"Maybe. Yes?"

The response hurt him. She didn't trust him anymore. *How could she?* But there would be time for that later.

"Ben, what the hell is going on? This is crazy!" She was whispering again, but her voice carried.

"Something's here with us. Please, let's go."

He saw the conflict in her eyes. She thought he'd finally snapped. She might be right for all he knew, but they had to get out. She could leave him if she wanted. He would keep her safe.

She stopped resisting, and they made the last few yards out of the room and into the hallway leading back to the lobby. They raced along as fast as Julia could. Phantom hands reached from behind him. Endless limbs grasping to pull him back to dinner, make him eat. He glanced back, expecting to see Howerton in the hallway, but found an empty palace. A priceless landmark devoid of life.

The walls closed in around him. The floorboards creaked above their heads. "Do you hear that?"

She looked at him, her brow furrowed, her eyes full of concern. She shook her head.

They burst out of the hallway and into the lobby. A nurse he'd never seen before sat behind the desk. "Is there a problem, sir?"

"Yes, I need my car." Ben's breath came in ragged spurts.

An orderly standing by the door walked over. Ben hadn't seen him before either. The man towered above him. Six-four if he was an inch. His hands were as big as Ben's head.

"I need my car," Ben said again when neither of them responded. Julia shifted on her feet. She wouldn't meet his eyes, wouldn't focus on anything. Her cheeks were red with embarrassment, and the way she glanced at Ben said it all; she was scared and angry.

"Are you hard of hearing?"

Again, the nurse didn't respond. Ben let go of Julia, and his hands tightened into fists. If everyone were in on it, he would fight his way out and save Julia. "Give me the keys. Now."

"Maybe you should just relax a bit, Doctor," the big orderly said. He placed a hand on Ben's shoulder. Ben spun on him, his fist flying into the man's face.

"Ben!" Julia screamed as the orderly stumbled backward. Years of playground fights had given Ben a mean straight punch. The orderly tripped and fell onto his butt a few feet away.

"Give me the goddamn keys or you're next."

If the nurse cared, she didn't show it.

"Ben!" Julia yelled again.

The orderly stood. "You're going to wish you hadn't done that."

"Think so, you big bastard?" Ben squared up. He would kill everyone in this place with his bare hands to save Julia.

"That's enough." Howerton strode into the room. "Get his car."

The big orderly looked at Howerton in confusion.

"I said get his car. Now."

The nurse reached under the desk, grabbed a keychain, and handed it to the orderly. He walked out the door with one last glare at Ben, rubbing his jaw. Howerton turned to Ben and Julia. "Dr. Kent, don't ever step foot on this property again. If you do, I'll have you arrested."

Ben edged toward the door, taking Julia by the hand and keeping his gaze on Howerton the entire time. He had the distinct impression of an audience watching, a thousand people standing on the balcony observing the play. They walked out, Ben looking all around, expecting an ambush.

"My god. What the hell is wrong with you?" Julia asked breathlessly.

"Not right now." Ben kept looking around, waiting for something horrible to present itself. These people— these things— wouldn't let him go that easy. The orderly pulled around in their car.

"Yes, right now, Ben," she said as the orderly stepped out.

"Next time you sucker punch me, I'll break your fucking neck."

Ben ignored him and walked to the car. "Let's go, Julia. We need to leave."

She shook her head but did as he said. Tears formed in her eyes as she slid into the passenger seat.

Ben sped out of the porte-cochere. He watched in his rearview, expecting the Home to shrink.

It didn't.

The building loomed just behind. He hunched down in his seat. It was following him. He put his foot down on the accelerator. It wasn't done with them. It wouldn't let them go.

"Ben, what are you doing?" Julia yelled as the engine roared.

He didn't respond. He needed to get them away from there, and the building wasn't going to allow it. Whatever malignant presence permeated the place wanted them as a permanent addition. He watched it all in his mirror, the peaked roof, the angels above the entrance, the dim windows. It grew closer.

"Jesus, Ben! Stop!"

Ben looked forward just in time to slam on his brakes and avoid colliding with the gate. The tires screeched as they came to a full stop only six feet from it. The guard in the gatehouse stared wide-eyed at them.

Ben opened his door and yelled, "Open the gate!" before slamming it closed again.

The guard did as he was told without thinking, and in no time, they sped away from the Home. Ben looked behind, expecting to see the building come around the bend and give chase. It didn't.

Julia sobbed. "What the hell is wrong with you?"

"They were going to poison us. They're a cult."

She shook her head as tears fell. "Do you even hear yourself right now? You sound like a mental patient!"

They'll lock you up in a place like this. He shook the thought aside. She didn't understand that he was trying to protect her, and she didn't need to. She had every right to be scared, but not of him.

"Didn't you smell what they tried to give us? Couldn't you hear that thing in the hallway? Jesus Christ, Julia, how did you not see any of that?"

"It smelled fine. It's all in your head. Something's wrong with you, don't you see that?"

"Nothing is wrong with me! I'm telling you, something is in that place. Those people know about it."

Julia began to reply when Ben glanced in his rearview mirror. The thing from the closet peered at him from behind his seat, its yellow eyes wide and terrible.

"Fuck!" He veered the car to the side of the road, slamming on the brakes. Julia screamed as they shifted forward in their seats, putting her hands up so that she wouldn't collide with the dash. When Ben looked back, the thing was gone. He put the car in park and leaned over into the back seat, frantically searching for it. "Did you see that?"

"No! No dammit, I didn't see—" She doubled over, grabbing her belly and groaning.

They poisoned my wife. I shouldn't have let her eat that food. "What is it?"

"I don't know."

"They poisoned you! We need to get you to the hospital."

293

She pounded the dash with her fist. "No! They didn't poison me. Listen to yourself! I'm nine months pregnant and I'm scared! That's what's wrong!"

He tried to form a response. His mouth opened and closed several times. "We need to go now. We can leave tonight—"

"No. No, we're not. Take me back to the apartment right now."

"Julia! We need to get the hell out of here!"

"Take me back home right now, Benjamin Kent! Right now!"

He stared at her in disbelief. She slammed her fist into the dash again. "Take me home!"

What if she's right?

She could be right about everything. He might have lost his mind already. Hearing things, seeing things. He might not be able to trust himself anymore. The gravity of it pulled his stomach down to the floor. He thought he might be sick.

He found the shifter and put the car into drive without saying another word. He didn't look in the rearview, afraid of what he might see. They drove back home with Julia crying silently in the passenger seat.

He stared at the road, unblinking, waiting for the Home to make its presence known again.

Julia tore out of the car as soon as it came to a stop. Ben shut it off and chased after her.

"Julia, wait!" He needed to make her understand.

If she heard him, she pretended not to. She hurried into the building. He walked after her, breaking into a jog when she entered the elevator. He ran through the lobby just in time for the door to close in his face.

"Trouble in paradise, huh?" Harry asked over the novel in his hands. Ben ignored the comment and strode to the stairs, throwing the door open and taking them two at a time.

He'd just passed the second floor door when the lights went out. His heart skipped a beat as he froze. Images of a million terrible things closing in around him in the darkness raced through his head. He willed his shattered nerves down. Now wasn't the time for panic.

He grabbed the railing and started feeling his way, inching up the steps one at a time. The sound of a wet foot slapping a stair above him rang in the darkness. Then another. Soon the noise of something closing on him echoed all around. They began slowly, but the pace picked up with each step. A cascade of noise washed over him.

Every hair on his body stood on end. He pictured his mother, her wet corpse rising from the bathtub, the cuts on her wrists thin and bloodless. He broke into a mad dash, blindly moving up the steps to the fourth floor, a race to see who would get there first. He stumbled as he jumped up the last three steps to the landing, the echo of wet footsteps only a few feet away.

He could almost hear her voice. *"I'm so alone, Benji. Don't leave me alone again."*

He closed his hand around the handle and flung the door open, diving through as the sound closed in. He imagined fingers reaching for him as he spilled into the hallway's light. He landed hard, turning immediately to engage whatever monstrosity had followed him.

He saw only the stairwell's looming darkness. The door slammed suddenly, and without any force acting upon it. He jumped to his feet and ran to his apartment. The hallway lights began to flicker as he shut the door behind him and locked it. The light from the peephole vanished as he did.

"Julia!"

No response. He searched the apartment. He'd drag her out if he had to. "Julia!" he yelled again in the hallway.

"I'm in here," she said from behind the closed bedroom door.

Ben turned the handle. Locked. He put his face against the door. "Julia, please listen. We need to go." She had to listen. He had to make her see.

"I'm not going anywhere. You need to calm down. You're scaring me." He could hear the tears in her voice.

"Please, just get in the car and let's go." He waited for a response but didn't get one. "I promise, as soon as we get to New York, I'll check myself into a hospital. Please, Julia, I think something's here with us."

She laughed, but it didn't sound like her. It came out bitter, mean. "You're losing it. There's nothing here. You're imagining things."

He tried to open the door again as he glanced behind him, expecting something in the hallway. The big orderly in the Home come to take him away, or the thing from the closet gazing at him. Nothing there. Not yet. "Please!"

"I'm not going anywhere with you until you calm down. I can't deal with this right now. Just leave me alone. We'll talk in the morning."

The light in the hallway flickered, and Ben's heart leapt into his throat. "Come out!" He pounded on the door in frustration.

She started to sob. "I don't know what to do. I'm scared of you right now!"

The words cut through him. Auditory hallucinations, phantoms in the stairwell. That could be exactly what happened to his mother. A vision of her seeing things in her rearview flashed through his mind. Locking herself in the bedroom to get away from the demons. Cutting her wrists to get out the bad blood.

"I'm telling you, something isn't right here. I…" *What? Am I going to tell her something chased me up the stairs?* Words failed him. A sudden bout of clarity put him in her shoes. He wouldn't believe her if their positions were reversed.

I'm not crazy.

Unfortunately, every crazy person said that. He'd heard things, he'd seen them. Not in some half-light, or some trick of perspective, but full frontal. Things were coming to get them. He'd heard his dead mother calling his name.

I heard my dead mother call my name.

The utter insanity of it hit him all at once. Dead people didn't speak. They didn't chase their children down stairwells. Julia saw what he couldn't— something was wrong with him.

"Okay. Okay. I'll stay out here on the couch. Just promise me you'll talk to me, face to face, in the morning."

She didn't respond.

"I'm scared too."

The silence dragged on for a full minute before she spoke. "Promise me you'll get help tomorrow. Not next week. Not when we get to New York. Right away."

Hot tears stung his eyes. If he ended up like his mother, his son would know what it was like to grow up without a father too. "I will, I promise." He would say anything to make sure she never looked at him the way she had in the car ever again. "Will you open the door?"

"No. I need to be alone right now. Sleep on the couch."

He hung his head, trying to choke back tears at the thought of going insane like his mother, the thought of his fiancée and child terrified of him. "Okay. Okay."

He took a deep breath, trying to steady himself, and turned around. The hallway stood empty. He walked back into the living room, moving slowly, fearing what might be there. Again, nothing.

The same feeling he'd experienced earlier, as if a party was going on around him that he couldn't see, still plagued him. He wished he had the gun, but it was locked in the bedroom with Julia, and he doubted she'd be willing to hand it out to her crazed fiancé.

He took off his tux coat, sat on the couch, and pulled the cover over him. Despite the bit of sleep he'd gotten the night before, he felt as exhausted as ever. He wished now that they'd bought a TV. Anything would be better than waiting in the living room for the next horror to descend on him. He wanted an out.

His eyelids grew heavy, and he slipped off. He shook himself awake. He wouldn't sleep again until they left Tennessee. The nightmares only made things worse.

Something walked down the hallway outside the apartment. Steps moved from the far side of the hall to just outside the door. He glanced at the clock. It was still early. *Just a neighbor. Nothing wrong with that.*

The sound repeated itself three times over the next five minutes. The footsteps came from the far side of the hallway near the elevator, approached the stairs, and entered the stairwell. Ben tapped his foot nervously. *Maybe one of them has kids that play on the elevator.* But he hadn't heard the elevator doors once. He rubbed his eyes. *Everything's fine. I'm just imagining it.* He stared at the wall and listened to the endless clomp of shoes on wood.

I'm not going to look. It wants me to look. It's messing with me.

Steps, maddeningly close. Nerve-wracking.

I won't look.

The invisible party closed in around him. Something unseen sat next to him, and he swallowed hard, ignoring it. The walker in the hallway continued his endless loop. Elevator. Stairwell. Elevator. Stairwell.

Ben stood up and paced back and forth, the couch cover wrapped around him. *Nothing's wrong. Don't bother Julia. She thinks you've lost it already.*

"I'm sick. I'm sick and I'm tired. Everything's going to be fine soon."

His steps mirrored those of whoever was in the hallway, and he stopped immediately. *I'm not going to play this game.* He peeked into the peephole. The hall light was still out, but a dark shape walked past his door. *Just a neighbor. Maybe they called the repairman.* The logic didn't stick.

The phantom gathering moved in a little closer. His thoughts grew manic, and sweat formed on his brow. *I'll just go out there and ask him to stop.*

He unlocked the door and eased it open, freezing in stunned horror at what he saw.

It's not real. I'm not seeing this.

The door opened onto the short hallway outside of his office at the Home. The janitorial closet was opened a crack. A pair of long, black fingers reached around the closet's doorframe. Ben slammed the front door as the lights flickered and died above him.

"This isn't real. This isn't happening."

A loud click and a squeal emanated from the apartment hallway.

"Julia?" Ben's voice cracked. Nothing responded.

Ben curled himself into a ball on the floor. Tears fell down his cheeks. "This isn't real," he said. "This isn't real. This isn't real." He shut his eyes as tightly as possible.

The squealing stopped, and a wet slap of feet on hardwood made its way toward the living room. *"I'm so alone here, Benji. Don't leave me alone."*

"This isn't real!"

The footsteps closed in on him. The ghostly party loomed overhead, watching him break down.

"This isn't real! This isn't real!"

The footsteps stopped only a few feet away. Heavy, wet breath heaved above him. The thing from the closet leaned over and spoke in Julia's voice, *"Yes, it is."*

Ben threw the blanket off. He was still on the couch, his clothes soaked through with sweat. He jumped up and looked around frantically. Night reigned outside, but the lights above him were on. He put a hand over his open mouth, his eyes dry and lids heavy.

"Ha, ha! Ha, ha, ha! Not real. I knew it wasn't. I knew it!" *Just a bad dream.* The laughter tapered off slowly, then stopped abruptly. Sanity wasn't a victory he wanted to celebrate. Not now. He put his head into his hands and let out a heavy sigh.

The phone began to ring. He moved to get it only a split second before remembering he'd tore it off the wall. *The phone's gone.* He peeked at the kitchen from behind his fingers. The ringing came from the trashcan where Ben had disposed of it.

He stared at it, watching the trashcan move slightly at every ring. *Just another dream.* He shivered from cold and fear. *Doesn't matter. It's not real.* He would answer the phone and wake up again.

He inched into the kitchen, taking the baby steps so common with the patients he'd seen in school. He reached into the trashcan, pulling the whole phone out, disconnected wire and all, and placing it on the table.

"I just have to pick it up," he said aloud. "And I'll wake up. Everything'll be fine in the morning. We can get out of here, Julia and me." His hand shook as he grabbed the receiver. He lifted it slowly to his ear. In the distance, someone hammered on a piano, the tune discordant and ugly.

"Hello?" His voice shook.

"Ben? Ben, please help me! Please, Ben! Please, Ben!" Julia was crying, terrified. "You were right! I just want to get out of here!"

"Julia!" His eyes, stinging from lack of sleep, widened. "Where are you!"

"Ben. No! No, please! No—" Her screams cut off, and the sound of the receiver hitting the floor blared out of the other end. Something picked it up and breathed raggedly into it.

"All mine, Benjamin."

Ben dropped the phone and ran into the hallway. The bedroom door stood slightly ajar. He pushed it open so hard it banged against the wall and broke through the drywall, sticking there. Something covered by the blanket stood on top of the mattress. In the darkness, he couldn't tell if it was Julia. He flipped the light switch to no effect.

"Julia?"

Whatever stood on the bed didn't move. A thousand dead patients watched him from blackened corners and open doors.

"Julia?" he asked again. He reached the edge of the bed and with a shaking hand tried to grab the blanket. The door slammed behind him and shook the apartment.

Dozens of dead faces crowded around him. Before he had a chance to scream, the thing on the bed threw the blanket over him.

Chapter 13

The morning sun woke him. He jumped off the couch and looked around wildly. The beautiful early morning glow did little to erase his horror.

"Am I awake?" He bit down hard on his finger, hard enough to draw blood. It hurt terribly but confirmed that he was conscious. Relief flooded him, making his legs weak. He sat back down.

Okay. Okay. It was a dream. Dream or not, it felt real. He shook his head. His eyes were heavy and dry as bone, and he had little doubt that if he looked in a mirror they'd be red-rimmed with bags underneath. He ran his hands over the two-day stubble that had grown into a ragged beard. The sweat from his nightmare had soaked his undershirt, turning it dull gray around his armpits.

He let out a heavy sigh and glanced into the kitchen. The phone sat on the table where he'd left it in his dream. Disbelief shocked him into action.

"Julia!" He dashed into the hallway. The bedroom door shook in the frame as he tried to enter. Still locked. "Julia!" He heard movement from inside. A few seconds later, the lock clicked and Julia opened it, staring at him bleary eyed. She looked terrible.

"What?"

He opened the door further and walked into the room. Everything was fine. "Are you okay?" He held her by the shoulders and looked down at her.

"I'm fine," she snapped. "Why wouldn't I be?" She brushed past him and toward the bathroom. Halfway there, she stopped and grabbed her belly. He rushed to her side.

"What's wrong?"

"I don't know," she said as she doubled over.

"We're going to the hospital." He moved toward the bedroom to grab some clothes.

"No." The dead calm of her voice stopped him in his tracks. "I'm not going anywhere with you."

He stared at her stupidly. "What?"

"You've fucking lost it. Screaming all night. Running all over the apartment." Another wave of pain washed over her, and she grunted. "I'm not doing another goddamn thing with you until we're out of here."

Running all over the apartment? It was just a dream. It was all just dreams. He thought of the phone sitting on the kitchen table. "Julia, look at you. You look like shit, and you might be having contractions."

"You're one to talk." She walked into the bathroom and closed the door.

"Let's go to the doctor."

She didn't respond.

"Goddammit! I'll call an ambulance and have them come here then." He turned to head toward the kitchen before he recalled they didn't have a phone.

"I'm fine. Just leave me alone," she said through the door.

But she wasn't fine. Nothing was fine. If she wouldn't talk to him, maybe he could call someone else. He glanced at the clock hanging on the wall in the hallway. Seven AM. He could call Regina. Maybe she wouldn't be at work yet. Julia might listen to her.

His resolve hardened as he grabbed a pair of jeans from the packed box. One way or another, he was going to get her to a doctor, and then get them both the hell out of town.

"Slow down," Regina said over the lobby phone. The guard— not Harry, but the other one—kept peeking over his fishing magazine at Ben, no doubt at his haggard appearance and crazy tone. The guy must have thought Ben was off his rocker, but at that moment he could have thought Ben was a space alien for all it mattered.

"I need you. Julia won't listen to me, and I think something might be wrong."

She hesitated before she spoke, obviously uncomfortable with the conversation. "Then you need to take her to a hospital. You know that."

"She won't listen to me. She thinks…" He couldn't tell Regina what she thought of him. "Please. I'll explain when you get here."

Regina didn't say anything.

"I don't have anyone else to turn to here."

She'd only known him a week, and he'd been raving about ghosts half the time. *She thinks I'm nuts too. They should all start a club.* It didn't matter. He'd never have to show his face in this town again.

The silence dragged on for several more seconds. "I'll need to call in late to work. I'll be there in about thirty minutes." Her voice conveyed her displeasure.

"Thank you." Ben hung up and took the elevator back to the apartment. He didn't know how he would convince Julia to get out of town, but making sure she was okay was a start.

When he got inside, he found Julia sitting on the couch, staring straight ahead at the wall. She didn't notice him.

"Julia."

She didn't respond.

"Julia," he said with more force.

"What?" The same cold voice from earlier.

"Regina is coming over."

"Great." She continued staring at the wall, seeing something Ben didn't.

He watched her gaze into nothingness. That wasn't how she normally acted, and it wasn't normal for pregnancy either. He furrowed his brow. "I'm going to make you something to eat." He went into the kitchen and made eggs and toast. When he finished, he set it on the table. He didn't make anything for himself. He couldn't have kept down food if he tried. "Food's ready."

No reply. She just stared as if it held an answer to some unasked question. Of all the things he'd seen over the last few days, that scared him the most. He wanted to go over to her, to hold her hand and comfort her. She wouldn't have it now.

A knock sounded on the door. When Ben opened it Regina examined him up and down.

"You look terrible." She said it not in the nonchalant way a co-worker might, but the way someone with serious questions about his well-being would.

He shook his head and opened the door further. Julia didn't look up when Regina walked in. Regina gave Ben a questioning expression. He shrugged and shook his head again.

"Julia, sweetheart? Are you okay?" Regina asked.

Julia's gaze drifted up to meet her. "Hello, Regina. When did you get here?"

Regina sat next to her and put a hand to her head. "How're you feeling?"

"Pissed off." She glared at Ben.

Regina glanced up at him then focused back on Julia. "Is everything okay?"

"Can we talk alone?"

The question hit Ben like a slap in the face.

"Why?" Regina asked.

"Can we talk alone?" Julia repeated.

Regina questioned Ben with her eyes, but he was at a loss. *Has she had enough? Is that what this is? Is she done with me?* Sleepless and afraid for himself and his fiancée, his mind worked slowly.

"Ben, is there somewhere we can talk alone?" Regina asked.

He pointed to the bedroom and walked back into the kitchen. He couldn't look at Julia right now, couldn't bear the loathing in her eyes. Regina helped Julia to her feet and they walked into the bedroom, closing the door behind them.

Ben heard their voices but couldn't make out what they said. He stared down into the congealing mess left over in the pan where he'd cooked the eggs. Even the smell of the food made his stomach dance. He couldn't tear his gaze from the dirty dishes. He wanted to break down. He wanted to get into his car and away from this place and all the problems in his life. He wanted to end the stress and find some little place in the middle of nowhere where he'd be all alone.

But no matter what was going on in Julia's head, he wouldn't leave her. He couldn't. He always thought she felt the same.

He hoped that was still true.

Ben tried to keep himself busy, but after the first twenty minutes, he ended up sitting on the couch and staring at the wall as Julia had. The door in the hallway opened, and Regina walked into the living room. She gave Ben a look of clear displeasure.

"What's going on?" he asked.

"A lot, actually. She's in and out of it, and what she's saying isn't making a lot of sense."

"What do you mean?"

"Well." Regina's gaze drilled into him. "She said you hit her last night."

Ben's eyes widened, and he jumped off the couch. "I would never!" He shook his head in disbelief.

Regina held up a hand. "I don't think you did. Her story changed three times while we talked. But you've been acting erratic. She said you started a fight last night at dinner. She said you thought monsters were chasing you out of the Home."

Ben sat back down and cupped his hands in front of him. He looked down at the floor. He couldn't hold Regina's gaze. "I don't know what's going on anymore." Shame coursed through him, reddening his face.

Regina licked her lower lip before biting it in frustration. "I don't know what to do for you two. Something is going on around here."

"I'm telling you. Something is wrong with that place, Regina. Something is happening to us because of it."

"I've worked there for ten years. I've seen some spooky stuff, I've heard some spooky stuff, but there are no monsters in the Home. Whatever you think you're seeing is in your head, and I think you need help. She told me what happened to your mom. I think you need to get checked out."

There it was. *You have a family history of this? You need to seek help, man. You've lost it, Ben.* After worrying about hearing those words for so long they had no effect.

"What about Julia? You think she needs help too?"

"No, I don't. I think she's nine months pregnant and stressed out. That baby could come any time now. You two don't need to be leaving town."

"I'm not staying here. You couldn't keep me in this place if you tied me down."

Regina sighed loudly. "Look at me, Ben."

He reluctantly did as she commanded. It was harder than he wanted to admit.

"You need to think about what's best for her and your baby right now. Think about what's going on as a doctor. Think about everything you're experiencing. What would you say if you saw a patient like that?"

He shook his head and cast his gaze back down at the ground. "I think they did something to her."

"Who the hell are 'they,' Ben? Your co-workers? The people I've worked with for a decade? Listen to what you're saying."

He wondered what Theresa would say to all of this. He didn't think she was crazy anymore, not after everything he'd seen over the last week. *Will that be me if I get checked out at the hospital? Will they lock me up for thirty years and tell me I'm crazy? They put something into her to get to her baby. What if they did the same to Julia?*

311

His blood went cold. He stood up and looked Regina in the eye. "I'm doing what's best for my family by getting out of here. I called you over here because she won't talk to me. What should I do, huh? Let her have the baby locked up in a bedroom by herself? Stick around here stewing in this apartment all day until one of us finally gets sick of it and walks out?"

Regina didn't back down an inch, but her face did soften. "She won't go to the hospital. She says she's fine, but she looks terrible. My advice? Let her rest. If she keeps acting strange, call an ambulance and make her go regardless. But whatever you do, stop scaring her. That isn't going to help anything. You need to get a grip. If not for you than for her."

He could see the same fear in her eyes that he'd seen in Julia's the night before.

"You need to get help. You aren't well."

He suddenly regretted calling her. Of course Regina wasn't going to help him. He barely knew her, and he was raving like a madman. The kneejerk reaction to Julia's condition and indifference was to call for outside help. He didn't know what he'd expected, but he certainly didn't think that Julia would lie to someone. *Why? Does she want to get away from me?*

"Thank you for coming, Regina." He sat back on the couch and resumed staring at the floor.

"I don't know what you want from me." She walked to the door, closing her hand around the knob. "If you need anything you can always call. Make sure you dial 9-1-1 if she goes into labor." She opened the door and stepped out. "And think about what I said. It wouldn't hurt to get checked out."

He wanted to go into the room and ask Julia why she'd lied, but it wasn't the right time. Nothing good was going to happen while they were still in Tennessee. He sat on the couch, staring at the same place on the wall that Julia had for the better part of an hour, mulling over the best course of action.

He could stand one more night in this place for Julia's sake. When the movers arrived on Friday, it would be easier to get her to leave. She wouldn't stay in an empty apartment by herself. At least he didn't think so. It felt underhanded, like he was plotting behind her back to whisk her away. But he needed to get away from Umber Gardens, and Julia did as well.

One more day in this terrible place. Friday afternoon, we're out of here. Julia won't be mad once she's home. I'll get checked out, we'll start over in New York, and everything will be okay.

He wanted it to be true. He needed it to be true.

He didn't bother Julia, and she never left the room. When his watch read half past three, he finally worked up the courage to knock on the door and walk in. He didn't want to ask her about anything she'd said to Regina, he just wanted to make sure she was okay. "Julia?"

She sat on the edge of the bed, her shoulders slumped. She wore the same nightgown she had been earlier, and she looked worse than she had that morning.

"Are you okay?"

She didn't respond.

"Julia?"

Finally, she glanced up at him, her eyes bloodshot. "What?"

The tone of her voice hurt him, but he did his best not to let it show. "Are you hungry? Can I get you something?"

"I'm fine." She rolled over into bed, turning her back to him.

"You need to eat."

"I said I'm fine. Leave me alone."

He stood in the doorway and watched her. *What the hell am I supposed to do here?* He couldn't remember ever feeling so adrift in the sea of his own life. There was no roadmap for this, no guiding star for getting through fear and insanity.

That's when he noticed it. The gun sitting on the dresser next to the bed. Something about it sitting next to her was obscene. *Why the hell would she pull that out?* She couldn't be that scared of him. *I'm her fiancé for fuck's sake!* He walked over and grabbed it, kissing her on the cheek as he did. Everything was spiraling out of control. He hid it under the blanket on the couch, not knowing what else to do with it, not knowing how else to react to Julia being terrified of him.

He'd make her something and bring it in to her. As apologies went, it sucked, but if she wanted to throw it in his face, she was more than welcome to. He went to the kitchen and opened the fridge. Nothing left but condiments and eggs. He closed it and grabbed the keys from the hook on the wall.

He locked the door and took the elevator. The security guard ignored him. Ben couldn't blame him for that. He jumped in the car and drove to a fast food joint a few blocks away, ordering two burgers and fries. He wasn't gone more than twenty minutes.

As the elevator opened up and he stepped off, he noticed the apartment door was open a few inches.

A cold lump dropped into his guts. He pushed the door open, his hands shaking. *I can't deal with any more of this. Please let this be the wind.* He walked into the living room. "Julia?"

She didn't answer.

He stepped deeper into the apartment. She stood by the kitchen table, swaying slightly, the unhooked phone receiver in her hand. She mumbled into it, speaking in a hushed whisper.

"Julia."

She hung up the phone and avoided his stare, her expression blank. "What?"

"What do you mean, 'what'? You were talking on a dead phone."

She glanced down at the phone and back at him. She didn't seem to understand what he was saying, as if he'd spoken to her in Chinese. "I thought I heard it ring."

He set the food on the table. "That's it. I'm taking you to the hospital if I have to drag you out of here." If he had to, he'd call Julia's family and let them deal with it. If it made everything better he'd leave her with them, as long as she got the help she needed.

Rage flashed across her face.

"You can be as mad as you want. I'm worried about you." He grabbed her hand. "I'm scared, Julia."

Confusion replaced anger as she looked back at him. "I'm fine. I really am. I'm scared too. I'm tired." She kissed his hand as he'd done to her a thousand times. She shook her head a little, as if clearing away the cobwebs. "I think the baby is coming soon." She sounded like herself again.

"Let's get out of here. Let's get in the car and go right now."

She sighed. "I can't. Not today. I can't handle it right now." She dropped his hand, and it fell to his side. "Let me rest today. When the movers come tomorrow, we can pack up and get out of here."

"I know you aren't supposed to travel when you're this pregnant, but staying here is worse."

"Okay, sweetheart. We'll deal with it tomorrow. I need some sleep."

She'd been sleeping all day, but at least she wasn't angry right now. He didn't want to screw that up. "At least eat something first."

Julia looked down at the bag on the table. She opened it up and took out a hamburger. "I'll eat in the room. I just need to lie down for a while." She moved past him back to the hallway. The bedroom door closed, and he was alone again. He took a deep breath and blew it out. One more day.

He cleaned up the uneaten breakfast on the table and made his way to the couch with his burger. He didn't want to eat, but he had to keep his strength up. He was taxed to his limit, and tomorrow would be the hardest. *Just one more day though. Just one more. We can be in New York tomorrow night.*

He managed to eat a few bites of his burger before sleep overtook him.

Chapter 14

He awoke to a boom coming from the bedroom. The darkness outside the window told him he'd been asleep longer than the moment he thought he had. He wiped the sleep from his eyes.

Another boom shook the apartment. He tried to think, but sleep had made his mind clumsy. *Someone was coming to help deliver the baby. Something.*

Julia is in the bedroom.

"Julia!" He picked up the gun and charged into the hallway. He grabbed the knob to the bedroom door; cold as ice and locked. "Julia!"

A creaking in the room responded.

He moved back and kicked the door as hard as he could. It burst inward, splintering the frame. He stepped inside the freezing room and flicked on the light switch. A wire shorted in the wall, and every light in the apartment switched off. The putrid stink of rotten eggs filled the room.

"Julia!"

Still no response. There was nowhere to hide in the bedroom. He threw open the closet and felt around in the dark, his eyes still not adjusted to the darkness. He yelled her name again and reached under the bed. Wherever that smell came from, it was worse under there. He didn't find Julia.

When he put his hand on the mattress to stand up, it came away damp. It didn't look like blood, but in the dark his mind leapt to the worst possible conclusion. He wasn't dreaming this time, of that he was sure. Julia was missing.

A loud thump came from the living room. He tore out through the door and stopped in his tracks in the hallway. Something covered by the blanket from his bed, seven feet tall and broader than Julia, stood in the center of the room. The stink gagged him.

"Julia?" he called out anyway as his courage left him.

It didn't move. Ben saw his breath as he exhaled. *I'm seeing things now. They're going to show up and take me away.* But he would find Julia first.

He strode toward the thing under the blanket. He didn't care if it hurt him. All that mattered was Julia.

As his fingertips touched the comforter, it collapsed.

The absurdity of it made black spots swim in front of his eyes. The room twisted dangerously under his feet, and he knew with certainty that he was about to pass out. He rubbed his eyes, trying to focus and remain conscious. His legs turned to jelly. *This isn't real.*

Something slammed into the back of his head, and he fell forward. Everything turned gray and fell sideways, almost in slow motion. The gun tumbled from his hand and drifted down to the floor. His head connected with the hardwood forcefully enough to make his ears ring. He retained consciousness just long enough to see Julia, still in her robe, step over him and grab the car keys off the hook near the entrance. Without looking back, she opened the apartment door and stepped out, dropping the remains of Grandma's lamp in the hallway.

Images moved in front of him as he wavered in and out of the waking world. Men and women filed past him, old and dead, rotten and stinking. Stains painted themselves onto the ceiling before his eyes.

The thing from the closet crawled past him on all fours. A spider in the vague shape of a man. It did laps around him, its head always in the same position, its neck moving at impossible angles to keep watch on him. Its rotten flesh hung in tatters from yellowed cheekbones. The oozing whites of its eyes stripped him down, unmade him, scoured the secret heart of him.

Hands gripped his arms and legs. A sudden burst of adrenaline awoke him as something pulled him in four directions at once.

The lights flickered throughout the apartment as the phone rang on the kitchen table. Invisible hands held him in place, pulling at his limbs, keeping him hovering several inches above the ground.

Something moved in the hallway, coming closer. It sucked the warmth from the room. He stared at it, mesmerized. He could almost see through it. A shimmering cloud of blackness. He couldn't think, couldn't do anything as he urinated in his pants; the hot stream warming his leg for a moment in the freezing room. Death. That thing was death come for him. An unknowable, unstoppable force of nature that would take him away from the world.

I'll never see Julia again.

Her laugh as he made fun of her grandmother. Her face when they saw their boy for the first time. The look in her eyes when she told him she loved him. All of that gone, taken away by the almost-there-thing.

He grunted and tugged with his arms and legs, trying to curl himself into a ball and break away from whatever unseen monster had him. He wouldn't lose everything. He would find Julia. He would get out of there and save his fiancée and child.

The trance that had gripped him fell away. Whatever held his left arm loosened as he twisted. It clawed at him, leaving deep, bloody scratches on his wrist as he tore free. His right arm followed, and he grabbed onto the door that Julia had left open. He dragged himself toward it, curling his arms to try to get away.

The thing's hold was failing. It let go with a scream that came from nowhere and left a ringing in his ears when it passed. Nothing on Earth could make a noise like that. His blood ran cold in his veins as he jumped to his feet, grabbing the gun where it had fallen and charging through the open door.

A horrible wail followed him as he ran for the stairs. He yanked the door open and flew inside as the sound of pounding feet chased him. He couldn't think. Fear had taken away any rationality. He felt his way forward as pursuit closed in.

He tripped halfway down and tumbled to the next landing, striking his head hard enough to see stars. The sounds of stomping on the stairs above moved him onward. He jumped up and rushed down the last few sets of steps, nearly tripping again. He had to make it. That thing catching him would be death, or something worse.

He reached for the lobby door. Locked. Footsteps slammed onto each step, no further up than the next landing.

He put a foot onto the wall next to the door and grasped the handle, tugging on it as he kicked off the wall. It didn't budge for half a second, and then with a snap it flew open, sending Ben onto his back and spilling the lobby's bright light into the stairwell. He got to his feet and dashed through the door, pulling it closed behind him.

Harry—of course it would be Harry—looked at him dumbly from behind a magazine as Ben hurried to the desk. "Did my fiancée come by here?"

He didn't respond.

"My fiancée, man, Julia! Pregnant woman!"

"Y-yes. She came through here ten minutes ago."

It didn't feel like he'd been out that long, but everything hurt, and it was impossible to tell anymore. His head throbbed with every heartbeat, full of broken glass. Ben sprinted out the door.

Their car was gone. *She went to the Home. It's inside her, and it took her to the Home to get out.* Everything Theresa said came back to him. *I should have listened. I should have left when we had the chance.*

He wanted to break down, to give up and run away screaming. He wouldn't, not yet. He ran back inside to the desk. The lights flickered overhead, and a distant boom sounded from the stairwell. Whatever was in the building with him wasn't done yet.

"What's going on?" Harry asked, his eyes wide.

Ben ignored his question. "I need to use your phone."

He didn't argue the point, just placed the phone on the edge of the desk. His stare didn't leave the gun in Ben's hand.

Let the old man piss his pants, Ben had bigger concerns. He picked up the receiver before he realized he didn't know who to call. *The police will think I'm crazy. They'll lock me up without even looking for Julia.* He remembered the note in his pocket with Regina's number on it and took it out, pounding the numbers in as the lights flickered again and loud crash arose from the stairs, much closer this time.

The phone rang five times before Regina picked up.

"Regina, I need your help."

Regina *tsked* at him. "I told you earlier, I don't know what you want from me."

"Listen, just listen—"

"Jesus Christ, Ben."

Harry stared at him. He sat so stiff in his chair he looked like a statue.

"Julia's gone. She took my car. I need you to come here and get me."

"What do you mean she's gone?" Urgency entered her voice.

"I mean she took my car and left. I think she went to the Home."

"What? Are you messing with me?" She breathed out hard through her nose. "Look, I want to help you, really, but this is crazy."

"Please."

Another boom from the stairwell, this time from the bottom.

"I think she might be having the baby. Something's wrong with her."

Harry finally plucked up enough courage to stand up. He stared at the stairwell door. "Hey. Listen, whatever is going on here, I'm calling the cops."

Ben ignored him. "I don't have anyone else. I'm begging you."

"I can't help you. This is crazy."

The words hit him like a blow to the chest. "I have nobody to turn to."

Her voice had been carefully emotionless, but she had apparently reached her limit. "This is fucking nuts. You need help." Another loud noise resonated from the stairwell. Harry's gaze darted from the door to the gun and back again. "I'm calling the police before you hurt yourself or someone else."

"Regina, listen—" Ben's words died in his mouth as a click marked the end of the conversation.

That's it. Declared crazy by the only friend he had in town as Julia moved further and further away. He wasn't though. He wasn't imagining the claw on his arm where the ghosts had held him, or the almost-there-thing that even now must be drifting down the stairs to get him.

"Give me the phone, son." Harry stared Ben in the eyes. His attention focused only on that and not on the gun hanging at Ben's side. Both of them jumped as another boom echoed in the stairwell.

The lights flickered overhead. On the edge of hearing, a whisper called from nowhere. He had nobody to turn to, no asylum to find. Everything was falling apart around him. His mind, his life, his family.

"I need help, Harry." His eyes misted over, and his breath became shallow. He wanted to break down and cry. "I can't do this on my own."

Harry remained tense, but his expression softened. "Just give me the phone, son. We'll call the police and get everything sorted out."

The police. He'd met the mayor on his first day at work. He'd seen the mayor and the police chief at that party. They were part of it. They knew what was happening. No harbor in this town could shelter Ben from the storm. If he wanted to find Julia, he was on his own. All the things he'd seen paraded in from of him in his mind. The phantoms in the dark. The endless arm reaching for him in the basement.

He wouldn't leave her to those things.

Ben dropped the phone. "I need your car."

"Hey, now. This doesn't have to get ugly." Harry raised his arms slowly, an old southern gentleman held up by a madman.

Ben suddenly remembered the gun in his hand, the killing tool he'd never felt comfortable keeping. He pointed it at Harry, though doing so made him sick. A doctor sticking up a security guard. The broken glass sloshed painfully in his head.

He'd do what he had to do. "Don't make this harder than it has to be. Give me your keys." A crash echoed from the stairs, and the elevator started dropping down faster than it should. Not free falling, but not going a floor at a time. "Give me your keys or I'm going to kill you." The words escaped his mouth before he thought them.

Harry shrank back against his chair. Ben didn't know if he was lying or not. He'd do anything for Julia. Anything.

"Alright." Harry started to shake. Ben recalled their first meeting, this kind old man welcoming them to their new home. "Don't kill me. I got a family." He reached into his pocket and pulled out a ring of keys, placing them slowly on the desk. "I got grandkids."

The elevator hit the bottom floor with a thud that vibrated the building. Both Ben and Harry looked over as all the lights in the lobby went out. "What's this about?" Harry asked.

Ben ignored him. His headache grew worse. The doors of the elevator began to open, but not on the automatic mechanism. They pried apart slowly, as if someone inside were opening them by hand. When they were halfway, they burst out, shaking the elevator as they slammed home into the walls.

"What's going on here?" Harry said.

Ben grabbed the keys off the desk as something moved inside the elevator. Not one something. A dozen somethings. A hundred. The dead party that had been in his apartment filed past them and out the lobby door. Whispers filled the room as they glided by unseen.

Ben's chest rose and fell as he started to hyperventilate. They were all around him. They closed in and suffocated him, trying to squeeze the will to live out of him. The whispers became an angry hiss in his ears.

"You're crazy."

"Too late to save anybody, can't even save yourself."

"You'll get Julia killed."

He pressed his eyes shut, trying to clear away the miasma. "Do you hear that? Do you see what's happening?"

Harry shook his head, but sweat poured off him. Even with only the dim light from outside illuminating the room, Ben could see the whites of Harry's eyes. He looked like a dog in a thunderstorm.

"Which car is yours?" Ben pushed everything else down. If he focused on it, if he let the voices in, he'd get lost in them and never find his way out. *Get out of my head. You're dead. You're all dead and rotten.* If they heard him, they paid no mind. The whispers continued.

"Br—Brown truck." Harry slumped back in his chair.

"Get out, Harry. Get out while you can." Ben ran from the building, the endless stream of dead breathing chills onto his neck.

It all stopped at the door. At the sudden change in atmosphere Ben stumbled and fell. He hit the ground heavy, his chin nailing the pavement and splitting open. Everything spun and his ears popped. Two people walking by on the street, a man and a woman, stopped. The young lady pointed at him and whispered something to her companion. Ben didn't notice. He lay face down on the concrete, the darkness of the lobby behind him beckoning. The ghosts wanted him back. They wouldn't come out, but they whispered to him, calling him.

"Aren't you tired of this? Wouldn't things be better in here?"

He shook as everything came back into focus, slowly at first and then quicker as he gathered himself up. The world wasn't better wherever those things lived. Both he and Theresa had seen through their veil. Any promise the dark things made was a lie. Maybe others couldn't see it, or maybe they didn't care.

He just wanted his family back. He stood and saw the brown truck parked near the front of the building. More people stopped and stared or just glanced as they walked by. He ignored them and climbed into the cab. Police sirens wailed in the distance. Maybe coming for him, maybe not.

Inside the truck smelled of dirt and old leather. Decades of hands had worn the steering wheel smooth. It had to be older than Ben. As he turned the engine over, he caught sight of the picture hanging from the rearview mirror. A slightly younger Harry with a whole gaggle of kids and young adults around him. He glanced back at the lobby. He didn't see anything, but he could sense it. Sense them. The puppets of the dark things gazing back at him from the darkness. He wanted Harry to be okay, but he wasn't going back in there to find out.

That thought hurt him as he backed out of the parking spot, the old truck sputtering but running strong. He'd threatened to kill the man and possibly left him to die. But he had to look after his family, he had to save them.

That meant going back to the Home.

The city and then the countryside slid by outside the windows. The road didn't provide any safety, and he hadn't expected it would. Shapes and shadows appeared and vanished on the shoulder. His headlights blinked out twice outside of the city, the second time almost leaving him in a ditch. He powered through, afraid to move on but more afraid to stop. It had touched him in the apartment, hurt him. Even now, the scratch on his arm pulsed as he gripped the wheel. Not daring to take his gaze off the road even to look in the rearview mirror, he fell inward to thought.

The stink of the urine covering his pants made him ill. More than anything else, that was a good indication that Regina might be right. He might have lost it. Wide-eyed, shaking, and covered in piss on his way to a mental institution to rescue his family from monsters.

"Please, God." He couldn't recall the last time he prayed. "Let Julia be okay. Please. Let all of this be over. Don't take her away from me."

Eddy had always laughed up his sleeve at religion. *"Prayer is the last bastion of the weak and the desperate."* Ben couldn't imagine himself more desperate, and he'd never felt so weak. Even when his dad died, even when his mom took her own life, he'd never been so hopelessly alone.

"Please, let all of this stop." His eyes misted as another shape half-formed on the side of the road in the darkness. It started as a patch of blackness on the ground, rose up as a kneeling man, and then melted back into the night. "Don't take her from me."

In some deep place, deeper than the thinking mind normally went, Ben knew it wasn't just about her. His sanity, his ability to recognize real from fiction, had been placed on the line. He had to be right, because if he was wrong, it was worse. It meant he'd done something terrible, and Julia had run away.

Whispers drifted in from outside his door. *"Just give up, Benji. Come home."* His mother's voice.

"Shut up." He caught sight of his red-rimmed, teary eyes in the mirror and quickly looked away. "I see what you are now. I see what you want. You won't get my family."

The voice laughed and faded into nothing behind him.

He wiped his eyes. He couldn't cry now. The dark things weren't done with him yet. He didn't need to hear voices on the side of the road to know that.

He didn't know what to do when he reached the Home. The gate would almost certainly be guarded. Six bullets and a beat-up truck weren't going to get him very far. For all he knew, they had guns too.

Another whisper came from outside the door, this one unidentifiable. He'd never been so tired. Every muscle in his body fought him for control. The only option that came to his addled mind was to sneak in. Park the truck up the road from the Home and climb the wall. Even once he got over it, he'd have to find a way inside.

One thing at a time.

His decision made and his resolve set, he continued toward the Home. The shadows on and around the road multiplied, and the whispers droned endlessly from the countryside around him. Something moved in the bed of the truck, but he wouldn't look. He wouldn't give it the satisfaction.

It wasn't going to stop him now.

He parked the truck on the side of the road and killed the engine. Nothing had appeared or whispered after he entered the forest. If seeing monsters was bad, not seeing them was worse. They were still around, still waiting at the edge of sense. But here, in their domain, they had fallen silent.

He took a deep breath and stepped out of the truck, holding the gun in his hand like a lifeline. The gate to the Home was right around the next bend in the road. He pocketed the keys and stepped into the absolute blackness of the nighttime Tennessee wilderness. The angry clouds overhead blocked the moonlight. He couldn't see his hand in front of his face, but he knew he wasn't alone.

He stumbled and broke branches, cut himself on foliage, as he slowly made his way through the brush. Stories came to mind of people getting lost in the woods at night. Direction became impossible to tell in the darkness when all the trees looked alike. He drew in a deep, shaking breath. He wouldn't get lost. He couldn't.

Seven feet tall and shrouded in shadows, a lumbering shape passed without making a sound only ten yards in front of him. It vanished behind a tree that should have been too small to cover its hulking form.

It's not real. He tried to convince himself. *It doesn't want me to get to Julia. It knows I'm close.*

He squeezed his eyes shut and willed it to be true, but the now dried and crusted cut on his arm disagreed. Those things could hurt him. For all he knew, they could kill him.

The sound of a panting creature running straight toward him raised the hair on his neck. He turned around, the gun pointed outward. The woods and twilight revealed nothing. Off to his left, a little closer, the panting thing ran by again. Ben spun to face it, his breath coming in ragged gasps. Again, nothing.

Caution gone, he turned back in the direction he'd started and ran. The sounds of pursuit sprang up all around him. Things on all fours, and bigger things that stomped with each step, hounded him. Branches and trees snapped and fell as they danced around him, toying with him. A crack like woody lightning ripped through the night. He tripped and stumbled, barely holding onto the gun. He hit the leafy floor of the forest hard enough to knock his breath from his chest.

It saved his life. A tree just in front of him slammed down close enough for its branches to tear into his face. It hadn't descended slowly, it had shot down hard. Something huge, impossibly large, had knocked it over as if it were a child's toy.

He stared at the tree on the ground in front of him. *They can do more than just hurt people*. Theresa had been wrong. She'd said that those things couldn't affect the world. These things walked in it as if they owned it, strode across its face.

He caught his breath, looking into the foliage. All the sound had ceased as abruptly as it started, but they weren't gone. They were never gone. They were brain aneurisms. Cancer. Madness. Endless anxiety in the back of the mind while humanity slept. The monster in every child's closet. The fear in every new parent's eyes when they looked down at their child and knew one day she would die. He couldn't win.

"Then why don't you come home, Benji?" His mother's voice again, or some cruel mockery of it. He shut his eyes as tight as he could, not wanting to see it take her shape. *"You started all of this. You came here. Isn't this what you wanted all along?"* Her voice bled down softly from the tallest tree and squirmed out from beneath the dirt. *"It's in your blood, Benji."*

He rose from the ground. He wouldn't respond. He wouldn't talk to it, wouldn't give it the power.

A small break in the clouds flooded moonlight through the trees. Behind every one stood a figure. The Hemsworth woman from the basement, her sagging flesh making her face look like a frown, peeked out from behind an oak. Robbie, pale and white-eyed, blood staining his gown. Ben's father, twisted and broken like the day he'd died in the car wreck stood on legs that couldn't possibly have supported his body. His mother, her arm up, her finger beckoning him, the cuts from her suicide standing out like exclamation points. A thousand more. All staring. All wanting.

His mind numbed at the sight. The cruel mockery of his dead family froze him in terror.

"Don't fight it."

"You can't win."

"Come home, Ben."

"We can be together, son."

They came closer with every word, drifting over the ground without moving. Beckoning. Needing.

It wasn't them. They were dead and rotting. Just the dark things pulling his strings, making him insane. "No!" He ran past them as they drifted closer and reached for him. His loved ones in a sick play of life, the same fakery he'd seen in the closets and doorways of the Home. The moonlight glinted off the top of the building in the distance. He could see it now. He made for it as fast as he could.

"Ben! Mommy misses you! Come back, Benji!" The voice fell into the distance behind him, but that was just an illusion. He could feel the thing on his heels, a cold breath on the back of his neck.

The lights of the building appeared through the forest as he drew closer. He could make out the wall. The Spanish moss. The cracks. The dark things circled around him, but made no move to stop him. He tripped again and caught himself before he fell. He needed to be out of the dark. Caught in the eternal gloom, the endless midnight, made it all worse. Being out there was no better than being stranded forever on the fourth floor. The image of him wandering the endless twilight of the hills and forests of Tennessee closed in on him, trapping him.

He approached the wall, but drew short, panting and glistening with sweat. He couldn't possibly jump it, but low branches from nearby trees grazed parts of it. One branch was only two feet above his head and sturdy enough to support him. He tucked the gun into his pants and grabbed the limb, drawing himself up and cutting his fingers on the bark.

It hurt, but he didn't care. Nothing hurt as much as being in this place. He had to find Julia and get out. He managed to climb onto the branch, which bent under his weight. From there he could almost reach the wall. He stretched for it.

"Don't go, Benji."

His mother stood just below, watching him with her pale eyes and bloodless face. He didn't mean to look, but he couldn't help it. She was only a few feet away. *"Don't leave your momma again."*

He glanced down at her, caught in her eyes. Only a truly terrible god could create a world where this could happen. Those eyes cut a hole in his heart. They tore out his grief and left it raw and fresh in his hands. The same old guilt and self-loathing stabbed at him as he stared down.

"Please, just go away." He tore his gaze away and reached for the wall, getting one arm and then another over the top and using it to steady himself as he stood. He started to pull himself over.

Her voice became higher and rough. *"Don't leave Mommy, Ben."*

The thing grabbed his foot and tried to pull him back over. Tugging at him like it had back in the apartment. The bones of its fingers locked into his muscle.

"No! Please! Stop!" He screamed at the thing that wore his mother's face. He tried to kick at it with his free foot, but his shoe passed right through. His breath came out as a terrified whine, a noise a child would make when he saw something he couldn't understand. "Get away from me!" His worst living nightmare, his mother come back to take her revenge for him leaving.

"You left me all alone. I died because you left me." Teeth bit down into the hard calf muscle, breaking through and pouring out hot blood. He screamed and pulled toward the wall with all his might, gaining a precious few inches.

The hands vanished. The teeth disappeared from his leg, leaving only pain. Still hyperventilating, he tugged himself over the wall, falling headfirst and tumbling down. He didn't care if he broke his neck. Death would be better than being here.

He bounced off the wall and managed to fall side-first instead of on his head. The ground rushed up and struck him, shooting a sharp pain up the entire left side of his body. He howled as he impacted, his ankle twisting the wrong way. Not breaking, but coming damn close.

He turned onto his back as soon as he caught his bearings, yanking the gun out of his belt and aiming it at the top of the wall behind him. Any second, his mother and father, Robbie and the other spirits of the Home, would rain on him like the wrath of an angry god.

It didn't happen. Nothing happened. He pointed his gun and waited anyway, shaking and panting. The endless calamity was more than any human was meant to bear.

After two full minutes of watching, his heart slowed a little, and his hand shook less. It wasn't following him. He'd made it to where he needed to be but never wanted to go. He took a deep breath and rolled over, getting his hands under him. His ankle threw lightning bolts of pain through his entire body.

He looked up at the Home. He'd come in at the side, where the parking lot was hidden from the front of the building.

There, sitting in the closest corner spot, was his red Sportwagon.

Chapter 15

Ben knew it would be there, but that didn't lessen the shock of seeing it. *This is really happening. Julia is inside there right now.* He stared at the car. She was there. She was inside, and whatever it was, it had her. Favoring his right leg, he limped over to the vehicle. He reached out with trembling fingers and touched it.

This is here. I'm not imagining this.

He leaned against the car. He'd made his bed by coming here, he'd created the situation, and now it was crawling back to him. *I should have listened to Julia. We should have gone to New York.*

Nothing on the dark property moved. The lights cast shadows from the hedges that bled off into the night. Soon, those things would come back for him. They wanted to finish it. How or why he couldn't fathom, but he knew with a certainty that chilled him to the bone. It wouldn't let him leave. Even now, they circled just outside of the range of human senses. Going round and round like a shiver of sharks. They had eternity, he didn't. For all he knew, it was already too late. Whatever terrible purpose they wanted Julia for might have already passed.

That thought drove him to action. He pushed off the car, wincing as some of his weight shifted onto his bad leg. He didn't have time to feel sorry for himself. Julia couldn't wait. The only action available was possibly the worst one.

He'd go through the front door.

The parking lot met the edge of the building. He staggered around the line of hedges that shielded it from view in front. He might have a gun, but it wouldn't do him much good if someone got the drop on him. He didn't see anyone out front, and he pressed on.

It occurred to him that he didn't just have a gun, he planned to use it. Shooting someone, or at least shooting at someone. His stomach did a flip at the image, and the shock of it made him lightheaded. Taking sight of an orderly running at him. The squeeze of the trigger and the stink of the gun smoke. *How did it come to this?*

He walked down the path toward the entrance. The sweat on his palm made the pistol grip slick. He fingered the cylinder as adrenaline built up. For all he knew, ten people were standing just inside the door. Ten people and six bullets. He breathed through it, moving closer and closer to the door. He had to come to terms with it, and fast. These things, and those people, hadn't hesitated to conspire against him. They hadn't thought of Julia's feelings when they did whatever they did to her.

He approached the portal, reaching out a shaking hand and grabbing the handle. Locked. He hadn't foreseen that. He considered what to do next. All the first-floor windows were barred, the doors far too thick to kick down, especially with a bad leg. Not knowing what else to do, he knocked. On the other side he heard the faint echo of it, but nothing more. He readied the weapon, squeezing it as hard as he could.

A heavy thud came from inside the door's handle as someone inside unlocked it. Ben's heart beat so hard he felt it in his fingertips. The headache that had started in his apartment throbbed in time. The door inched outward and then swung wide. A single orderly, an old man Ben didn't recognize, looked down at him. He opened his mouth to speak, but Ben pointed the gun at him before he had a chance.

"Move. Yell and you're dead."

The man stepped back into the lobby, slowly raising his hands over his head. Ben followed him in. He'd seen a bank robbery on television as a kid. The police surrounded the two men standing just outside the entryway to the First National Bank of Columbus. The men had looked terrified, like animals caught in a trap. Ben could appreciate that feeling.

There were four people in the lobby, not ten. A nurse sat behind the desk. Scott stood near the entrance to the west wing, Theresa just in front of him. All watched Ben walk slowly into the building.

"Benjamin?" Theresa squinted at him as if she couldn't believe what she was seeing. "Help me, please."

Scott held up a hand, and she closed her mouth. Her eyes spoke volumes. She was terrified. "What's going on, Doc?"

"Where's Julia?"

Scott shook his head. "I don't know what you're talkin' about."

A bold-faced lie. Adrenaline and fear made him jumpy. He switched the gun off the retreating orderly, focusing it on Scott. "Don't fucking lie to me. I saw the car!" Scott just shook his head again and took a small step toward Ben, who wiggled the gun at his chest. "One more step and I swear I'll kill you."

"I don't know what's going on here, but why don't you just put the gun down?" He licked his lips and raised his hands above his head. "Look, man. Look at what you're doing. Listen to yourself. Nobody here took your fiancée."

All the things that had terrorized him since the first day coalesced in his head. The things in the closets, the way the staff looked at him; all of it formed into a knot of rage in his guts. He didn't feel like himself. He was an other now, like a patient locked up in the Home.

"Why'd you take her? Were you after her the whole time?" He imagined his mother's voice in the woods, taunting him. "Did you want my baby? My fiancée? What the fuck are you people after?"

Scott opened his mouth to speak, but Theresa beat him to it. "Your baby?" She stared at him, puzzled. The light of recognition entered her eyes, followed by a stunned horror. "You brought a pregnant woman here?"

"Shut up," said Scott.

"After everything I told you?"

"I said shut"—Scott slapped her full in the face—"up."

Theresa staggered back a step and put her hands up. The nurse behind the desk gasped.

They didn't want him to know. Everyone else would lie to him. Theresa alone would tell the truth. "No. Let her talk."

Scott shook his head. "Listen to yourself, you—"

Ben walked forward, pulling the hammer back on the gun to emphasize his point like he'd seen in the movies. "If you touch her again, I'll kill you." He would too. He could feel it. After all the terrors of the last two weeks, he'd do anything to be done with this.

Scott's eyes went cold. He didn't like being threatened. *Good.* Ben didn't either. Maybe it was the adrenaline, or maybe the anger, but a giddiness rose up inside him. A delight at seeing the fear in these people.

He reminded himself that a gun didn't make him invincible, and there were things in the Home that didn't fear bullets. Still, these people had ruined his life and taken everything, from him in just a week. "What were you saying, Theresa?"

Theresa glanced at Scott, who never took his eyes off Ben. "They'll have her in the basement. How could you bring a child into this place?"

The sincere concern in her voice struck him. He hadn't known. He couldn't have known. Even now, he wasn't sure what was happening.

Scott spoke up as if he'd sensed Ben's doubts. "Look, Doc. You're listening to a woman who's been locked up in a mental ward for thirty years. A woman that killed her kid."

"Don't you talk about my family, you monster," Theresa said, turning on him.

Scott ignored her. "Look at yourself." He nodded at Ben, taking it all in. The scratches across his face and his arm. His gimpy leg and busted chin. The stains on his clothes and the smell of piss. "Just put the gun down. It isn't too late to make everything okay."

Theresa started screaming at Scott and pleading with Ben to help her. He couldn't hear any of it. Everything became silent as, for just a moment, Ben saw himself with perfect clarity. He really was listening to a mental patient. He could have let her get into his head. Julia could have come here on her own, scared and running when he started raving, having nowhere else to go. He might be just like his mother, but instead of killing himself, he could be terrorizing his family. He lowered the gun just a fraction.

The nurse stared at something behind him, but by the time he noticed, it was too late.

Everything rushed back into focus as the orderly that had answered the door tackled Ben around the middle, sending him sprawling. Ben held onto the gun, but it did little good as all the breath was knocked from him. They both hit the floor hard, Ben's head bouncing off it.

"No!" Theresa screamed.

343

Ben struggled with the man on the ground, trying to spin and face him. Dazed by his fall, he didn't see Scott approaching until he was right over him. Scott kicked for the gun, but Ben raised it and squeezed the trigger.

The shot hit Scott in the neck, and the room went still. Scott took a step back, his eyes wide. Ben looked up, and for the first time he saw it. The black spots in the eyes that Theresa had told him about. The place the soul used to be staring down from Scott's face.

Everything slowed down. Scott put both hands over the hole in his neck as blood flew all over Ben and the orderly. He watched Ben, his expression one of shock, even with the black eyes.

He'd just killed a man. Pointed a gun, pulled the trigger, and now he was watching him die. He wasn't a healer now, he was a killer. Shock numbed his whole body.

The nurse behind the desk screamed and ran toward the east wing, snapping him back into real time. Scott tripped over his feet and fell face first into a puddle of his own blood.

The remaining orderly grabbed Ben's hair and bounced his face off of the ground. His nose shattered and the gun went flying. Everything blurred as pain blossomed across his head and tears filled his eyes. The splash of blood on the ground had a spider web shape to it.

He was a doctor. This shouldn't be happening. None of this should even be possible.

"You bastard!" the orderly screamed. "You shot him!"

344

Ben struggled against the man's grip, but on his chest, on the ground, he couldn't do much. He wanted to apologize, to say he didn't mean it. It was all some big mistake. They'd wanted someone else. That gun—and the man who owned it—should never have come to Umber Gardens.

Instead, he struggled with the orderly, trying to get up so he could find his fiancée. He resisted as the orderly picked up his head with both hands and slammed it into the floor again.

"You motherfuck—" The orderly didn't get to finish the thought.

Inches from Ben's head, the deafening report of a gun firing blocked out all other sounds. Ben flinched, huddling closer to the ground, and cried out. The man on top of him went limp, and blood dripped down across Ben's head and onto the floor. Ben sat face down, trembling. He'd killed a man, and…

Someone spoke above him, but he couldn't hear. His ears rang from the gunshot. A slap in the back of the head bumped his face off the ground, stinging his broken nose.

"We have to go, now, Benjamin." A voice. Theresa's. Ben looked up. His broken nose blurred his vision, but he could make out Theresa standing above him, holding his pistol. The murder weapon.

"Get up!" She gripped his arm. She might be old, but her hands were still iron.

Ben rolled the body off him and stood on shivering legs.

"We need to go."

Scott still struggled in a spreading pool of his own blood. Weakly now, still trying to stop the bleeding, his legs kicking. His eyes had fixed on a point above Ben, staring at something he couldn't see. Maybe those black holes saw the many ghosts of the Home circling, swooping in to claim their newest prize. Ben couldn't tear his gaze away, couldn't stop the mad logic loop in his head. He'd killed a man. He had to do it. He'd killed a man. On and on it went.

Theresa slapped him across the face. The sudden jolt to his freshly broken nose made his eyes water. "We don't have time for that. Move!" She grabbed him with that iron grip and strode down the hallway behind the desk, Ben limping along just behind. He took one last look behind him.

Scott had stopped moving.

They navigated the big hall and branched off into a smaller one. It took Ben a moment to realize she had no idea where they were going. He stopped her. "What are we doing, Theresa? Where were they taking you?"

She turned to him, the look in her eyes crazed. "The basement. We're going to the basement. They said they had a surprise for me down there." She narrowed her eyes at him. He could see sadness there, an old pain hiding and waiting. "You brought a pregnant woman here?" The shock in her voice hadn't diminished.

"I… I didn't know."

She slapped him again. "I warned you," she shouted. "I told you that you were in danger. I told you what happened to me."

She had, but he hadn't put it all together. He hadn't believed her. Now that disbelief would ruin his life. It already had. "I'm sorry." He wasn't just apologizing to her, but to Scott as well.

"Couldn't you sense this place? What it was?"

He could, yes. He sensed it from day one, and yet he stayed on. His mind still tried to tell him it wasn't real, even after everything he'd seen and done. He was just as crazy as she was. Julia was the only thing keeping him going. "What are they doing to her?"

Theresa gazed into his eyes. "How far along is she?"

Ben shrugged and shook his head. "Any day now. Why?"

She stared for a moment longer before looking away. She furrowed her eyebrows and looked down at the ground.

"Why? Why does it matter?"

The way she turned away scared him. "They're going to do to her what they did to me."

Ben leaned away from her. "What? What does that mean?"

"They'll get inside of her. Get inside of your baby. It'll be born into this world."

"No. This isn't real. This isn't happening."

She raised her hand to slap him again, but lowered it as she stared, the pity plain in her eyes. "Yes, it is."

He thought of the crib in the baby's room and the park where he would have liked to walk him. All the things they would do together. He imagined himself and Julia watching as Little Ben graduated from college and started a family of his own. All gone. "Can we stop it?"

She turned to walk away. "We can try."

Ben placed a hand on her shoulder. "This way." He hadn't been at the Home very long, but he knew the way to the basement. It pulsed in his mind like a beacon.

Ben peeked around the corner and then moved back into the larger hallway, Theresa just behind. Shouting emanated from the direction of the lobby, but he saw no one.

He'd killed a man. Even now, the police would almost certainly be on the way; if Regina or Harry hadn't already called them. If they weren't in on the whole thing. If this conspiracy, this cult, ran all the way to the roots of Umber Gardens, there might not be a way out. He might make it to the basement and find Julia, but they had nowhere to go after. No place to hide from his crime.

"What are we going to do?"

"What do you think?"

He closed his eyes and took a deep breath before moving into the next hallway. Anything could be out there. The rules of reality no longer applied to this place. "I mean after. If we get Julia and get out."

"I'm not staying here another day."

Escape. Get out of the Home, a mental patient fleeing from confinement. "Go where exactly? Do what? You've killed three people." Scott kicking in a puddle of his own blood flashed through his mind. "I'm not better off."

"Then lie down and die, Benjamin. Take this gun and blow your goddamn brains out. I'm not letting that thing have its way. Not after everything it did to me and my family." The conviction in her voice, the venom, terrified him. Even if she was right about everything, she wasn't sane.

There was nothing to say. She was right of course. None of that mattered now. For all he knew, it was already too late to save Julia. That twisted his guts. He couldn't picture his life without her. It would be the end.

Voices rose and fell behind them. Ben moved as quickly as he could on his bad leg. Theresa still had the gun, and he had little doubt that she would use it if needed. What scared him more was the silence, the pressure building by the minute. The things from outside weren't gone, they were lurking. Waiting for the moment to strike.

"It's going to try and stop us," Theresa said. "Are you ready for that?"

He nodded, but he didn't feel ready. This old woman had steel in her. With her jaw set and her eyes narrowed, she looked like rage incarnate.

"Why isn't there anyone here?" Ben asked. The sounds of talking and shouting in the distance had all but totally faded. They were alone. "Why isn't anyone trying to stop us?"

Theresa ignored him and strode toward the door. He followed. It stood wide open, propped with a doorstop, almost as if inviting them in. The closer they drew, the colder it became. By the time they reached the door, Ben could see his breath. The ghosts were thick here, so thick they brushed against his skin, puckering it up into gooseflesh. "Do you feel that?"

"Yes." She stared ahead as they passed the threshold and into the hallway. "They're close now." She turned to look at him. "We have to stop this, here. If one of those things comes into this world, it'll make what Hitler did look like a car accident. They'll wash over everything like a plague. Do you understand what's at stake?"

He nodded.

"Do you understand why we have to do this?" Even through all the anger and determination, he could see the sadness in her eyes. This woman had lost everything. In another time, she might have really been Saint Theresa. Here and now, she was just a murderer and a madwoman. "God can forgive the righteous of anything, but he hates cowards."

She walked forward, returning to the task at hand. At the end of the hallway, only one flashlight remained on the hook. Ben took it and flipped it on. There were no lights down the stairs, and a foul smell rose from beneath them. Rotten eggs. Sulfur. The stink of decay. Gray tendrils of mist swirled in the beam of the light as he pointed it down. Theresa descended without hesitation. Ben followed reluctantly. For anyone but Julia he would have turned and left, but she needed him, and she was down there.

The room at the bottom was black as pitch, but he sensed movement in the darkness. Things flitted at the edge of vision. When he swept the flashlight past, they vanished.

Other things didn't. He briefly illuminated faceless people before they disappeared, their bodies opaque and deformed. When the light flashed past the walls, the shadows didn't fade and vanish.

350

They bled upward, a rainstorm in reverse. Seeing it froze Ben's blood in his veins and brought tears to his eyes. Even if it was real, it was still madness.

"Don't look. Don't pay it any attention. That gives it power, and the last thing it needs right now is more of that."

She moved on, and deep inside he found the will to follow.

Theresa apparently knew her way, because she led. The edges of the room bled blackness that flowed on the ground in streams. The gurneys and wheelchairs that littered the path contained silently thrashing phantoms. The long dead pleaded and reached for him, demanding an end to their eternal torment that he couldn't grant. He couldn't look away. He couldn't unsee them as Theresa pulled him ahead with her inexorable march forward.

A scream, not from anything living, ripped apart the quiet. It echoed off the walls and bounced back, never fading, just moving further off.

"What is that? What are these things?" Ben's hands shook so terribly that the beam of the light danced.

"The unquiet dead. Pay them no mind."

Even if he could have obeyed, there was no ignoring what came next. A groan, impossibly loud from something inconceivably large, exploded from below. Ben braced himself against a wall, thinking it was an earthquake. It grew deeper, as if some great animal below screamed in rage. The quaking moved the floor violently, nearly tumbling him over. A stream of the flowing blackness, silky but cold as ice, touched his hand. He jumped back, dropping the light.

By some small miracle, it didn't break. "Steady, Benjamin. We're close now." Theresa's voice scared him as much as anything. She didn't sound like herself. She wasn't a mental patient anymore, she was a British lord on safari, out to hunt monsters. She was Ahab, and she'd found her whale.

He considered going back. He could turn around and get out. Run away somewhere where the police would never search, and the Home would never find him. Find a place where nothing like this could ever happen again.

Instead, they pressed on. The passages they took, a twisting warren beneath the Home, began to look familiar to him. With a sense of déjà vu, he realized he'd been there in a dream. The one with his mother and Robbie. They'd shown him the path to the cave and then to a room full of pipes. They'd told him to burn the place down. He wished he'd listened.

"I dreamed this." His voice quivered as he spoke. "I dreamed about the basement, and about the things here. Robbie and my mother told me to burn the place down."

She stopped for the first time and faced him. "You should have listened. There's power in dreams. Sometimes they show us what we need to know. Do you remember anything else?"

The figure of a man, its eyes missing, moved behind her. He shut his own, determined to block it out. "A room full of pipes."

They were close now. The shadows grew so thick that they formed a fog. Ben and Theresa rounded the last corner and faced the hole in the wall that led to a stone cavern beyond. The wall had been blasted apart from inside at some point in the past. Pieces of broken masonry covered the floor. It was a dead end, and it looked as if the room had never been used for anything. Ben wondered if it had been there even when this was a hospital, or further back when it was a house.

Torchlight flickered inside the cave. The shadows and the bleeding walls came to a stop at the edge. Sacred ground. A place where not even ghosts dared to tread. Voices, a chant of some kind, rose from below.

"This is it." She looked him in the eyes. "I don't know what's down there. I don't know if your wife is alive or if it already has your baby. But if it does, we have to finish this. Do you understand?"

It took him a moment to realize what she was implying. "You want to kill my baby?" Just saying the words weakened his knees.

She shook her head, but the fire didn't leave her gaze. "I'll do what needs to be done to stop this. I sacrificed everything to make sure it didn't work last time. I'll do it again."

Underneath all the fear and insanity, a part of him knew it had to end here. If the thing could do this when it was trapped, he could only imagine what it might do if free. The havoc it could cause. But to understand and to accept were two different things. This was his family, not some theoretical unseen monster. His fiancée and their little boy. The one he wanted to walk through parks with. The one he'd killed a man for.

As if on cue, Scott's voice drifted out of the dim black fog. *"You killed me. You were supposed to help people."*

Ben shut his eyes tight, trying to block it out. Trying to numb the hole in his heart.

"Do you understand what I'm telling you?" When he didn't respond, she continued, "We'll save your child if we can."

"I'm not going to let you kill my son." The words were out before he could even consider them. There was no discussion on the subject.

"It'll be a monster. A thing. It won't be your baby boy. It'll look human enough, but the first chance it gets, it'll kill you and come back here. It'll grow up surrounded by the people who brought it into the world, and I have no doubt it'll turn on them too."

She hadn't come down here to help him, she'd come down here to get her revenge. It had locked her up for thirty years, and she would make it pay.

"There has to be another way." He became uncomfortably aware of the gun in her hands. Still four shots left.

She stood deep in thought, considering his words. She looked at him, but didn't see him. She was somewhere else. Maybe thirty years in the past seeing it all play out again. Maybe wishing she'd tried something else then. This crazy old woman wasn't going to kill Julia or Little Ben. She'd have to kill him first.

"This is pointless. We're wasting time." She passed through the cave entrance. He limped in behind her.

The sudden cold reminded him of a meat locker. The place where you keep the dead until you're ready to cut them up. The thought nearly made him ill, and he reached out to steady himself on the wall.

It burned him so badly that the flesh actually sizzled, the wall as hot as a stove. Ben recoiled, horrified. He glanced over to see that Theresa had gone further down the steep downward slope. Torchlight flickered in the distance. With a look at his already blistering hand, he pursued her.

The cave was roughhewn, unnatural. The stone, in an almost octagonal shape, looked as if something huge had burrowed through the ground in some distant, unknowable past. *What could have made something like that?* The size of such a creature terrified him just to think about it. He imagined seeing it at the bottom of the tunnel, waiting for him with an open maw. He thought of it cast down from the outermost reaches of the universe and slammed into the ground miles below Tennessee to live out a sentence for some unimaginable crime.

Another groan shook the cavern, echoing off the walls. He closed his eyes and stopped himself from touching the burning stone again just in time. He wanted it to be a dream. He wanted to wake up in his bed and find Julia next to him. Another nightmare was better than facing this.

As the last echo faded, he heard voices further down. He opened his eyes to discover he'd lost sight of Theresa.

Going faster now, afraid of what she might do, Ben tried to catch up. He passed the first torch, set into an iron sconce on the wall. They became more regularly placed, and the dim light revealed a type of black stone Ben had never seen before. The path curved gently, but ahead it turned sharply to the right. Theresa stood there, gun in hand, staring at whatever was past that point.

The voice could be heard clearly now, though the language was a mystery. He could almost recognize the speaker, but the foreign tongue's guttural sounds masked him.

The words conjured a deep disquiet. Images of sleek gray creatures running through forests of endless nights filled his head. Snakes with the heads of men working deep below the world, mining its core to make room for their masters. A great black shape rose from a hole in the center of New York, its flesh covered in teeth and eyes. The sounds and images were almost hypnotic, lulling him into a nightmare from which he'd never escape.

When the chanting stopped, Howerton's voice snapped Ben out of it. "Drop the bowl."

White-hot rage replaced fear in an instant. If Ben checked the trail of paperwork that had led to the Home hiring him, he bet he'd have found Howerton at the end. That man had ruined his life and taken his family.

He limped the last of the way to the turn in the cave. Around the corner, the tunnel continued for another thirty feet. It rose into a cavern that stretched up into a ceiling lost in darkness. At the far end of the room, torchlight revealed a gigantic black pit, a cliff to nowhere.

Howerton stood just behind Julia, who teetered dangerously, as if unaware how close she was. Vitalie stood on one side, his arms raised. On the other side was an old man Ben recognized from the dinner.

For a moment, he saw nothing but Julia. Her gentle sway, as if she were listening to music only she could hear. The crazy set of her hair. The robe in which she'd left the apartment. His heart ached watching her. He'd failed her miserably by allowing everything to come to this.

He grabbed the gun from Theresa's hand. She resisted, but he tugged it away from her. "Howerton!"

All three men turned. The expression on Howerton's face— eyebrows raised, eyes wide circles of surprise—made it clear he hadn't expected Ben. He looked past Ben at Theresa, then turned his attention back. Julia didn't move. She swayed gently back and forth, listening to the music for only the crazy and the damned.

"Get the hell away from her." Ben pointed the gun at Howerton.

Howerton glanced down at the weapon as if it were an extended hand he didn't feel like shaking. "You're interrupting something beyond your understanding, Dr. Kent."

Ben laughed. "You sick fuck. Get away from her. Now." He raised the gun higher.

Another groan from below, down that hole at the end of the room, shook the cave. Whatever this thing was, it wasn't far. Ben's headache exploded into a dozen tiny stars that danced in front of his eyes. His vision blurred. He stepped back, nearly falling over. He thought he might be having a stroke. That would be a great cosmic joke. Murdered by his body instead of the dark things. He kept the gun raised, but he could barely make out Howerton's shape.

When the groan passed, Theresa spoke behind him, but Ben didn't hear her. Once his vision returned to normal and the ringing in his ears stopped, he heard her repeat, "Don't listen. It gets in your head."

"You can hear it, can't you? You've seen it and heard its song. You are gifted. I knew you would be. That's why I chose you. You and your family fulfilled all the requirements. Can't you see what a great honor this is? Don't you understand what this means? You could be royalty in a new order. You could be the father to the ruler of the world." Howerton took a step forward.

"Don't move." Ben stood up straighter. He'd seen the thing. He'd heard its song. It wasn't a savior, it was a monster. "It's evil. I've seen it." He'd seen its true face. The black spots where the souls used to be.

Howerton tilted his head back to the ceiling and laughed as the other men looked on. When he returned his gaze to Ben, the same blackness Ben had seen in Scott's eyes was there. Unfathomable malice. An endless dark that made the night sky bright as day in comparison. "You are a child, and this is beyond you." His words echoed in the room.

Theresa stepped next to Ben. "Don't listen! Shoot him."

"Quiet!" Howerton's words drifted slowly to them, as if they were spoken underwater.

Theresa fell backward, landing hard and letting out a gasp of pain. Ben's ears rang. The room drifted away, and a loud keening masking everything. Behind it, far in the distance, Ben heard a woman singing. A slow siren song, dashing on the rocks all who came to her.

Howerton's voiced wafted to him over the ringing. "This is silly, Dr. Kent. We're all family here. You remember your family, don't you?" His voice poured from his mouth like honey and milk. He was right. With a voice like that, he couldn't be wrong.

Howerton moved a single step closer. Ben raised the gun to shoot, but he was so tired. His arms were heavy, and everything hurt. He didn't see the point anymore. There was no escape from this place. Theresa had said it herself: There was no happy ending to this story.

"You've been running your whole life. Aren't you tired?"

He *was* tired. So damned tired of everything. The endless tragedies, the eternal fear. Existence was one long attempt to hold onto things that always fell away, doomed to failure before it even began.

Ben's mind lulled as Howerton spoke in a hypnotic tone. His words came from the air all around. "What did you hope to accomplish here? Were you going to save the day?"

He was right. Nothing could ever be the same after this.

"You couldn't even save your mother."

Ben lowered the gun and stared at it. He could put it in his mouth and end all his problems now. One single, infinitesimally small second of pain and his troubles were over. He raised the weapon slowly, putting it to his temple. The great family tradition, ending too soon. Sparing yourself the pain of living. He stared at Julia across the room. She didn't turn around. She didn't as much as look at him. She didn't need him anymore.

"Yes. Let it be over now. We'll take care of everything."

Chapter 16

Ben's hand shook as the cold metal of the barrel pressed against his temple. He wanted this. He needed this.

"There you go. We'll take care of everything. Don't worry."

A hand closed around the one holding the gun. Theresa. She pulled it away from him, and the illusions fell apart like a dandelion in a windstorm. Ben snapped out of it as the man next to Howerton moved toward them. In panic, Ben pointed the weapon, tearing it from Theresa's grasp, and fired.

The shot missed by a mile, but the man jumped back. Another roar swept out of the hole in the floor, louder than the first. "Get him!" Howerton screamed over the cacophony.

The man dashed forward, but too late. Ben didn't miss with the second shot, which struck the man dead in the chest. He looked down at the gaping hole left by the bullet and took two steps back. With a horrified expression, he fell to his knees, then to his side. His black eyes drilled into Ben, open wide and seeing nothing as he moved no more.

Ben stared at what he'd done. Howerton paid it no mind. He ground his teeth, his expression full of rage. Ben didn't notice it at all. Two men dead by his hand. He really was a madman.

"Stephen." Theresa stepped forward. "You're going to pay for what you did to me. You're going to pay like Eric did."

Howerton smiled his condescending smile. "You think this is over?"

Ben gazed down at the gun. The damned thing was heavy. They never looked heavy, but once you picked them up, the gravity really settled in. A killing tool. Nothing good came from them. They had one reason to be, and they served that purpose well.

"Just put it down, son," Howerton said.

The light became too bright. Ben looked up to find himself in the lobby. Scott kicked weakly in the ever-spreading pool of blood. Dr. Vitalie had his hands over the wound, but it wasn't helping. A nurse nearby held her hands in the air as if she was being robbed. He didn't know how he'd gotten there. The fog of memory was thicker than usual. He recalled leaving the apartment with Julia.

No. That's not right. Julia ran away from me.

It all came flooding back. She'd run away, terrified of him screaming at the monsters in the apartment. She stood by the desk in the lobby now, crying. The older nurse, the one with the attitude, had her arms around Julia.

"This doesn't have to go any further. You're ill, Dr. Kent. We can get you help."

Theresa was nearby, two orderlies holding her in place. "Don't listen, Benjamin! It's a trick!" She struggled against them, but she was an old woman, and they were healthy men.

"What—" He lifted the hand with the gun, and everyone stepped away from him. Julia cowered behind the nurse. "Julia?" She wouldn't even look at him. "What's going on?"

"Please, Ben." Her voice cracked when she spoke. "Just put down the gun. Don't hurt anyone else." Her words were thick with tears.

"I didn't…" But he had. He'd shot Scott in the neck and watched him bleed. He'd created an elaborate fantasy, and now he was killing for it. The doctor in him, the healer, recoiled in horror. This wasn't who he was or what he did. "I don't know what's happening." He rubbed his face with his free hand.

"No! Listen to me. It's a trick. You're in the basement. They're trying to kill your family!" Theresa really looked like a madwoman now. Her hair flew out in all directions, and the circles under her eyes were as heavy as his own. She couldn't hide her mania. "They'll kill her!"

Julia doubled over as a fresh wave of contractions hit. Ben sucked in his breath as she grimaced in pain. "Julia!" He looked around at the assembled medical staff. "Someone help her!"

Nobody moved. They all stared at him, the crazy man with a gun. Scott's kicks weakened and grew further apart. He would be dead within minutes.

"Somebody do something!"

Howerton gestured to get his attention. "Listen, Dr. Kent. This doesn't need to end violently. I know things seem bad right now, but there is help." He put his hand out but didn't move closer. "Give me the gun. We can sort this out and get help for both of them. Just hand me the weapon."

That weight in his hand was an awful burden he didn't want anymore. He'd never really wanted it to begin with. "I don't know what's happening to me." Everything hurt. His nose throbbed in agony, and his leg ached as if a car had hit it. That hadn't been in his imagination; he'd felt those. He'd seen the dark thing pretend to be his mother in the woods outside.

For just a second, the world split in two. He saw himself standing in the lobby, holding the gun at his side. Only the smallest distance away from it, he saw himself in the basement, in that cavern. Howerton walked slowly toward him in both places, his black eyes gleaming.

Everything snapped back and he was just in the lobby again, terrified and surrounded by people.

Howerton took a few more steps, his hand still out. "Just listen to my voice. You're sick. You didn't understand what you were doing. You're seeing things clearly now. If you hand me the gun and let us help you, we can make all of this end. You want it to end, right?"

Ben did want it to end, but Howerton's words touched on something else. They'd been in the basement. Howerton wanted Ben to kill himself. He'd said it would feel good. Ben shook his head and aimed at Howerton. "I know what this is." His face twisted into a mask of agony. "I'm not crazy! I'm not!"

Howerton stopped, uncertain. "Just relax, Ben."

"What's wrong, Ben?" The snarky tone at the dinner rang in Ben's ears. Howerton had said his name like a curse.

"Don't call me that! You don't know me!" He screamed it so hard he felt his face turn red. Julia wept as she grabbed her abdomen.

"Yes! Look at them, Benjamin. Look close." Theresa struggled against the men holding her. One clamped a hand over her mouth.

The normally bright lobby became too dim. Most of the lights had gone out. What was left flickered like firelight. The ceiling wasn't a ceiling anymore, but the roof of a cave. Behind the desk a massive hole gaped in the floor, leading down to endless horror. The prison of some unknowable thing.

Fresh, burning anger kindled in Ben's chest. They wanted him to think he was crazy. From the first day, they'd been torturing him; first trying to get him to their side, then attacking him when they couldn't. "I see what this is! You want to get into my head?"

Howerton backpedaled, moving closer to the hole in the floor. "Don't do anything rash, Dr. Kent." He raised his hands over his head as the floor beneath him turned to stone. Julia stood behind him, but the nurse vanished along with the orderlies. They were back where they'd been. Back in the real world.

Rage clawed its way up Ben's throat. All that fear. All that anxiety. All of it just fuel for his fury. "You like to play games with people?" Maybe something drove their actions, maybe not. Maybe they couldn't control themselves, and once that thing got inside, you became its puppet. They were the ones hurting Julia though. Their hands tried to take her from him.

Howerton showed Ben his palms as if he were surrendering. "Dr. Kent, please. You've let Theresa Parker get into your head. She's done it before. She killed a nurse she'd sucked into her delusions. She's very charismatic. Think about it. Think about what you're doing!"

All the illusions had vanished. Julia stood still as stone near Howerton. They weren't in the lobby, and nobody was with Howerton except Vitalie, who stood quietly nearby, watching.

Ben snarled at Howerton as the torchlight reflected in the blackness of his eyes, the holes where his soul used to be. "Let's see how you like it when someone gets inside your head."

Three feet away, Ben couldn't miss. He squeezed the trigger, and in a flash, the left side of Howerton's face vanished, replaced by a ragged red crater in his skull. His mouth moved open and closed, looking every bit like the puppet he was. He took one jittery step forward, and fell backward onto the stone.

The shot echoed around the room and faded. The smell of gun smoke filled the air as Ben stared at the remains of the man who'd tried to take everything from him. Another roar shook the world. Angry this time. Vengeful, but powerless.

Theresa walked toward Vitalie. He fell to his knees in front of the pit as she approached, quaking in fear. Even through the black of his eyes, something human shined. He folded his hands in front of him in a prayer position. His mouth contorted into frown.

"Please. I didn't want to do any of this. It gets inside of you. It makes you think what it thinks and want what it wants."

Ben never tore his gaze from Howerton's corpse. Pink bits of brain had sloshed out of his cranial cavity and onto to the floor. A puddle of blood, not unlike the one around Scott, formed beneath him. "You think that excuses you? You think that makes this okay?" Despite his harsh words, his anger was spent, replaced by a nervousness that made his hands shake.

"Julia?" Ben went and grabbed her around the waist, pulling her away from the edge of the chasm. She looked at him, a hint of recognition touching her features. "It's okay." He brushed a sweat soaked piece of hair from her eyes. Her vacant expression struck him like a blow to the chest. She didn't know who he was.

Then, as if a shadow had passed from over her eyes, she saw him. "Ben?" Her gaze darted around their surroundings. That moment of recognition ended, replaced by fear. "Where are—" She doubled over in pain, clutching her abdomen just as she had in his nightmare vision. "I think he's coming, Ben."

He hoped she meant their baby. He gently held her wrist, taking her pulse. "It's okay. We're going to get you out of here." Her heartbeat was erratic and weak. They needed to get her to a hospital, and fast.

Vitalie kept talking, even though Ben wasn't listening. "I couldn't help it." He looked down at the ground, avoiding Theresa's stare as she came closer. "You can't control yourself when it's in you. Please. Please, help me."

Ben shook his head. There couldn't be a God in Heaven if things like this happened on Earth. All of it was pointless. People were just pawns in a nightmare game. He guided Julia toward the cave entrance. She screamed as another wave of contractions wracked her body.

"I can help you!" Vitalie yelled at Ben. "I can help her!" He pointed at Julia.

Ben turned toward him, but Theresa was already standing in front of Vitalie. She looked down at him, her face twisted by disgust. "This is for my baby, Vincent."

"Don't!" Ben yelled. Vitalie had said the only thing Ben cared to hear, but it was too late. He tried to rise, but she moved fast for an old woman. Her kick couldn't have been very hard, but it was enough. Vitalie tripped backwards, but there was no ground to catch his fall. He screamed as the black pit swallowed him. He never hit the bottom. Maybe there was no bottom to find. His cries just faded into the distance.

"Why?" Ben stomped toward Theresa as another roar rattled the Earth. "Why! He could have helped us!" He took her by the shoulders and spun her around. He didn't know what would happen to Julia, and she'd just thrown off a cliff the last man who might. He shook her and ground his teeth. He wanted to throw her off after him.

She looked him dead in the eyes, not shying away from his pain. "They lie. If that thing is in her"—her gaze drifted past Ben to Julia, still standing by the entrance to the cave—"then it's too late."

Julia let out another scream. He let go of Theresa and ran back over to her. He'd never heard a cry of pain like that before. Birth was painful, but not like this. Julia's whole body shivered as if she were in the throes of a seizure. The events of the last few weeks had rendered him helpless, and this was no different. Doctor or not, he couldn't help her. "What can we do?"

Theresa stared down into the pit. She was in another world, far away. "We burn it down. We kill it before it gets out." When she looked up at Ben, sadness darkened her eyes. "Burn the building to the ground." The words from the dream of his mother and Robbie echoed back at him. Theresa walked over and gently took Julia from him. "Collapse the whole thing on top of it."

"Will that kill it?" He couldn't lose Julia too. Not after all of this. He wanted to drop to his knees and pray that God would deliver him, but he wasn't sure he believed in God. There were twenty patients upstairs, and who knew how many staff members, but he didn't care. They could all burn if it meant saving her. He'd do anything to make the suffering stop.

"I don't know that anything can kill it. I don't know if it's alive. But it may stop it." Theresa caught his stare with hers. "We're out of options. If it's inside her. It might already be too late."

He knew what he had to do. "Don't hurt her." He didn't want to leave his fiancée with this woman, this mad old lady who'd killed

369

two people right in front of him, but he had to. There was no coincidence here, and no choice. He'd seen it in his dreams. Ben reached into the pocket of Julia's robe, relieved to find the keys to their car. "Take these. It's the red car parked in the corner of the lot. Go left when you get out of the building. Do you know how to drive?"

Theresa took the keys. "I can manage."

"Will you be able to get out on your own?"

"We're its mothers. It won't hurt us."

He shuddered at her words, his skin dancing under his clothes. The idea that an unknown monstrosity had violated his fiancée nauseated him. "There are people up there too." He opened up the gun's chamber, examined the inside, and slammed it closed. "Two shots left." He handed her the weapon.

She looked down at it and back up at him. "Are you certain?"

He wasn't, but he didn't care what happened to him as long as Julia escaped. He'd known it all along, but to act on it made his head spin. "If you hurt her, I'll find you." The threat was empty. He didn't think he would be walking away.

She took the pistol. "I won't."

He guided them up the slope of the cavern and back into the basement. Julia could barely walk, and both he and Theresa supported her. His mind filled with images of Theresa dropping her, unable to pick her back up. Of Julia giving birth to their baby with a face like the phantoms he'd seen, or horns sprouting from its head, tearing Julia apart. He pushed them out as best he could and grabbed a torch from the wall.

"Take this." He gave her the flashlight as she took one of Julia's arms under her shoulder. Julia cried out in pain as she leaned against Theresa. The old woman looked ridiculous. Carrying a woman giving birth, with a gun in one hand and a flashlight in the other. "Get her to a hospital. Don't wait for me." He took a torch off the wall.

He felt it, from his skin to his bones. This was the only way. If he could bring the place down as he'd been told to in his dreams, if he could crash it on top of the hole where that thing lived, it might cut off its connection to the outside world. It might save his baby. It might end this.

Theresa nodded, holding his gaze for a moment longer. Without a word she shuffled off the way they'd come. He watched them go, the torch casting everything in shade.

Alone again. The invisible party waited in the corners and cracks. He felt them pressing in. Just inches away from him, taunting him. They would be angry at the violation of the sacred place below. They would come for him.

He moved in the opposite direction from Theresa. *Let them come.* Nothing would stop him.

371

Chapter 17

The walls that far into the basement were bare brick with old drywall crumbling in huge chunks. The ceiling overhead was devoid of any attempt to cover up the floor above or the bundles of pipes and wires that ran throughout. Shadows hung from the ceiling like cobwebs, dripping blackness down onto the floor. In other places, they moved up the wall, creeping slowly; a wound bleeding in reverse. The shades of people moved along the brick. Murals come to life for some unspeakable purpose, their features obscured in the darkness. When the light of the torch touched them they melted away and reappeared further down the passage. He tried to keep his gaze ahead.

"Haven't you hurt your momma enough?" a voice whispered behind him. He shut his eyes, wishing it away. *"You'll kill me twice, Benji."*

Her voice took on the same harsh tone it had outside. *"You'll hurt Mommy."*

The unmistakable certainty that a claw was reaching for the back of his neck overcame him. He spun, expecting to see the dark puppet of his mother bearing down on him.

Instead, he stood in the hallway to the east wing on the first floor. A woman sang from somewhere behind him, far away and sad. Clumsy hands slammed on a piano, accompanying the singing with a jarring melody that scratched at the inside of his skull. He could see the lobby from where he stood. Scott's still form soaked in a pool of its own blood. Howerton lay face down, part of his skull missing. Vitalie's body was nearby, his neck twisted at an obscene angle.

Ben closed his eyes to make it all go away, but when he opened them, it hadn't. He let out a soft groan. "It's not real. It's not real."

He shut them tighter, willing it away. When he looked again, the hallway in the basement was empty, with no sign that he'd been anywhere else. He turned back to press on, but something blocked his path. A wall of blackness that his light didn't penetrate.

One great yellow eye, as big as Ben's head, opened at the top of the mass. It blinked once, and a thin line he hadn't noticed before yawned wide halfway down. Rows of dull black teeth gleamed in a hole that descended forever.

Ben froze. All the laws of reality were so casually cast aside that he must have lost his mind. No other explanation made sense. His fear had gone so deep that it emerged on the other side in a place where nothing was real anymore, taking him along for the ride.

He stepped back, trying to distance himself from the dark thing, but it drew closer. He tripped over a broken piece of masonry, falling and landing hard on his tailbone. An explosion of pain ripped through his wounded leg.

"You aren't real!" He denied it, refused to accept it, but it kept coming.

He thought of Julia and their baby. He hoped they'd get out. It was all he could muster anymore. The calm he felt as the thing swooped in surprised him. He thought there would be fear, but there was just a feeling of acceptance, not unlike what he imagined the Buddha would have felt on his deathbed. The only weapon he had left was his light.

Out of options, and out of time as it closed in, he reared back and threw his torch at it. The one eye widened as the flame passed through it. Another scream came from below, this one long and angry, as the shadow thing shattered into scraps of night and fluttered into the darkness.

The pieces vanished one by one, leaving the hallway clear. The moving shadows on the wall evaporated into nothing. The clouds of blackness that hung overhead broke apart and disappeared. The sensation of someone breathing down his back stopped as abruptly as it started. He exhaled heavily, his heart beating so hard it hurt, waiting for the monster return.

After a long moment, nothing came.

He didn't want to get up. Life had shit on him since day one. He'd never stood a chance. Nothing good would ever come for him. It was in his blood, written large across the stars that marked his birth. He'd been fucked from the word go. Poor white trash with a dead dad before middle school and a suicide for a mother.

"Why does it have to be like this?" His voice sounded rational. Scholarly. A man asking a question of a wizened sage.

The answer didn't come from any of the things in the Home, but from the distant past. From a trailer in Ohio where a woman worked two jobs to make sure her son didn't suffer. He suffered regardless, but that didn't change the fact that she'd been there for him when she was alive. *Life is hard sometimes.* That was a fact. That didn't mean you gave up. That didn't mean you stopped trying for the people you loved.

He got up on shaking hands, his leg barely supporting him now, and retrieved the torch. He didn't want to touch it after it had been through that *thing*, but he didn't have a choice. Unclean as it might be, he couldn't wander around in the dark. It was no longer an expectation that something would happen, it was a certainty. Ben knew it wasn't over the same way he knew the sun would rise in the morning.

Theresa had hit it dead on. You might stop things like these. You may slow them down. But evil—not the manmade kind, but the kind that moved like a force of nature—could never be killed. It would change forms. Wait. Rest. And come again. The best a person could hope to do was survive it intact.

As he stood back up, he saw what he was looking for. Old, rusted pipes coming out of the floor filled the room to his left, relics that had managed to stay unreplaced for half a century. In any other situation, Ben might have found it funny that a place that threw its wealth around so freely would neglect something so important.

He limped into the room and let his torch illuminate everything. Rusted or not, he wasn't going to do much with his hands, and beating a gas line with a torch was crazy even by his failing standards. He lifted the light over his head and noticed a pile of pipes the size of baseball bats lying in the corner. He walked back into the hallway and tossed the torch down as far as he could. He wouldn't get much done if he blew himself up the moment he busted open the lines.

When he turned back toward the room, he again stood in the lobby. The front door was open, and a steady downpour of rain had started. He watched the road that led away from the Home as his red Sportwagon zoomed along, leaving. He didn't understand what he was seeing. He looked at the floor. Someone had stepped in Scott's blood and tracked it all over the lobby. It looped by the desk, toward the west wing, doubled back, and…

And ended right where he stood. He'd been wandering around in a daze, doing nothing but making circles, slack-jawed and empty-eyed. He'd never been in the basement. He imagined it. Howerton's brain leaked out of his skull, but his one remaining eye stared at Ben from where he lay. Accusing him. Damning him.

"No!" Ben screamed. He refused to believe it. *"No!"*

He squeezed his eyes shut. When he opened them again he was back in the basement, in the room with the pipes. He put his hands against his temples and pressed as if he could get the thing out of his head. It had to stop. He imagined what it would be like if this kept on even when he'd finished. If ten years from now he'd still see himself standing in the lobby, forever circling his crimes as the bodies of those he had killed rotted away.

He picked up one of the iron pipes, praying to a god he wasn't sure he believed in that this would end. The first few bashes had no effect at all. The lines were thick. The old iron in his hands pinged off them, vibrating his arm and rocking his broken nose painfully. He kept beating at it to no effect. He expected the voices to start up again, to taunt him and tell him he was worthless. They didn't. Somehow, that was worse.

Huffing and sweaty, he backed away. It was hard to see in the dim light that spilled from the corridor, but there didn't appear to be any way to release the gas without breaking the pipes. The only valve was an emergency shutoff. He smashed again, the jolt of metal on metal making his leg hum with pain. Frustrated, he struck harder each time.

Finally, after what felt like an eternity, the first crack appeared with a loud hiss.

For the next ten minutes, he struck the old pipe over and over. A joint came apart, tearing the entire line from its moorings and shooting so much gas into the room that it made him lightheaded within seconds. It occurred to him that this might not be necessary. Just lighting the drapes on fire on the first floor might be enough, but he wasn't going to risk it.

He would end this with such finality no one would find anything but ashes. There would be an empty field where a hundred-year-old house filled with monsters once stood. People would pass it in the woods and spread urban legends about it around campfires. Nobody would ever dig up its horrible secrets. A spectacular fireball would mark the end of the story.

Ben dropped the pipe, which hit the floor with a clatter. He coughed as the gas filled the room. He limped down the hall and picked up the torch, moving back toward the entrance.

"This is real. I'm not crazy. This is real." He repeated it aloud. If a man couldn't trust in his own sense of time and space anymore, he wasn't really a man, just a floating consciousness. Something like that, a disembodied idea, would make him just like the thing in that hole. That terrified him more than anything.

His unease grew, something he thought impossible only a half hour before. Not knowing was worse than fear. The uncertainty gnawed at him, ate away at his center until he began to doubt everything.

When he got back to where he'd parted ways with Theresa and Julia, his nose started to bleed. He felt the first warm trickle on his lip and reached up with an unsteady hand, brushing it away. He set fire to the equipment he passed. Cloth seats of wheelchairs, old mattresses, and stacks of ancient paper kindled and burned with just a touch of the torch. By the time he reached the larger room where he'd fled from the unseen thing the week before, the hallways behind him were ablaze, and smoke filled the air. He coughed as it entered his lungs.

His vision split, showing him both the room in the basement and the first floor as he wandered the passages. He saw himself lurching through the Home as he lit another box of loose papers in the basement. He tracked Scott's blood across an expensive rug as he went into the records room he'd seen in his first week, lighting everything inside.

He staggered out of the records room in the basement, and at the same time moved closer to the basement on the first floor, still wandering in a daze. The double vision made his headache pound. Anxiety fluttered in his chest. He had no energy left. Not even enough to care anymore. He'd done what he had to do. He set more things alight as he closed on the stairs.

When he entered the final room that would lead to his freedom, his upstairs self entered the back hallway. Both moved ever closer to the middle point where they'd meet. He wondered if he would die when they touched. Finally find the end he'd seen coming this whole time. The final calamity that would bring sweet relief.

He wanted to care. He wanted to scream and cry. He'd do anything to feel something, but it was all gone, burned away like the basement around him. He coughed again as he entered the stairwell. Through his other eyes, he was passing the door to the basement hallway. They'd meet at the top of the stairs.

He took them slowly, his hurt leg cold. As long as Julia was all right, if he'd managed to save their child, he'd die with a smile. All of it would mean something. Everything they'd been through would have some worth. He passed the halfway point on the stairs as his glassy-eyed, blood-tracking self moved closer to the basement door. Almost there now. No turning back.

He reached the top and grasped for the door handle. Before he could touch it, the knob turned, and the portal yawned open in front of him. He stared at himself through two sets of eyes. One of him covered in soot and dirt, the other bloody and crazed. The pain in his head hit a blinding crescendo. He fell forward onto his knees, passing through himself instead of colliding, and vomited in the hallway. Everything screamed at him. The ringing in his ears deafened. He yelled, but couldn't hear himself over the sound. He put his hands to his head to block it out.

He'd die like this. His brain would swell and explode in his head, unable to cope with the cognitive dissonance in front of him. His entire body vibrated, ready to shake itself apart.

And then it stopped, leaving him shaking and gasping for breath.

He gazed down into the green and yellow puddle of sick on the hardwood in front of him, a line of drool hanging from his mouth. He wasn't dead. The sensation of invisible monsters floating around him, the feeling of impending doom, all gone. The headache, near constant for the last week, faded first to a dull throb and then nothing at all. He wiped his mouth and rose to his knees, pushing himself up as smoke billowed from the basement behind him.

He wasn't relieved. He didn't have it in him. He'd become a clay mold into which the world could pour its shit.

Fire alarms blared. At their piercing shriek, he jumped and came down hard on his bad leg, certain the thing in the basement was coming for him. When he realized what it was, he let out a weary sigh and limped toward the front of the building. He had to get out. He didn't know if the whole thing was going to explode when the gas reached the fire, but he didn't want to be there to find out.

He heard the frantic shouts of people from that direction and decided the back door was the better choice. He left the basement hallway to find the body of a man shot in the chest lying near the rear entrance. Ben stepped back, pressing himself against the wall and taking in a deep breath. The orderly had crawled toward the back door after he'd been shot near the basement. The line of smeared blood looked like a snail trail. Theresa had killed another man. That made three in the last few hours.

Julia and Theresa had made it out. That was enough, even if she'd had to kill every living thing in the Home to do it. He moved away from the wall and walked faster toward the exit, ignoring the pain in his leg as best he could. The back door stood slightly ajar, a ring of keys sticking out of the lock. Ben pushed it open and walked outside. It was raining as it had been when he'd seen the lobby in the basement through his other eyes.

He limped through the mud, making a beeline for the parking lot. "Please, let them be gone. Let them be at a hospital already." He clenched his fist, not sure who he was talking to anymore. "Please, let all of this be done."

He rounded the corners, but vehicles blocked his view of where his car would be. He navigated the lot, his heart pounding. The monsters might be gone, but it wasn't over yet. Something in his gut told him…

Then he saw her.

Julia, on the ground, her robe bloody, leaned against the tire of a truck near where the Sportwagon had been. There was no sign of it, or of Theresa.

"No." He said it quietly as he looked at her. "No." His leg almost buckled under him, but he didn't care. He started running, each step causing his leg to tremble. "No." *This isn't real. This isn't real.* He chanted it in his head. He had to be right. He was still in the basement. He had to be.

Julia stirred as he approached. Her eyes, unable to open all the way, fluttered weakly. "Ben?"

"No, no, no!" Tears blurred his vision. He wiped them away, slamming the back of his hand into his eyes so hard it hurt. His mouth hung open. It couldn't be true. This was another bad dream. Another stupid cosmic joke some monster was playing on him.

He knelt down with no regard to his own pain. "Julia, baby. What happened?" His hands hovered over her, afraid to touch her and cause more pain. He couldn't see again. The salty drops from his eyes fell and mixed with the red on the ground. Theresa had left the gun sitting near her right hand like some cruel joke.

Maybe not a joke; maybe a last resort.

Julia tried to sit up, but failed. Blood soaked the lower half of her robe, dying it crimson with her cruor. "Ben?" Her eyes didn't focus on him, and her expression turned quizzical, as if he were a riddle to be solved. "It hurts so much." Her head lolled to the side but she lifted it back up, grimacing with the effort.

"Shh, shh, shh." He grabbed her hand and brushed the hair from her eyes before leaning in to kiss her forehead. His tears dripped onto her face. The entire world swayed beneath him. "You're okay. We're going to get you out of here." His insides twisted. All the blood around them looked unreal.

She took her hand from his and tried to push him away as shouts emanated from the front of the building. "No. No more, please. No more hurting." She said it with pain and fear in her eyes, as if he were the one responsible for all of this.

"It's okay." He pulled himself next to her and put his arms around her as she struggled. "I'm going to make it all okay." He buried his face in her neck and rocked her back and forth, stroking her hair, taking in her scent. A clear certainty that this would be the last time he'd ever do it put him over the edge. A groan escaped his lips as he rocked her, stroking her. "What happened?"

She stopped struggling and dropped her arms to her sides. "You did this." The calm in her voice stabbed him in the throat. Choked him.

"No." The word barely escaped his lips. He couldn't breathe. "No."

She took three short breaths. She'd lost too much blood. "I want to see the baby, Ben." Her lower lip quivered. She shook with cold. He hugged her closer, willing this to be fake. It didn't go away.

"Bring me the baby." She pointed at something in the shadows of a nearby vehicle. A small form, lifeless and still. Its umbilical cord was wrapped around its neck, the bloody remains of a placenta not far away.

Ben squeezed his eyes shut, not wanting to see anymore. Not wanting to feel anymore. He'd told Theresa he'd find her and kill her if she hurt Julia, but he'd been the one that left them alone. He'd been the fool who hadn't been thinking clearly and had left his family with a crazy murderer.

"No. He's fine, baby. You'll see him soon." He sobbed into her neck, rocking her back and forth.

She didn't speak for a long moment. Her breathing struggled. The only sounds in the entire world were the shouts from the front of the building. People hurried in and out, trying to save the patients. A deep whoosh vibrated under Ben's feet, and the sound of breaking glass drifted from the rear of the building as the gas lit.

Ben didn't know if that would kill the thing, but he'd pray at its altar every day if it could give him Julia. "I love you so much." He cried into her hair. "I'm so sorry."

She reached up a bloody hand and clasped it in his. No words. Her energy was spent. There wasn't a place for words anymore.

"Please don't leave me. I can't go on without you." He'd done all of it for her. Without her, it had no worth. He had no worth. "Don't go."

She shook harder for half a second, gasped, and moved no more. He continued rocking as if he hadn't noticed. If he ignored the horrible truth, it wouldn't be real. It couldn't be real.

"Julia?"

She didn't respond. He stopped rocking.

"Julia?" He saw the eternal stare of her eyes. She was gone. "Please don't go." He wiped his tears, smearing blood across his face. He shook her, trying to wake her up, to make her look at him.

Police sirens wailed in the distance, moving toward the Home. They couldn't save her though. Nothing could anymore.

Only one option was left.

He untangled himself from her and closed his hand around the pistol. One more moment and he'd be with her. They could be done with all of this, free in a way that they could never be on Earth.

"I love you, Julia."

He shut his eyes, afraid that looking at the gun would steal his nerve. With one final breath, Ben put the gun to his head and pulled the trigger.

The click of the hammer on the empty chamber made him jump. He pulled it again. Then again. He continued pulling, more frantic each time. "No. No, please." He slammed the gun onto the ground, pounding it into the pavement as if it were to blame. His small finger shattered under the blows, but he didn't notice.

The sirens grew closer. Vaguely human shapes watched him from the windows of the Home. His mother. Howerton. Julia.

He screamed into the night, wanting everything to end.

It didn't.

Remember, authors make their living thanks to readers such as yourself. If you enjoyed Ben's story, please take the time to leave a review on Amazon. Help someone else find this book.

From the Author

I'll say thank you to my readers (Yes, *you*) before I say anything else. I owe a lot of people more than a handshake for this book coming together, but none of it would mean anything without you to enjoy it. Seriously, thank you for taking the time from your busy day to sit down with my book. I hope you had as much fun reading it as I did writing it.

Next comes my editor, Jenn Loring. My novel has significantly less weasel words thanks to her. Thank you, Jenn, for taking the time to answer a fledgling writers many, many, many questions, even when they fell well outside of what you had to do as a book doctor. You should start a support group for frazzled authors.

My good friend Ernest Dempsey, also a writer, gave me a ton of good advice about how to get this book together so I could get it to readers. Thanks for taking the time to walk me through how to make this happen, Ernie. His thrillers are amazing, check them out.

All of the people who put up with me throughout this process deserve a medal. Megan, Adam, Brian, Trevor, Leslie, everyone at Dojo Chattanooga, everyone at Rhythm and Brews, and all my Island of Misfit Musician friends—Thank you. I know when I'm caught up in my work I'm a downright unpleasant bastard to be around, but you folks took it all in stride. I couldn't have done this without your support. Trevor's words of wisdom are the only reason I had the guts to publish anything at all.

Last, but not least, I'd like to thank poor Ben and Julia. They suffered through horrible fate after horrible fate, horrible draft after horrible draft. Sorry you didn't end up in a romance or a comedy. You drew the short stick. I'll write a secret book nobody will ever see where everything turns out good for you two.

You'll live happily ever after, I promise.

Al Barrera

October 2014

www.ingramcontent.com/pod-product-compliance
Lightning Source LLC
Chambersburg PA
CBHW070724280626
47159CB00023B/2373